CIRCLE OF FIFTHS

JAMIE B TANNER

Integrity Arts Press
Changing the World with Words

ISBN: 978-0-9830506-4-3

Library of Congress Control Number: 2011935984

Any references to historical events, real people, or real places are used fictitiously. Names, characters, and places are products of the author's imagination.

Front cover design by Tanya Leone.

Book design by Tanya Leone.

Printed by IngramSpark, in the United States of America.

First printing edition 2021.

Integrity Arts Press
www.integrityartspress.com

for Beck

Contents

I

Full of Grace

I stood in the tall grass and stared at the sky, trying to see behind the blue because that's where God is supposed to be. Sister says we must be very good people because God watches each of us from Heaven. He knows all of our names and everything we do and say. But we can't see God because He is invisible.

The blue was the exact color of my favorite shirt and there were no clouds. The sun was behind me, warming my back. I wondered if God had anything to do with the weather and determined that of course He does. We must have been very good children to get such a nice warm, sunny day. I wished that it wasn't recess, though. If it were after school we would have so much more fun outside without Sister hanging around. We'd be able to laugh really really loud. We would imitate her yelling at us. We would stick out our arms and fly around. The boys would fart.

I thought about religion class as I shuffled my feet in left field. No one ever kicks this far so I always volunteer to play outfield where I can daydream. I was confused about religion. Again. Just before recess, Sister told us that we should be prepared to be dead. We should even wish to be dead because that is the only way that we can be with God in Heaven. When we die, we get released from our physical bodies, and then our souls get to meet God. In person. We are our souls, by the way, not our human bodies. And in order to go up to Heaven instead of down to you-know-where, we must be in a state of grace. You never know when you might find yourself flying out of your body on the path to Heaven, so being in a state of grace as often as possible is a very good idea for our salvation. And salvation means being saved from the fires of you-know-where. Which is hell, in case you don't know.

Sister Regina seemed pretty happy about the prospect of being dead. She smiled a lot when she told us about it. She also explained that there are many hurdles to get through before arriving in Heaven and that we should not expect a free ticket. One of the hurdles is how many sins you're carrying around on your soul. If you think pure thoughts and go to Confession a lot and stay in a state of grace, your chances of getting in are fairly good. Sister says we should constantly be ready to die, and in order to be ready, we have to confess to the priest and become purified. Even though God is always watching, we are going to mess up sometimes and sin, but thank goodness there is Confession because then all is not lost.

Since there are so many people on earth, there are always a few souls flying through the sky on the way to heaven to be with God. No matter how hard I looked from left field, I *could not* see them. Or God. All I saw was the green field, the blue sky, the few wispy clouds, and my classmates running around playing kickball. I felt a little bit left out, even though it was kind of peaceful without any balls whizzing at me. In left field, I could just think my thoughts and try to spot souls zipping through the air. Every so often I thought I saw something flash past me, and I wondered if it might be a soul going to Heaven. But I could never be sure. I still don't know what a soul looks like.

Of course, if you are a pagan baby, you will go directly to purgatory without even a chance at Heaven because the negligent heathens around you did not baptize you. Our class prays for pagan babies every day, and on Fridays we each place a dime in the tin can and when

Sister Regina determines that there are enough dimes, she will send them to Africa to help the missionary nuns persuade the people of Africa to get their babies baptized into the One Holy Catholic and Apostolic Church. This is so that the babies can then go straight to Heaven instead of purgatory, which is just another name for a part of you-know-where. It's a little higher up and does not burn you in the flames for eternity. Purgatory is supposed to actually be almost kind of pleasant, but it's still sad because God is not there and you will never get to be with Him because of the strict baptism rule.

While I was puzzling through the intricacies of Heaven, purgatory, and you-know-where, this is what happened to me:

Suddenly Elly was screaming, "Look out! Look out, Lennie!" I heard her warning about one second too late. WHUMP! I took a kickball right smack in the belly. Sister *always* kicked to left field. I should have been paying attention instead of pondering my eternal salvation. I could maybe have caught the ball for an out, which would have meant an instantaneous end to recess and everyone would have been mad at me. Instead, when the ball smacked into me at five hundred miles an hour, the wind was knocked completely out of my body. I crumpled to the ground with my eyes wide open, and my mouth too. My eyeballs came to rest at ground level, watching Sister's black clodhopper feet rounding the bases, sending up little puffs of dirt with each heavy step. As she headed for home, Anthony Didonato ran over to retrieve the ball, which was lying innocently right next to my head.

"Are you dead, Kuklinksi?" he yelled.

"No," I rasped. "I don't think so!" Even though I was prepared to be dead, like Sister told us.

Anthony gave me a look that seemed to be full of admiration mixed with pity. "OK. Good." He grabbed the ball and made a valiant effort to throw Sister out at home plate. Even if he made it, we know that Sister would declare herself safe and her team would win the game. Then we would go back to class and glare at Sister's teammates of the day, and they would look at the floor because it was never fun to be on

Sister Regina's team.

While Anthony and Audrey Fremont tried to tag Sister out, Elly ran over to me from right field to see if I was OK. By the time she got to me, I was breathing again. My stomach felt like a million bee stings.

"Can you get up?" She looked terrified.

"I don't know." I liked having my face in the grass. And I was afraid to move in case something besides my belly hurt.

Sister Regina, triumphant from her home run kick that almost killed me, shouted from the sidelines. "Leonore Kuklinski! Get up right this instant! You are completely fine—it was just a little ball! Let's stop the drama right now, shall we?" She placed her hands on her hips and announced to my classmates: "Leonore's slight discomfort at this moment is INSIGNIFICANT compared to what Our Lord went through upon the cross. Keep this in mind! Whatever pain we experience in a game of kickball is ABSOLUTELY NOTHING compared to what He endured NAILED to the cross!"

That kickball, propelled by her giant killer leg, had hit my belly with the impact of a gunshot. But I wasn't going to be able to argue that. And Sister is a big—well, a person, I think, and I am a small kid. I told Elly to not help me up from the ground because I knew Sister would yell at her if she did. I stood up slowly and put my arm across my stomach. The stinging was not going away very quickly. I still couldn't take a full breath.

"There we are now, Leonore! I hope you're planning on going to Confession today! It appears that God has used my home run as a lesson in paying close attention to one's faults and sins! What is it that caused you to put yourself in the way of my strong, healthy home run kick?" Sister's eyes glinted at me all the way across the field.

Did she have to yell this in front of all my classmates? I was never going to hear the end of it. I got up and began to trudge toward her. She was lining everyone up to go back inside. My classmates were sneaking glances at me, and I knew everyone was thanking God it wasn't them getting yelled at by Sister Regina.

"I can't HEAR you, Leonore Kuklinski!" Sister paused in her herding duties to focus on harassing me. "ARE WE GOING TO CONFESSION TODAY?"

"Yes, Sister," I said, louder than I normally talk, but I wanted her to hear me.

"Yes, Sister, WHAT?"

"Yes, Sister Regina." I cast my eyes downward like any repentant sinner would.

"Ah, that's much better."

Anthony Didonato was behind me and I distinctly heard him whisper, "Yes, Sister Vagina."

We had had many lessons in how to say Sister's name. It was pronounced Reg-EYE-na, not Reg-EE-na. The first day of school, she made us say it about fifty times, all together now class: Sister Reg-EYE-na.

I did not know there was a word that rhymed with Reg-EYE-na.

"Shut up!" Audrey whispered to Anthony. They were both laughing but trying not to.

Sister told us to go inside, sit down at our desks, and be quiet. There were no further instructions to get out a certain book or a pencil or our bibles. Uh-oh. This could mean only one thing, one very, very bad thing: Sister was getting ready to tell us a story. And it was going to be about Jesus or saints—or Jesus *and* saints. And probably how they were killed. For us. For their unwavering faith in the True Church.

You could always tell when the storytelling was about to happen because she would pace across the front of the room, clearing her throat. Then she would look up at the ceiling. There wasn't much up there—peeling white paint, some cracks, and a ceiling fan that never worked. It was like she had her own personal view of God, and we, being little, couldn't see Him. She would start breathing deeply and very loudly. Finally, she would begin: "Children, I have something to impart to you," she'd say. And we'd know that we were in for another bloody, gory saint story.

None of us knew what "impart" meant, except maybe Angela Santini. Her vocabulary was unnatural for our age. The rest of us just sat there, looking at Sister expectantly. And warily.

A long, nasal inhale, and then: "Today, you will learn the story of our beloved Saint Ursula and the eleven thousand virgins. You will learn why she is so important to the history of the Holy Catholic Church and why she is so very special that we named our beautiful parish for her. Dear, beloved Saint Ursula." Sister looked right through us, beaming.

My stomach still hurt. I wanted this to be a good story so that I could get my mind off the stinging pain in my belly.

There was a faint snicker from the back of the room. It was Anthony Didonato reacting to the word virgin, and that could only mean that the word was dirty and had to do with sex in some way. We would have to get the story from him in the alley after school because for sure Sister Regina was not going to tell us any of the good parts. Of course we knew all about the Virgin Mary and that she was different, a clean version of virgin. I decided to ask him about vagina, too, since it seemed related somehow.

Sister Regina swished around the front of the room, her habit swishing and her rosary clinking. Her eyes were closed, but she didn't crash into anything. Finally she stopped pacing and in slow motion turned to face us. There was a smudge of dirt at the bottom of her habit. Kickball dirt.

"So, my dear children," she began. Oh no! This was going to be a long one. "In the fifth century—do you realize how long ago this was? Over one thousand four hundred years! So close to the time when Our Dear Lord walked this earth! Yes, it has been more than fourteen hundred years since our wonderful St. Ursula lived!"

One thousand years, one million years. What did it matter to someone who was seven years old? One time my grandpa spread a thousand dollars from the racetrack across the table and it seemed like a lot of money. Probably one thousand years ago they didn't have electricity. Also, Ursula is kind of a weird name. No one is named Ursula these days.

"Ursula was the daughter of a Christian king in Britain, which is known to us today as England." Sister smacked the tattered world map that was tacked to the wall near her desk. Her hand slapped somewhere in the Pacific Ocean. I knew this was nowhere near England. So did everyone else, but no one would dare tell her.

Another deep inhale. "There was a pagan king whose son asked for Ursula's hand in marriage. Ursula wanted to remain a virgin, and so she asked for a delay of three years time before she would marry. She also asked for companions and received 10 women of noble birth who would serve as her ladies-in-waiting." Sister Regina began to stride around the front of the classroom again, deep in her story. I was fascinated by the rhythmic way her rosary swayed as she paced. Her hands were buried deep in her habit. She looked as though she had no limbs—she was just one large human blob on legs. You couldn't see them, of course. Her legs. She glided around the front of the room and she could have had wheels for all we could tell. Only her face was apparent because the rest of her head was mostly hidden under the complicated habit-hat contraption.

Sister Regina looked over at Angela Santini, the teacher's pet, the miniature saint. "The names of the dear maiden virgins are as follows: Ursula, who you know as our patron saint, beloved martyr, and child of God. Her maidens were Sencia, Gregoria, Pinnosa, Martha—" at this point we all swung our heads to stare at Martha Babcock, a blond, quiet girl who ate cucumber sandwiches for lunch every single day "—Saula, Britula, Saturnina, Rabacia, Saturia, and Palladia."

Sister Regina took yet another deep breath. How could she have all of those strange names memorized? She'd rattled them off effortlessly.

"Each of the 10 ladies-in-waiting was accompanied by one thousand maidens, all of whom were virgins as well. There were also a thousand virgins to accompany Ursula herself. Hence, that is why there were eleven thousand virgins." Sister turned to face us. We all beamed back at her, struggling desperately to understand what this story meant. Our second-grade minds were trying to grasp the scope of eleven thousand. I had no idea what eleven thousand of anything might look like. More than my grandpa's race track money? I was much too scared to ask Sister Regina to explain the significance of this number to us. Maybe someone bolder, someone like Elly, might ask.

"All of the virgins including St. Ursula boarded ships and sailed around the sea for three years. When it was time for the pagan king's son—" Sister Regina sniffed some disapproval each time she uttered the word pagan "—to claim her, a big storm came up from the sea and blew the ships to Cologne, where all of the dear virgins—God rest their souls—were murdered by the Huns, who hated Christianity. To be more specific, each one was beheaded, one after the other." She slowly turned her head to face us with a somber glare. "They were led to the gallows, one by one. Slowly up the wooden stairs they went. They kneeled down. The executioner swung the blade and—" Sister Regina slammed her hand on the big oak desk: Whomp. Whomp. Whomp. Each whomp came in a slow, deadly rhythm. I could practically see the heads rolling after they'd been chopped off. Whomp. Sister looked at us, her eyes bulging. Whomp. Then she turned away, and we heard her whisper, "May the heathens be forever damned to the fires of hell." Whomp!

One thing we knew for sure about Sister Regina was that she liked to include the details of martyrdoms whenever possible. We had heard enough stories about saints being boiled in oil, roasted alive, buried alive, disemboweled by lions, and burned at the stake to require at least a few future years of therapy each. Now we had chopped-off heads to add to the list.

"And this, dear children, is why Christopher Columbus named

the Virgin Islands so, to honor St. Ursula and her voyage with eleven thousand virgins." Christopher Columbus? Sister Regina clasped her hands together and raised her eyes to heaven above for a moment. "Thank God for Christopher Columbus."

"Niña, Pinta, and Santa Maria!" exclaimed a beaming Angela Santini. Sister looked at the floor while her hand grabbed the edge of the desk and her knuckles turned white.

"And so, children," she said, pinching the poor desk really hard, "You are to pray for the eternal rest of all eleven thousand virgins and thank them for the service they provided to mankind."

I was really confused. What did they do besides ride around on boats for three years? I looked over at Angela and her expression was what my mother would call a "long face."

Elly raised her hand. Sister got this look on her face like it was going to be a trying experience to answer Elly's question. "Yes, Maria Elena," she said. When she called Elly by her full name, she was near the end of her rope.

"What did the virgins eat for three years on the ships?" Elly's face looked concerned.

"Whatever God provided them," Sister pinched her forehead with her right hand, like it hurt to even consider this question, which I thought was brilliant.

Audrey Fremont's hand flew up into the air. I think Sister pretended not to see it, but finally she said, "Audrey? And this had better be a serious question."

"Yes, Sister. I was wondering who gave the maidens to Saint Ursula? I mean, I didn't know people could give other people away to someone else."

Sister looked at the floor. Then she looked back up and her eyes bored into Audrey's. "The times were much different one thousand four hundred years ago. And some things are not ours to know."

Audrey began to say something, and Sister's hand shot out like a crossing guard's to stop her. It worked.

Anthony Didonato raised his hand. He could look angelic if he tried. He knew it, too. Anthony lowered his voice, like he was being respectful. He asked, "Where were all the men?"

Sister's face began to turn crimson. "There were no men accompanying St. Ursula and her virgin handmaidens. They were virgins! There WERE no men!"

Anthony looked confused. But he thought better of saying anything else, thank goodness.

Angela Santini raised her hand next. Uh-oh. "Were all of the maidens considered nuns, Sister?" Angela had her hands clasped in front of her on her desk. She appeared to have understood the story about Saint Ursula and was pursuing something more current. This was not a second-grade question. It was further evidence that Angela was some sort of Catholic child freak who was really an adult in a child's body.

Sister Regina looked out the window. "Yes, my dear. In a sense, they were also brides of Christ."

Whenever Sister said "Brides of Christ," Anthony Didonato would whisper, "Brides of Frankenstein." I looked over at him and he had his head down on the desk, which meant that he was trying not to laugh because of course he'd get in big trouble.

Elly looked across the room at me, and I translated her expression to mean that we were going to have to investigate this Saint Ursula thing. Also, virgins and vaginas, whatever those were, but we'd find out from Anthony. We would discuss it on gig night, as we did all things important, by flashlight under a blanket. And if we couldn't figure it out ourselves, we could always ask my Aunt Liddy.

Elly has been my best friend since the day we were born—September

30, 1959. We met in the hospital room our mothers shared. We had heard the story so many times we could tell it as if we remembered, which we didn't. When we were a few hours old, the nurses brought us to our mothers at the same time to be fed our formula. Formula was the only acceptable, civilized way to feed children of our era. No, absolutely no breasts for us.

"Here are your chemicals in a bottle," my mother Frankie whispered to me the first time she held and fed me. She didn't buy all the hype about formula feeding but caved in when my grandmothers crowded around and hissed at her that bottle feeding is progress and the advancement of the human condition. Human women shouldn't have to be so base as to use their breasts anymore to feed their young. Formula was a miracle! If only they'd had it when they were young mothers!

We were slurping away contentedly at our miniature baby bottles when Elly's dad Frank and my dad Ted arrived to stand around uncomfortably and look at us. Yes, Elly's dad's name is Frank and my mom's name is Frankie. It's pretty easy to tell them apart, though. Besides, his name is officially Frances and hers is Francesca.

Our dads couldn't believe that they contributed to our existence in our mothers' arms. Rosa, Elly's mom, looked positively radiant; Frankie was more rumpled and tired looking. We were all a little exhausted but trying to get our bearings with each other.

Rosa and Frank were cuddling little Maria Elena, who is named for her grandmothers. One of them is dead (Maria) and the other one (Helen) is a mean, bigoted old woman who is mad that her boy Frank married that spic Rosa. When we asked Aunt Liddy what a spic is, she spit out a little bit of the wine she was drinking. She said we were never to say that word—it was a mean thing to say to a Puerto Rican person who is just a person like the rest of us only some people don't like them. Who could not like Rosa just because she is from Puerto Rico? Sometimes adults don't make sense.

Ted convinced my mother to name me Leonore—after the overtures, of which he (Beethoven, not my dad) wrote three. Leonore, as far as either of them knew, was not a Catholic name, and it was certainly not a Polish name. But my father loved classical music and Beethoven almost more than he loved playing dance tunes and polkas for money, and he desperately wanted me to be called Leonore. It was an awfully big name to saddle an infant with, Frankie thought, but it was interesting and unusual, so she agreed. My Auntie Liddy took one look at me lying there in my swaddling clothes and had a fit about my name being so ridiculous for a little baby girl. She immediately started calling me Lennie, and it stuck. I didn't know until years later that my father let it stick because in this way I honored two composers with my name: Beethoven, of course, and also Leonard Bernstein, who—as you know—was called Lenny by the world. My father told me he would take me to meet his hero someday, introducing his Lennie to the famous Lenny.

And I was the one who eventually gave Elly her nickname. I could not even come close to saying Maria Elena. It came out as Maweelaida or something African-sounding like that, when we were two and just learning to say things out loud. One day I just announced her name: Elly! I stopped even trying to say Maria Elena. And soon everyone else began to call her Elly. Even the nuns, once we started going to school. We were the two little unfortunates who were stuck with non-Catholic names, and for that we got some pity and a fair amount of attention.

Religion took up the whole afternoon on Fridays, so when religion was over, school was over. And on Fridays we had to go to Confession. Sister Regina escorted us over to the church to make sure we all walked through the door. She interrogated anyone who went home instead, even though she did not have official jurisdiction over us once we were outside the school building. Sister slapped Kleenexes on the heads of wayward girls who forgot their hats or veils. This was usually me and Audrey Fremont.

While I waited in the Confession line, I wondered again about the ships full of virgins sailing around the ocean, eating whatever God provided them. What could that be? Fish, maybe. Donuts? Probably not. And they floated around for three years. That was almost half my lifetime. What was the point? Did they go swimming? Did they play checkers at least? If Ursula didn't want to get married, why didn't she just say no? Why did she have to sail around with a bunch of women for all that time?

Oh, God, I thought. Having this thought is probably a sin. I added it to my list.

"Bless me Father, for I have sinned."

Father Chaslowski listened to my story of stealing a piece of candy right out of the bin at Orr's Department Store. A chocolate caramel in a bright foil wrapper. It was really easy to unwrap it and pop it in my mouth without anyone seeing it. But I was dying of guilt because I knew my guardian angel was probably flapping around in the background, telling me that stealing is a sin. I knew she was saying it, but I couldn't hear her because she's invisible. I could not resist the temptation. I also had to tell Father that I thought badly of Saint Ursula because I questioned her judgment about dragging a bunch of virgins around the high seas for three years. Father started coughing and couldn't talk for a minute. Then he took a long time to speak, and when he did he gave me five Hail Marys and told me to look up Saint Ursula in the Catholic Encyclopedia so I could understand her story better. This intrigued me because I didn't know it was legal for penance to be something other than reciting prayers.

I went to the pew and knelt down and said the Hail Marys as fast as possible while waiting for Elly. And then I overheard Father through the wooden door, telling Elly that her penance would be seven Our Fathers. I was a little scared that eavesdropping would be considered a sin, but I wasn't sure. I knew that in the previous week, Elly had smacked the neighbor kid Bart and stolen two of the same exact kind of candies from Orr's Department Store (the day after I did because I told her how good they were). One for her and one for me, so maybe I should have confessed again? Elly had also shouted at her mother.

Apparently these were greater transgressions than mine, and she had to pray directly to God the Father, whereas I could get off with just talking to the Virgin Mary, relying on her to get the message over to God for me.

Waiting for Elly, I thought more about the mysteries of absolution. Sister was teaching this to us because, she said, we were SECOND GRADERS and needed to understand exactly how it worked because the salvation of our eternal souls depended on it .

With the Sacrament of Confession come Absolution and then the State of Grace, which is the big lead-up to the Sacrament of Communion. Sister Regina's face, crimped by the habit that squished her expression into a square, turned pink and her eyes rolled heavenward as she explained to us that the state of grace is that glorious moment when your soul is absolutely clean (get it? absolutely/absolution!). It is pure white, unadulterated by the poisonous dark sins that foul it and turn it black (very, very black if you never confess your sins and receive the cleansing of absolution—like all the heathens and people who live in China). Because we are such imperfect and fallible human beings, the state of grace is temporary and lasts only until the first thought comes along to destroy the bleached, clean whiteness. We were to visualize our souls like clean white sheets drying on the line. They were perfect and perfectly white until the first speck of dirt flew through the air and landed on the whiteness, ruining its flawlessness. Therefore, we should pray directly after being absolved. No thinking, just praying, and praying as long as possible to keep the specks of sin from landing on our clean, white-sheet souls. The more you pray, the more you keep your thoughts away and the longer you get to be in the state of grace. Hail Marys were good, one after the other like a rosary. Or just do a rosary! Say the rosary one million times! That would keep you in the state of grace for a long time.

And the most important thing, Sister Regina told us, is that we should also pray to meet with an unfortunate accident immediately after being absolved because then our souls will go directly to heaven to be with Our Heavenly Father. If we were lucky enough to be in an accident on the way home from Confession, we would be pretty much a shoo-in to get into heaven. The fate of our souls would be sealed if, for example, we were to be run over by a truck and killed while crossing Eighth Avenue. The corner of Eighth and Broad was the busiest intersection in town, and there was some sort of accident there at least once a month. Just think, we'd even be in the newspaper because it was such a popular accident location! We would be run over and then our clean and unblemished white souls would fly right up there to heaven, completely bypassing Purgatory because penance, absolution, and the state of grace would have purified our souls and given them a green light to march directly to Heaven.

While I waited for Elly in front of the Saint Bernadette statue, I thought of a plan for how we could get to heaven in a state of grace. Then I said a few earnest prayers asking God to help us get run over at the intersection of Eighth and Broad on the way to my house. After that I prayed, as I always did, that the statue would bleed or cry or smile or have any miracle of its choice, and I would be the one to spot it and tell the Monsignor. (In case this actually happened, we could put off being run over for at least a week.) I kept praying and looking, praying and looking, and still nothing happened. St. Bernadette was as unmoving as ever.

When Elly was finished with her Our Fathers, we genuflected and then headed toward the foyer of the church where the really big statue of St. Ursula is. Our eyes were at toe level with the bottom of her skirt. Robe. Whatever that thing is that saints wear.

"Do you think she was really this big?" Elly whispered.

"I don't think so. She would have been a giant!" I had a momentary confusing image of eleven thousand giant women sailing around in giant ships.

"Then the bad guys wouldn't have been able to kill them all."

"I didn't think of that." Sometimes Elly was extremely smart.

We both experienced Sister Regina sneaking up on us and smacking the backs of our heads for talking in church. Thwap! Thwap! Then she swished away toward Frank Didonato, who was very obviously chewing something. Eating in church is a sin that sends you right back into the confessional, even if you've just done your penance, and it was a much more serious infraction than merely chatting in church.

"What did you get?" Elly asked me. Sister was out of earshot, pulling Frank out of the pew by his ear.

"Five Hail Marys," I replied.

"I got seven Our Fathers!" she said. I didn't let on that I already knew in case eavesdropping really was a sin. "And I prayed that we would get killed on the way to your house."

"Me, too!" I said. "And I figured out how we can do it!"

"You did! How?!" Elly's eyes brightened.

"All we have to do is cross Eighth Avenue without looking. I got the idea from Sister Regina! If we cross without the light, some car will come and run us over, and then we'll go straight to Heaven."

"That is a great idea." Elly's face sparkled, in spite of her imminent death. "We could be martyrs! Except we don't have to get burned at the stake or boiled in oil! We can be mowed down by a Cadillac!" Elly was up on many death methods of the martyrs because she got a copy of *Lives of the Saints* from her grandmother Helen Wojechowski. It was the only present she ever got from her grandmother in her entire seven years of being a live human being.

"Should we do it today?" asked Elly.

"I guess so." I had a momentary feeling of sadness at missing Friday night macaroni and cheese, but I figured we could probably get some in Heaven when we got there, possibly any time we wanted, since it would be Heaven where all things are possible.

We said goodbye to Saint Bernadette and Saint Ursula and stood on the front steps of the church. We made a pact to keep walking at all the intersections between the church and my house. There would be a special focus on the one at Eighth and Broad, conveniently located on the route home. Elly was coming over because it was Friday and our fathers (naturally) had a gig, so Rosa, Elly's mom, would be coming over later. She would probably bring a bag of weed, which was our mothers' latest pastime during our dads' band gigs. They told us that they were smoking clove cigarettes, which we didn't realize was a lie until we were in high school.

We started walking past the rectory on the corner of Sixth and Broad. We glimpsed Mrs. Kovach in there preparing dinner for the priests, banging pots and singing to herself. The dinner smelled like fish, which of course it would have to be since it was Friday. As planned, we stepped into the street without stopping to look both ways. Of course, our attempt to be run over could not really happen at this corner because it was not a busy street. And besides, there was a stop sign. We did it anyway so that we could practice. My heart pounded as we ignored our training and did not stop, look both ways, and listen. Elly grabbed my hand as we plunged onward.

I began to have a gnawing feeling that ignoring pedestrian laws might be some sort of a sin and could possibly get in the way of our direct route to Heaven. Even if it were a small sin, it would affect our state of grace by putting a few dark blotches upon our souls. I did not mention this to Elly as we were getting closer to Seventh Avenue. Maybe it was not a sin since she hadn't said anything. She was more up on sinning than I was because she was smarter about the religious things and paid attention to the nuns more than I did.

Elly marched steadily toward Seventh Avenue. She took my hand again and we plowed into the street. Our courage was burgeoning, a good thing since we were only a block from The Big One. A white Pontiac was slowing for the stop sign and we were right in front of it. "Please hit us," I prayed, even though I was sure it would hurt. But the car stopped and the woman beeped the horn to shoo us away faster. Then she smiled. I was momentarily confused. Was she nice or was she mean? I made a mental note to ask God about this sort of mixed message when we arrived in Heaven.

One half-block left before Death Street. I prayed to my guardian angel (who I had named Georgy, after *Georgy Girl*) to make it not hurt too much and to please shoot me straight to Heaven because I certainly didn't know the way without some directions, especially after we left our flattened bodies behind on Eighth Street. And to please keep Elly and me together because that was the whole point to eternity, right? To be with those you love as well as Our Heavenly Father. I was assuming, with a bit of excitement, that we were probably going to be able to fly. I thought maybe I'd need some flying lessons or at least a push in the right direction. Elly and I were both going to need Georgy's help! Except that we'd have Elly's angel too, whose name was Santa Lucia. Maybe they'd fly us all together in a line, like Peter Pan and Tinkerbelle did with Wendy and the other kids.

Elly grabbed my hand for the third time. I was positive she was having similar thoughts. I wondered what she was saying to Santa Lucia and if she'd be kind enough to help Georgy Girl and me, too. We were passing the Shell station on the corner of Eighth and Broad. Oh no! Grampa Kuklinski was there buying gas. He spotted us! He would have to witness our deaths!

"Hi Grampa," I said.

"Come on, girls. I give you a ride." He never really smiled with his mouth, just with his eyes. He had a strong accent. I liked how he spoke English, just using the words that he needed, not a bunch of extra ones. And he was always really nice, especially if Grandma Kuklinski wasn't around.

"NO!" said Elly. "We HAVE to walk."

"Right," I agreed. My grandfather looked perplexed.

"Well, you could give us a ride, but we have to cross Eighth Avenue first. You could pick us up at the 7-11," I suggested. This only baffled him more.

I knew this would ensure him seeing the big accident, but I thought it might buy us enough time to get run over.

"OK, girls. Whatever you say. Is a busy corner, eh? Please to be careful."

I didn't say we'd be careful because that would have been a lie and definitely canceled our ticket to Heaven with giant black lie blotches on our souls.

Elly smiled a sly, knowing look in my direction. We set off for the curb when Grampa went in to pay.

We stepped into the street with not one glance either way or at the traffic light. My heart was slamming around in my flat little chest. In the crosswalk. Step by step. Sweaty little hands clamped together.

Then we heard it. The horn, the screeching of brakes. A '62 Chevy Impala was inches away from our plaid skirts. It was happening!

Except that we were frozen in place. We had stopped walking and stood, rooted, in our tracks. The car was only a couple of inches from where we stood. People were running toward us from all over. Cars were stopping everywhere in both directions.

"What's the matter with you kids! Don't they teach you anything about red lights in school?!" A frightened looking man in a business suit was yelling at us. His Impala was at a weird angle. We could hear cars still screeching as they braked to a halt behind the Impala. There were skid marks everywhere.

A woman in a blue print dress scolded him. "Can't you see that they're just little girls! You apologize to them this *instant*! Look! They're scared to death!" She was red in the face and waving her arms, but her blonde helmet of her hair didn't move the whole time.

Indeed, Elly and I came out of our daze in the middle of the street, paralyzed yet trembling, and very much alive. We were not in Heaven, as we had planned. We were still very much on Earth. The other cars began to blow their horns, but we couldn't move.

And then my grandfather scooped us up in his arms and dragged us the half block or so to his car. "What were you thinking?" He actually said *tingkingk*. "Don't you girls know how for to crossing street? My God, wait until I tell your mother." He was truly angry. I'd never, ever seen him angry. He was probably truly frightened, too, but that possibility didn't occur to me until many years later.

Grampa deposited us in the kitchen after a silent ride home from the Eighth Avenue intersection. Being a man of few words, he stopped yelling, having said everything he had to say in a couple of syllables and the expression on his face. My mother was at the stove making macaroni and cheese AND crab cakes. (Thank God it wasn't Mrs. Paul's fish sticks—I really hate those.) My father wasn't home from work yet. Grampa steered us into the living room and then he went back in the kitchen to talk to my mother. We sneaked to the doorway and tried to listen but all we could hear were accented whispers. And then the bang of a spoon hitting a pan.

"Leonore! Maria Elena! Come in here this instant!" Uh-oh. You know what that means when she calls me Leonore and not Lennie. And I had never heard her call Elly Maria Elena before. Ever. I didn't know that someone else's mother could yell at a kid that was not hers.

Uh-oh, uh-oh. We tiptoed into the kitchen.

"What in God's name were you doing? Trying to get yourselves killed?" She was holding a wooden spoon in one hand. The other one was on her hip. Hand, not spoon.

"Yes," replied Elly.

"What?" My mother was thrown off the track. "What the hell are you talking about?"

Elly blurted out the entire story of us learning all about absolution in religion class. Because of what we were learning, we thought it was a great idea to off ourselves at the Eighth Street intersection so we could go straight to heaven in a state of grace. I stood by, quietly staring at the black and white linoleum floor.

"What?! WHAT??!!" my mother kept shouting. "I don't BELIEVE this!" I was waiting for her to tell us what a wonderful plan we had devised. Instead, she smacked the spoon on the pot. She smacked it on her palm. There was an interesting percussion piece developing with her spoon and the pots. She paced around.

"Do you realize that you would be DEAD? Do you realize that you would never see your family again? That we would be so very, very sad because you'd be gone?! Do you understand how terrible this would be? Do you? DO YOU?!" She actually shook me by the shoulders a little bit before she pulled me close to her. With her other arm, she grabbed Elly and pulled her close, too. It was weird, being smooshed by my mother in the middle of the kitchen. She made little sniffy noises and I realized that she was actually crying! My grandfather leaned against the fridge, an unlit cigarette in his fingers. I could not decipher the expression on his face.

My mother let us go, and then she disappeared into the breakfast nook with my grandfather. Elly and I exchanged worried glances. Then Frankie dialed a number, picked up the receiver, went into the pantry, and shut the door. The phone cord stretched all the way across the kitchen, making a squiggly clothesline through the air. The pantry was the only place in the entire house where you could have a conversation on the phone with no possibility of being overheard due to all the cans and jars and bags of flour in there absorbing your words. This came in quite handy when I reached high school and my life depended on the telephone.

Grampa took up the pacing. "Don't you know that you should not pray for to being dead? That the Good Lord get insult if you take matter of life and death into your own hands? No matter what the crazy nun say."

Elly and I stood side by side, backed up to the fridge, staring at him. Neither of us had ever heard the words "crazy" and "nun" uttered in such close proximity to each other, in the same sentence and even in the same breath. Panic crept into my belly. It hadn't occurred to me that we could be doing something wrong, especially since Sister Regina had been so passionate about it. And that's who my mother must be talking to on the phone in the pantry. Sister Regina! Oh Dear Lord Oh My God, as Sister Regina herself would say.

Elly and I stood there watching the stretched out phone cord that led to my mother's ear inside the pantry behind the thick wooden door. Every now and then the cord would wiggle around a little. We heard the murmuring of my mother's voice. Once we heard, "And how COULD you?!" Then it got quiet for a few more minutes. My Grampa just wandered around, the same beat-up cigarette twirling in his fingers. He was too polite to light up in the house.

Finally we heard the door to the pantry creak open. My mother hung the phone up and ushered us into the breakfast nook. She sat us down and took a deep breath.

"I would like your promise that you will never ever do such a thing again," she said. Clearly, "such a thing" meant trying to get run over or accidentally killed in any variety of ways. Before we could promise out loud, she continued, "Elly, I'm calling your mother right now. We'll have to have this talk with her when she gets here. Do you understand?"

Elly nodded. You could always count on Elly to understand and to tell the absolute truth. I nodded too, in solidarity with my friend.

"All right then," my mother said. "No more praying to die and no more plans to have an accident. Am I clear on this? And more importantly, are the two of YOU clear on this?"

More nodding from the two of us.

"Sister Regina understands this also. There will be no more misunderstandings about penance. Is this also clear?"

"Yes, ma'am," I said. My mother liked it when we said that.

"Your job is to be alive and live your lives. Understood?"

I didn't really, but we both nodded again.

My mother scooted us out of the kitchen. We retreated to my room to discuss what happened. I hoped that the crab cakes and mac and cheese were still on the menu.

"I don't get it," said Elly. She lay on my bed, staring at the ceiling.

We were supposed to revere nuns and priests above all other human beings. Sister Regina had told us with all seriousness about the state of grace, and so we took her word for it. And now my mom and my Grampa were more upset than I'd ever seen them because of something a nun said and my mom even called up Sister Regina. On the phone! I didn't know you could even do that! I did not know that nuns talked on the phone—it was beyond my imagination that a nun could do anything human like that. Eating? Talking on the phone? Watching TV? Peeing? Oh my God, I had to stop thinking about that right now!

When Rosa showed up carrying a bottle in a paper bag, our moms retired to the breakfast nook and started talking in low voices. When they went in there, we immediately snuck outside to our special spying place underneath the window where we could hear everything they said. We tucked ourselves behind the bush and drew our knees up to our chests. We listened as Frankie told Rosa the whole story, every single detail of our plot to have ourselves killed after Confession. She patiently explained every detail of Grampa at the gas station watching helplessly as we stepped into the intersection against the light.

Rosa exclaimed in Spanish, the glasses clinked, their voices rose and fell. We could almost hear them sipping whatever was in the mystery bottle during the spaces in their conversation.

Frankie described her phone conversation with Sister Regina. After the part where Sister Regina had explained to Frankie that it was her God-sworn duty to teach us the truth and it was not her responsibility how we interpreted it, we heard Rosa say, "Jesus Christ. What if they—Can you imagine, Francesca? They could be dead! Jesus, Jesus, Jesus." We heard some noises, like she was hitting the table or something.

Frankie said, "I'd sue that goddamn nun. I'd sue the entire Vatican."

We got really still. My mother was going to burn in hell for saying "goddamn nun." I was thrilled and scared at the same time.

"Frankie, I might want to be dead, then, too."

"Oh, Rosa, don't say a thing like that."

Then there was a long silence. We had to be extra careful not to make a sound so they wouldn't discover us hiding out under the window. Elly did not look at me, and I did not look at her. There was no chance of the giggling that usually gave us away. My heart was pounding, but I wasn't really sure why.

"They're just babies," Frankie said. "I worry about everything. I try so hard to protect her all the time. But this! How can you protect a child from something like this?"

"I don't know," was all Rosa said.

"And to think they could have been killed because of that stupid, ignorant, horrible, mean old woman. What is WRONG with nuns, anyway?"

I think Frankie started to cry. It got really quiet for a few minutes, and then our moms started talking about when we were born, when we were actual babies. I had a funny, warm feeling in my stomach when Frankie talked about protecting me. I liked it and felt surprised at the same time.

2

Our Pope Who Art In Heaven

For the first two years of our lives, Elly and I spent time in playpens or on blankets or on the floor together. We got to know each other in a way that hardly anyone else does. Like siblings, but closer. Without knowing what we were doing, we listened to each other breathe, copied each other's movements and attempts at speech. We felt each other's feelings, knew when we were happy or upset or hungry or tired. We tumbled into each other's rhythms, falling asleep within seconds of one another and waking up almost simultaneously. We held hands all the time. We never hit each other. We locked eyes often, and through our eyes, we could sense each other's thoughts. We responded to Frankie and Rosa in similar ways, though it was clear whose mom was whose and who we belonged to.

As we spied on them from outside the window, I felt like I had two mothers.

"They're like sisters," we heard Frankie say.

"Sí," Rosa agreed.

"We are, too, aren't we?"

"Family," Rosa said.

No other children besides us ever arrived in either family. Ever. We didn't know that our mothers were suspect in our parish because how can a good Catholic couple produce only one child? The truth is that Rosa miscarried four times after Elly was born. And Frankie had had an ectopic pregnancy that blew out her left ovary. The right one apparently never worked after that, either. So it was Elly and me for our entire childhoods together. We became the blood sisters that we never officially had.

Elly reached over and took my hand. We sat there in the dirt underneath the window for a long time, long enough for our moms to finish whatever was in the bottle and then start talking about what to eat for dinner.

"I made some macaroni and cheese," Frankie told Rosa.

"From a box?"

There was a pause. "There's another way?"

Rosa began to laugh, and then our mothers argued about what to get on the pizza they were about to order in place of the processed mac and cheese. Of course! It was gig night! And we didn't seem to be in trouble anymore for trying to get run over in the intersection.

On gig nights, Elly and Rosa almost always stayed over. We would eat Catholic Friday food and watch the Movie of the Week and then Elly and I would read books and cuddle up, and when our moms fell asleep, we would keep talking under the covers. Our dads would not come home until it was almost morning, and then we would all tiptoe around while we made pancakes and decided what we would do all day while they were sleeping and getting ready for their Saturday night gig.

The Continentals played gigs all the time. That's what bands do. Our dads dressed up in shiny red shirts and black pants, and they loaded up Frank's van with all kinds of black cases and music stands and wires and other mysterious stuff. They would kiss us all goodbye and then roar off to their gig, and we wouldn't really talk to them again until Sunday night. Or maybe even after school on Monday.

We were not sure if our moms liked our dads being in the band or not. They complained all the time about the gigs, but we always had so much fun together on gig nights. There was always something interesting to eat. Our moms got happy. One time I saw Frankie counting out little pink pills on the table. She never took medicine except on gig nights, and the medicine seemed to make her and Rosa so happy. I did not miss my father on the weekends. When he was around, he was usually mad and scary. So I liked it OK when he was gone.

My dad was happy only when he was practicing his sax or listening to music under his big headphones in the den. Every now and then, when she wanted to get his attention or ask him a question, Frankie would go over and lift one earphone off my dad's ear. He usually got really mad, answered the question in one syllable, and then closed his eyes and refused to communicate any further.

One time when this happened, Frankie sat down in the kitchen and told Elly and me the story of their wedding and how my dad and Frank played in the band instead of being grooms at their own reception. She was better than the story-hour librarian in the children's library. She was better than our Girl Scout leader telling ghost stories around the campfire. Frankie sipped a highball and wove the wedding tale with big eyes and waving hands.

"Our wedding got evacuated," she began. Our parents got married during the same wedding mass at St. Ursula's. Frankie said it saved three hours of her life from having to sit through another wedding mass for Rosa and Frank.

"What's evacuated?" asked Elly. But I already knew from watching *Attack of the 50 Foot Woman* at Aunt Liddy's. In the movie, the whole town had to get evacuated because a giant lady was going to step on everyone and their houses. She turned into a giant because of a nuclear accident. She went around stepping on everything, so everyone ran away from her.

Frankie explained why places get evacuated and then went on. I was admiring my mother. She looked beautiful and her eyes danced. Her hair was all soft and bouncy. She never sprayed it. And she didn't wear red lipstick like all the other mothers. She looked so happy. I went and leaned against her and she put her arm around me. "It was New Year's Eve, and the church was packed, which was good because it was so cold. The high mass was over three hours long, and I had to pee really bad by the time it was over. I had to wait until we went outside—it was crazy to go outside, it was probably below zero—but everyone wanted to throw rice at us before they came back in to the fellowship hall.

"That's when the trouble started. During the rice flinging, something blew up in the kitchen. Then the firemen came when all the guests were starting back inside. Your Aunt Liddy realized what was happening and started screaming: "FIRE! THE KITCHEN'S ON FIRE! GET OUT! FIRE! FIRE!"

Elly and I ran around the kitchen yelling, "FIRE! FIRE!"

Frankie smiled from behind her highball glass. The back door opened and Rosa came in with a box of pastries from Groman's Bakery. We pounced on them while Frankie made her a drink and explained that we were reenacting their wedding. Rosa rolled her eyes.

I got out the canister of rice and threw it on my mother and Rosa. There was a second of shocked silence and then they got into the act. Frankie put a dishtowel on her head and Rosa grabbed the flowers from the vase on the table.

Frankie kept going with her story. "The kitchen was on fire! The pot of stuffed cabbage fell over on the gas stove and caught fire. The flames jumped over to the trays of golumpkies and pierogies and the nutrolls, but the hruschikis were like dry tinder. The flames hit the ceiling and then the champagne exploded!"

"What a mess," Rosa said.

"And I still had to pee," said Frankie. "I thought I was going to have to pee in my wedding gown!"

"Eew," said Elly.

Frankie adjusted her towel veil. "So your grandfather went down the street to the Moose Club and explained about the fire, and the Moose people said to bring our party down there!"

Rosa told us how all the wedding guests trooped down the block in their fancy clothes while the church kitchen burned in the background. And about how our dads ignored our moms and jumped onstage and started playing with the band and the Moose Club food ran out and Frank's mom, Elly's future grandmother, stomped out of the wedding reception because she couldn't stand that Rosa was a spic and that the wedding got evacuated and surely that was a sign from God that he was mad about the interracial marriage. Then our moms got really drunk on whiskey from Grandpa Findley's flask, which Grandma Findley had stuffed in her purse and produced in the ladies room where Frankie and Rosa went to be mad at their new husbands.

By this part of the story, Elly and I were rapt, sitting on the rice on the kitchen floor. It hurt our butts but the story was too interesting to move.

"And then you two came along not too much later." Frankie exchanged a look with Rosa. They didn't share the meaning with Elly or me.

A long time later, we figured out that we were probably both conceived on that unbearably cold New Year's Eve night because we were born within three hours of each other at the Sacred Heart of Jesus Hospital in East Bedford exactly nine months later.

"Why doesn't Grandma Wojechowski like you?" Elly asked. "Why did she think God was mad at you and Dad?"

"Oh, niña, we've been through this. Your grandmother has different ideas about people, that's all."

Frankie snorted into her highball.

"And here we all are," Frankie said, meaning nothing in particular.

"Would you get married again if you had a choice?" The question just flew out of me. Sometimes I wondered if Frankie really wanted to be something besides a mom.

She didn't look me in the eye. "Of course I would, Lennie. Of course—because I would want to have you." And I believed that part was true.

"Your mother wanted to be a doctor," Rosa revealed.

I felt immediately proud. "Like Dr. Kildare?" I said.

"Yes, like Dr. Kildare," Frankie admitted.

"But—"

"Your grandparents wouldn't pay for medical school. They said girls can't become doctors." Frankie poured some whiskey into her highball glass.

"You can be anything you want to be," said Rosa. "Don't ever forget that."

Frankie didn't meet anyone's eye. She sipped her drink and looked out the window. Since it was dark, I wasn't sure what she was looking at.

"I'm glad you didn't become a nun," Elly said to her mother.

Rosa blanched. "A nun?" She grabbed Frankie's dishtowel and pulled it tight around her face. She looked like Sister Regina, only pretty.

"AAAAHHHH!!!" Elly and I had the same reaction.

The beginning of June. It was the best time of the school year because we didn't have much real work to do, and the nuns gave us snacks a couple of times. Sister Regina stopped telling martyr stories and would bring in too-sweet cookies that were usually overbaked. When the nuns do cookie experiments in the convent, they feed the results to us. We were happy though, because any diversion at all from the Baltimore Catechism and being-burned-at-the-stake stories was fine with us.

On Tuesday, June 4, Elly and I got to school just like any other day, and we compared lunches. She had tuna and I had PB & J. We decided to trade each other a half sandwich. We pooled our Hostess cupcakes and carrot sticks. She had Yoo-Hoo and I had Hawaiian Punch. We usually pour these drinks on one of the healthier looking shrubs that line the schoolyard. We don't want to poison a weak one.

The whole class was sitting there as usual, waiting for the day to begin. A few brazen things were going on, like Frank Didonato throwing paper airplanes and Audrey Fremont threatening to lift up her shirt at James Schneider. This had the attention of the rest of the boys in the room; they completely ignored Frank's aviation attempts.

Nine a.m. came and went. The planes stopped flying and Audrey investigated her lunch, bored with her exhibitionism. Nine-fifteen. Audrey crunched up her lunch bag and strolled to the front of the classroom. She launched into an imitation of Sister Regina. We were shocked into silence, but Elly couldn't contain herself and started laughing. Audrey can somehow get her face to be all red like when Sister is mad at one of the boys. I couldn't believe she was doing this when the door might open at any second.

Which, of course, it did. Audrey flew through the air to her seat with amazing speed and grace. She cancelled the red in her face and looked as angelic and expectant as the rest of us. But Sister Regina didn't walk through the door alone. She was flanked by Father Chaslowski and Mother Superior. We were in big trouble. I felt my stomach drop straight to the floor.

"Children," Father Chaslowski began. He did not sound mad. He looked at us and his eyes looked teary like he'd been crying. But do men cry? Do priests?

"It is my solemn and sad duty to report to you that our Dearest Father, Shepherd of all Roman Catholics on Earth, Pope John the Twenty-third, has passed from this life into the next." He pulled a white handkerchief out of his pants pocket and covered his face with it for a moment. Then he blew his nose with a loud honk.

We all stared straight ahead. We had only a vague idea of he was talking about.

Mother Superior must have intuited this. "What Father is trying to say, children, is that Pope John has died and he is now in heaven with God the Father, Jesus, Mary, and the Holy Spirit."

There was a small gasp from the classroom. Popes can die? Popes are infallible, the right-hand man of God, the Head Guy of the Roman Catholic Church. I always assumed that they lived forever, just like nuns and priests. How could a Pope be completely dead? I bet that his soul was completely white and blemish free. I looked over at Elly. I knew she was thinking the same thing, only she raised her hand and asked Sister out loud right in front of everyone how a Pope could die. Sister's eyes misted over and she started to cry, right there in front of us!

Mother Superior answered. "Dear one, all humans die and wait for the return of Jesus to give us everlasting life. The difference with our dear Pope is that he does not have to wait as we do—he has gone straight to Heaven to be reunited with God." We only had this particular Mother Superior for a couple of months. I really like that she called everyone Dear, but unfortunately she only lasted a short time.

This explanation didn't quite satisfy Elly. And I still felt bewildered. "Does that mean that Pope John flew up to Heaven to be with God?" Elly was so sincere and so earnest in her question that Sister Regina and Father Chaslowski didn't call her impertinent.

"No child," Father Chaslowski said. "It just means that his soul receives special dispensation upon arriving at the Gates of Heaven. His mortal body is still here on earth."

Then the most amazing thing happened:

"Gather all your things, children," Sister Regina instructed us. "School is over for the year. I want you all to go home and fall on your knees and pray for our Dear Pope John the Twenty-third." We all noticed that she was calling people "Dear" now, too.

I was thinking to myself that if Pope John is already up there with God, what do we have to pray for him for? I mean—he probably didn't have to stand in line with regular people or anything. Something in me said that I should not ask this question out loud. So I didn't, I just thought about it in the privacy of my own head.

Frank Didonato looked way too happy about the dead Pope. I sent him an emergency ESP message to stop smiling or else Sister would make us do something like clean erasers or write something one million times before we leave. But Sister and Mother Superior and Father Chaslowski didn't even notice. They conferred with each other in a huddle, dabbing at their eyes with their habits and handkerchiefs. Father and Mother Superior left us with Sister Regina, who collapsed in a heap on her squeaky oak chair. Then she did an inexplicable thing: she got up and walked out of the room without saying a word to any of us.

We were left alone. A room full of eight-year-olds. No one knew what to do or say.

"Is she coming back?" Leslie Feinberg said, breaking the silence. Leslie was a suspect Catholic because of her name. Every time roll was called, the Sister calling it would say, "Are you certain you're a *Catholic*, Leslie *FEINBERG*?" And Leslie would say, "Yes, Sister, I am, I definitely am a Catholic." And then the nun would go on, casting occasional suspicious looks at Leslie. In spite of her dubious Catholic status, Leslie was braver than most of us, maybe because she had to work so hard to be accepted by the nuns. Leslie would definitely be the one to figure out whether or not anyone was going to see to us escaping from school. We sat there in stunned silence for a few minutes, the now-abandoned third-grade class of St. Ursula's Parish Parochial School.

Frank Didonato got courageous first and peeked out into the hallway from his desk, which was closest to the door. He told us that it was empty out there. "I don't think anyone is going to come for us," he said. He looked scared, like he might cry. Frank Didonato never cried. He didn't even cry when he got hit in the head with a baseball bat and needed five stitches.

Leslie took matters into her own hands. She got up and went to the cloakroom to get her stuff. Angela Santini followed her. So did the rest of us after a few moments of hesitation and whispered discussion.

It was strange that Sister Regina was not there to tell us to line up. She always valiantly helped whoever needed to zip or button jackets or sweaters as we lined up, and we depended on her helping us even though it was scary to be that close to her. She told us that helping us was her cross to bear, just like Our Dear Lord Jesus who had the real cross to bear for our sins. Sister Regina's cross was insignificant in relation to his, and we should think about what our own crosses might be. I thought mine might have something to do with my dad's mad moods, but I wasn't sure that would qualify.

The third-grade class was scared and silent as we gathered our things, closed up our books and desks, and found our jackets and lunch boxes. Audrey Fremont was the first one to step out into the hall as the rest of us hung back, not really believing that we were getting out of school for the entire year.

"All the other classes are going, too!" Audrey told us. "Let's get out of here!" She was the first one out the door, followed by Angela and then Leslie. The rest of us poured out when we thought the coast was clear. As we raced past the convent, we could see all the sisters gathered in the main parlor. Not one of them looked out the window at the 200 students of St. Ursula's School as we ran home, freed by the dead Pope.

We walked to Elly's house because we figured Rosa would be cooking something really good for dinner and hopefully cookies for dessert. She didn't seem surprised to see us. There was a special news broadcast on the TV instead of "The Price is Right." And Rosa *was* cooking something really good—pierogies, of all things. Frankie showed up at the back door with a bottle of wine in a paper bag. I don't know if she thought she was hiding it or something.

"Here's to the conclave," Frankie said, pouring wine for herself and Rosa.

"What's a conclave?" I asked her.

"It's where they fight over who's going to be the new Pope," Rosa answered.

"How irreverent!" my mother said, rummaging around for the corkscrew.

Rosa gave her a smile and continued bustling around the kitchen while Frankie opened the bag and then the bottle inside. We were not offered any of the mystery liquid, of course. So Elly and I excused ourselves to run around the block and yell. Suddenly it was summer and we really had a lot to do.

School was officially cancelled for the year, which really only amounted to one more week. Our mothers watched the television for news of who would be the next Pope, and our fathers went to work and came home and practiced their music. We went a little stir crazy, not knowing what it was OK to do or not to do since the Pope was dead and we thought we were supposed to be respectful. It came as a complete surprise on Friday night when we were loaded, along with our mothers, the drums, and a few assorted instruments, into Frank's van and were driven over to the Moose Club on Center Street. The Moose Club was an old building that was pretty much one big room. It was hazy and dim in there, and we could see a little stage at the far end as we walked in. People were milling around, and the bartender guy seemed very busy clinking glasses and bottles of beer. Our mothers staked out a table near the back exit, piled their purses on top, and instructed us to stay where they could see us at all times. Then they went to the bar and got us some sodas and themselves each a drink that looked like iced tea with a little red cherry on a stick. I watched Frankie sip hers, and a little smile came across her face. She looked happy, and I liked when she was happy.

Elly and I were very quiet as we watched The Continentals set up their music stands (special cardboard ones that had THE CONTINENTALS spray painted in red sparkles on each one). Frank arranged his matching silver-red sparkly drum kit very carefully in the center of the band. My dad Ted warmed up on his tenor sax by playing scales and difficult-sounding riffs. I heard him practice all the time at home, but here he sounded like a formidable, famous musician. We watched the bass player and Mr. Kimball the trumpet player set up their stuff, and they winked at us a few times. And then all of a sudden, without any perceptible signal, the band launched into a swing tune, "String of Pearls."

Wow! It was loud, louder than anything we had ever heard before. And it was amazingly beautiful! There were our dads, playing this loud, wonderful music. The band was like one person playing. We stood at the edge of the stage, and the music blew right over our heads, practically making our hair stand on end. We'd heard these tunes a million times but nothing like we were hearing them now. Our dads turned into magicians, making the notes dance, which in turn made the people dance. We were at an official Continentals gig!

Soon the hall was filled with cigarette smoke and people drinking things that looked a lot like our moms' iced teas. Our mothers were camped out together at our table, talking and laughing. Sometimes people we didn't know came over and laughed with them. They kept their eye on us in case any of the drunk men came too close. Elly and I pretty much stayed glued to the edge of the stage, though. We couldn't believe that our fathers and those lively musicians up there were actually the same people.

My Aunt Liddy showed up and had a couple of Long Island Iced Teas—that's what they were called—with Frankie and Rosa. For a minute, they huddled over the table and it looked like they were taking some aspirin pills or something, but Elly whispered to me that they were the same kind of pills that made our moms happy. I thought it was the iced teas, but maybe it really was the pills. I wondered if Frankie took one when my dad Ted got into one of his mean moods. It couldn't hurt, right?

Then Aunt Liddy showed us how to dance. She was smiling really big the whole time she was teaching us. We carved out a space on the dance floor, and Aunt Liddy showed us the polka: "One-and-two, one-and-two, step-skip-step, step-skip-step." She was so good at it and so patient that pretty soon Elly and I were zooming around the dance floor, a miniature couple polka-ing with the best of them. We could dance in between people and get around the dance floor faster than anyone else because we are so small. We danced over in front of our dads, who never acknowledged us, but Mr. Kimball winked and smiled at us a lot, even while he was blowing notes out of his trumpet.

The band took a break. Our fathers headed straight for the bar and our moms just stayed put at our table. Conversation in the hall rose to a booming level without the music in the background. The smoke got thicker, and it seemed like the crowd expanded, milling around the dance floor but not dancing. Elly and I slipped out the side door. It wasn't any cooler outside, but at least there was less smoke. We held hands and wandered around the parking lot. A few cars had couples in them making out. Elly wanted to go right up to the windows and look in, but I thought that might not be such a great idea.

"Kissing is so weird," she said. "I don't know what the big deal is."

I agreed with her. There were a lot more interesting things to do—like stealing an iced tea and seeing what that particular fuss was all about.

We rounded a blue station wagon, and there was my Uncle Andy. He was leaning against a red Firebird that was not his. Elly squeezed my hand tight. Uncle Andy is my father's brother, who Aunt Liddy calls a "good for nothing lazy bum."

"Hiya girls," Andy said. He swigged his beer. Neither of us said anything.

"We have to go back in," Elly announced. I could feel her being afraid of him, and that made me really afraid of him.

"That's too bad, girls. I thought maybe we could have some fun out here."

My voice decided to make an appearance. "Our moms said if we weren't back in five minutes, they were going to come after us." That was kind of a lie, but I decided that I would not confess it because it was a lie of desperation. There must be some kind of official confession exemption for this kind of lie.

Andy put his hand in his pocket. "How about a kiss for your uncle?" he said, squatting down so that he was eye level with us.

"No thanks, " Elly replied for both of us. I concentrated on disconnecting my shoes from the asphalt where they seemed to be glued. She tugged me, and I started after her. But in the fraction of a second before I started to run, I felt Andy's hand slip under my dress and into my underpants. Just for one second. Ok, maybe two seconds. His hands were clammy and rough. And they didn't belong there. Elly kept pulling me and I must have run, because suddenly we were back in the smoky hall and the band was back onstage. I almost started to cry, but then I wondered if I had really felt the hand or just thought I did.

Frankie had her hands on her hips. "WHERE have you two been?" She acted a little mad but mostly relieved to see us. "It's time to go," she said before we could reply. I noticed that the band was playing "These Boots Are Made for Walking," but it sounded strange and distant to me because my head had a weird buzzing in it. I looked at the stage and saw our dads playing the music that I could barely hear through the buzzing

We were bundled into the car with Rosa and Aunt Liddy. Andy was still lurking in the parking lot. He saw us and raised his beer in greeting. He had a little smile on his face that made him look like someone I would not want to talk to.

"Lazy son-of-a-bitch," Aunt Liddy said under her breath. That seemed meaner than good-for-nothing-lazy-bum, and I liked that she said it.

The car felt like a safe cocoon, and I felt like I could breathe again—even though Frankie was having a hard time finding the ignition and Rosa had to help her and we sort of sideswiped a car on the way out of the crowded lot.

"Is this what our fathers do when they go to gigs?" Elly asked. She seemed agitated, probably because of Andy and also from drinking about six cokes throughout the evening.

"Yes, honey. This is what they do every weekend, all weekend, sometimes four or five times in one weekend." Frankie was slurring her words a little. Actually, a lot. "Don't you miss your daddy on the weekends? Sometimes it's like you don't have a daddy and I don't have a husband."

"Sí," said Rosa. "But us girls, we are a big family, no?" Rosa was speaking Spanish and English mixed together. I loved when she did that.

I asked, "Why do they do it?" I figured it was a fair question.

"Because they love music and they get paid," said Rosa.

"Do they play the same music over and over?" I wondered.

"Yes, they do. Over and over and over and over. Again and again. Goddamn 'Moonlight Serenade.' Goddamn 'Pennsylvania 6-5000.' The goddamn 'Smile at Your Honey Polka,'" said Frankie. "And guess what? They don't smile at their honeys. Never."

The car was speeding up and slowing down, sometimes getting a little too close to the curb or the parked cars. I felt vaguely alarmed about this.

I decided to keep Frankie talking. It seemed to straighten out the car. "Then why do they still like it? Isn't that boring?" There was something that didn't make much sense to me about playing the same songs over and over.

"And why didn't they wink and smile at us while they were playing like Mr. Kimball did?" asked Elly.

"Well, well. Maybe we'll ask the band that question at the picnic next weekend, what do you think, Rosa?" Frankie blew right through a red light at Eighth and Broad, the Famous Intersection of Death.

The Band Picnic! Elly poked me in the ribs. We loved the Band Picnic. It was one of the funnest days of the summer.

"Cuidado, Francesca, we're almost home," said Rosa. She was

gripping the dashboard.

Our mothers fell silent until we pulled into the driveway of our house. The car got parked outside because Frankie couldn't figure out how to get it into the garage. Aunt Liddy was snoring in the back seat, and we wondered if we should just leave her there.

"Did Mr. Kimball really wink at you?" Frankie asked us before we got out of the car.

"Yes, he did," replied Elly, truthfully. "About 100 times."

I wanted to tell about the hand but I couldn't. And they seemed mad enough about Mr. Kimball winking. I didn't know what they would think about the hand.

Rosa and Elly stayed over, as usual. Our dads didn't get home until it was light, clomping into the kitchen with their gear. Rosa got up and went home with Frank. Elly and I watched them leave, staying really quiet so we didn't wake my mom. We snuck down to the kitchen and made two bowls of Cheerios. We ate our breakfast outside, watching the paperboy wobble around on his banana bike, whipping the East Bedford Bugle onto porches.

We were the only ones awake for hours. I wanted to tell Elly what Andy did to me—and I didn't. I mostly wanted to forget about it. I tried to get interested in packing my stuff for Girl Scout camp, but I kept feeling the hand where it didn't belong.

3

Lennie and Lenny

Frankie sipped a highball. She and Rosa were talking about our grandmothers, and it was the second time I ever heard the word "bitch." We were sitting around the pool at the Band Picnic, and Elly and I were finally allowed to play by ourselves anywhere we wanted, even in the water for the very first time ever. We splashed around in the shallow end but inched slowly toward the deep end while our mothers sunned themselves on lounge chairs and kept us within visual range. Suddenly, Elly flew through the air and into the water, creating a big splash.

"HEY! You have to be careful! NO RUNNING! NO JUMPING!" My cousin Jenny had gotten her lifeguard certification two days before, and she had been hired as the Official Lifeguard of the Band Picnic. She blew her whistle and yelled at Elly. She seemed to be intent on dampening our fun, but in reality, she was probably just Being Important.

Jenny walked around the pool swinging her whistle (a present from her father, my Uncle Henry, the leader of The Continentals before our fathers staged a coup and took over) and looking very concerned and busy. When Elly surfaced, Jenny ran over to us and made us promise to be really careful and stay in the shallow end of the pool. She didn't want to have to worry about us, and since we were the youngest kids, we were the biggest risk to her reputation. She wanted to be known as never having anyone drown on her watch.

"But you've only been a lifeguard for two days," Elly pointed out, wise beyond our eight years.

"Shut up," Jenny commanded. And then she promised to teach us how to dive if we didn't cause any problems for her all day. No more jumping cannonballs, no swimming underwater to see how long we could hold our breath. No excess frolicking anywhere in the pool.

We decided to be very, very good and followed all her orders all day long because we really wanted to learn how to dive. We splashed and cavorted in the baby end of the pool and didn't even venture over to the deep part, which had several red "9s" painted around the edge, indicating that the water was so deep that we would undoubtedly die immediately if we fell in near one of the 9s. We hung around near Mrs. Kimball, the trumpet player's wife, and their latest baby, which she dipped into the water and then made cooing noises at. It was fascinating. We could not discern whether the baby was a girl or a boy because she called it Pat. Such an unlikely baby name. Not Patty or Patrick. Just Pat. She appeared to really love this little creature as evidenced by the many lipstick tattoo marks all over its little face and arms. We sat with them at the edge of the pool with our legs dangling into the water and eavesdropped on my other cousin, Robin, complaining about the excessive size of her boobs.

"This isn't my suit, it's my puny sister's," she explained to Elly's glamorous cousin Susanne, nodding over to where puny Jenny was striding with her whistle. "It's like trying to squash cantaloupes into Dixie cups," she laughed, obviously pleased with her analogy. Then they both laughed really loudly about the ridiculousness of the idea of Robin's giant breasts fitting into the orange suit. There was never any explanation about why Robin had to wear Jenny's little suit instead of one that might actually fit her. I was busy trying to figure out what cantaloupes were when one of those very breasts exploded right out of the too-small-suit.

There was a lot of screaming. But in the very few seconds before it started, Elly and I were face to face with a huge—and to us, very mysterious—piece of anatomy.

"Wow," Elly whispered. "That was BIG."

I couldn't speak. I swished my legs back and forth in the water, listening to all the yelling and screeching. This had attracted the attention of the men, who were in the field playing touch football. One by one, they streamed toward the pool.

I was fascinated with the marvelous looking boob, which was by now covered up again. I had never, to my knowledge, ever seen a nipple. At least not that close up. It was interesting and intriguing. I stared at my cousin, seeing her in a new way. The breasts were hidden inside a t-shirt for the remainder of the afternoon. I looked at them often. I wanted to see the other one, too. If Frankie had known about my fascination, she would undoubtedly have attributed it to me having been deprived of breastfeeding. In that case, boobs and nipples would have been no big deal at all. But there I was, delighted and enthralled.

The football players were disappointed that they'd missed the show, and they taunted Cousin Robin to do it again. She turned red and shooed them away. The other women seemed jealous, especially Mrs. Kimball, who seemed in danger of letting the ambiguously gendered baby slip into the pool as she glared at her husband. And Jenny, who had reluctantly relinquished some of the attention she'd been gathering by being the Official Lifeguard.

When the men went back to their football game, Susanne dragged Robin off to where they kept the food and liquor. They poured themselves large plastic cups of something that—the more they drank, the more they laughed. During one of these laughing spells, Robin succumbed to something Susanne said and raised up her t-shirt. I got my wish. Oh my God, I saw THE breast again and also the twin breast, two of them at once! Brown nipples, beautiful roundness. I don't think Robin saw me looking, but Elly did. I had a funny feeling in my stomach, a kind of thrill and a kind of twisty feeling. It was a wonderful new sensation. All I had to do to make the feeling happen again was to imagine those breasts appearing before me.

For the rest of the afternoon, Elly and I played our new game called Beautiful Ladies. We pretended to be gorgeous, rich, society ladies out for a stroll. Our imaginary route took us through gardens and patios and over a bridge on the grounds of our estate. In our game, the bridge gave way just as we stepped upon it (the edge of the pool) and the Beautiful Ladies were thrown into the water, soaking their designer dresses and ruining their hairdos. There would be much screaming as we plunged into the water. We laughed at how foolish the Beautiful Ladies were, and then we did it all over again. Jenny glowered at us from the other end of the pool and finally came over to sullenly give us our diving lessons, since she really had nothing better to do.

When our skin turned blue and puckered, we got out of the pool. We were enraptured with ourselves and the Beautiful Ladies so much that we made a tent out of our beach towels and invented our own world. The Beautiful Ladies lived there, and nothing bad ever happened. Our world was surrounded by trees and parks with elaborate jungle-gym equipment. Kids could have their own houses. The Beautiful Ladies could eat anything they wanted, and they didn't have to do any work, ever. They could read books that they got from the library and listen to records they bought through the mail. There were all sorts of animals there. And the very best thing was that there was music everywhere. You didn't need radios or anything—you could just think it and there would be whatever music you wanted, playing right out loud.

Frankie was suddenly standing over us, tugging at my towel.

"Hey, prune-girls, it's time for you to get changed into your clothes. It's getting dark." Frankie looked so happy. Her green eyes twinkled. She fluffed up our heads.

We didn't even argue with her. We were clammy and tired, and if we were lucky, our moms would let us roast marshmallows over the grill when we were all dry and dressed. Frankie nudged us toward the barn, where our regular clothes were hanging up in a former horse stall. No animals lived in this barn anymore. It had been converted into a sort-of playhouse for adults. There were chairs and a pool table, and the stalls were now changing rooms, swept clean of horse poop and straw. It still smelled a little bit of horses, though, which I liked.

Elly ran and I chased her all the way in. It was dim inside the big barn, no matter what time of day. We tiptoed around even though there was no real reason to. Elly found our stall, and we started peeling off our wet swimsuits. In mid-strip, Elly stopped and stared toward the door of the stall, one foot in and one foot out of her little blue suit. I followed her eyes and I saw him—Uncle Andy, leaning against the doorway with a beer in his hand. His other hand was down his pants, except that there weren't any pants. His hand was *down there* and he was holding onto something. There was a slow dawn of realization as we figured out what it was.

His hand was on his thing, and it was slowly going up and down. His shorts were halfway down his thighs, where the elastic held them from dropping all the way.

The air went out of both of us in a rush. We were stunned by the unfolding scene of his hand, his thing, up-down-up-down. Neither one of us had ever seen a real live thing. Neither one of us knew what to do. This was not right, him standing there looking at us, his hand touching his thing.

I caught his eye. He looked at me in a brazen, frank, unfamiliar way. His gaze drew me in like a tractor beam. He dared me with those eyes, and I finally had to look away. Elly was squeezing my hand so hard I thought I might have to scream.

Andy took his hand away from his thing and then he put both of his hands on his hips like Frankie does sometimes when she's mad. The thing just kind of hung there but it was sticking straight out, pointing directly at Elly and me. It was surrounded by a patch of dark hair, like fur. It looked like some out-of-place appendage on a rare, weird animal, one from Africa or Borneo or somewhere exotic that you could only see in a National Geographic photo. Then he started moving toward us. We were frozen to the floor.

"It's OK," he whispered in a really weird voice. "Don't you want to see it up close?"

"No!" yelled Elly, emphatically. Apparently my voice was frozen, along with my body. I couldn't get a squeak out.

"How about you, little niece-y. Would you like to touch it? It's very warm." Andy kept inching closer, and I couldn't move. I could smell the beer on his breath. I was scared his thing was going to make contact with me.

He reached out for Elly's hand, and I could tell he was going to make her touch the thing. Not me, her. It was slow motion for a few seconds, him reaching for her hand, panic spreading across her face, her mouth opening—

"MOM!" Elly suddenly screamed. This was not your usual scream. This was a supersonic scream. If you walk over to a piano and hit the very highest note, which is a C, you'd get an idea of the pitch. As for the loudness, imagine an air horn going off next to your ear. There you have Elly's alarm scream.

Elly's screaming triggered something in me, and I started shouting. I don't really have the kind of voice you can scream with. I didn't really know what I was shouting, just that all of a sudden I was. This spurred Andy into action. He whipped his shorts back up to where they belonged, dropped his beer bottle on the ground, and grabbed Elly's arm. Hard. Then he shoved her up against the rough wood of the barn wall. When he had her pinned against the wall, he stuck his arm out and punched me in the stomach. Hard. I felt the breath in me get sucked out so that where there had been air, there was nothing. Tears welled up in my eyes and I tried to get my breath back. I felt like I would never be able to breathe again because it hurt so bad.

"Mama!" Elly started screaming again in spite of Andy holding her against the wall. I think my gasping for breath scared her more than Andy bashing her against the wall.

"You little shitheads. You little crybaby shitheads." Andy picked up the beer bottle and flung it against the far wall where it smashed into a billion pieces. "If you ever tell anyone about this, I'll beat the living shit out of you," he hissed. Then he disappeared into the shadows of the barn. I could see the glass glittering on the floor where the dim light hit it. I wondered if we should try to clean it up before anyone saw.

Aunt Liddy came flapping into the doorway, her flip-flops making a lot of noise. I'd never seen her move so fast. She looked frightened. "Is everything all right?" she asked, peering around as though she knew that Evil Andy had just been there with his thing out, punching me and slamming Elly.

"I'm stuck," Elly said, showing Aunt Liddy how tangled she was in her swimsuit. She was making something up so we wouldn't have to tell Aunt Liddy about Andy and then he would kill us! By this time I was breathing almost normally again, but I knew Elly wanted to divert attention from me in case I wasn't. I wanted to cry, too, but I knew this would be a bad idea. I was scared of Andy, and I was amazed at how strong my friend was.

I felt the sudden, unspoken agreement in the air between Elly and me, that we would never tell about what had just happened. We would lie about it if we had to. I knew without a doubt that Andy would keep his word about beating us up, and so did Elly. Except we sort of knew that Aunt Liddy suspected something. She kept looking around the barn. "Was there anyone else in here?" she asked, knowing that there was. "Why is all this glass on the floor? Did you break something?"

"No," Elly answered, a little too quickly. "But it's scary because it's getting dark. And there might be giant ants or something!" She was trying to get Aunt Liddy to laugh because we always watched the late night giant insect horror movies with her when we stayed over at her house. Elly always pretended to be afraid of the fake giant ants, and this always made Aunt Liddy laugh.

But Aunt Liddy didn't laugh. She took one of the towels and rubbed us both down, warming and comforting us without realizing she was doing exactly what we needed in that moment. Rosa and Frankie came in, drinks still in their hands. "Dios mio, such noise about nothing! Maria Elena, don't you know how to dress yourself?" A look of relief washed over her face when she realized that we were OK. Except that we weren't. Not at all. I felt a lump jump into my throat. I wanted to throw myself in her arms and cry. But I couldn't, or she would know about Andy. And then we'd be in big trouble.

Rosa helped both of us into our warm clothes and led us out to the grill where Ted had speared far too many marshmallows on sticks for us. I saw Andy, now holding a new beer, lurking around behind everyone. He was looking at us with his mean eyes, and I knew he would really do what he said about hurting us. Now we had to be careful. We would have to be careful forever and ever, amen.

In the car on the way home from the Band Picnic, I curled up in the back seat with Elly and both of our moms. We were in Frankie's car, which was big and comfortable with a huge back seat. We clung to each other in the dark, and I knew she was thinking about Andy just like I was. Our moms were on either side of us, cuddling us up, too. I vowed that I would never let anything bad happen to Elly, no matter what. I would never say one thing about what happened. My belly hurt where Andy hit me, but I pretended that it didn't. There was marshmallow goop on my face and I distracted myself by trying to stick my tongue our far enough to lick it off.

Safe between Frankie and Elly, I let my mind wander and started thinking about breasts. Robin's dark nipples hung before my eyes. I imagined that the flesh surrounding them would be soft, like a pillow. And then I had the terrible horrible thought that if Robin had those round nipply soft things, then possibly all women did. I felt my own flat, nonexistent ones. I had a vague idea that they would grow eventually. I thought of my mother's, always hidden away, but now and then I bumped into one and wondered uncertainly about it. And Mrs. Weingarten, our old neighbor down the street. Hers were enormous bombs beneath her floral print dresses. When she hugged us, they pressed around our heads as she leaned over. I smelled her older woman brand of perfume and enjoyed being gently pummeled by all that flesh. The idea of different shapes and sizes hadn't occurred to me before Robin's accidental exhibition. It was a slightly disturbing, mostly delightful thing to think about.

Rosa had breasts that were just the perfect size. They weren't too big or small, and they had substance. I once saw her rushing from the shower to her room, towel flapping, one breast partially exposed. I was more interested in her furry crotch, but Elly wasn't at all intrigued, so we went off to play in her room. Now, riding home in the car, I wondered more about that—breasts as a source of fascination. It gave me another little thrill in my belly to consider it.

We pulled into the driveway, and my parents were sort of whispering. I wasn't quite asleep but kept very still because I knew if they thought I was sleeping, my dad would carry me upstairs and tuck me in and I wouldn't have to brush my teeth. Which is exactly what happened. I even got tucked in in my clothes. I felt my dad's hand brush through my hair, and then he left, leaving the door ajar like he always did.

I tried to sleep for real, but I kept thinking about Andy in the barn. It was creepy and scary to think about. Seeing his thing and him almost making Elly touch it was just not right. I couldn't get the picture of it out of my mind. Images flashed through my head: breasts, which were nice. And Andy's thing, which was really scary. I didn't want to see it, it was private like breasts, and no part of me ever wanted to see it. When I thought about him holding it with his hand, I got a barfy feeling in my stomach. I couldn't stop thinking about it, and I couldn't sleep even though I was so tired from playing Beautiful Ladies all day long. I stared at the ceiling even though I couldn't see it. The house was quiet. Every now and then I heard some little noise that told me my parents were still downstairs.

The quiet was broken by voices that were getting louder and louder. This scared me because my parents never spoke to each other loudly, so I thought someone else had come into the house. But it turned out to be just the two of them. They were arguing about more children. My mother didn't want any. My father did. It was the middle of the night and they were fighting about children?

"Isn't Lennie enough?" my mother shouted. It didn't sound like her voice. It sounded weird, like a shrill version of my otherwise intelligent and composed mother. By this time I had crept to my little perch at the top of the stairs where I could hear everything but no one knew I was there.

"Enough? It's not about enough! Children should not be ONLY children!" my father yelled back.

"We don't have enough money! And you're never around! You're always with that damn band! If you want more children, you'd have to be a better father!"

"Oh, so you think I'm a bad father? Because I'm gone a lot?! Are you just saying that I don't take care of Lennie? That I can't be a good father because of MY MUSIC?! Huh, Frankie? IS THAT WHAT YOU'RE SAYING?!"

Then it got really quiet. My little knees were knocking together. So I was expensive. So my father was a bad father. So I shouldn't be an only child. What is an only child?

When I heard the kitchen chairs scraping the floor, I snuck back into my bed. I knew they'd be heading upstairs, and I needed to fake sleep, which I wasn't very good at. I usually laughed when I pretended to be asleep and I saw them open the door and look in on me. Then they'd come in and laugh with me and tickle me and tell me to go to sleep, young lady. This could not be a night like that, though. There would be absolutely no laughing. But no one came in to check on me. There was just quiet, and a heavy tension that blanketed the whole house. When I got up in the morning, there was a pile of blankets on the couch. I don't know which one of my parents slept there, but it went on for a few nights. No tickling, no pretending to be asleep. Just tense silence.

My stomach hurt for days. I could not stop thinking about Andy and his thing. I could not stop thinking about my parents fighting. It was my fault, I knew this, and I didn't know what to do about it. To make matters worse, I didn't get to see Elly for three days. She had to go to her grandmother's, and I knew that was terrible for her. Her Grandma Wojechowski still wouldn't let Rosa in the house, but she demanded that Elly stay with her on some weekends. We knew that we wouldn't get to see each other after the Band Picnic, but I needed her. I needed to talk about Andy the Terrible with her under the blankets with a flashlight. This is where we figured everything out. But Elly was being tortured by her grandmother who made her read the Bible and gory saint stories and who said mean things about Elly's brown mother. I was so lonely that my body ached, and I couldn't eat any food because that would make it ache more.

My parents weren't really talking to each other, which meant they weren't talking to me very much either. All three of us lived in the house, and it was weirdly quiet except for my dad practicing and my mom listening to the radio while she read books. For some reason, we all went to the grocery store one evening together. Silently. Usually Frankie shopped alone or took me with her and sent me on missions to find tomato paste or molasses. She was the only mother I knew who cooked with things like molasses or maple syrup instead of white sugar, which she insisted was poison.

But this night all three of us piled in the station wagon and went over to the Acme. The place was dead. It was one of those summer evenings when people were doing other things, like taking walks or going to hear the Municipal Band at the Rose Garden. The Acme was only open for a few more minutes, so we were there with other people who really needed stuff before the next day and were rushing in before they closed the doors.

Out in front of the store there was a boy holding a cardboard box. He was an older kid. He looked like he could be in high school or or maybe older. As we approached him, he started dragging the box over toward the dumpster at the side of the building. My father stopped in his tracks and watched him.

A little yelp came from the box. My father sprinted toward the boy. "What the hell are you doing?" he demanded. Frankie and I froze and watched.

The boy said something to Ted. A little puppy face peeked over the side of the box, which by now was in a tug of war between my dad and the kid. When I realized that the boy was on his way to tossing the box containing the dog into the dumpster, I wanted to scream just like Elly would, if it were physiologically possible for me to scream, which it was not.

Frankie took my hand. We watched the boy surrender the box to my dad. We saw his face scrunch up and start to cry, in that way that boys cry, knowing that they want to and they have to but they're not supposed to. We heard him tell my dad that his mother made him bring the whole litter of puppies to the Acme and give them away or else she was going to kill them, one by one, with a hammer. There were eleven of them. The boy managed to give ten away, and there was one left and he had to be home in ten minutes and he didn't want to bring the puppy home for his mother to murder.

Frankie was squeezing my hand so hard it was going numb. My ears were buzzing. I couldn't believe this was happening. I couldn't believe that a person on the earth would actually do such a thing as kill puppies with a hammer. I couldn't believe that this boy had to live with a person like that.

We stood there and watched as my father reached into the box and took out the little black puppy and cradled her to his chest. The boy broke down sobbing. My father patted the boy's shoulder. He asked his name.

"Jeffery," the boy said.

"That's a good name," my father said. They shook hands. Jeffery wiped his nose on his forearm. He forced himself to stop crying.

"Thank you," he kept saying to my dad. He patted the puppy on the head, and then he ran away.

We never did go inside the store. We got back in the car and I sat between my parents in the front seat, which I never got to do because it was "unsafe," and the little black puppy, oblivious to her near demise, curled up on my lap.

When we got home, Ted played a recording of the Piano Concerto Number 21 by Wolfgang Amadeus Mozart, and we watched the puppy romp on the floor near the speaker. The piece was majestic and melodic, fitting for the dramatic rescue of the puppy. Ted explained a few things about Mozart to me, that he was a child prodigy and a genius. I was so happy hearing the music and playing with the puppy and having my dad talk to me that I wanted to live in those moments for the rest of my life.

"Can we name her Wolfie?" I asked Ted. After Wolfgang Amadeus Mozart.

"I think we can," he said. He actually smiled at me. My heart swooped.

There were no more fights about children because Frankie's ectopic pregnancy happened about three days after my dad rescued Wolfie. Frankie was rushed to the hospital while I was in my room playing with Elly. When we went downstairs, Frank was sitting by himself in the living room, his face ashen. "Your mom got sick and your dad and Rosa went to the hospital with her," he told me. He didn't mince words, just told us the facts. The puppy was on his lap. I felt like I should cry because I knew something was terribly wrong but didn't comprehend it.

"Are we staying here?" Elly asked. She took my hand. It was a very adult thing to do.

"Yes, honey," Frank said. He kept looking at the television. There was a baseball game on but the sound was off.

Elly ran into the kitchen and rummaged around. Then she led me back up to my room. She produced a candle, placed it on the dresser, and lit it. She asked the Virgin Mary to take care of Frankie. She said the Our Father, the Act of Contrition, the Apostle's Creed, and seventeen Hail Marys in a row.

"That ought to do it," she said, when she was finished.

In the morning, Aunt Liddy was in the kitchen making waffles. My father was still at the hospital and so was Rosa. But Frank had gone to work. Since it was summer, we didn't have to go to school. So Aunt Liddy fed us waffles and then took us to the movies where we saw *Dr. Doolittle*. When we got home from the movies, she made more popcorn and found a movie on TV about giant wasps. We didn't laugh as much as usual about the bad special effects because we were still worried about Frankie. But she came home the next day, a little wobbly and high on some kind of painkillers. And after that, no one mentioned anything about her having any more children. Ever again.

So I was officially an only child, and Wolfie the dog became something of another child for my parents and a sibling for me. We slept together and got in trouble together and played in the yard together. She waited for me after summer catechism class. She loved Elly like I did, and Elly loved her. And one time I saw Jeffrey the boy at the park. He was with a black dog. It wasn't until I got home that I realized it must have been Wolfie's dog mother. And I was so glad all over again that Wolfie was not killed with a hammer. I tried to tell Wolfie about it—we had seen her mother and did she miss her? But Wolfie only wanted to play with her tennis ball, which was fine with me.

The Friday just before school was going to start again, we were instructed to skip Confession and go straight to my house after the final summer catechism class.

"We have never skipped Confession before," Elly said worriedly as we trotted along Broad Street on our way to my house. "And we are not exactly in a state of grace."

"I know," I said. I was vaguely worried that all the stuff we did at Girl Scout camp was not exactly free of sin, but I wasn't sure how to confess it, and I hadn't said anything in Confession all summer. Stuff like spying on our counselor and putting Saran Wrap on the toilets and stealing Angela Santini's bra. I'd been putting off confessing until the week before school started, and now I'd have to carry the sins around even longer.

"This means we can't go to Communion on Sunday, you know." There was a little flutter of panic in my chest.

Elly stopped in her tracks. "What is going on here?" Our weekly routine had been seriously disrupted. "I should have asked Sister Anne. She would know what to do about skipping Confession." Sister Anne was the newest nun in the convent, even newer than the new Mother Superior, and we had her for summer catechism. She was also the youngest and the most willing to talk to us about almost anything. She wandered around a lot trying to be helpful wherever she could. The most amazing thing about Sister Anne is that she doesn't wear a regular habit. She wears a skirt that stops below her knees so you can see her actual legs. And she wears a veil thing that doesn't cover her whole head. Her hair is brown and it is real. We spent quite a lot of time marveling at the fact that Sister Anne seems to be an actual Real Person.

There was no mac and cheese at my house. Our mothers and fathers were all there and they were all dressed up in their church clothes. It was more than highly unusual that our parents would be together, dressed up, in the same house, and our fathers not getting ready for the Friday night gig.

"What is going on here?" Elly said again. I could feel her fear jump right from her chest over to mine.

"We're going Somewhere," my dad said.

"WHERE!?" I demanded in a more squeaky voice than I intended.

"You'll see," he said.

Oh no, not again. Not another Somewhere.

"Are we all going?" Elly asked, calmly, in adult mode. I could almost see her as a grown woman, with a flower print dress and breasts and lipstick.

"We're all going, Elly," Rosa said. I could tell by looking at her that she wanted to just level with us about the big mystery. But by some prior agreement, she couldn't. She was going to have to watch us squirm.

The parents ushered us into Frankie's big Chrysler station wagon, and my dad got behind the wheel. (It would be unheard of for my mom to drive with my father in the car, even if it *was* her car.) This was the car we used when we went to church or to some other event where we had to dress up. It was the big boat of a car that she couldn't fit into the garage after The Continentals gig. The best part about this car was that me and Elly could sit in the way back seat which faced out the back window instead of in the direction the car was heading. Elly and I crawled in and held hands. Frank and Rosa got into the regular back seat that faced the regular way, and Rosa patted Elly and me on the head as we backed out of the driveway.

It was weird to see Mr. Frank Wojciechowski dressed up. His neck seemed trapped by his shirt and tie, straining to get out. Rosa looked beautiful, like my mom Frankie. They looked like Glamour Magazine photos. And my dad Ted looked very serious and a little scared, but he would never admit that. He always had everything under control.

The car hurled down Route 22 and passed by all the familiar landmarks, like Liberty Bell High School, The Cup, St. Ursula's (where our friends were still in the Confession line), and the Stewart's Root Beer drive-in where you could get Scramburgers. When we crossed the river into New Jersey, we squeezed each other's hands. We were going Somewhere far away with dressed-up parents. We were eating peanut-butter-and-jelly sandwiches because there hadn't been time for a real dinner. We didn't know what else to whisper to each other, so we fell silent and eavesdropped on the parents' conversation.

"You don't have to worry about me driving in Manhattan, Frankie. I've done it for years now." Ted had that tone which meant, Do Not Talk To Me About This Anymore, I Will Not Answer You.

"Yeah, don't worry, gals," Frank said. He had his arm around Rosa's shoulders in a possessive way. There was something icky about him doing that.

Neither Elly nor I knew what or where Manhattan was. But it was apparent that it was a scary place to drive in, so we scooched closer to each other and held hands even tighter. The landscape was completely unfamiliar as we traveled east on the freeway, wondering where the actual Somewhere might be.

It began to get dark and we cruised into an area where millions of cars whizzed by and it was hard to tell how many lanes there were to the highway. We started to see the skyline of New York City half in and half out of the dark. There were lights twinkling from some of the tallest buildings and shadows of others. You could tell immediately that it was New York—even we could tell, even though we've only seen New York City in books and photographs. We did not get that there was a connection between New York City and Manhattan. There was the Empire State building and the Chrysler building, and Frank was pointing out the Statue of Liberty. In minutes, we were IN the city, in those lights and traffic and millions of people. If New York City was the Somewhere, then it was going to be very, very good.

The Chrysler moved at a snail's pace through the streets and traffic lights and pedestrians. I had never seen so much life and activity and brightness in one place before.

"Where are we going?" I couldn't contain myself. It was a little weird that our parents were taking us on our first trip to New York and not saying one single word about it. We even had to figure out that it was New York all by ourselves.

"Sssshhhh! Your father has to concentrate on his driving," Frankie said. She turned around for emphasis.

"My driving is FINE, Frankie." My father said this with his teeth clamped together, meaning that it was possible his driving was not really fine at all.

A brand new terrible thought sent a shock through my body. "Maybe they're going to give us away!" I whispered to this to Elly. Why else would we come to this bustling hive of humanity with dressed-up parents who wouldn't tell us a thing if they were going to continue to keep us as their children? What other explanation could there be? I could tell that Elly was considering this because her face was scrunching up a little in that way that it does right before she starts crying.

"Why do they want to give us away?" whispered Elly back to me.

"Because there are big orphanages in New York, and we'll have a better chance of getting new families if they leave us here." I don't know how I knew that. I just did. New York was big enough to have things like that plus other places that we couldn't even imagine, probably.

"Maybe we'd be able to get in the same family. Then we could be sisters like we almost are." Elly was squeezing the life out of my hand.

"¡Dios mio!" Rosa said, "Do you hear what they are thinking? We have to tell them!" Rosa was snapping and unsnapping the clasp of her clutch purse. "Niñas, we are not giving you away! Where on earth do you get such ideas? Ay, those nuns . . . ."

"No, don't tell them anything!" Frank insisted.

My mom rolled her eyes toward the car ceiling. My father didn't say anything. Rosa kept up the purse snapping. Frank turned away from us, happy with the game. He was actually laughing. "Hey, I never thought of that! How much do you think we'd get for them?"

"¡Dios mio! Don't be so cruel!," Rosa said. Her neck was all red, and I could tell that she was furious. Her dark eyes flashed around the car, from us to Frank to my parents all the way up front. Rosa actually took Frank's arm from her shoulder and flung it away from her.

The car swung hard around a corner, and we all slammed into the person we were next to. Rosa slid across the seat and whammed back into Frank, who just laughed. Elly and I used this opportunity to clutch each other. Maybe they weren't going to give us away, but the alternatives were still mysterious and scary.

"Here we are!" Ted informed us as he whipped into a parking lot and paid the attendant. We were in a canyon of tall buildings, one of which had a marquee announcing this evening's concert by the New York Philharmonic. This is the building we walked towards, our moms smoothing their hair with one hand, purses dangling, while they held tight to our hands with the other hand. Our dads led the procession, somber in their Sunday suits. No one said a word.

We entered a gigantic lobby filled with people who were also all dressed up, way more than us. OK, so it was clearly not an orphanage. Ladies in black and white handed out programs and took our tickets. Next we were in a giant hall filled with seats and red ornate wall hangings and three balconies. The many seats on the stage were filling up with musicians who had violins, cellos, flutes, trumpets, and all sorts of other instruments. They made amazing sounds as they warmed up. They sounded vaguely like my dad playing his tenor sax, but much more exotic. Right in front of all the musicians' seats was a big box with two steps up to the top. I knew immediately that this is where the conductor would stand while he waved his baton at the musicians. I knew this from watching Leonard Bernstein on TV explaining music to kids.

This is how we sat in row 14, seats A–F: Frank, Rosa, Elly, me, Ted, Frankie. As soon as we sat down, Ted took on the role of orchestra tour guide, explaining everything to Elly and me. He practically hadn't said one word in two hours, including where we were going and why or anything. Now all of a sudden there was his voice, and I felt mad that he'd deserted us until he felt like talking.

"OK, the oboist just came out. He's going to tune the orchestra when the concertmaster comes out—the concertmaster is always the very last musician to come onstage—OK, and there's the timpanist. He's tuning his drums to the right pitch—see how he puts his ear right next to the drum?"

"Dad, why didn't you tell us we were coming here?" I was still dismayed about how we were taken from our ritual Friday evening and driven all the way to New York City, wondering if we were going to be dropped off at an orphanage and given away to new families.

"Lennie, I have my reasons. Now pay attention. There's a lot to learn here. I want you to be ready when Mr. Bernstein comes out."

A sparkle of fireworks went off in my head. "You mean LEONARD BERNSTEIN is HERE??!!" Now this was too much. We were going to see a television star in person? We were going to hear the NEW YORK PHILHARMONIC???? I forgave my father immediately because Mr. Bernstein was a hero for both of us, and apparently he was going to be right here, right in front of us, only a few feet away. In the flesh. On the podium! We watched Mr. Bernstein every time he came on TV to teach kids about music or to have a special program for grown-ups about the orchestra. I thought he was more fascinating than God, but I would never admit that to Sister Regina or Father Chaslowski. Ever.

My father just sat there with a smug look on his face. "Yes, this is Mr. Bernstein's orchestra." He didn't even look at me. He stared straight ahead at the stage, smug and self-satisfied. I stared at him and demanded, "WHY DIDN'T YOU TELL ME?" He would not turn his head. I thought he looked mean and sad all rolled together in the same expression.

People taking their seats looked over at us. "Lennie," my mom whispered. "You can't talk that loud in here." She looked worried, as though we might get kicked out because of my loudness. She seemed surprised because I am not usually a loud kid. Or maybe we'd be kicked out because of my kidness. Elly and I were the only kids in sight. And I was so excited that I was squirming around and poking Elly and practically jumping out of my seat.

I could hardly contain myself. Mr. Bernstein was nice to kids. His orchestra played things I now recognized, like *Night on Bald Mountain* and Mozart's *Jupiter Symphony*. I had no idea that kids could go and see the orchestra in person. I had no idea that there were hundreds of other orchestras in the world besides the New York Philharmonic. I had no idea that the actual New York Philharmonic was within driving distance of my house. I love Mr. Bernstein and the smiling, gentle way he talks to kids, as though he really understands us. Not like we're stupid because we're kids.

More and more people came and the seats filled up. Elly and I were still pretty much the only kids in our section of the audience, which was so close to the orchestra that we had a good view of the musicians' feet. We did spot one fat little girl a few rows over who was eating a huge lollipop. Even I knew you weren't supposed to eat in the concert hall, but maybe she had the lollipop to shut her up. I could have used one myself.

Suddenly the lights went down. A guy holding a violin came out and the audience applauded. The violin guy turned his back on us and looked at the orchestra. My dad poked me and said simply, "Concertmaster." The oboe player played the tuning note which is A=440, which is the A above middle C on the piano, in case you didn't know. Everyone should know this. This A is the Official Tuning Note of symphony orchestras.

Then the whole orchestra burst into tunes and riffs and arpeggios and long tones all dancing around the A=440. Then as suddenly as they started, the musicians stopped playing. A big quiet settled over the whole auditorium—which, by the way, was Carnegie Hall, but we didn't realize the significance of that until quite a few years later. The quiet was for us to get ready to listen and for the musicians to get ready to play.

Then, Mr. Leonard Bernstein bounded out of a door behind the percussion section, strode through the violin section, and jumped up on the podium. He bowed his head hello to us, raised his arms, and the auditorium burst suddenly into sound. I practically jumped out of my seat—I'd never heard anything so loud and so beautiful all at once. Elly grabbed my hand. We were listening to Shostakovich's *Festive Overture*, but we didn't know it was called that. The strings were playing a million miles an hour and the winds were answering with chains of notes flying around everywhere, with brass fanfares bringing up the rear. The music sent chills up and down my spine, not the cold kind of chills but the electric kind, where every cell of my body stood at attention and couldn't contain their excitement.

In my brain I tried to synchronize the orchestra from the television to the orchestra onstage before me in person, with Mr. Bernstein just a few feet away from me. It was real now, but it wasn't real on TV. Or was it? My mind was overwhelmed because the orchestra was so real, and on TV it was so remote. Here we were, just feet away from the violins and trombones and Mr. Bernstein himself.

The *Festive Overture* ended with a huge bang and everyone in the audience clapped and some people yelled Bravo! Then the musicians scattered around the stage while some serious-looking guys dressed in all black wheeled a piano out from somewhere backstage. The musicians had to scrunch their chairs back farther on the stage to make room for the piano. Mr. Bernstein was nowhere to be seen while this was happening. My mom leaned over and whispered, "Are you happy, Lennie?"

"I am really happy, Mom."

"I thought you might be." She smiled at me really big. My dad did not turn his head away from the stage. But I knew he was happy deep in there somewhere, too. His lecture had stopped the moment the orchestra tuned. I wondered when he might speak again. It could be days. I wanted to know why he'd brought us here, why he didn't tell us anything about it, why he didn't talk to me about important stuff like this unless he felt like it. Why did it have to be a secret? Why did everything with him have to be a big secret? He even got Elly's parents in on it, too, and they went along with it in the car so that we thought we were going to be orphanage dwellers. I felt mad at my dad and happy at him all at the same time.

The lights went down again, and then some clapping started. A beautiful woman in a white swishy gown came onstage and sat down at the piano. The gown was actually wisps of fabric swirling around her. The straps were tiny, and her breasts caught my attention because they seemed to want to jump right out of the dress, like Robin's. Then the music started again, and this time it fell down from the ceiling around us in all different colors. When the piano began to play, I felt like crying. I just held Elly's hand tighter and I knew she felt like crying, too.

The woman's name was Miss Ludmilla Michalowski and she was from Russia. She was 34 years old, it said in the program, and she had recently defected from The Soviet Union. She had hair like you would see on someone in a shampoo commercial. It swished around down her back as she was playing. Miss Michalowski and Mr. Bernstein looked at each other while the music was playing, and they were saying things to each other with their eyes. First the music was fast, then it was slow and very beautiful, then fast again, and the woman's fingers flew around the keyboard. It was a concerto by Mr. Rachmaninoff, who is no longer alive. He is in heaven with Pope John and President Kennedy.

I decided right then and there that I wanted to play the piano like that. I might even want to BE Ludmilla Michalowski, even though I didn't like her dress all that much because it seemed like you could get very cold wearing it because your arms and shoulders would be sticking out. I pretty much hate all dresses. I was thinking that you could probably play the piano in pants. Actually, if you played that well, you could probably wear anything you wanted.

I looked over at Elly who was maybe even more entranced than me. She was watching the violins intently, not the pianist or Mr. Bernstein. Her eyeballs were following the violinists' bow arms, which were all going the same way at the same time—sort of like synchronized swimming but with instruments.

The music ended with a giant chord and people jumping up shouting "Bravo, bravo!" Miss Ludmilla in her white dress went offstage and came back on five times. Someone gave her a huge bouquet of roses. My hands were sore from clapping so much. My father stood and pounded his hands together, staring straight ahead. I never felt so connected to him but so separate. Did he want to be on the stage with those kinds of musicians? This possibility intrigued me, but I couldn't bring myself to ask him.

Intermission at Carnegie Hall involved much rustling about by women in fancy dresses and fur coats and men in black suits. Perfume wafted around the air, and it was not terrible perfume like Audrey Fremont's mother wore. It was soft and pretty perfume, and I made my nose bob around like Wolfie's, smelling the different smells. Some of these well-dressed people were getting cocktails from the bar in the lobby and sipping them as they laughed and chatted with each other. It was all so marvelous—music and well-dressed people in the most amazing building I'd ever been in.

Our mothers took us to the ladies room where the line was a mile long, out the door and down the hallway. It was a great place to experience the perfume. We stood behind two old ladies with white hair and hats with genuine feathers sticking out of them. I wondered how the people sitting behind them could see the orchestra.

"Look, Sidney," one of them whispered to the other one. "A cleaning lady has shown up for the concert." She pointed at Rosa and smirked to her friend. "She's a little early for work, isn't she?" The woman did a little sniffy thing with her nose after she said this. The other old lady chuckled in a snotty way.

Rosa blanched and looked down at her black dress, which I thought made her look beautiful. Then she ran out of the ladies room. We were fourth in line by then.

"Listen, you old wrinkly-faced, too-rich-for-your-own-good bitch . . ." —my mother Frankie was actually saying this out loud— "keep it to yourself in the future and realize that the person you just insulted is, in fact, a human being. Which is more than I can say about you!"

There was a very big "Hmmmmph!" from the lady who had said the mean things about Rosa. I was morbidly entranced by the foxes running around her neck biting each other. It was a terrible realization to understand that someone had killed them for the sole purpose of decorating a mean old woman. I had a vague idea of why she had called Rosa a cleaning lady, but I couldn't believe she'd said it out loud. Elly was standing next to me, staring at the floor. Her hand was clamped to mine, squeezing hard.

My mother did not budge from the line in spite of being stared at by Mean Dead Fox Woman, who did not say anything more, but we knew she was steaming inside and thinking more mean thoughts. She turned her back on us dramatically and whispered something (probably very mean) to her friend. It was about my mother. I could feel my fists wanting to punch her and my feet wanting to kick her. I was more comforted than alarmed by the potential violence inside me.

We stood our ground in the line because we had to pee really bad. I tried to imagine the rest of the music to come and couldn't wait. When the two old ladies disappeared into stalls, Elly turned to Frankie with serious eyes.

Frankie was red in the face and tapping her foot on the tile floor of the ladies room. This may have been because of the exchange with the fox ladies or because she had to pee so bad, I wasn't sure.

"Anytime, honey," Frankie said, and pulled Elly close. "We're a family, and don't you forget it. No small-minded bigoted people are ever going to get to us." She said this part a little extra-loudly, possibly in hopes that Mean Dead Fox Woman would hear her.

Then all three of us went into the stall when one opened up. We politely looked away when the pee-er was peeing. It took Frankie the longest because she had all of that hosiery equipment to deal with. It was OK, though, because in that small space, we were a team.

Rosa was back at our seats, talking with Frank and Ted. Her eyes looked smeary and the rest of her looked like she was trying to be small so no other mean ladies would notice her. Frank had his arm clamped around her. This time it seemed like a good thing, not icky at all.

"Rosa," Frankie began.

"No, no, don't say anything. It's OK," Rosa said to my mom. "I'm used to it."

What? Elly and I exchanged a look. She was used to people being so cruel to her?

"Well, you shouldn't be used to it." Frankie was still steaming.

"Girls," my father began authoritatively.

"DON'T call us girls, Ted," my mother interrupted. She traded a look with Rosa that I think said, "I could slap my husband AND that mean old lady and stomp right OUT of here."

"The lights!" said Elly. "Look!" In the lobby, the lights were flicking off and on. This is how we learned about the signal for the end of intermission. It means hurry up and sit down, the music is about to start.

The second half of the concert was taken up by a very long piece called *Pictures at an Exhibition* by another dead guy named Mr. Modest Mussorgsky. It is about going to a museum and looking at all the paintings there. Each painting has a name and its own little piece of music and they were all strung together. It was like a movie without the screen. It was so much better than a movie because I could make up the scenes in my head as the music played. The musicians swayed all around as they played those millions of notes, and the colors flew from the rafters again, changing depending on the sounds that were made. Mr. Bernstein danced on his special little box in front of the eighty players. Magic things would happen when he waved his arms a certain way, and sparkles of silence would happen when he dropped them to his sides. I thought I might hit the ceiling with excitement when they played one of the sections called *The Great Gate of Kiev*, it was so loud and amazing and strong. At the end, again, there were more Bravo! shouts and wild clapping and people standing up, which made the applause sound even louder.

I could not believe that this amazing thing had happened to us in place of Confession and macaroni and cheese. And instead of a gig. Why did our fathers not have a gig?

The car ride home was quiet and still, like we were floating on the sea of that music all the way home. Ninety miles, Ted told us; it was an even 90 miles from our house to Carnegie Hall. I would think that thought the whole time I was growing up. Ninety miles and a lot of practicing might get me to Carnegie Hall. Ha-ha.

And then no one spoke the rest of the way home. Elly and I held hands and finally fell asleep with our heads on each other's shoulders, dreaming of a hall filled with unbelievably beautiful music and nice people only.

4

E-G-B-D-F

Elly's father showed up after work carrying a violin case. With his hat and his trench coat, he looked like a gangster coming up the walk, swinging the case. Elly and I watched him come toward the house.

The door squeaked open. Frank walked in slowly. We held our breath. "Here," he said, handing the violin to Elly. He didn't even say hello.

"For me? Really? Is it mine?" Elly was jumping up and down just a little. I could tell because the hardwood floor made that chirpy noise where she was stepping.

"Yes, it's yours. Why else would I bring a damn violin home?" Sometimes Elly's dad was really crabby. Today was one of those days. Elly's mom said that he sounded mean but that didn't mean that he really *was* mean. He still scared us.

"Oh, thank you, Daddy. Gracias, gracias!" gushed Elly.

"Speak English, Elly." Frank hung up his coat and went toward the kitchen. "You'll be taking lessons from Sister Regina starting next week."

Oh no, Sister Regina! We thought we'd gotten rid of her after third grade! Poor Elly, alone in a room with Sister Regina! And she only had one week to get used to the idea.

We took the violin over to the couch. There were three latches on the black lid, and one by one, Elly gently opened them. She raised the lid, and lying there on a bed of red velvet was the most beautiful violin in the world. It looked exactly like one of the New York Philharmonic violins, brown and shiny and like it would sing if you breathed on it.

Elly ran her fingers over the wood. Smooth, cool. A marvelous, shimmering chocolate. She touched the D string and felt it quiver under her finger.

"Dammit! Don't touch it! Sister Regina will show you how to hold it. Until then, don't you dare touch it!" Elly's dad had come back from the kitchen with a beer. He came over to us and slammed the lid of the case down roughly. He took it and placed it on his desk. "Understand?" he demanded.

"Yes," said Elly. Her voice was so sad. She nodded, her eyes still glued to the black case with the magic inside. "When is my first lesson?"

"I don't know—ask your mother." Frank the dad put his feet up on the coffee table and snapped the newspaper open. "And if you touch that violin again, you won't have a lesson at all. Ever. Do you hear me?"

How could she not hear him? He couldn't prevent her from dreaming about it, though. She told me about it the next day as we were hanging out on the playground spying on Sister Regina. We were wondering out loud if she was the same as she used to be or if she had miraculously changed into a nice nun over the summer.

Elly stayed awake late into the night, so excited about the violin on the desk downstairs that she couldn't close her eyes. When she finally fell asleep, she dreamed that she was in an orchestra full of violins and they were playing the Nutcracker Ballet. All of the arms of all of the violinists were moving the same exact way, and her arm automatically knew how to do this. She felt very proud of herself.

Our spying indicated that the summer had had no effect on Sister

Regina. She yelled as much as ever, and she still said, "Dear Lord oh my Dear God" all the time, especially when something happened that she didn't really know what to do about. Like when one of the first graders skinned a knee. "Dear Lord oh my Dear God, what shall we do? Perhaps a Band-Aid is in order." Or when one of the sixth graders hit a ball into the cafeteria window, shattering glass all over the place. "Oh Lord oh my Dear, Dear God, look what has happened. Just look, Dearest Lord!" As if Our Dearest Lord couldn't see for Himself and miraculously fix it if He so chose.

"She still talks to God all the time," Elly said. "She talks to God more than she talks to real people. Except she doesn't yell at him, just at kids."

The bell rang and we ran in to Sister Lucy's class. Sister Lucy was so old that we were scared she was going to keel over and die any minute. She hadn't been the same since the day Mr. Martin Luther King, Jr. was murdered and she told us she was afraid for mankind and the evil that was taking us over, one by one. She looked sad and defeated all the time after that, and then when Mr. President Kennedy's brother was also murdered, Sister Lucy vanished entirely for a day and we had to have a sub who wore plain clothes. We stared at the sub lady's legs all day long because it was so weird that they were out there in public beneath her dress for everyone to look at.

One day in class, Sister Lucy fell asleep during a movie and it took kind of a while to wake her up. With Sister Lucy, things always went pretty slowly. She also never noticed our hand signals across the classroom or the notes we passed to each other. We grew increasingly bold as the year went on and our writing abilities got better and better. One time I even brazenly threw a note through the air to Elly, barely skimming Angela Santini's hair as it flew by. Sister Lucy never blinked.

One Saturday, I was put in the car for another one of those mystery drives, during which my father would not speak except for one word answers to my interminable questions. I know that my mother refused to go on a mystery drive unless she was secretly told the destination beforehand, like the New York Philharmonic concert. I was never so privileged. My father somehow thought it was fun for me to be driven around and tortured, desperately wondering where on earth we'd end up. The best of the mystery drive times included ice cream. The worst times involved old people, like the time we went to see Mrs. Hadley, who was something called a Rosicrucian. Frankie found her and talked my dad into going to see her. Mrs. Hadley had special powers and told my parents psychic things while I sat on her couch and ate chocolate mint candies from a bowl on the end table. I do not like mint, but I ate them because they were sweet and chocolate was involved. And I was bored but also a little scared of Mrs. Hadley. She had a little rat dog that sat on the floor in front of me and growled if I moved too quickly. That was not a fun mystery drive day. Weird and sort of interesting but not exactly much fun.

We pulled away from our house and went in a direction that I didn't recognize. "Where are we going?" I tried, knowing it was completely fruitless.

"Somewhere," my father said.

"Dad!" I thought momentarily about somehow cleverly using the word Fuck, which I'd learned from Audrey Fremont, but then thought better of it.

"You'll see."

"AAHHHHH!"

"Lennie, don't scream." It looked like my mom was trying hard not to laugh.

"If I hear that sound again, we will turn around and not go where we're going," my father said. Like this was a threat of serious proportions, not to go wherever we were going. He was gripping the steering wheel like it could get away from him.

"Well, if I knew where we were going, maybe I wouldn't have to scream," I shot back. I was frustrated but also slightly excited. We were not going to either grandparents' house. We could be going anywhere. It could be good or it could be bad. I prayed that we were not going to the doctor because I did not want to get a shot. Even though it was Saturday, I wanted to be sure.

A dead silence filled the car. Uh-oh. It had obviously been the wrong thing to say.

"Lennie," was all my mom said. My dad stared straight ahead. His knuckles were white from grabbing the steering wheel.

"Mom, please. Tell me! Where are we going?" I whispered this, thinking that somehow this might make a difference. I made sure that she knew I was whining even though I was whispering very softly.

"To a place," she said. "Now, DROP IT." She was as frustrating as my father. She had that sort of smirky look on her face that told me she was in a good mood. She was not ruminating about some world problem, or some nurse thing, or some parent thing. She was in a good mood but didn't want to push my father, whose moods were always unpredictable. He had a way of making fun things into serious things, like the gig and the concert in New York.

I sat in the back seat and tried pouting. We passed the Western Electric plant where Auntie Liddy worked and made a lot of money. We passed Jim's Hot Dogs. We passed the Ritz, a really great place to get ice cream because the scoops were so huge. We were soon in a completely unrecognizable section of Allentown. My father parked the car on a street lined with stores. I scrambled out. He was already striding down the sidewalk, not waiting for me or my mom. He turned and walked into a store, my mother behind him and me trailing two steps behind.

The store was full of furniture. I realized immediately that it wasn't brand new furniture. There were couches other people had sat on and dressers with big scratches that had held other people's clothing. There were also dinette sets with ripped vinyl. Coffee tables with rings from glasses. I instantly worried that we had suddenly gotten poor and that all the furniture in our house would go away and we would get an ugly floral print couch and a bent-up set of kitchen chairs.

My father was already in the back recesses of the store. "Mom," I tugged on her coat sleeve, "what are we doing here?"

"You'll see," she said, infuriating me. She paused to look at a bureau with very ugly drawer handles. Oh God, no, I thought. I do not want that bureau in our house.

I ran to find my father and there he was, standing in front of a huge old upright piano. I could see right away that several of the keys were broken and one of them even had the whole top missing so that it stuck out like a bad, rotten tooth.

"Would you like to have a piano?" my father asked.

Would I like a piano? My heart leaped. OF COURSE I would LOVE a piano. With a piano, I could begin my dream of becoming Ludmilla Michalowski! Uh-oh. But not this piano. I wanted a grand piano. I wanted any piano but this one.

"Yes!" I said, thinking maybe this piano would have nothing to do with the piano we would eventually get.

"OK, then," he said. And a salesman materialized and shook my dad's hand and said, "That'll be fifty-two thirty-seven."

I watched my father count out two twenties and one ten and some ones and some change and then three days later a truck came to our house and deposited that very big ugly piano in our dining room because that was the only room in the whole house it would fit in.

I felt sick to my stomach looking at it, taking up an entire wall of the dining room. I didn't go near it the first day. I just glanced at it from other places in the house. You could see it from everywhere. It had a huge presence in our little house, even bigger in one room of it. It stood against the wall and dared me to come closer.

It was light brown. Almost a flesh color. Not the color of any piano

I'd ever seen. Someone had painted it with the kind of paint you put on walls, not on furniture. Especially not on pianos. It was not shiny brown like Audrey Fremont's. Or shiny black like Angela Santini's baby grand. It was fleshy pink-beige and it looked bad. Very bad.

"Aren't you going to play it?" my father asked.

"Dad, I have no idea HOW to play it." I said this as sarcastically as possible. How could he think I would ever want to play this ugly thing?

"Here, let me show you." And he took my fingers and pounded out Chopsticks with them. Then he sort of wrapped his hands around but under mine and we played something hard, something like Ludmilla Michalowski might play. It sounded good. It was me, I was making this sound and it was GOOD. I did it all by myself then, picking out the Chopsticks notes without him even helping me. He slipped away, and I picked out a couple of other little tunes. And then I was hooked. I was now officially friends with the pink/beige piano. It made great sounds and it vibrated a little when I had my hands on the keyboard. I tried out chords – a whole bunch of notes at once. And they sounded really good. So all of a sudden it didn't really matter what my piano looked like; it only mattered what it sounded like. The inside is what matters, I realized, kind of like with a person. Because a person can be kind of ugly and still be a good person inside. That's how my piano was. Weird pink on the outside and magic on the inside.

The next Wednesday after school, I went to my new piano teacher's house. Actually, not one, but two piano teachers lived in the house. They were sisters. And they were extremely old. Possibly older than Sister Lucy. I couldn't tell, but they might have been in their fifties, or they could have been a hundred. Both of the old ladies were named Miss Ashley. Beatrice and Bernice. Miss Beatrice Ashley and Miss Bernice Ashley.

Both of the Miss Ashleys were on hand to meet me and my parents. The elder Miss Ashley (well, I assumed she was the elder because her hair was completely white) was very short and very round. She made it clear right off the bat that she only took the more advanced students. Her studio was actually the entire living room of the house. There were two grand pianos nestled up to each other and they took up all the space in the room. There was also a pilgrim-type bench next to a table upon which was a dish of chocolates. I noticed the chocolates right away. I had a weird feeling of wanting some but was too terrified to actually figure out how to pick one up and stuff it in my mouth without being noticed. It had been a lot easier to do this at Miss Hadley's house, in spite of being stared at by the growly rat dog.

The other Miss Ashley was very tall and very skinny and had grey hair, also in a bun at the back of her head, which was a little pointy at the top. (Her head, not the bun.) She also had a pointy nose but very friendly eyes. She told me that my lesson was not to happen in the living room full of pianos. Instead, she ushered me through the living room, through the dining room and up a dark staircase at the back of the house. At the top of the gloomy stairs, there was a much smaller, much brighter studio surrounded by windows, which sort of looked like a closed-in back porch. Miss Ashley #2 had a small upright piano that she explained to me was a studio piano. It was black and looked somewhat official, just like Audrey Fremont's piano. A little schnazzy. I could not wait to touch it. My parents had stayed behind in the living room with Miss Ashley #1. I was excited to officially learn how to play the piano so I pretty much would have followed anywhere Miss Ashley #2 led me.

We sat down in front of the shiny little piano. I sat on the bench and Miss Ashley #2 occupied a little chair to my right. She had a mug full of very sharp pencils and a pile of notepads on the piano in front of her.

"Now then," she smiled at me. "Shall we begin?"

Miss Ashley #2 showed me that middle C would be shared by both of my thumbs and that on the staff, Every Good Boy Does Fine and All Cows Eat Grass and everyone has a FACE and Good Boys Do Fine Always.

"What about good girls?" I asked her. This was clearly unfair.

"Oh my goodness, no one has ever asked me that before." She looked kind of flustered. I didn't want to upset her, I just wanted to know where the girls were in all of this since boys had already had two mentions. I'm a fourth grader. I don't like boys. I don't know yet that I will never really like boys. Not in *that* way, anyway.

"There's a G on the treble clef. Maybe it could be Every Girl Bear Doesn't Fly. Or, All Cows, Even Girls! for the spaces on the bass clef." I desperately wanted her to think I was very clever and smart. And I wanted girls to get equal time, at least.

"My, my. I suppose you are right," said Miss Ashley #2. It took me a while to catch on that she never used contractions. She always said every word in its entirety. She regained her composure and told me that it didn't (did not) matter *how* I remembered the lines and spaces of the staff, I just had to know them all by next week. Both clefs. This gave me lots of leeway to make up as many mnemonics as I wanted.

"When do I get to play a concerto?" I asked.

There she goes, flustered again. "My, my goodness. How wonderful it is to have such an enthusiastic student. I do not believe a concerto will be within our realm for quite a while, however."

I did not know what a realm was, but I did know that my father loved the Grieg *Concerto in A Minor* and the Rachmaninoff *Concerto #3* and we both love Mozart *#21*. So I naturally wanted to learn to play them all. We listened to his recording of the Philadelphia Orchestra playing the Grieg with André Watts over and over. And we had heard Miss Ludmilla Michalowski play Rachmaninoff *in person*. When we listened to the record together, sometimes my dad conducted, and sometimes he let me conduct with his real baton, which he kept in a special box on the top shelf. I loved that Grieg concerto. It seemed quite do-able to me; I thought I just needed a few basics of piano playing before I could manage it.

When we were finished with the names of the lines and spaces and learning which fingers played which keys in the C major scale, Miss Ashley escorted me down the stairs and back into the living room studio. My parents, strangely enough, seemed to be beaming at me.

"You have a very fine little student here," said Miss Ashley #2. "She would like to play a concerto soon. Isn't that precocious?"

I could see my mother redden a bit and my father stare at the floor. Whatever precocious meant, it could not be good. They would not tell me in the car on the way home. They just told me to practice and not talk so much when I went to Miss Ashley's house for lessons. Which is what I did from then on, once a week. Thursday afternoon became my favorite time of the week. Within the week I was playing "In the Canoe" proficiently. I was quite proud of myself and thought I was a genius because no one else in my fourth grade class was taking piano lessons. And Elly was the only other kid taking lessons of any kind.

The phone rang one day after school and it was Miss Ashley #2 calling to ask my mother if I would play "In the Canoe" in the Spring Musicale. It was unprecedented for such a new student to be included, but my progress had been rapid, according to Miss Ashley #2. My mom put her hand over the mouthpiece of the phone and asked me if I would.

"OF COURSE," I told her. And from that point on, I was convinced I was headed for Stardom. Just like that kid that Leonard Bernstein was talking about on the last Young People's Concert. And just like my hero, Ludmilla Michalowski.

Elly told me about her first lesson with Sister Regina. She learned how to hold the violin bow on the frog. I did not know there was such a thing as a frog on a violin bow. But it is very important. It is not like an actual frog. And its name came from when they made the first violin bows and bow frogs were carved to look like real frogs. Years later, when Elly started studying violin with Raphael Bernhard of the Philadelphia Orchestra and she found out that Sister Regina had not only taught her the complete wrong way to hold the bow but also fabricated the entire story about the frog, she was furious and called up the convent to yell at Sister Regina just like my mother had done years before about our near-death incident. When Mother Superior answered the phone, Elly hung up on her. What was she going to do, ask for Sister Regina and then actually yell at her? Elly set about atoning for the hang-up call by correcting everything wrong that Sister Regina had ever taught her. Which was, actually, just about everything. And Elly began to realize that her talent, not Sister Regina's teaching, had landed her with a prestigious teacher. That was pretty sobering.

At her very first lesson, Sister Regina had made Elly pray that she was not too talented, and would not become too proud. When learning her scales, Sister Regina insisted that she play at least one note way out of tune so as not to offend God with perfection. Not that perfection was even possible, but you didn't want to take the risk of bugging God in any way. I wondered why she didn't think that God might actually be offended by the way-out-of-tune note, but I was too chicken to ever ask her. Elly and I discussed it many times. We thought if God gave you the gift of being an excellent violinist, why wouldn't you play the best you possibly could? Why would you pretend to make mistakes? We couldn't delve into this quandary too much because it seemed too blasphemous at the time.

Elly's first song was "Dark Eyes." She could play it perfectly right away. I loved that song immediately. It was mysterious and wonderful. She brought her violin over and we invented a duet. I found some notes on the pink piano that matched her violin ones and away we went. We practiced it over and over, and then we pretended that we were on the stage at Carnegie Hall. We bowed before we began playing, and then we bowed again at the end. We pretended that the audience was clapping and cheering. We did not curtsey. We held the side of the piano and bowed the way Miss Ludmilla had bowed, sweeping her whole body down and holding it there while the audience went wild.

Elly had the brilliant idea to put on a concert and charge people money to come. It was going to be held between our living room and dining room (I would play the piano which was in the dining room and Elly would stand in the doorway to the living room). We convinced Frankie to let us move the dining room table out and set the chairs up audience style. Here is who attended our concert: Frankie, Rosa, Ted, Frank, Grampa and Gramma Kuklinski, Aunt Liddy, Audrey Fremont, Angela Santini, and Leslie Feinberg. Grandma and Grandpa Findley couldn't come because they were in Europe as usual, but Elly had the brilliant idea that we could make them a tape and then Grandpa Findley would be all happy and tell us what talented girls we are.

The audience clapped for us as we came down the stairs in our best clothes and entered the Carnegie Hall stage. First on the program was "In the Canoe," then "Dark Eyes," then the improvised "Dark Eyes" duet, and then the grand finale, the "St. Ursula Polka," which Elly and I had composed ourselves, in honor of our fathers. And St. Ursula, too, of course.

At the end of the polka, we bowed and ran back upstairs. Elly put her violin away carefully, and we ran back downstairs for ice cream. Aunt Liddy grabbed us both and told us how proud of us she was. She spilled a little of her wine on my shirt but I didn't really care. It was white wine so it didn't really show.

Frank came up to us and said, "Listen. You need to know about polkas. That wasn't a polka, OK? That was a mess."

We stood there, motionless. Shocked.

Ted added, "Yeah. Polkas are always in duple meter. You know what that is, don't you?" We had no idea. "Obereks are in triple. You called a triple meter song a polka. And that is incorrect. It is so incorrect that it offends me." He made a little mea culpa thump on his chest like you did in church when you were admitting to God what a sinner you were. Then Ted and Frank went out into the kitchen to get more beer. You weren't allowed to have beer in the real Carnegie Hall, but we didn't say anything to them about it. We stood, rooted to the floorboards. Our fathers were offended by our music.

Aunt Liddy materialized again and dragged us both into the living room. "Listen, you two girls were good. Very good! Don't worry about what they said." She said this several times while tying a paper napkin in a knot. Her eyes flashed and glanced toward our fathers. She asked us to play our songs again. But we didn't. Elly packed her violin away and I closed the music on the piano. They were our professional musician fathers. We had to worry about what they said.

The dress rehearsal for the Spring Musicale was the best thing ever. It was in a recital hall on the campus of the Pennsylvania Center for Musical Arts in Allentown. In the recital hall was the biggest, longest, shiniest piano I had ever seen. It was a Steinway, a huge, nine-foot concert grand with the lid propped all the way open. It looked like a magnificent living being. The air shimmered when you pressed a key. The sounds that came out of that piano were big and round and different colors. They vibrated right through to my heart.

My turn to play came right after a scrawny little girl who played "The Daffodil Song." I stared at her, finally realizing that the Miss Ashleys actually had other students and this is what one of them looked like. She was reptilian in her movements, slow and darting at the same time. "The Daffodil Song" was not very inspiring because it was a string of single notes in a row. At least I had advanced to the point of playing chords. When Scrawny Girl was finished, I raced up to the stage. Miss Ashley #2 almost had a coronary.

"LEONORE! WE DO NOT RUN ONSTAGE!" Her voice was like a bullhorn. She made me go back to the seats and practice walking "gracefully" up to the piano. It was the hardest thing I ever had to do. She stood at the edge of the stage with a stern look on her face and didn't move away until I was seated on the piano bench.

"In the Canoe" sounded like a Mozart Concerto to me. I did not want to get off the piano bench when I was finished, so I didn't. I started to play scales and "Spinning Song" and "The Happy Farmer" and even the "St. Ursula Polka," which, as we now know, is not an official polka. I was so dazzled by that enormous piano that I never wanted to leave it.

Miss Ashley #1 clapped her hands. "Leonore! LEONORE! You must not play more than your recital piece! Please! Other students are waiting." She stood at the edge of the stage with her hands on her little puffy hips. "Please come away from the piano this instant!" Miss Ashley #2 was sitting there with her head in her hands.

"You can call me Lennie," I said to her as I jumped off the stage. I know I was kind of pouty, but I really did not want to leave that amazing giant piano.

Miss Ashley #1 turned all red and ordered me back on the stage so that I could practice my curtsey. By this time, all the other kids had stopped whispering and were staring at me because I was clearly a Problem. Miss Ashley #1 instructed me, step by step: "Get back on the piano bench—DO NOT PLAY THE PIANO ANYMORE—we're pretending that you've just finished your piece. Now get off the bench, bow—no, not like that—one hand across your belly and the other folded behind you—yes, bow, and now curtsey. What's that? Yes, I do realize that the boys do not have to curtsey. But the girls must. That is the proper etiquette. Yes, you have to. If you do not curtsey, you may not play in the Musicale."

She pronounced it "mew-zee-cal." If I did not do this weird curtsey thing, I would not be allowed to play the beautiful gigantic piano. That was blackmail. I knew it in my little nine-year-old heart. And so I did it. I sold out. I practiced curtseying. It was not easy. It is a very unnatural kind of movement. I got really mad at the boys who could just bow and then leave. Why did the Miss Ashleys make the girls do this peculiar and embarrassing thing? I decided then and there that when I get to play with the New York Philharmonic, I will not curtsey. I will only bow.

We stopped to pick up Elly on the way to the real recital. Elly was going to be my own personal fan in the audience and then come over and spend the night. There was also a rumor about stopping for ice cream at the Cup after the recital. I hadn't been able to stop thinking about the piano all last night and all day at school. I could not wait to play it.

"Are you nervous?" Elly asked.

"What?" Nervous to play "In the Canoe," which I had already played 40,000 times? Which I had already performed to huge acclaim at our house concert?

"Are you scared? Sister Regina said it honors God to not be too cocky when performing in public. It's better if you're scared." Elly delivered this statement with appropriate skepticism.

This was a new one. "We already know that Sister Regina has some crazy ideas." I enjoyed any opportunity to refer to Sister Regina as crazy, seeing as how we could have been killed by her advice. I also knew Elly knew it too, but she had to be on better behavior since Sister Regina was now her violin teacher. "So I'm not scared, OK?"

"OK. Just don't get God mad at you."

When we got to the Pennsylvania Center for Musical Arts, all of the Miss Ashleys' collective students were milling about in their best clothes. Some were wringing their hands, and a few were wearing mittens. I realized immediately why they did this and thought it was the best idea in the world.

"Mom," I said, pulling on her skirt. "Did you bring my mittens?"

"Lennie, it's May."

I knew this. But you never know what mothers have in their purses, so it was at least worth a try. I decided from that moment forward to always wear mittens before I practice so my hands will be really warm when I play scales and technical exercises.

I was shocked by one of the older girls bursting into tears. "I can't," she wailed. "I can't do this, I'm too scared!"

"God probably likes her," Elly whispered. I was too entirely mystified as to why anyone would be scared to play the piano since it was so fun. We watched the girl run out of the hall and into the night, her parents chasing her and ordering her to stop and get right back in there this instant. She never did come back in, and when it was her turn to play, Miss Ashley #1 got up and announced that Candace Walters was indisposed and unable to perform.

"What's indisposed?" I asked my mother.

"It means she's doing something like throwing up in the bathroom and can't come onstage," she replied. Frankie had the tiniest grin on her face. I thought she looked beautiful in her polyester mom outfit. It was burnt orange with a paisley blouse. And she was trying out a new hair-do, with bangs and flippy things around the back of her head. She looked great.

The audience lingered about before the Musicale, choosing seats, encouraging children, and fanning their faces with programs. Eventually, Miss Ashley #1 herded all of us students into the front three rows, which were decorated with blue bows on each end. I was shocked to see her in a glamorous black dress and actual jewelry. Even lipstick! There was pink lipstick on her usually pale, thin lips. She looked like an entirely different and very glamorous Miss Ashley #1.

According to the Spring Musicale program and the dress rehearsal, I was the first performer. Miss Ashley #1 gave me the signal (a solemn yet subtle bow of her head as she seated herself) and I went up onstage. I made the sounds hit the ceiling and fly around the room. The notes danced and sparkled, a different sparkle and color for each of them. I was quite captivated with myself. I wanted "In the Canoe" to go on and on. I thought about playing it twice as I reached the final cadence. But as I paused on the last note, the audience erupted into applause and I couldn't just start it over. So I got up from the piano bench, walked to the edge of the stage to uphold my part of the blackmail bargain and curtsey. Which I almost did, except that I really misjudged where the edge of the stage was and I fell over the side, flat on my face. I collapsed in a little taffeta heap on the floor. There was a giant collective gasp from the crowd, and Miss Ashley #1 came running toward me, her large bosom swaying from side to side. Miss Ashley #2 trailed her, her hands clasped over her mouth. "Oh my goodness, Leonore, are you alright?" they said in unison.

But I was already standing, uncrinkling my communion dress. "Oops," I said. I tried to smile. Miss Ashley #2 whisked me away and pushed me into a seat next to two smirking high school students.

I sat there for the rest of the recital. I heard all kinds of music, some of it nervous and terrible, and some of it talented and exciting. I could tell the difference, it was easy. At the end of the concert, my parents and Elly collected me at the back of the hall. I was sporting a band-aid on my knee that Miss Ashley #2 had materialized out of her purse. See what I mean about purses? She could have had a pair of mittens in there, too.

"And I come from Al-a-bam-a with a band-aid on my knee . . . ." I sang to them, glad to see them after a whole evening of music that had been sometimes boring. Elly cracked up. But neither of my parents even smiled. OK, so it was really corny. I said this and then laughed out again. My father scowled even bigger.

Uh-oh, I thought. This cannot be good.

"Lennie, that was uncalled for," my father said.

"What was uncalled for?" Uncalled for always meant something bad done on purpose.

"Falling off the stage? Being clumsy and calling attention to yourself? Slapstick comedy has no place in a music recital." My father smashed his lips together and when he did this, he looked very mean.

"But I didn't mean to fall! I just fell!" I felt this icky snake feeling crawling up my stomach. "It was an accident!" What is slapstick comedy?

"Leonore, you're in fourth grade," said my mother. Her eyes looked misty. I was supposed to understand that fourth graders did not fall off stages because they were too old to be so foolish. And I didn't like this part of my mother that took sides with my father. It was like sometimes she put her real personality away when she was around my father, and the two of them were these two old unrecognizable proper stuffy people. It was bewildering to me.

"But how did I play?" I tried.

"You were great!" Elly confirmed.

"Fine. You played fine," my mother Frankie said. Ted my father said nothing. Absolutely nothing. Then we started walking out. I was convinced that they had been taken over by some aliens from one of Aunt Liddy's movies and turned into someone else's parents during the course of the recital.

The Miss Ashleys intercepted our departure. "Leonore, you were very good!" exclaimed Miss Ashley #2. "Very, very good for your very, very first Spring Musicale!"

"Yes, very, very good! And hopefully not injured!" smiled Miss Ashley #1. I saw my father take a step toward her and whisper something in her ear. She nodded, first up and down and then back and forth. Then she looked at me with sort of a pitying look in her eyes. He was apologizing to her for me! For my clumsiness!

I would never be able to forgive him for that. Me falling *off* the stage was more important to him than me making music *on* the stage. I had a sick feeling, like I might have to barf right there, right on the floor. I grabbed Elly's hand, and its warmness kept me connected to the ground I was walking on.

In the car, no one said anything. I watched the front of the car make familiar turns. I knew I should not ask where we were going, but I really, really still wanted to go to the Cup—to drown my sorrows in a hot fudge sundae.

My dad stayed silent as he drove. I knew he was ashamed of me. It was an accident! He didn't say anything about my piano playing. Well, damn him. Yes, I know what damn means. Sister Regina told us to damn all the terrible people when we say our prayers. And I am now not going to learn the Grieg Concerto for him. I am going to play only what I want to play. "Georgy Girl" is now at the top of the list. He bought me an ugly piano that I didn't want but then I learned to play it and I'm pretty good at it and now he's ashamed of me. So, damn him! Damn him and the commies that murdered Mr. Dr. Reverend Martin Luther King, Jr., which Sister Lucy talks about during early morning prayers. We were supposed to pray for his soul and for the eternal damnation to hell of all of the murderers in the world, since there were getting to be so many. I thought for one spiteful moment about lumping my dad in with all those awful people, that's how horrible I felt.

The car pulled into the parking lot of the Cup. My father got out, slamming the door and leaving the rest of us in silence. This meant that we were going to get whatever he got us, even if it was pistachio. While he was gone, my mother turned around to look at us. "He just wants you to be the best musician you can be," she said.

"But I am! I played "In the Canoe" perfectly!"

"I know, Lennie. But you have to remember that your father does this for a living and there's a certain way it has to be done."

Whatever that meant. "He's ashamed of me." I looked down at the floor of the car. Wolfie's fur was all over the place.

"He's not ashamed of you. He just doesn't know how to say what he means." Wow, I couldn't believe my mother was making excuses for my dad.

He came back with hot fudge sundaes, phew. My parents hardly talked. It was too weird. They scared me. And they hardly ever scared me. We ate our sundaes quietly. They were good, but not as good as they would be if people were laughing and talking.

"I don't want you girls staying up talking until 2:00 A.M. Understand?" my mother ordered. I did not like this new unfriendly part of her. I thought maybe it was because she was going to have to deal with my dad and she didn't want to. I wouldn't want to be alone with him either, that's for sure.

"We understand," Elly nodded solemnly. Then she and I climbed the stairs to my room.

I think that was the very beginning of us against them. On some level, both Elly and I recognized it and felt it but we didn't know how to talk about it. We were starting to fear our parents and grow on our own, away from them, and it was weird.

We crawled in the bed and snuggled up close.

"Was I terrible?" I asked my best friend, knowing that I really was not, that I really was very good and I could even have played a much, much harder piece and made it sound great. I knew that playing the piano would figure into my destiny, even though I wasn't completely clear on what destiny was.

"No, you were great."

"Thanks." I looked earnestly into Elly's face and she looked just as earnestly back into mine. It was strangely like looking in a mirror.

"I have to play in the violin recital next week. I hope it's not on a stage," she said.

"Yeah, you could fall off and have your father hate you for no reason."

"Yeah," said Elly. She pulled me close to her.

"What did I do wrong? Why is he so mad at me?"

"I don't know. Maybe he thinks you fell down on purpose so that you would get a lot of attention."

"I didn't!"

"I know. I think God probably thought it was a good deal because you didn't make any mistakes. So falling was a good way to not be too perfect."

I thought about this for a second. She had something there.

I clicked off the light and we looked at each other in the dark, even though we couldn't exactly see. But we could sense that little light that everyone has in their eyes and we kept looking at it until we got too sleepy, but we knew it was there even in our dreams.

In the morning, my mother made us pancakes. Then I showed Elly how to play "In the Canoe" on the piano, but she didn't catch on very fast. That's OK though, because I know I would never be able to play "Dark Eyes" on the violin.

"I don't want to hear that anymore," said my father after he came up from his basement workshop. "You're going to have to start playing some real music instead of that tripe."

"What's tripe?" I asked. I saw Elly get that scared look on her face again.

"Don't ask stupid questions." He slammed out the back door.

At my next lesson, Miss Ashley #2 complimented me on my playing in the Spring Musicale. I then apologized for falling down. I even got real tears in my eyes.

"Why, my dear Leonore, that is all right."

"My father was mad about it."

"Oh no, I am sure that he was not, dear. He was simply worried about his daughter!"

"No. He was mad. I know it." If I had looked at Miss Ashley #2 at that moment, I might have registered her expression of complete surprise and a tinge of sadness. Instead, I focused on the new piano music she had up on the music rack. Something called a Sonatina written by Mr. Muzio Clementi. He is dead. He wrote the Sonatina several hundred years ago. When I first looked at the title, I was sure it said Snotatina. Miss Ashley #2 pronounced it so I didn't have to ask. She definitely said "Sonatina." But secretly after that, I always referred to it in my mind as the Snotatina I was working on. Sometimes I had to clamp my teeth together to keep from laughing out loud during my lesson. And then a couple of months later, there were Mozart and Beethoven Snotas. Just my own little joke with the dead composers. And a very good secret from my father, whose forehead vein would stick out of the redness of his face if he ever heard anything so disrespectful.

5

Public School

Ted walked in one night after work and announced that I was not going to go back to St. Ursula's in the fall. Instead, I would be shipped off to William Penn Elementary. And after that, I would be going to Ben Franklin Junior High. And then Liberty Bell High School. I was officially going to be a Public School Kid. The news took me completely by surprise, and I automatically started to cry. I was going to be a traitor, a defector. He had already arranged the whole thing and I would have no say in the matter.

"This is nothing to cry about, Lennie. They have music in the public schools. Much better music, as a matter of fact." Then he stuck his headphones on and that was that. Frankie tried to calm me. She claimed that Ted was still mad at Sister Regina for almost killing us, but she secretly thought that Ted didn't want to pay tuition anymore because he could almost quit his day job and do the band full time. So. I was going to be the sacrificial martyr giving up my school for Ted's full-time gig. There would finally be a saint named Lennie.

Going to public school was not a big deal in itself, but it was really bad because Elly and I would be separated. She would still be going to go to St. Ursula's until eighth grade. Then she'd be going to St. Francis

Academy for Girls for high school. And if all of that wasn't bad enough, now I was going to have to wear actual regular clothes. This scared me more than just about anything. There's a real advantage to those plaid skirts and off-white blouses and kneesocks, the same outfit day after day. I had no idea about fashion in the real world, and girls who pick out their own clothes frightened and intimidated me.

Elly and I decided to pack some sandwiches and run away from home for a while so we could process this whole terrible turn of events. We needed to make a Plan. There was nothing in the fridge, so we ended up making mustard sandwiches—bologna sandwiches without the bolgna—and cherry Kool-Aid. We packed a baggie full of Milk-Bones for Wolfie and announced to Frankie that we were leaving. Possibly for good.

"OK girls. Just be back in time for dinner. We're having a barbeque. Fresh corn. Fresh tomatoes. And ice cream from the Cup."

"You don't understand," I said. "This is serious. If I can't go to the same school as Elly, what is the point of living?"

Frankie started to reach out, maybe to hug me. It will be OK, her eyes said.

"Ice cream from the Cup," Elly whispered to me. "See you later," she called to my mom. We headed off to the band shell at the Rose Garden. There's a hideout there behind the vines with just enough room for the two of us and Wolfie. We had an excellent view of the intersection at Eighth and Broad, where we were almost killed that day after Confession.

"I'm scared of public school," I confessed. I moved closer to Elly.

"I'm scared of St. Ursula's without you," she admitted.

"What are we going to do?" I wondered.

"Talk on the phone a lot. And there's always gig nights."

"Right," I said. There's always gig nights.

On the very next gig night, our mothers accosted us to have the most horrible awful conversation you can imagine. The conversation had a title: The Facts of Life. We were trapped at Elly's house, the ploy being pizza and *The Sound of Music* on TV. It was the one night of the year *The Sound of Music* came on TV, and before we could sit down and watch it, we had to endure this onslaught of disgusting information from our mothers, who, we didn't know at the time, had purchased some primo hash for the occasion.

"So, that's how—"

"No! Stop! Don't finish that sentence! We GET it!" Elly's eyes were big and wide and her hands were ready to clamp themselves over her ears.

"You get it?" Rosa seemed relieved.

"Do YOU get it?" Frankie pointed the question at me.

"If she gets it, I get it, OK?" I did not want to hear *again* from our mothers how the penis enters the vagina and all the swimming sperm valiantly fight their way to the one egg that was lying in wait for the strongest, surest of them all. I could not possibly associate this image with my parents. I'm sure that's why Elly was looking semi-hysterical next to me. She had once seen the act in person, and it wasn't pretty.

We'd already heard it all anyway from—who else—Audrey Fremont, in the alley after Girl Scouts one day. We screamed and tried not to believe her, and we tried not to listen, but it was too fascinating to run away. It was even freezing cold outside and we stood there and shivered while Audrey took her time with the gory details. Our mothers were doing the same thing, lingering over those embarrassing words that I will never ever say out loud. We wanted to put it out of our minds immediately because Julie Andrews was coming on in minutes and we had to get to the living room.

"So, no questions about the Kotex or anything like that?" Rosa was clutching a pink box filled with menstruation equipment. The outside of the box said "Especially For My Daughter" in frilly script. My box was lying next to Frankie, who had pretty much ignored it the whole time they were lecturing to us. I never wanted to open that box. I pretended it didn't exist.

Elly began a high-pitched scream as Rosa finished the question.

"Why are you screaming, niña?" Rosa's face looked like a combination of amusement and panic.

"I'm not DOING that!" Elly wailed. Julie Andrews is just moments away, I was trying to psychically tell her. Moments. Shut up and we'll be free! *The Sound of Music* will be our escape!

"Doing what, honey? You're gonna have to get your period. Every woman does. Even Jackie Kennedy, may her husband rest his soul. Even Marilyn Monroe."

"ALL women? You mean it's not an option? You mean that old Mrs. Weingarten does it? And Goldie Hawn? And Julie Andrews?"

"Yes, honey. All of us." Rosa told her somberly. I noticed that Frankie was looking away with her lips squashed together, which meant she was trying not to laugh. They had just ruined our lives with this information, and she thought it was funny?

"This is completely disgusting." Elly had this expression on her face like when you tried to get her to eat tapioca pudding. She clamped her hands across her chest. "I refuse," she announced. I felt so proud of her in that moment, so much so that I was distracted from the idea that blood was going to come out of my body on a regular basis and be absorbed by some official wads of cotton called Kotex which had to be positioned just right between my thighs.

Stayfree Ultrathins were decades away. There was an urban legend in the 1960s that no one under eighteen could use a tampon and survive. It was clear that we were going to be doomed to bleed into giant mattresses strung between our legs. Rosa was pulling the Kotex and belt contraption out of the pink box and showing us how it all worked. The only time previous to this that I'd ever seen a Kotex was at Camp Frontierwood when we made a torch out of about forty of them, soaked the whole thing in kerosene, and then set it ablaze on the last night of the summer. It burned bright for four hours—and this was the item that was going to hang between my legs and collect blood? Just exactly how much were we going to bleed, anyway?

As I was thinking these things, I watched Elly's face grow more and more stony. She finally said, "I refuse to go through with any of this," just like some professor or movie star or person making a keynote speech.

Our mothers looked at each other with an indecipherable-to-us adult expression. I could see Julie Andrews in the distance, running through the mountain meadow. It was starting and I didn't even care anymore.

"Fine. You let us know how you accomplish this, OK, Elly?" said Frankie. Rosa was trying hard to swallow a smirk. She seemed a little bit mad at us, too. Did she think we were going to welcome this news? That we were going to say Oh, how fabulous it will be to be Women?

I went over to the TV and cranked up the volume in time to hear that the hills are alive with the sound of music. Elly and I took our places on the floor right in front of the screen. Our moms came out of the bedroom and parked themselves behind us on the couch, rolling their hash cigarettes and noticing that their hands were shaking ever so slightly when they picked up their wine glasses. They were proud of their strong-willed daughters and scared for them all at the same time. The speech had not gone exactly as they'd planned, and they were puzzled by our refusal to welcome our female destiny.

Our moms crashed on the couch even before Baron von Trapp rescues the family from the Nazis. When the movie was over, we covered them up with a blanket and tiptoed up to Elly's room. Our dads wouldn't be home for hours.

"I'm not doing it," Elly said when we crawled into bed. "I can't believe God would make us do something so horrible."

She had a point there. "Do you think the nuns do it?" I wondered.

Elly was quiet for a while. "I really don't know. How could they? They might not have any regular parts, we don't know."

I was pretty sure they had breasts, from being hugged by Sister Anne and Mother Superior. They felt like regular women, and I'd been considering breasts fairly regularly since I was six.

"It will be OK, Elly," I tried to comfort her.

"I don't see how," she said. "The main thing is, I'm never, ever going to be pregnant. That would be even worse than all that blood."

"Me either." I could do blood, but not babies or marriage. I didn't see what was all that great about it. I knew subliminally that Frankie wasn't too happy to be married, even though she loved me.

We fell asleep with our arms and legs tangled up in one another's. I woke up in the pitch dark and decided to wake our mothers before our dads realized what they'd been up to while they'd been gigging. I hid the pink boxes, and Elly tucked the homemade cigarettes into the special tin box that Rosa kept in the kitchen.

Everyone got there at around seven on the Friday night before school started. Frankie was letting me have a summer slumber party to celebrate going to public school and we were going to sleep out in the screened-in porch. As it turned out, Audrey Fremont was going to William Penn Elementary, too. I felt happy about that. It was weird with Audrey—she scared me and thrilled me at the same time. She looked at me funny sometimes, like she knew something about me that I didn't know myself. I liked hanging around with her because you never knew what she was really up to.

First we ate pizza for dinner, and then we played Life and Monopoly and Hearts, which was the most fun. Auntie Liddy was there for a while and she taught us how to play Michigan Rummy. When our mothers were out of earshot, Aunt Liddy told us it was Real Gambling. We got into it, and I won the most pennies, about five dollars worth.

Audrey Fremont, Leslie Hammer, Barb Murphy, Angela Santini, Elly and me were there. Just six of us. Around 11:00, my mom got out the popcorn and told us three scary stories. Then she turned off the porch light and went inside.

It was very, very dark, one of those hot, muggy, Pennsylvania nights. There were fireflies everywhere. No one was inside their sleeping bags—we were all lying on top of them.

"How old are you going to be when you do it first?" Audrey Fremont asked. We could not tell who she was talking to, even though our eyes had adjusted to the darkness and we could make out the forms of each other around the porch.

"Do what?" Angela Santini asked. She never got anything. You had to explain everything except math to her.

"IT! IT! YOU KNOW!" Audrey yelled.

There was laughing. Of course we all knew what IT meant.

"I'm going to be 16," Barb said with conviction.

"I'm waiting till I get married," Leslie Hammer said. Her father is a minister. She had to say that.

"I'm never doing it," Elly announced. "I saw my parents doing it and it's gross."

I knew this story but was shocked that Elly would share it. She was completely traumatized the night that she tiptoed down the hall because she heard strange noises and decided to go and get her dad. When she peeked into her parents' bedroom, there he was on top of her mom, legs everywhere, going up and down on her, and there was moaning and grunting. Elly had a good view because there were two candles lit and she could see everything. She told me all about it the next day, and it took only a little while for us to figure out exactly what she saw.

There was a momentary silence among us. We were, of course, all imagining our own parents doing such a thing. And then thinking,

"EEEW! EEEEEW! UGH! BARF BLEEAAH!!" And then saying it.

And in the middle of all of this, I thought of Uncle Andy and felt sick to my stomach.

"What about doing it with a girl?" Audrey totally shocked everyone.

"You can't do IT with a girl!" Leslie pronounced this with authority. Maybe her father had explained all the possibilities to her.

"Yes you can."

I didn't immediately recognize whose voice said that.

Then all of a sudden there was a hand coming up my leg. It was kind of squeezing my thigh, and then it started poking its way into my crotch. At first I was too stunned to do anything, and then I started screaming. "Get off! Get away from me! Stop it!"

The hand went away. There was some weird kind of laughing and then someone else, Angela, I think, started shrieking. And then there was running and jumping and sort-of laughing but really scream-laughing because we were all pretty frightened.

It turned out to be Audrey Fremont. She tried to feel all of us up, one after the other. Barb said she was a pervert. I learned what a pervert was from Uncle Andy, who had taken several other opportunities after the Band Picnic and the Gig Parking Lot Incidents to rub his crotch on me and then tell me he would kill me if I told anyone. So here is Audrey Fremont doing a similar pervert thing. And I was too freaked out to run in and tell my mother. But here's the weird part: I was not that scared and in reality, I liked it. So I suppose that made me a pervert, too. Doing it with a girl. What an amazing thought.

When we finally settled down a little bit, Leslie Hammer proclaimed to Audrey Fremont that she should not be doing such things to her friends, and if it happened again, we would go straight to the authorities. I suppose that meant our parents, but with Leslie you never knew. It could mean the entire clergy of the Presbyterian churches of Allentown. (Actually, it was a miracle that Leslie could even play with us because we were all Catholics, and I once heard my grandmother taking my father to task because he let his daughter associate with a Presbyterian. Of all things.) It could also mean the cops, since her uncle was the police chief of the entire city. In our opinions, Audrey Fremont could possibly be in big trouble for being a pervert.

There was a tense silence for about two minutes, and then Barb suggested that we try to levitate someone. Angela got nominated, probably because she was the smallest one of us. Also the most pious. She would not let Audrey touch her anywhere except her head, so the rest of us made a circle around her and chanted the levitation chant and Angela rose into the air. She wrecked it, though, because as soon as she started going up in the air, she freaked out and we all started screaming and collapsed in a heap on top of her. That was the end of our paranormal journeys for the evening because my mother appeared at the door and looked at us. She didn't have to say anything—we just knew it was time to shut up.

Pretty soon after the failed levitation, all my friends started drifting off to sleep. You could tell by the way the breathing changed. I was not sleepy, though. I was thinking about that hand on my leg. It felt good. And where was it headed? I mean, I know. But what was it going to do when it got there? Do I even really like Audrey Fremont? I was mostly scared of her yet fascinated by her. But she had a big mouth, and if you didn't invite her to parties and stuff, she could really make your life miserable. So, what if the hand had belonged to someone I definitely liked? Like Elly? I would trust Elly to put her hand on my leg and not do anything I wouldn't like. Or Leslie. I liked Leslie a lot, and sometimes when she smiled I got this sort of warm, tingly feeling in my belly, and I thought about how pretty she was. I would probably like Leslie's hand on my leg, going to wherever it wanted to go further up.

Frankie got a new job and the first day of her being a nurse was my first day as a 5th grader at a brand new school. She was going to be a surgical nurse, one of those people that smacks the scalpel into the palms of the doctors. Frankie admitted to me that she really had wanted to be a surgeon herself and be the one who got her palm smacked, but my Grandpa Findley didn't want to pay for medical school because he figured he'd be wasting his money since Frankie would get married and not even use her education. Women were not supposed to do important jobs like surgery. So for now, this would do.

On that first day of everything, when I was going to William Penn and she was going to St. Joe's Hospital on Pine Street, she was wearing scrubs as she saw me to the door to get the schoolbus that would surely be filled with pimply, mean, scary, public school boys. And Audrey Fremont. That was the only good thing—Audrey was going to be there, too. I was wearing an outfit that looked a lot like my St. Ursula's uniform, and it was comforting to be dressed that way, at least at first.

"Where's your nurse hat?" I asked Frankie, more sarcastically than I meant.

"Nurses don't have to wear hats anymore." Frankie really had been instrumental in getting those nurse hats declared obsolete at St. Joe's, but she wouldn't accept credit for it.

"You look like Dr. Kildaire."

"Thank you."

"I think you'd be a good doctor." I said this earnestly, mad at my Grandpa's cheapness.

"Thank you, Lennie. Maybe someday I will." She smiled at me, a nice relaxed kind of smile that I hardly ever saw on her ever, especially when my dad was around. "Happy school." She smiled at me like a mom on television would smile at their kid. And I felt happy and not quite so scared to go to the new school.

William Penn turned out to be not so bad. Even though Audrey was in the other 5th grade class across the hall, it wasn't so terrible. It was actually kind of fun. I was way ahead of everyone else because of the strictness and discipline of Catholic school where we actually learned stuff. I felt a little sorry for the public school kids who spent their time messing around in class instead of learning. But that was their problem. I made a friend in my class immediately, a nerd girl whose name was Evelyn. What a terrible name for a 10-year-old girl. She was much cooler than her name. We hung out at recess and talked about music. She played the viola, which is a sort of large violin that has a lower voice. No one else bothered us, and we played together at recess and ate our sandwiches together at lunch. I felt lucky to have a school friend—Evelyn the viola player, and a best friend—Elly the violin player. Evelyn told me all about the alto clef, which is unfamiliar to piano players and just about everyone else on earth. Pretty much only viola players use the alto clef, and that makes them special in the music world. I found this interesting and felt drawn to her because of that out-of-the-ordinary fact. And Audrey, my Catholic school friend was there, hovering in the background. I knew it was a little hard for her to adjust because she didn't have anyone to boss around right away, but she found a third grader to bully until someone in her class finally responded to her that way.

I got used to public school pretty quickly and started getting a reputation as the smart music kid because I always finished my work ahead of everyone else. I got stared at because of that. One day I was in the middle of a daydream that involved playing a concert on a brightly lit stage. The audience was chanting, "Lennie! Lennie!" and I began to play a Mozartian version of "Close to You" in a medley with "You've Only Just Begun" and "Rainy Days and Mondays." My reverie was interrupted by Mrs. Thompson instructing everyone to close their books and line up at the door because we were going to have a Special Experience. I looked particularly hard at her red lipstick mouth because when she was angry, her lips turned into two very squiggly red lines, as though someone drew them there with a sharpie pen. But her lips were the regular size and so she couldn't have been mad. I could not for the life of me figure out what our special experience was going to be. As I looked around our classroom, it seemed that my classmates were equally puzzled. Most of them were jockeying into position so that they could walk in the line next to their favorite person and avoid their most unfavorite person who was either Susie Snot or Michael Mineo. Susie Snot's real name was Susie Baker, but the snot name stuck the day that she let a big stream of it course its way down her face and onto her dress. And Michael Mineo was commonly thought of as a retard, even though we had no idea what that meant. Michael just had what Mrs. Thompson called "fits," where he screamed and threw things and knocked his whole desk over, scattering papers, pencils, and crayons. He did this at least weekly.

I got stuck in the two-by-two line next to Ruth Walchonski, even though I was trying to negotiate for a spot next to Evelyn. Ruth would not shut up the entire way down the hallway. "Where are we going? Where are they taking us? What are we going to do? Look, we're going down the stairs!" Duh, Ruth, I am thinking to myself, our classroom in on the second floor, we have to go down to go anywhere.

"We're going into the gym! The whole school is going into the gym! There's my brother! He's in kindergarten. Even the kindergarten is going to this. What are we going to do?" Ruth looked straight ahead with a panicked expression on her face. She wasn't talking to me, she was just talking. Teachers walked up and down the line, shushing us. There was to be No Talking! I didn't really care what was about to happen, I was just glad to be not doing math and not sitting next to James Schnieder, who usually smelled even though he was very good at math.

As we were herded into the gym, I caught a glimpse of Audrey whispering into a blond girl's ear. The girl looked frightened. I wondered what mean thing Audrey was saying to scare her. I could not catch Audrey's eye in order to telepathically tell her to stop it. Not that she'd telepathically listen to me or anything.

Each class in William Penn Elementary School was led into the gym and seated in rows according to size. I marveled at the arrangement of students because nothing like this would ever happen in Catholic school. The kindergarteners were up front, then first grade, and so on. The fifth graders were near the back of the room. We had to sit on the cold wooden basketball floor, which wasn't great. The teachers arranged themselves around the room in folding chairs. Mark Snyder kept trying to look up Miss Atlantica's skirt. That was her name, the beautiful second grade teacher who wore skirts shorter than any of the other teachers. This made sense because she was the youngest, for sure. And she was by far the most beautiful. Mark Snyder was a too-big-for-his-clothes sixth grader, and he was the source of all sexual information at William Penn Elementary School. He was a lot like Frank Didonato but mean.

William Paderewski was poking Anita Pojoli in the ribs with a stick. I thought about telling, but I was pretty sure he was going to get caught anyway by Mr. Neupauer, who was our only guy teacher of the school. He was kind of tough and seemed to like being the only man around. Most of the boys of the school respected and feared him, even Mark Snyder. I was interested to see him get caught and hoped it would cause a big scene. William was always poking someone with something; pencils, sticks, his finger. Always, he had to poke someone with something.

Just as Mr. Neupauer was walking toward our class with his eye firmly on William, the principal, Mrs. Geiger, walked up in front of everyone. Mrs. Geiger was friendly and soft, like a big cuddly pillow, and she wore squashy clothes and gave hugs if you ever had a problem, like someone chasing you around the playground with a rock for no reason. She was tough on the chasers, though. They did not get a hug. She could yell as well as she hugged, that's for sure.

Amazingly, the kindergarteners were the first to shut completely up. That's probably because Mrs. Geiger looked at them very friendly-like, and they thought they might all get hugs. Then the first graders shut up, and all the way down the line until the sixth graders, who shut up fast, trying to be good citizen examples for the rest of the school. Mrs. Geiger cleared her throat and told us how excited she was to have such special guests for an afternoon performance at William Penn Elementary. She gestured to the four empty chairs, each with a music stand in front of it. There was a piano parked near the chairs. And a movie screen was set up behind the seats. A big flash of excitement flew through my body. I wasn't sure what an afternoon performance was, but it had the promise of being very interesting and different.

"Today we welcome the Broadway Ensemble, here to play for you! The Ensemble is very special because they play music for silent movies! I know you'll be the best good citizens and listen carefully and appreciatively to the concert!" Mrs. Geiger had on her biggest, politest smile. She always spoke in exclamation points.

I was beside myself! Music played by real live musicians in front of a movie! I had never heard of such a thing. I looked around and did not see Miss Williams, our music teacher who wore way too much perfume. If you had to stand next to her, it was hard not to gag. Your eyes would always water, that was definite. But she would know how to explain the music that was about to happen in our school gym.

Mrs. Geiger said a few more things about how we were to be very good citizen audience members and then she said, "Welcome, Broadway Ensemble!" Mrs. Geiger swished her arm to the left, and four people dressed in black walked out to the pretend stage area in the William Penn gym. Of course, it was not a real stage, it was just the floor, but we got it that this is what it was supposed to represent. They took their places and got ready to play.

There were two men and two women. One woman sat down at the piano. One man had a violin, another woman carried a cello, and the last man had a trumpet. Miss Williams had pictures in the music room of these exact instruments. The cello woman had grey hair and red lips like Mrs. Thompson. The violin man had stringy black hair that was kind of long. My dad would say he looked like a hippie rat. And the piano woman had blond fluffy hair and she was pretty but looked tired. She touched the piano in a soft way, intimate, like it was a pet, or a person she loved very much.

The cello lady pulled her bow across her strings and made some soft, low sounds. She adjusted the peg things on top of the cello. She did it again. And my belly felt all warm and furry feelings. I loved that sound. I wanted to run up there and put my hand on the cello and touch that sound, but I knew I'd get in big trouble if I did something like that. So I sat there, very straight and still, letting the low, sweet sounds wash over my body. The trumpet guy hit some staccato high notes in the background, punctuating what was going on around him.

I had no idea that it was the group's fourth gig of the day and that they were tired and bored and hungry. To me they were magicians. Even when they accidentally touched the strings of their instruments, it sounded like a song. They started to play together. The four people became four extensions of the wood and brass and strings. This beautiful, complete, complex sound rose up from them and drenched us William Penn-Schoolers. I didn't even notice that my classmates squirmed and whispered and poked each other and giggled the whole time the quartet played. Mrs. Geiger patrolled the sides of the gym, warning kids to behave themselves and be good citizens.

The movie started, a black and white film that was interspersed with the words people were supposed to be saying. I could hear the boys around me making fun of it because it was a really old movie, made before they figured out how to include sound on film. They thought it was stupid. I was the only person enthralled with the way the music told the story that we couldn't actually hear. I watched the piano woman so hard that I thought I might faint. She became an athlete when she played. I never knew that a body could move like that. Her fingers were strong and exact. Her arms were like two graceful swans. Her black flowy clothing swayed with the string bowing and the music. And her hair—that was best of all. It would swing and move back and forth. It was wild and it was rhythmic at the same time. Her face became beautiful with concentration, and she smiled a small smile when the harmony fit just so, just perfectly.

I decided I wanted to be her. I wanted to embrace a piano while playing it. I wanted to make those exact sounds. I wanted to play the piano with violins and cellos more than anything else in the entire universe. I could just see Elly and me playing this very music, maybe in Carnegie Hall in one or two years.

At the end of the very special experience concert, we were told to stand up, and then the teachers herded us back to our classrooms. I couldn't believe it was over. I watched the musicians pack up their instruments and continued to stare at the pianist until Mrs. Thompson pushed me right out the door. The sounds kept flying around in my brain for the rest of the afternoon, which, thankfully, was only another hour. During personal reading time, I mostly pretended to read *Harriet the Spy* because I was really listening to the music all over again in my head. I was imagining myself with a grand piano, playing for a room full of people. This was very unusual because *Harriet the Spy* was my very favorite book of all time and I could read it over and over. I didn't care a thing about Harriet that day, only the fluffy pianist.

Ted didn't say very much when I told him everything about the Special Experience concert. He asked what instruments they had and I recited: piano, cello, violin, trumpet. "That's a stupid combination," he said. I asked him if we could please, please, PLEASE go to New York City again and see another famous pianist playing with the orchestra. I told him I wanted to be a real piano player myself and I wanted to play the piano in Carnegie Hall so bad.

"Concerts cost a lot of money," was all he finally said.

I kept pleading with him.

"Look, if you don't shut up about it, we'll never go again, understand?"

Frankie kept glancing at my father, saying something with her eyes. But Ted sat there, stone-faced as usual. He acted like he hadn't heard a word I said.

"Lennie, your dad had a bad experience with that kind of music a long time ago and—"

"Frankie, SHUT UP! Do NOT say another word! You DO NOT understand! And if you don't understand, how do expect HER to?" My father slammed his hand down on the table. He looked like he might slam his other hand down on something—or someone—else. But he stomped out of the room and went to his usual place in the den and turned up the music really loud. He didn't even put his headphones on.

How could anyone have a bad experience with music? I turned to my mother and almost asked her out loud, but I was too scared.

"Lennie, your dad wanted to be in a symphony. But his parents wouldn't send him to music school. He tried to get a scholarship and he was turned down. Do you understand what that all means?" Frankie whispered this so my dad couldn't hear.

"Yes," I told her. It meant that he didn't get to have his dream.

6

The Attic

"Do you remember how to get to Miss Ashley's from school?"

"Yes!" Frankie was going over the instructions for the tenth time.

"Do you remember how to get to your grandmother's from your piano lesson?"

"Yes!"

"What time am I picking you up?"

"5:30! Can I go now?" I waved goodbye to my mother and ran to the car. Audrey Fremont's mother was driving us to school in her Caddy. After school I was going to walk to my lesson and then my grandmother's house where Frankie would pick me up after work.

For my first piano lesson of the school year, I was surprised to discover that I would no longer be going up to Miss Ashley #2's studio; I had been promoted and would be staying in the living room with the two snuggled-up grand pianos and Miss Ashley #1. I didn't even have one second to get sad about Miss Ashley #2 because Miss Ashley #1 started right in with scales as though we'd been having lessons together for years. I loved the bigger piano and the sounds it made. My lesson was over in what seemed like five minutes. Miss Ashley #1 gave me three new pieces and assigned the major sharp scales from the circle of fifths. It was a lot of work for me, but I was up to it, especially since public school was going to be a piece of cake in terms of homework.

I shuffled through the leaves on the way from the Home of the Miss Ashleys to my grandparents' house on Garrison Street. It was one of those fall days when the leaves drift slowly from the trees to the ground, and then you swish through them with your shoes. It was gently raining oak leaves all the way down Union Boulevard. In spite of all the piles of leaves, I was feeling scared and unsettled in my stomach. It was weird to go somewhere other than home after school and my lesson. I missed Wolfie. I missed Frankie. I wondered how surgery training was going and if she had seen any real blood or guts yet. I walked really slowly, watching all the feelings swirl around inside me, like they weren't quite part of me but I couldn't exactly get away from them, either.

When I got to my grandparents' house, the only person around was Andy. I got really scared, thinking my grandparents had left me alone with him. But then I spied Gramma out in the yard with a basket full of laundry, clipping it onto the line. My worst nightmare was to be alone with Andy anywhere. I don't know what he really does in his life besides hang around and bug people. That is probably what a lazy slug does. I do not know exactly what a lazy slug is, but I heard my dad tell Aunt Liddy that Andy is a lazy slug and mooches off my grandparents who will not tell him to get off his butt and get a job. He sits around watching TV and drinking beer all day. He sometimes yells at and argues with the people on TV. Every now and then he goes out to the garage and does things to his motorcycle. I don't understand how he can own a motorcycle if he doesn't have a job to earn money to pay for it.

On this Piano Lesson Day, Andy and I were, unfortunately for me, the only two people inside the house. He was yelling at *The Match Game*. I wish I had just quietly taken out my homework and started working on it, but I made the mistake of asking Andy where Grandpa was. This meant that he noticed me. He switched off the TV and came over to where I was standing in the doorway to the kitchen. He smelled like beer and cigarettes. That was the other thing—he smoked. Gramma didn't let him smoke in the house, though. This was the only thing she put her foot down about.

"How about a kiss for your favorite uncle?"

I got a really terrible tight feeling in my belly. Here we go again.

"No, thanks." I was clutching my pile of schoolbooks and my bag of piano music. I thought I could use all the books as a shield between him and me. He kept coming closer and closer until his face was an inch from mine. The beer and cigarette smell was overwhelming, along with another, unidentifiable, foul smell.

Something clattered in the kitchen. Andy backed away for a moment. Thank God for my grandmother. She had somehow gotten back inside, and now she was coming out of the kitchen, wiping her hands on her flower print apron.

"I'm out of flour. Andy please, can you go to the store?" She didn't kiss or hug me hello, like she usually does, probably because the flour was on her mind.

Andy made a face that I couldn't interpret. "Come on," he said. "You come with me."

My Gramma handed him some money. My stomach did a little flip flop. I'd never been alone in a car with Andy before. It was possible that my nightmare was partially coming true.

"You get Lennie a little candy, too," said Gramma. She was feeling guilty. I could feel it.

Andy dragged me into the garage, even though his ratty car was parked on the street. The garage was one of those garages that was separate from the house. It only had a couple of tiny windows up near the roof, so it was always dim in there. It smelled like beer, cigarettes, and cars—a lot like Andy but not quite as awful.

"Why are we in here? Your car is out there." I tried to stay as close to the door as possible.

"Come here, Lennie. Show your favorite uncle how much you love him." Andy's voice was insistent. We were standing just inside the door next to the workbench. I still had my music bag in one arm. He took my free hand and placed it on his crotch. Something in there was very firm and his pants were stretched tight across it. The thing.

My body stiffened completely. I could not believe what I was touching. I could not look at him and could not move. We both stood there, sort of frozen. You are not my favorite uncle, I was thinking.

"That's good, Lennie. Good."

What was good? Standing in a half dark garage with my hand in a place it should not be? This was definitely not good. It was weird and awful.

I heard the screen door of the house slam. Andy jumped and pulled me behind him out of the garage. My grandmother was standing on the porch. There was a moment that seemed to stretch forever. A moment where she looked from me to Andy to the garage, then back to Andy.

"What were you doing in there?" she asked.

"Showing Lennie my Honda," Andy replied, without missing a beat. What a liar! He did have a beat up motorcycle in there but we didn't go anywhere near it. My heart was doing cartwheels. We went in there so he could put my hand right on his thing. The crappy motorcycle in the corner was completely ignored. I began calculating his Confession list in my head: making me touch his thing and then lying about it through his teeth. He would have hundreds of Our Fathers, at minimum.

Then I had a horrible thought: What if I had to confess it, too? Did I actually do something wrong? Did I just do a sin in the garage?

"Get some milk and some bread, too," Grammy instructed. Then she slipped back into the house. Andy led me to the car, a wrecked-up Pontiac.

He looked straight ahead at the road and he told me, "We were just fooling around. It's what bigger kids and grownups do. And I don't want you to tell anyone about it, understand?"

I said yes, and then I thought about all the other times he told me not to tell or he would do something terrible to me, Frankie, and Wolfie. I didn't understand why he was being sort of nice about it.

I followed him around the grocery store and we got milk, bread, and flour, and a Hershey bar for me. When we got back in the car, he tried to get me to sit close to him like a girlfriend, but I wouldn't. I sat by the door with my hand on the door handle. I know this made him mad. All the way home he lectured me about keeping our "game" a secret. He was being really weird. Weird and nice combined. I didn't tell him that I didn't think it was a game because it wasn't fun at all. I knew it would just make him madder.

I didn't forget about it during the week. I thought about it a little, and I made up a plan to try and help Gramma cook dinner after my next piano lesson. Maybe I could just attach myself to her so I could stay away from Andy.

But of course it didn't work out that way. He was too smart. He dragged a desk (that he found at a garage sale) up into his attic room and told Gramma that he was going to help me with my homework. She bought it.

"No, it's OK. I'd rather do it at the table," I tried. And then I looked over. The table was already set for dinner. Andy, the lazy son-of-a-bitch, had done it himself, I knew it.

"It's OK, Lennie. Just go ahead and work with Andy," Gramma said, abandoning me to a fate worse than death.

I had no choice but to follow him up the stairs.

Who lives in an attic? It was stuffy and dark. I'd never been up there before, never wanted to venture into his territory. He had a bed and a

TV and a couple of chairs and the garage-sale desk. There were posters on the walls, and on his closet door there was a big picture of a woman with no clothes on. Her breasts didn't even look real. Her lips were too red, but who would look at those? And her eyes – there was no sign of life in them. I looked away from her really fast. My first glimpse of a centerfold. I caught the caption at the bottom: Miss April. It was September.

Andy took my books and piled them on the desk. Then he said we were going to play the game again. I already knew that, but hearing him say it made me want to throw up.

He came over to me. I backed up and he kept coming toward me until he had me trapped against the wall. His beer-sweat-cigarette smell was overpowering. My stomach did a flip, my head started to ache.

He put his hand on my chest. "I know you want to play our special game with your favorite uncle. I know you do." His voice was low and growly. His big hand was heavy on my chest, holding me against the wall. I couldn't get a good breath in. I was scared, so scared that he'd punch me and knock the wind out of me again. I could still feel that terrible feeling even though it had happened years before.

"Whatsa matter, you scared of your favorite uncle?"

I was terrified, and for the millionth time, he was most definitely NOT my favorite uncle. I didn't answer him. I felt like crying, but I was determined not to. I knew that it would not be a good thing if I cried.

He relaxed his hand, but before he took it away, he ran it over my chest. "You ain't got any titties," he announced.

Shocked, I looked at the floor. I wasn't *supposed* to have any yet. I knew I'd get some, but give me a break. I was only ten. I told him that.

He laughed a smelly beer laugh in my face. "Get on the bed," he ordered. I was not used to being commanded about like this by someone besides my father. So I walked over to the bed and sat down. I thought for a second about trying to run out the door, but there were too many obstacles in the way, including Andy himself.

All of a sudden he was on top of me, touching me, dragging my skirt off me, almost ripping my shirt as he tugged it off me. In a few seconds, I was naked and he was sitting on top of me. I willed myself not to cry. I struggled. This was worse than anything I could every have imagined.

"What are you doing? Why are you doing this?" I'm not even sure if I said this out loud. But I kept thinking it, over and over. Why? He didn't look like himself, he looked like a horror movie person. He WAS a horror movie person because he was in complete control of me. His face was red and his mouth was hanging open.

I protested, I fought him. He stopped being nice and smacked me across the face, and he threatened to punch me in the stomach. And then a very terrible thing happened, which is that he got his thing out of his pants. There it was, right there in the daylight. I felt the air leave me and another big wave of fear take its place. I tried to grab the afghan my Gramma knitted, the one that's on the bottom of his bed, so that I could cover myself up. He pulled that away from me and shoved me back down. What was happening? It made no sense and it made terrible sense.

He started pushing my legs apart. He was making these grunting sounds. I tried punching and kicking at him but he was too strong for me. He started shoving the thing between my legs. I tried to scream but he clamped his hand over my mouth. He grabbed both of my arms and pushed himself between my legs. He was transformed into this werewolf kind of thing and he was hurting me. Him on top of me, his thing trying to push its way inside me where there was no room. I couldn't breathe, I couldn't move. I could barely cry.

At some point I understood, with a clarity that devastated me, what he was actually doing. I understood, exactly and clearly, and that is when the thoughts in my head and the feelings in my body whooshed together and propelled my little self up into the safety of the highest corner of the attic rafters. From way up there, I was not attached to myself, and the hurt he was doing to me was something I couldn't feel. I don't know how it happened, I just know that it did and I knew I had to go there to survive this.

He kept trying to shove himself inside me, up me, but I was too small. He made more grunting sounds and said a lot of swear words. He drooled beer spit onto my face. He slurped at my nonexistent breasts. He finally settled for rubbing his thing between my thighs while the rest of him pinned me down so that I could barely breathe. I felt suddenly ashamed. It must be happening to me because I deserve it. Of course, I must have done something bad. It's the only possible explanation.

The grunts and the thrusts got faster and faster and louder and finally stopped when he shot some wet goop out of himself and all over the bed. I thought it was pee but it – wasn't. He fell forward on top of me and I had to breathe in little gulps if I was going to breathe at all. It took a few minutes but he finally heaved himself upright. As soon as I was free, I grabbed my clothes and clattered down the wooden stairs and into the pink bathroom and locked the door.

Uncomprehending, in pain, in fear, I couldn't even look at myself in the mirror. The tears finally came and I cried them all out. My legs were red where he rubbed himself on them. My little private place was raw where he tried to force his thing up me even though it wouldn't fit. Shaking, I pulled my clothes on. I washed my face. I sat on the toilet, hugging myself. I forced the tears away and the lump in my throat down. I pushed the burning in my eyes away. I brushed my hair with my Gramma's brush.

He was banging on the bathroom door. "Get out here! Right now! Before I break the door down!" he ordered in a loud whisper. He stopped thumping for a few seconds and then tried again, "Come on, Lennie!"

"NO!" I was not going to let that happen again. Never, ever, never again. I wondered how it would be to jump out the bathroom window. We were on the second floor. I could possibly break my leg or something, which might be OK, but my Gramma's rose bushes were right underneath the window. Getting stabbed to death by thorns would be a little too much. I was completely trapped.

Then Andy got really, suspiciously, nice. "Come on, Lennie. I'm not going to touch you. I just need to tell you something really, really important."

I was still shaking. I didn't answer him. I stared out the window at the rose bushes. If Wolfie were with me, she'd bite him, I knew for sure that she would. I looked at myself in the mirror and then I looked away. I looked like some kid I didn't know.

"Lennie, my favorite niece, come on out. I have to tell you a really important thing. Come on, baby."

"Don't call me your baby. I am not your baby."

"Yeah, I know. It's just something you call someone you really like."

This confused me. How could you do something like this to someone you really like?

There was a tap on the door and I jumped. And then, for some unknown reason, I took a deep breath, unlocked it and went out. The very first thing I noticed was that his ugly thing was zipped back up in his ugly pants where it belonged.

Of course, I should not have trusted him. I should have stayed locked in that bathroom until my mother Frankie came to get me or until he broke the door down, because he grabbed me and dragged me up the stairs to the attic again. He sat on the bed and I thought he was going to do it all over again but instead he pulled out a gun from somewhere behind him and he showed it to my wild eyes which, this time, were starting to cry on their own in spite of what my brain said.

"If you EVER tell anyone about this, I am going to come over to your house and first I'm going to shoot your goddamn dog and then I'm going to fuck your mother the professional nurse, and then I'm going to shoot her in the head. Then I'm going to cut your goddamn father's balls off and then I'm going to beat the living shit out of you before I kill you. And you're going to know I mean it because you'll be watching the whole time as I kill your precious mommy." His beer breath was making me gag and his words were making me feel like I was going to pee all over the floor. Tears were spilling down my face. I wanted to grab the gun and shoot his thing off. But I just went limp. I knew down to the core of my being that he could and would do those things. And now I had an image of him doing that awful thing to my mother Frankie. I would let him do it to me again a million times before I'd let him get near my mother.

"Do you hear me, little girl? Do you understand me?"

"Yes," I said, sobbing.

He slapped me again. "Cut that shit out. NOW!"

I didn't know how to stop crying. So I held my breath. I held it for so long that my eyes started to go dim and I got a little dizzy. But I stopped crying.

He sat down in a rickety chair across from me. He put the gun down on the desk in plain sight. It was pointing at me.

"Shit," he said, "I don't want to be mean about it."

"Then don't," I squeaked.

"Do NOT push me, Lennie."

I shut up. I couldn't figure out how *I* could be pushing *him.*

"Just keep your mouth shut about this. Do you understand me?" He stared at me. I could not stand to look at him.

"Yes, " I said.

Then he told me to go downstairs and watch TV. He said he would come down right after me. I was supposed to show Gramma the homework he had helped me with. I was supposed to make up a story, a lie.

I crept downstairs really quietly. He went into the kitchen to get another beer. The top of the gun was sticking out of the back of his pants. I thought maybe it wasn't a real one. How are you supposed to know? I had never seen a gun before except on TV. What was wrong with him that he thought he needed to scare me with a gun? His words were bad enough.

"Do you understand your homework now, Piano Girl?" he said from the kitchen in a fakey voice. The fridge door slammed and the things inside it clinked around. Grammy was still in the kitchen, stirring something on the stove.

"Yes," I peeped.

"I can't hear you," he was coming back into the living room.

"Yes," I said, the same loudness.

I wanted to run away or hurt him or disappear into thin air. Any of those things would have been fine. I could not figure out a way to hurt him because he had that scary gun sticking out of his pants. What if Grammy saw it? Plus, I didn't want to touch him. Ever, ever, again.

He took a $5 bill out of his pocket and stuck it into my book bag. "Buy yourself some Hershey's," he said, in a voice I almost recognized. He knew I loved Hershey bars. Something inside me revolted. He could have given me a five million dollar bill and it would not have paid the price for what he did to me. I was mad at him for trying. I sat there, paralyzed. I wanted to take the money out and throw it at him, but I didn't move. I started thinking about what I could do with $5, which was a lot. The first thing I would do would be to hide it in my piggy bank. I would never spend it. There was something really wrong with him paying me money for what he did to me. Maybe I'd just put it in the donation box at St. Ursula's. God would know what to do with it.

Andy flipped the TV on. I sat on the couch as far away from him as possible and got out my math homework, trying to pretend that nothing had happened. Right. It was impossible. I looked at the numbers, which were comforting but strange, like their meaning had just changed to something I couldn't understand. So I got out one of my piano books and opened it to the Clementi Snota I was working on. The notes looked the same. And I suddenly discovered that I could hear them in my head by just looking at them. Then I got my fingers in the act by pretending to play the notes I was seeing on the page.

Uncle Andy stared at me while I was doing this. I sucked in my breath, instantly fearful. He looked at me and kind of snort-laughed and then turned the TV channel. It was 5:20 p.m. I watched and listened to the notes until I heard my mom come in the front door.

"Remember what I said," Andy said in a low voice. Then he grabbed my butt as I leaned over to pick up my books. A bolt of fear shot through me, and then my mom Frankie walked into the room. She looked very tired and preoccupied—and suddenly concerned.

"Where are your parents?" she asked Andy.

"Mom's in the kitchen," Andy said.

"Your father hasn't been here at all?" She stared at him really hard.

"Nope," he said, not even looking at her.

She looked at me. "Everything OK?"

"Yes," I lied. The biggest lie of my entire life so far.

"Except that she reads her music book just like a regular book," Andy said snidely. "I'd get that checked out if I was you."

"Reading music is just like speaking a whole other language. Something you wouldn't understand," my mother told Andy, who instantly looked like he would kill both of us. My heart pounded even harder than it had for the last hour. The image of the gun flew around in my head and I knew that he could and would kill us, exactly the way he described it.

I knew that my mother did not like Andy, even though she has never said this out loud. I was suddenly afraid that she would ask something about what we'd been doing and then I'd have to tell her the truth and then Andy would kill us both like he promised. I was anxious to get us out of there as soon as possible before he did something to us with that gun—or worse, his ugly horrible thing. I didn't know it but I was breathing really hard and my mom noticed.

I tugged on Frankie's sleeve like a four-year-old. She didn't say anything, probably because she didn't want to be there any more than I did. She looked from Andy to me back to Andy. I knew she was thinking something and I didn't want her to say anything. My heart was hammering and I could feel sweat all over my body. As soon as she said "Let's go," a huge flutter of relief washed over me. Tears jumped to my eyes, but I pushed them away fast. We were on our way out of the house, getting in the car, driving to our house where it was safe. I had never felt more grateful for anything in my whole life.

It was going to have to be my secret, a knowing I carried around with me that no one else could possibly ever find out. I was never going to be able to breathe a word of it, so I decided right then and there in the car on Broad Street that I would stuff it into this little-used place inside me where no one could ever get at it. I had only one other thing in there, and that was how good it felt when Audrey Fremont put her hand on my leg. So I had one good thing and one very, very bad thing stored in there. I figured I could live with that, especially since my mother's life depended on it.

Everything in my life turned strange after that Piano Lesson Day. I was scared a lot and I couldn't figure some things out, like why would someone do that anyway, and why did he pick me? Pictures of it would come into my head at odd times, like when we were taking a multiplication test or when we were playing dodgeball in gym class. One thing could make the thoughts and pictures go away: imagining myself playing the piano. The pretend piano strategy wasn't always convenient, especially when I was playing dodgeball, but I tried it anyway. One other thing that worked was imagining myself listening to the Grieg *Piano Concerto in A minor*. When I finally figured this out, school got a lot easier.

The thing that worked the very best was to actually play the piano, which I could do if I was at my house. I wasn't sure why this was, only that it worked and was the only reliable thing that could keep my mind away from The Awful Thing Andy Did to Me. The pink-beige piano became my best friend. My life depended on it, kind of like how my mother's life depended on me keeping my mouth shut.

I also began to plan my revenge. Since I could not tell on Andy because he was going to kill people, my mother and me in particular, I had to figure out how to do something that would make him stop doing it or else hurt him in the worst possible way. The best idea I had was to get him to just go away. Somewhere far away, like Alaska or Thailand. I had no idea how to accomplish this, only that I had to try.

The first thing I did was to light candles the next time Elly and I went to Confession. I saved up a bunch of nickels and lit fifteen candles. Elly was amazed.

"You must want something really bad," she said, expecting me to tell her what it was. But of course, I didn't. I couldn't.

So all I said was, "Yup, I really want something. Really bad." And then I gave her that look that we shared between us sometimes, and she understood that I just couldn't tell her. And then she did a wonderful thing, which was to take all the change she had in her little plaid pocket and light the rest of the candles, about twenty more of them. I knelt down in front of the now raging candle blaze and begged St. Ursula to make Andy go very far away. "My first choice is Thailand because is it a foreign country," I reminded her, "but Alaska would be fine also. Please make him go away and stay there and please make him live alone so he won't hurt anyone else. Thank you and amen." St. Ursula was so gigantic that I thought she must have some extra pull with God; otherwise, they would have made her into a regular-sized person statue. I believed this fervently as I implored her to help me get rid of Andy. I stared at her for a few seconds after I finished praying to make sure she wasn't bleeding or oozing oil or anything. It was a little intimidating because she was so huge, but nothing happened. So we admired our candle inferno once again and then we went to Elly's house.

It was really quiet in her house, which was weird because Rosa usually banged the pots and dishes around when she cooked. And there would be salsa music on the record player or the radio. But this day it was completely silent. And then we realized that no one was there but us. It was strange, coming home to no one, and we tried to figure out what to do. The only thing that seemed to make sense was to grab a bunch of food and go up to Elly's room.

We did our homework for so long that it started getting dark outside. We had never been alone in either of our houses by ourselves for this long before. When the phone rang, Elly jumped on it.

It was Frankie. "You two girls go to our house, right now. I'll be home shortly." She didn't ask how school was or anything. She did say to get there as fast as possible because it was getting dark. "I could call Andy to pick you up. Do you want a ride?"

"NO!" I shouted, much too quickly. I had to remember to be normal where Andy was concerned, as if that could ever be possible.

"OK, honey. But you and Elly run, OK? I don't like that it's almost dark out."

We promised to race the few blocks as fast as we could. Frankie also made us promise to not speak to anyone on the way, and, obviously, we were to be very, very careful.

When we got there, Frankie was just pulling into the driveway in the big Chrysler. She told us that Rosa had been to the emergency room because Uncle Bill had beaten her up. Just like that. She said it like Rosa had skinned her knee or something. Beaten up? Uncle Bill is Frank's brother and Elly's uncle. He has a fat potbelly because he drinks so much beer. He is loud. Elly hates him. When we go to parties or the Band Picnic, we stay as far away as possible from Uncle Bill. Uncle Bill is like Uncle Andy, only older and fatter but just as creepy.

Elly started crying when Frankie told us about Rosa. "Why? Why would he hurt my mother? What did she do to him?"

Elly was crying, but I was mad. I thought of ways to steal Uncle Andy's gun. I thought we should march right back to the church and change the candle prayers so that both of the uncles would be sent to Thailand. I was not liking uncles at all, not one bit.

Frank and Rosa came in the back door with my dad, who looked like he might murder someone on the spot. I hoped that the person he killed would be Uncle Bill—and then Uncle Andy, if he had a little extra energy. Elly ran to her mom, who held her, and they both cried. Rosa had purple bruises all over her face, and one of her arms was in a sling.

Frankie handed me a plate full of peanut butter and jelly sandwiches. There were at least ten PB&Js stacked up. "Get some milk and go eat in your room. Elly can stay with you tonight." This was our signal to get out of the way of the adults. I was never allowed to eat in my room. I didn't point this out to Frankie, and I didn't tell her that we had already raided the fridge at Elly's house and we weren't really hungry. Frankie had already turned her back and was reaching into the top cabinet where the whiskey lived. Elly and I slipped out of the kitchen and went up to my room, but we snuck back out and crept down to the landing where we could eavesdrop on our parents in the kitchen.

Frankie demanded to know what exactly had happened. We could hear Rosa sniffling, which meant she was still crying.

"She must have mouthed off to him or something," Frank said. His voice sounded tight and small. I could feel Elly tense up next to me.

"Goddamn pig!" Frankie said. It was more like she yelled it while trying to be quiet.

"Frankie, that's not necessary," Ted said.

"Yes it is goddamn necessary. The man is a menace."

"He was drunk," Frank said.

"Don't defend him! As if that's an excuse." My mother's voice sounded brittle. "Look at her! A broken arm! Bruises everywhere! Two broken ribs! It's a good thing you showed up when you did, Frank Wojciechowski. She could be dead!" The last word caught in Frankie's throat and she began to cry.

"Uncle Bill is very bad," Elly whispered to me.

That did it for me. He was definitely going to have to go the way of Uncle Andy. A creepy, icky feeling started to snake around in my belly, occasionally making little stabs outward to my arms and throat. It was icy, chilly and slimy all around my insides. It dawned on me that maybe Uncle Bill tried to do to Rosa what Uncle Andy was trying to do with me, did to me. It was a slow unfolding of realization, clear and cold behind my eyes.

Our parents started moving into the living room, so we tiptoed back to my room and kept the door cracked open. Wolfie the dog was very interested in our sandwiches, so we gave her one of her own. Dogs always seem to have such a good time with peanut butter.

"I know I shouldn't have to say this," Frankie was saying, "but you'd better keep your kid away from that monster."

I could feel Elly stiffen when Frankie said this.

"Damn right we will," Frank agreed. "He's not welcome in our house anymore. At least for the time being."

We couldn't see my mother rolling her eyes, her ubiquitous response to anything she considered ridiculous. "For the time being? For the TIME BEING? I would NEVER let that asshole in my home again."

"Frankie! That is enough! This is Frank's home we're talking about," said Ted.

"Frank's home? How about Rosa's home? Huh?" I loved when my mother got belligerent and righteous. I felt scared about it now, though.

"It's alright, Frankita," Rosa sniffled. There were some shuffling sounds.

"NO IT IS NOT ALRIGHT," my mother was yelling now. She started banging chairs around. We heard one of the dads trying to reason with her in a low voice.

"What about the cops?" Frankie kept pushing "Why haven't you filed a report? Pressed charges? Are you going to let him get away with this?"

"He's my brother, for Christ's sake," said Frank. "I can't have my own brother arrested."

"But you'll let him beat and rape your wife!" Frankie would not let it go.

"That's enough, Frankie," said Ted. "That is enough."

"Good God," said Frankie. "You two are spineless. He could have KILLED her! He's crazy! No one should ever be alone with him! But of course, you can't call the cops on your dear, drunk, abusive brother now, can you?"

"That is ENOUGH, Frankie. I mean it."

"Jesus Christ. Jesus CHRIST! What is wrong with you two? What kind of men ARE YOU?!" Something crashed downstairs. It was probably Frankie's glass of whiskey. We scampered under the covers then.

"Elly! Get down here!" Frank commanded, stomping into the living room. Elly had had only one bite of her PB & J. She stayed frozen in my bed.

"Quick! Be asleep!" I snapped the light off and we pretended to be sleeping. Even Wolfie faked along with us. We left one sandwich on the plate and tucked the other ones around us under the covers.

Ted's heavy steps clomped up to my room. The door creaked open and he paused for a moment, looking at us. We were well-practiced at slowing down our breathing and feigning sleep. And there was no possibility of us even thinking about laughing at a time like this.

"Shit," he whispered under his breath. Elly squeezed my hand under the covers.

"They're asleep," he said when he got to the bottom of the stairs.

"Let her stay," pleaded Frankie. "Go home and take care of your wife," she said to Frank.

Then it got really quiet down there. The front door opened and closed. We stayed immobilized under the covers. After about ten minutes, Frankie came up and peeked in my door. "I know you're awake," she whispered. "Do you want some ice cream?"

"Sí," said Elly, answering for both of us. "Por favor."

We crept out of bed. I accidentally brushed my hand on Elly's pillow and it was all wet. We sneaked past my father in the living room, but we didn't need to be that careful because he had his headphones on and was probably listening to Benny Goodman or Mr. Bernstein and the New York Philharmonic. He didn't open his eyes as we passed him. He wasn't even in the world when he got like that.

Frankie dished out rocky road and said, "Your mom will be fine."

"I know," Elly said. "But what did she do to get beat up?"

I knew she was trying to get Frankie to tell us the whole story, but it wasn't going to happen. You could tell because Frankie's jaw was set. She wasn't about to talk.

"She didn't do anything. She did absolutely nothing. No one deserves what happened to her. There are just some people in the world who do terrible things to other people. And your—your uncle is one of them."

And Uncle Andy is another.

7

Circle of Fifths

At a Thursday piano lesson I was assigned a brand new Clementi sonata (snota) and then had to go to my grandparents' house afterward, as usual. It was one of the days that Andy tried to be nice to me. On this particular day he tried to get me to let him put his thing in my mouth. No matter what, I could not do it, even when I thought about biting it really hard. Even though there was the threat of him murdering Frankie and me, I could not get my face near it. I started gagging. Then I started to almost puke but nothing came out. I sobbed uncontrollably. Andy cursed and smacked me and shoved me down the stairs from his attic room. And then he didn't come near me the rest of the day. I had over an hour by myself, hiding in a corner of the living room and watching the second hand of the clock move around, minute by minute. I did not read my music, didn't crack open my homework, didn't turn on the television or go into the kitchen to find a snack. I just sat there, frozen, and waited. And while I waited, I made up a prayer-chant in my head. The Circle of Fifths. C, G, D, A, E, B, F# the same as Gb, C# the same as Db, Ab, Eb, Bb, F, back to C, Hail Mary, full of grace, the Lord is with thee. Blessed art thou among women, and blessed is the fruit of thy womb, Jesus. Holy Mary, Mother of God, pray for us sinners now and at the hour of our death, C, G, D, A, E,

B, F#enharmonically the same asGb; C#enharmonically the same as Db, Ab, Eb, F, Hail Mary, full of grace, C major no flats and sharps, G major one sharp, D major two sharps, A major, three sharps—

I chanted this, the Circle of Fifths and the Hail Marys, as I watched the clock. I said it 372 times in a row before I heard Frankie open the front door. She looked really tired. And there was some actual blood on her scrubs. Eew.

"Ready to go?" she said to me.

I already had my coat on.

"What's the matter, Lennie? You look—I don't know, strange. Did something happen at school today?" She had an alarmed expression on her face.

"I'm fine. Nothing happened," I said in my best bravado. "I'm trying to memorize the circle of fifths." I, of course, had it way more than memorized.

"What's the circle of fifths?" she asked. She looked really interested.

I explained it to her. The major keys make a circle, starting with C major, no sharps or flats. Then you move to G major, a fifth above, and its key signature has one sharp. Then D major, anther fifth above with two sharps. And so on.

Frankie's expression of interest transformed into one of bewilderment.

"Your grandparents not here again?" she asked, changing the subject.

"Nope," I said, even though sometimes Gramma was there but she wasn't, really.

"Andy?" she asked a question without asking it.

"Having a beer in his room."

Frankie didn't say anything, but I knew she didn't like this.

There were two and a half more months of school. Eleven more piano lessons. I'd added it up in a different part of my brain while I was chanting and waiting. I knew I could handle it, and then I was going to figure something out for the summer and the next school year. And maybe by that time Andy would be in Thailand or Alaska or even Ohio. Ohio would be better than nothing.

I discovered that I could practice almost nonstop if I put one of the puffy couch cushions on the piano bench. I started spending most of my time at the piano. Sometimes the TV would be on and sometimes not. I even ate food while playing, chewing in time to the music. I knew that the Miss Ashleys would be outraged, but I did it anyway. Sometimes I piled all the other pillows around me and made a Fortress of Solitude. But mine was not made of ice like Superman's; mine was soft and comfortable, and I pretended that it was impenetrable. I had plenty of stuff in there to zap intruders and villains. In my fortress, I made it so that kryptonite could not get in. There could be nothing in there that would harm me. Also, there were no boys allowed and definitely no men. Wolfie would lie down next to me and guard me. She knew it was really important.

Elly wasn't around as much as usual since her mom had gotten beaten up. She went right home after school, and so did I, and we wouldn't see each other until gig night. Things weren't feeling right anywhere in our lives, and we weren't depending on each other like we usually did. So I hid in my music fortress. My mother got more and more concerned.

"Lennie, you can't spend your entire life at the piano," she said one day. "Do you want to invite your friend Evelyn over? Or how about Audrey?" I had never been alone with Audrey Fremont, and that thought intrigued me. Evelyn was beginning to bore me. I missed Elly and I was scared of Andy and the only place I felt safe was in my piano fortress.

"I don't spend my entire life here," I said snottily. My mom looked great in her green scrubs, but her face was so anxious that I immediately felt bad for being sarcastic.

"The amount of time you spend here is unhealthy," Frankie said. "I know most mothers would be happy about their child practicing the piano, but there has to be a limit. You need to be a normal child sometimes." Frankie's hands were on her hips. I wished I could tell her that my normal childhood got interrupted by my Uncle Andy.

"You look good in your nurse outfit," I dodged. "You look just like a doctor."

"Thank you, Lennie. And I still think you need to come away from there and join the rest of the world."

I was not going to do that. My fortress was the most protected, healthiest place in my life. "I like it here," I said.

Frankie sat down, dislodging the north wall of my fortress. "Why do you like the piano so much?" she asked.

"It's warm and safe," I answered truthfully, leaving out the part where I chanted for the disappearance of Andy, and now Bill, as I went around and around the circle of fifths.

I saw her left eyebrow lift and immediately regretted what I'd said. "And I love music. It's my destiny," I told her, not quite sure what I meant.

"Hmmmmm," eyebrow higher and then a sigh. "OK," she said, peering at me.

No matter what, I was not going to tell her about the circle of fifths or the heartbeats. Like when my heart would race and pound really hard. Sometimes when that happened, I would shake and feel like crying. Or I would cry and I wouldn't be able to stop. It wasn't so bad in my Fortress of Solitude. It never happened when I was playing the piano. But other times, I could never be sure.

All of my piano lessons passed the same way as all the previous ones. Music, pianos, a dish full of chocolates at the Miss Ashleys' house, and then walking as slowly as possible to my grandparents' house. There I'd face Andy and whatever things he would do to my body while my actual self hid up near the cobwebs on the ceiling of the attic. Then Frankie would come and pick me up and we would stop and pick up food for dinner from Barney's or, on the days she was the most tired, McDonald's. I would talk to her about math class or art class and she would smile and the closer we got to home, the happier I would be. I was very good at pushing what Andy did to me out of my brain into that secret place inside me. I was determined to not say one syllable about it to anyone. I took my responsibility for their safety very seriously. No one, especially my mother, would ever find out.

Elly and I went flying through the back door of our house. We had big news.

"Angela got kidnapped!" Elly's face was flushed and her hair was wild from running.

"Yeah! She got kidnapped! And now she's dead!" I was out of breath from trying to run as fast as Elly. We were scared. We were shocked.

My mother put down her cooking utensil—she actually called it that, and not a spoon or a spatula—and asked Elly to explain. Elly told her that Angela had not come home from school the Friday before, except we knew this because it was in the newspaper and then teams of volunteers went out looking for her. One of the eighth graders finally told the cops that he saw Angela being dragged into a car near the school. That meant that she was kidnapped and now the police were involved and there was going to be another picture of Angela's parents in the paper, crying.

I had been in catechism class waiting for Sister Anne to come in and tell us something new about Jesus that we didn't already know. Elly didn't have to go to the after-school classes because she got enough religion during the day at St. Ursula's, but apparently I didn't since I was now a public school kid. So on Wednesdays, Elly waited for me out on the playground and we made faces at each other through the window without Sister Anne seeing. This very day, though, Sister Anne came in looking very pale and told us that all of the nuns were gathering in the parlor and she had to go. We were going to be dismissed without having Catechism. The last time the nuns gathered in the parlor of the convent was when Pope John the Twenty-third died. And this time they were there because the news broke that Angela Santini's body had been found in the field behind the 7-11, which was completely surrounded by houses, yards, and barking dogs. I did not immediately believe it. I didn't even believe that she was missing, in spite of the being-dragged-into-a-car story. I really thought that she was just hidden away somewhere, doing extra homework or praying piously for all the pagan babies. I thought it was just another one of Audrey's mean stories, made up to scare us to death.

But it was *true*. One of the neighborhood dogs found a part of her (no one would tell us which part, and, as a result, a million rumors flew about). Then they roped off the whole field for two whole days, brought in backhoes, and kept lights on all night long. Barb Hammer lived there and told us every detail. Her yard backed onto the field, and she could see everything, including when they pulled a lump of clothing out of a hole in the ground and then loaded it into a big plastic bag. It took her a while to realize that the lump of clothing was Angela and not a pile of clothes after all. When this realization hit her, she ran screaming into the living room and had to be held by her mother until she could stop crying. Mrs. Hammer, feeling helpless, called the police department just to confirm what Barb had seen. Yes, it was true. She had seen the dead girl being "removed."

Elly and I both got out of an afternoon of school to go to the funeral. This was not as bad as the viewing, which had happened the night before. A whole group of girls and their parents went to McConnell's Funeral Home on Broad Street to see Angela in her coffin. I overhead my mother and some other ladies in the restroom discussing how they could possibly have a viewing for a body that had been buried in a field for five days and then dug up by a dog. But then there was Angela Santini, lying in a long white box in her school uniform. Her face looked weird, it was powdery and very white. The rest of her body was under a blanket. There was no way to tell which part of her the dog had found since she was all tucked in and hidden away.

People were lining up to go past the open casket. The mothers hovered protectively around their—thankfully, still alive—daughters. Some of the fathers paced around in the parking lot, not even going in to pay their respects to the late, pious Angela Santini.

It made no sense, her being dead. She was the most obedient, quiet, respectful, religious child of all of us. If this could happen to her, being so good and perfect and everything, what was going to become of the rest of us?

Elly grabbed my hand and we stood in the line of mourners. I learned that this is what you officially call weeping for a dead person: mourning. Our mothers stood behind us. They were holding hands, too. Rosa was softly crying, which made my throat get all tight like I was going to have to cry, too. Rosa would cry at most things, and this was one of the more appropriate things. Frankie was stone-faced and looked furious. I knew that she wanted to hunt down whoever would do such a thing and kill him. Angela really liked my mom, and I think Frankie respected Angela's earnestness.

We stood side by side and looked down at Angela. She was wearing her plaid St. Ursula's uniform. There was a teddy bear tucked under her arm. Her face was smiling, sort of. It was that perfect, innocent smile that was a trademark of Angela's. She always looked like she was in direct communication with God or at least the angels. I had this weird thought that she would now be able to see and hear everything that we do down here on earth. Sort of like God, but she would not be all-powerful—she would just be more influential with all the angels. She'd be able to report on us to God, only it would be way more impressive than when she did that same thing with the nuns in class.

Dead. D-E-A-D. There is the body that used to be Angela—and sort of still is, I mean, it *looked* like her—lying there in a white box. Coffin. I tried to make my mind understand it, but the rest of me was too scared. Like if I ever understood, then I would know something I'm not supposed to know, and I'd be dead also. Looking intently at Angela—or the body of Angela, or whatever, even after we sat down and the priest got up to say a few words (which sent Angela's mother into a crying fit that was so bad she hyperventilated and had to be escorted out of the room), I kept trying to find her. She was going to sit up any minute. She was going to sit up and say something and then we would all go home, relieved that it was all a big mistake.

From the adjoining room we heard, "My baby, my baby! Why did they take my baby?" This was highly uncharacteristic behavior from Angela Santini's mother, who looked a lot like Mrs. Cleaver, the Beaver's mom, right down to the little pearl necklace. When I heard her wail like that, something inside me wrenched up and I wanted to wail, too. But I didn't. I sat there with my classmates and their moms, who all looked as though they were trying to hold something inside themselves for fear of acting just like Angela's mom. No one was acting like themselves except for Frankie.

I could not believe that Angela was not going to wake up. There was now this enormous difference between her and me, mainly that she was dead and I was not. When the viewing was over, we lingered out in the lobby while our mothers talked to some of the other mothers in very hushed voices. I happened to glance into the viewing room and I saw the two undertaker guys lower the lid over Angela. The breath went out of me. Elly saw, and she knew instantly what had happened. Her face became very scared and I felt her suck in a breath. The lid was down and Angela was IN there. What if she wakes up? It would be worse than anything I'd ever seen in one of Aunt Liddy's movies, waking up inside a dark coffin and being alive and trapped in there with all that dirt on top of you and no way to get out.

So when we went to bed that night, I was scared to turn off the light. Elly stayed over, as she did most Fridays, but this wasn't your typical Friday. We didn't talk much; we tried to act sad. Then we tried to entertain ourselves by checking our breast progress. We did this periodically in front of each other and the mirror. Elly's boobs were far bigger than mine. In fact, everything on her looked more in proportion. I was skinny and had muscles. Elly was also skinny but she had the beginnings of curves like you saw on models and movie stars. She had excellent breasts. Mine were there, but were mere shadows of hers. She always reassured me that more of them would show up as we got older.

On this night, we admired each other's breasts for only a few seconds and then fell back on the bed. There was an underlying creepy feeling in my body. I felt weird thinking about Angela so much, especially since I had witnessed her last moments of being a person on the earth before they shut the lid on her. I knew I wouldn't be giving her a second thought if she were across town, still alive. So now I thought about her constantly because she was dead and this made me feel guilty and scared. I had no idea how to translate this to Elly.

"What do you think it feels like to be dead?" I wondered. I didn't tell her the rest of what I was thinking, which was that someone exactly like my Uncle Andy had killed Angela because she had told on him. A cold, eerie feeling churned around in my belly. I was absolutely positive that this is why Angela was murdered. Beyond a shadow of a doubt, I was certain.

"I think that's the whole point," Elly said patiently. "You're dead. You don't feel anything. You're not in your body anymore."

"I still think she could wake up, and if she does, she's going to be really scared."

"I know. But she's really dead. I could feel her deadness." Elly could feel things like that. She always knew what people were thinking, which is why I had to be so careful about the subject of Andy so she didn't figure it out from my thoughts.

"Maybe you really don't go anywhere when you're dead. You just are dead and everything stops," I wondered.

"No, you go to heaven and have fun with Jesus." Elly crossed her arms, which I knew meant that she was not going to budge on this point at all.

"Well, how do you get out of your body? No one's ever seen that happen. No one really knows that you can actually get out and have life everlasting."

"You become invisible. You rise from the dead out of your body but humans can't see you anymore because you're invisible to them. Only God and the angels can see you." Elly acted like it was an effort to be patient with me.

"Well, how are you supposed to see them, or anything, without eyes?" This is the part that scared me the most, not being able to see. Angela's eyes were closed in the casket. She wasn't seeing anything earthly, that's for sure. All I could think of was that her eyes might pop open and there she would be in the dark. And she probably wouldn't be able to breathe, either. This was getting worse by the second.

"You don't need eyes to see when you're in your eternal body!" Elly seemed suddenly exasperated with me. "You can see everything in the universe!"

"Did Sister Regina tell you that?" I was going to be suspicious of Sister Regina forever.

"No, Father Chaslowski did." That stopped me in my tracks for a moment. I pretty much believed Father Chaslowski.

Elly had it all figured out. I just knew that being dead was not what I wanted at all because it was too scary, and the living people all around you got very weird. They talked about you like you were the best person in the world, which we knew Angela was anyway. And they cried, and they had masses for you. Some of them stood around and whispered things and then shook their heads and said things like,

"Oh, what a terrible shame." And they cooked a lot of food, much too much for one family to eat, especially when they weren't hungry at all, they were too busy crying.

At this point, we didn't really have any idea of the real reason why Angela turned out to be dead. Except, of course, for my own personal theory, which I was not about to share with anyone. There were all kinds of rumors. Everyone had their own theory, including me, but I never spoke mine out loud. I was too scared that the same thing would come true for me. I did secretly ask Wolfie to dig me up, should that need ever come to pass. I didn't want a strange dog to find me, especially the slobbery Lab from down the street. I think Wolfie understood me, and I knew I could count on her. Then I got really scared and couldn't sleep, thinking about being dead and not being able to see, and being trapped in a coffin with the lid nailed shut. No matter what Elly said, I was scared out of my mind.

After the funeral, thoughts of Angela came to my brain all the time. I tried to get her to talk to me from heaven, but I never heard anything definite. I wanted to know if it was true, if she had had someone do those things to her and then she told on him and now she was dead. I wondered if she might help me out so that I could stay alive and survive until the end of the school year. I knew she'd have influence with the types of angels who handled these sorts of things. I thought she might understand and help me.

I pushed the Uncle Andy thing further and further inside me. He kept doing it to me, week after week, after every piano lesson. When it happened, I hid in the place inside of me that I created in my brain. It looked exactly like my Fortress of Solitude, and I knew that it was just a matter of time and that it would stop eventually and I'd be OK for the most part. I would go to my piano lessons and I knew what was going to happen afterward and I stopped caring anymore. I learned how to shut him out and let him do whatever he wanted to me. He actually even began to be nice to me about it, and once he even said he was sorry, but he just couldn't help himself. Of course, the next week he got mean again and showed me the gun again, just to remind me that he still had a plan to murder all of us if I told.

No matter what, I was not going to end up like Angela, dug up from the field by a dog. I had to make sure my mother was safe, and the only way I could do that was to stay alive, and the only way I could do that was to never tell anyone in the universe, ever.

Everyone looked at me when the office messenger brought a note to our class and Mrs. Reynolds read it out loud after saying, "This concerns Lennie Kuklinski and no one else." It was as if someone clicked a remote control and they all swiveled their heads around so they could stare at me. At St. Ursula's, this would never happen because the nuns instructed us to never turn around if there was a commotion behind us. And if someone did, they would get whacked on the head and called a "Looky-Loo" by the nun doing the whacking. A Looky-Loo was very bad because they were fair game for Satan. If the Looky-Loo didn't have enough self-control to resist looking at whatever was causing the commotion, how could they possibly have enough self-control to resist Satan's other devious manipulations? But in public school, being a Looky-Loo was no big deal. An office message was an unusual thing, and one that was read out loud was fascinating for everyone.

"Lennie, you are to leave your last class at 2:30 and meet your mother at the main entrance to the school. Do you understand?" Mrs. Reynolds gaze bored a hole into me. What was there not to understand? I had to leave early for some mysterious reason and there was going to be a crowd lingering around the main entrance at 2:30 to see me get into Frankie's Buick. Then there were going to be one million rumors about where I was going.

"Mom, could you have told me this before I left for school?" I said as I slid into the front seat, watched by at least fifty pairs of eyes. I waved at my classmates just to let them know I wasn't going to be intimidated by being stared at and rumored about. "And where are we going, anyway?"

"Oh, I realized it was time for your check-up," Frankie lied. She was a much worse liar than me.

We were heading toward Allentown, in the opposite direction of Dr. Frescatti's office. "We're going the wrong way then." I wasn't going to make this easy for her. My heart was pounding, and I had to try and distract it. Wherever we were going, I could absolutely not have the heart-pounding thing going on.

We pulled into a parking lot of an office building that was surrounded by tall sycamores. They all looked like good climbing trees. I didn't say anything as I followed Frankie into the building. She had on a white nurse outfit, not surgical scrubs. It didn't look quite right on her, but I figured she wanted to look as medical and professional as possible if we were going to the doctor.

"What kind of check-up is this?" I loved Dr. Frescatti. Why weren't we going to her? Why would we go to a strange building in Allentown surrounded by nice trees? I thought there might be a slight possibility that Dr. Frescatti had moved, but couldn't she just TELL me?

Frankie didn't answer. We opened a door with a whole bunch of names on it. Something Something Family Practice, and a list of doctors. The waiting room was full of toys and little kids. I decided right away that I would not go near the little kids. I found a *Highlights* magazine and pretended to read it while I begged my heart to stop hammering.

"Mrs. Kuklinski and—Leonard?" A woman from behind the reception desk gestured to Frankie. "The doctor will see you now."

"It's Leonore," my mother whispered to the woman. Leonard, my God! I was so glad none of my friends heard this.

I decided that my mother was not going in there with me. No way. But no one heard or listened to my protests. We were led down a long hallway and stopped in front of a wooden door. The reception lady knocked softly on the door, which said Dr. Carolyn Butler, M.D., Child Psychiatry.

What is Child Psychiatry?

"Come on in," a muffled voice said.

Frankie and I walked into a room with a desk and a bunch of furniture. It did not look like a regular doctor's office. There were no stethoscopes or tables or cotton swabs. There was a sandbox, though. That seemed weird to me.

"Hi, I'm Dr. Butler," the woman said. She had very red hair and about five million teeth, all of which were very large, much too big for her mouth. She smiled and there they were. And they were not exactly white. In fact, she bore quite a striking resemblance to a horse.

Dr. Butler shook my hand, which is the first time anyone did that to me. She said, "Welcome. I understand your name is Lennie."

At least she hadn't made the Leonard mistake. "What's to understand about that?" I asked. I crossed my arms and looked her in her horse face.

"Lennie!" Frankie exclaimed, pinching me on the arm. OK, so it was a little rude.

Dr. Butler asked us to sit down in chairs that faced her desk, which she sat behind. "So," she said. "What brings you here?"

I didn't say anything because I was bewildered about what we were doing there. The thing that brought me—dragged me—was my mother. I tried to assume a defiant air, and then I let the ball bounce to Frankie's court. She didn't say one thing. She just looked straight ahead. Dr. Butler just sat there looking at us and smiling with all those enormous teeth. I was very confused because there was no examining table and no cotton balls and no jar of lollipops. Was I going to have to take my clothes off? I decided to refuse to do that.

"OK," Dr. Butler finally said. "Why don't I talk with Mom first, and then Lennie and I can chat after that?"

"Sure," said Frankie, looking relieved.

Dr. Butler pressed something on a box on her desk. The door opened and I was escorted out by the reception lady. She handed me a different *Highlights* magazine and asked me to sit down in a kid-sized chair in the hallway. Apparently, separating parents and children was a common occurrence here in this weird doctor's office.

I read about Goofus and Gallant and then tried to pick out the hidden items in the picture on the next page. By the time I had seventeen out of twenty, the door opened again, and Frankie and I traded places. I was mad at her. I felt betrayed. So I didn't look at her as we passed in the doorway.

I sat in the chair across from the desk again. My feet didn't touch the floor. Dr. Horse Teeth Butler smiled at me again. I steeled my resolve to not tell her anything. She could just ASK ME if she wanted to know anything about me.

"Well, Lennie, I understand that a terrible thing happened to one of your classmates recently." Dr. Butler put her pen down and looked into my eyes.

"Well, I guess it's pretty terrible if you're dead." I felt swirly in my belly, scared that she was going to ask me something about being dead.

"Yes, I imagine it would be."

"I wouldn't like it if I couldn't see anything." Uh-oh, she got out her pen again. Apparently that was something worth writing down.

"Yes, I imagine I wouldn't like that either." She stopped writing and looked at me again.

I felt the swirly feeling so I decided to try and be tough because that seemed to keep the feeling away pretty well. I made a frown face like my dad did all the time.

I know she was watching my face get all serious and nasty. I tried to look just like my dad in one of his mean moods. She took a deep breath and said, "Lennie, your mother tells me that you enjoy playing the piano. And as a matter of fact, you play the piano all the time. For hours and hours, even." Wow, those teeth! I want to count them! She could come right over to me and bite me and I would probably be killed.

"Well, yes I do." Something clamped shut inside me. I was not going to tell her anything. It was none of her business. My fort is my own personal place. I felt completely betrayed that my mother had to tell a strange child psychiatrist doctor about my fortress, like it was some crazy thing and I needed to be cured of it.

"I see," said Dr. Butler. "Now we seem to be getting somewhere."

"Where?" I said, as snottily as I could.

"Why, the road to understanding, of course." Dr. Butler wrote something down and then she looked at me and smiled.

"Jesus Christ," I said. It was the first time I ever took the Lord's name in vain. But I wanted to shock her. The road to understanding? Was she kidding?

Dr. Horse Lady wrote something else down. "Are you fond of swearing?" she asked.

"Only in front of adults," I replied. I had the feeling that I was going to be in big trouble if I kept this up so I decided to try and behave myself.

"So, what kind of doctor are you, anyway?" I asked. "Are you going to listen to my heart?" I tried to divert her.

Her smile got bigger, as if that were even possible. "I'm the kind of doctor that children talk to. We talk about all kinds of things in here. Sometimes we play with toys in the sand, or we just talk."

"YOU play in the sand? Do you get paid for that?"

"Well, Lennie, usually I just sit here while kids play and they tell me stories. Sometimes I do play, though. I enjoy the sandbox."

She was too weird for me. A lady who plays in a sandbox with kids and toys? I was getting a visual that was just too peculiar. Dr. Butler playing in the sand in her polyester suit.

I wanted to make the teeth go away. And I was not going to talk to her about anything important, but I didn't tell her this. I looked around the room, thinking that the toys she had all over the place are baby toys and I almost told her this. The sandbox looked intriguing, but I wasn't going to admit this to her. I just sat there, swinging my legs back and forth.

"Why aren't you going to listen to my heart?" I asked again.

"I'm not going to listen to your heart, today, Lennie. I'm just going to listen to your words. OK?" The teeth began to fade from view as her smile seemed to transfer from her mouth to her eyes. She seemed nice enough, but there was no way I was going to trust her enough to tell her things that were not her business. My father said this all the time, that family things are none of any other people's business. I decide to follow his example. Ted would think my life was none of Dr. Butler's business, but Frankie was the one who was making me be here, so maybe it *was* her business. It was all too confusing.

"So," she was trying again, "do you want to tell me about your piano playing?"

"What is there to tell you?" I asked, feeling betrayed by Frankie. "I'm a good piano player and I do it as much as possible."

"Your mother told me that she was worried about you. That you weren't spending much time outside or with your friend Ella."

"ELLY! Her name is Elly! ELLY, OK?!" I felt protective and like I might start to cry all at once. "I play the piano a lot. Every chance I get. It's what I do."

"Do you like playing the piano?"

Duh! I've only said it fifty times. "It's my very favorite thing to do," I said, to clarify.

"Do you like your piano lessons?" Dr. Teeth Woman wrote something else down really fast like she didn't want me to know she was doing it. She wrote while she was looking at me and not the paper. I decided that I would have to try that myself sometime.

"Miss Ashley is the best teacher in town," I told her. "There are actually two Miss Ashleys, but I have the more advanced one. The other Miss Ashley just teaches beginners."

"Oh, I see." A little more writing.

"I have performed in the Spring Musicale," I informed her. "Several times."

"Oh, you have! Well, you must play very well, then."

"I do," I agreed. "If you had a piano in here, I would show you." I'd much rather play the piano than play in a sandbox with some red-haired lady with way-too-many-teeth looking at me.

"And I would enjoy that!" She looked like she really would enjoy it. But, oh well.

Then we sat there looking at each other. I was not going to say anything more. And she seemed to not want to, either. She did write a few more things down on her secret piece of paper.

She looked at her watch. "Well, Lennie, we only have a few more minutes left together. Is there anything you'd like to talk about? Or would you like to play with anything I have here?"

"No, thanks," I said. I was feeling a little bad about having been snotty earlier.

"Well, alright, then." She escorted me out to the hallway. Frankie had been waiting for me in the same chair reading the same *Highlights* magazine that I'd had. She looked very worried.

We said goodbye to Dr. Butler and the reception lady, and when we got in the car, I tried to stop myself from screaming. Instead, I said, very calmly, very nicely and not too loud, "Mother, why did you take me there?" I had never addressed Frankie as Mother. She had only called me Leonore two or three times when she was really mad. So I hoped she got the message that I was really furious with her.

"Lennie, I've been worried about you because you LIVE on the piano bench. You don't DO anything. I don't know when you do your homework because you're always practicing. I'm probably the only mother on earth who thinks her daughter practices the piano too much." She was gripping the steering wheel really tight. "And you never call me Mother."

She did notice the Mother thing. So I decided to try it one more time for effect. "I am perfectly fine, Mother." I said it the way I thought Elly would when she was impersonating an adult.

"I don't think you're perfectly fine, Lennie. I think something is the matter."

IcannottellherIcannottellherIcannottellherIcannottellherIcannot tell her IcannottellherNONONOIcan'ttellherICANNOTTELLHER. She couldn't know about Andy, no one could, and I gritted my teeth because it was too hard to keep it to myself but I HAD to, it was a matter of life and death, and in that moment, something tightened around the middle of me like a belt, keeping it all inside. That is the way it had to be.

"There is nothing wrong with me," I tried to be as emphatic as possible. I still wouldn't look at her. Let her think I was upset about Angela, please God.

Frankie took a deep breath. She finally looked away from me. She started the car. "OK, Lennie. I have no choice but to believe you. If there's nothing wrong with you, then I want you off the piano bench and acting like a normal little girl. OK?" I sensed that she didn't know what else to say. She started driving but way too slowly.

"OK," I agreed. "I am perfectly fine," I added, for some insurance. "AND I am not a little girl." Just to make that part clear. I didn't even care about the crime of lying. Lying is a venial sin that I'm supposed to confess. I made a decision in that moment that lying would be an OK sin, and I was going to have to think fast to replace some piano time with "normal little girl" time. Whatever that was.

As we turned onto Hamilton Boulevard, Frankie looked over at me long enough to scare me because she wasn't looking at the road. "If you say so, Lennie." Finally, she looked back out the window. "You do know that you can tell me anything, don't you? Anything at all?"

"Yes," I lied. I could tell her anything except for one very important thing because if I told her then she would be dead and so would I. "Can we get Barney's for dinner?" I thought maybe I could exploit the moment.

"Sure, Lennie. Of course we can get Barney's, and we can go over to Elly's house, OK? I miss them."

I never went back to see Dr. Butler and her many teeth. Frankie never mentioned it again. I never mentioned it again, and for all I know, my dad never knew anything about it.

I almost told Aunt Liddy once. Lots of times on Friday or Saturday nights, Elly and I would stay over at Aunt Liddy's to eat popcorn and watch horror movies. *Them* and *Attack of the Fifty-Foot Woman* were our all-time favorites. *Them* is the one about giant ants and it was on TV all the time. Of course, the giant ants terrorize the town and kill and eat people. *Attack of the Fifty-Foot Woman* is about a woman who gets exposed to radiation and grows to be—of course—50 feet tall. She goes around stepping on cars and houses. I wondered out loud how her clothes grew with her—this detail was never properly explained in the movie. It seemed to me that the townspeople could look right up her skirt. Both Aunt Liddy and Elly seemed aghast at this idea, but it really puzzled me. There were crowds of men looking straight up between her legs throughout the whole movie. I just wondered exactly what they could see.

In the morning, Aunt Liddy would make us waffles, which we would smear with butter and her homemade black raspberry jam instead of syrup. Then we'd talk about the movies and act out our favorite parts. I was an excellent evil robot.

The night I almost told Aunt Liddy, the movie was about giant grasshoppers, and it wasn't scary enough to scream at, so we weren't really paying attention. Somehow, Aunt Liddy got on the topic of her good-for-nothing brother who, of course, is Andy. The popcorn got stuck in my throat because I thought he might be coming over or something. I stopped breathing for a second.

"Why is he good-for-nothing?" I asked. Still trying to extricate that lump of popcorn.

"Because he doesn't DO anything. He doesn't have a job and he drinks beer and watches TV all day. And your grandparents LET him." I could tell Aunt Liddy was a little drunk and a lot mad because she never talked like this. She only had good things to say about people. "Don't you ever be like him, Lennie," she warned me.

"Oh, don't worry, I won't," I answered, a little too quickly.

Aunt Liddy looked at me sharply. "So you don't like him either."

I wanted to tell her so bad because maybe she could protect me and protect Frankie from Andy and the gun. I almost said it out loud, that he was hurting me and scaring me, and that sometimes I couldn't sleep or eat or even breathe because of it.

"He keeps saying that he's my favorite uncle, but he's not," was all that I told her.

"You only have one other uncle," Aunt Liddy reminded me.

"I know. Neither one is my favorite." This is true. Uncle Henry is loud and smells like beer—and pipe tobacco and aftershave—but at least he doesn't touch me. That might make him the favorite by default.

The grasshoppers were jumping down the street and people were screaming out the windows of the buildings along the way. Every now and then, a grasshopper would grab one of the people and eat them. I thought it much wiser to stay inside and scream, but there they were, all hanging out the windows. It seemed weirdly like me and Andy. I knew what was going to happen to me when I went over there, but I went anyway. Just like the people who were getting swiped out of their windows by the grasshoppers. We were all doomed, in a way.

That Saturday I went to the library to get more information about the whole Andy thing. Frankie dropped me off, thinking I was doing a book report. Elly didn't want to go, so I spent an afternoon by myself hunting for clues in the stacks of the East Bedford Library. I had to sneak into the adult section, which isn't really all that hard to do, but they don't like kids in there so you have to be really quiet and devious. No problem for me.

I pulled lots of books off the shelves and went to hide in one of the corner carrels. I took a few other books like *A History of Western Civilization* and *The Growing Trends of Warfare* to disguise the top of my stack of human sexuality books. I didn't find much, except that sex is something that happens to married people. We already learned this in the Horrible Conversation. It also happens to unmarried people, and there's a lot of religious debate about that. There are lots of apparatuses that prevent babies, which just adds to the religious arguments about unmarried sex. And there are complications, like being too young or there's a pregnancy anyway or there's jealousy and sometimes someone ends up dead. And if one person, pretty much always the woman, doesn't want the sex, then it is called rape.

So. That's what they call it. As I walked around the world with that knowledge, that new word, I began to feel tainted. Broken, sort of. Mad underneath it all, too. The whole thing is awful and confusing, I had no one to discuss it with, and there was nowhere to put these feelings except in the box I had nailed shut at the edges of me.

8

Charm School

In the lobby of Ben Franklin Junior High there is a sculpture of Mr. Franklin flying a kite with a key attached. A lightning bolt carves the entire sculpture in two and Mr. Franklin is smiling in spite of this. The lightning bolt is a swirl of shiny gold and silver and it is the coolest, most imposing feature of the statue. I stood there gawking at it for a long time on the first day of seventh grade. There would never be such a thing in a Catholic school. I pondered for a moment about whether a statue of a non-Catholic person could ever bleed or drip drops of oil or anything else of the nature that might compose a miracle. Probably not. Even though he was smiling, I thought Mr. Franklin looked like he might be happier in a museum than in a junior high full of pimply adolescents. I felt a little sorry for him.

"And just where do you belong, young lady?" A mean looking man teacher sporting a pointy crew cut was glaring down at me. He was very tall. He had one long eyebrow stretching all the way across his forehead.

My heart started pounding as I pulled out my wrinkled schedule. "Chorus," I peeped.

"Well then, hadn't we best be on our way?" What? Was he coming with me? I felt a stab of panic that I was in big trouble. I was also scared because I'd lost all sense of direction while studying Ben Franklin and his lightning bolt.

Mr. Crew Cut Man folded his arms across his chest. The heat of embarrassment began to rise up my torso to my face, so I skittered away toward the music room. He cleared his throat behind me and when I turned around, he was pointing down the opposite hallway. I was SO lost.

I scampered in the direction that his huge finger pointed. How could he be so much like my father and I'd never even met him before?

The chorus room was silent when I clattered through the door. I froze in my tracks. Uh-oh. Every single pair of eyes was looking at me. I was pretty used to Looky-Loos by this time, but there was something more intense about this group. I knew they had been talking about me.

"Well, well! Come right in! Don't join the chorus, do go straight to the piano, Lennie!" I knew the teacher's name was Mrs. Rohrbach, but I'd never laid eyes on her before and I was confused about how she could possibly know my name. She was smiling. She had about ten layers of makeup on her face. Her glasses were enormous pink circles around her dark eyes and her hair was a sprayed helmet that didn't move at all. It was clear that she had already somehow commandeered the respect of the entire seventh grade chorus, all of whom had been sitting silently during the two minutes of class that I'd missed.

"Can you play this?" Mrs. R—that's what we began to call her that day because we were all desperately in awe of her and we all wanted her to like us—asked me as she played a C Major triad and then played each note individually. Up the triad, then back down. Next she went up half a step to the C# Major triad, repeating the same pattern. And so on. Of course I could do this, and I took over on D Major. I accompanied my classmates up and down the chromatic scale while they sang their la-las. Mrs. R wandered among them, waving her arms, listening intently. My classmates stood up straight on the risers, paying close attention.

Mrs. R. put some music in front of me. "Your reputation precedes you, Lennie. Let's see your stuff." She smiled again. My reputation precedes me?

She spoke to the class: "We'll be reading the soprano part only; don't even look at the alto. Let's go." She looked at me. I played the introduction to *Both Sides Now*. Piece of cake. The chorus stood there and sightread the words and the melody. It was a rush to hear my playing combined with voices. It sounded great, better than great. The music was so easy that I added in a few notes of my own here and there, rounding out a few of the chords. I saw Mrs. R throw me a look from behind the pink scaffolding on her face. Her eyebrows made twin fermatas above the frames. We shared the secret of music making in that instant. Then she winked at me.

After class, a little crowd of my peers surrounded me.

"Where did you learn to play like that?" a fat girl named Dorothy asked me. Her eyes were wide.

"I take lessons and then I actually practice," I told her.

She looked immediately at the floor. I hadn't meant to sound snotty. It was just the truth.

Meanwhile, another girl with very black hair and a mouthful of orthodontics narrowed her eyes at me. "Other people around here play the piano, too," she kind of spat at me.

I hesitated. "OK," I said. I backed away from her.

All of a sudden Audrey was beside me. "Hey. Leave her alone," she commanded the metal mouth girl, who turned on her heel and left.

"You didn't have to do that. I can take care of myself," I told Audrey.

"Sometimes you act like a doormat," she told me. "Don't you know that you're the best piano player in the whole school? You're probably the best piano player in the entire town. You should act like it."

A warm feeling flooded me. I liked that Audrey was being my

bodyguard. I don't know why, just that I liked it. And the best piano player in the whole town?

We both had gym next. For the first time ever, we were going to have to change into official gym clothes for phys ed class and take real showers afterward. Audrey and I got locker baskets right next to each other. I watched her blatantly watch all the other girls get undressed and then dressed again in gymsuits. After a couple of minutes, I started watching, too. There were all sorts of techniques for getting the one-piece gymsuit on without divulging too many peeks at underwear or body parts.

Our teacher, Miss Chesney, was young and tough. Her name, courtesy of Audrey, quickly became Miss Lezney, and every time I heard anyone say this I'd feel a little rise of heat up the back of my neck. Audrey had given us the definitive lecture on lesbians one day after a Girl Scout meeting. Then she took me aside and told me that she'd like to be one, but she swore me to secrecy because she didn't want to deal with getting mocked about it. So I swore.

Dodgeball was the game of the day. We had to go through the excruciating process of picking teams, but Audrey was picked to be a team captain and of course she chose me first. This gave me plenty of time to size up the rest of the girls in the class. The other team captain was a girl whose real name was actually Bunny. She looked like my Aunt Tammy because her hair was teased and sprayed, she wore lipstick, and she had giant breasts. Bunny's boobs weren't really pointy like Aunt Tammy's, but they were enormous. I couldn't believe she and I were the same age. She looked like a 40-year-old in a seventh-grade gymsuit.

Our bright white gymsuits quickly took on various spots, streaks, and sweat stains. But the worst discoloration of all happened to a girl named April Potts (whose name instantly became Pothead). As we were wildly throwing balls at each other and hitting our classmates in tender places, someone noticed that Pothead was bleeding profusely. She soon had a saddle of red spreading throughout the crotch of her gymsuit. Astonishingly, she seemed to be unaware of this. She kept whipping balls around and yelling threats to the opposing team, and all the while she was menstruating freely and obviously.

"POTTS! LOCKER ROOM!" Miss Lezney finally yelled to her, in the voice of a Marine drill sergeant.

Pothead stopped throwing balls and opened her arms in a "why?" gesture.

Miss Lezney actually pointed down to her own crotch. Then she blew her whistle for no apparent reason.

Pothead looked down and saw herself bleeding. There was no breath in the gym. The dawn of awareness came over Pothead and she let out a high-pitched scream that would have been effective as a train whistle. The rest of us just stood there, dumbfounded, all thanking God that it hadn't been one of us. Pothead was going to be marked for life.

"DODGEBALL, GIRLS! DODGEBALL!" Miss Lezney blew her whistle and yelled to us. "It's just life, it happens to all of us. Now throw!" Miss Lezney waved her arms and wailed on her whistle. Her neck and ears were all red.

"Jesus Christ," Audrey said. "That was gross."

I thought about it all the rest of the afternoon. I would have been mortified if it had been me, of course. But Miss Lezney and my own mother plus Elly's mother had made it a point to highlight the fact that "it" happens to every single one of us females. Every last woman on earth has the potential to dye our gymsuit red with the blood of— what was it the blood of? Potential halves of future Catholics? We were doomed to it. I was just shocked to see someone actually *doing* it.

It hadn't happened to me yet. Elly got it and pitched a fit because she'd had to wear the giant mattresses for four days. We talked about it in the dark and she was mad and grossed out and told me I was lucky. But the truth is I was scared to death. I was worried that what Andy had done to me had either broken me or—a terribly frightening thing to contemplate—had somehow made me pregnant. All the right parts had been involved. I'd even seen some of the goop that came out of him. So maybe some of his potential future Catholics had made their way inside me to my stash of eggs and I was secretly pregnant. I might have been pregnant for a year or more and not known it. When the fear began in my head, it sometimes blew into a mushroom cloud of panic. Frankie was going to want to know how it happened and I would have to tell her and then Andy would begin his killing spree. And the thought of an actual baby was too much to contemplate.

The dread began to gnaw at me so much that sometimes I wouldn't hear a single word the teacher said in class. Then it got complicated by the fear that I could NOT let it show—the fear or the baby—or else Frankie would take me back to the child psychiatrist who plays in the sandbox. I waded through my layers of terror and started relying even more on my piano. The only time my head was clear and my stomach wasn't scared was when I was practicing. That meant in the evening and sometimes a few minutes in the morning and also during third period chorus. I could feel safe and breathe then. The rest of the time I worried, and sometimes I would shake and other times I would feel tears in my eyes for no reason whatsoever, like during a movie in Social Studies about China or in PE class being chased around the obstacle course by Miss Lezney and her whistle.

The trembling fear went on for weeks, maybe months, until one day I went to the bathroom to pee and found my favorite blue and white flowered underpants spotted with blood. Since Frankie was downstairs, I contained my screams of joy, but I thanked God and St. Ursula (who I had been petitioning to make me an honorary virgin despite my experience with Andy, which I knew cancelled out any possibility of real virgin-ness, but couldn't she see that it hadn't been my idea and didn't she think that eleven thousand virgins could maybe plead my case to God and please please please give me special dispensation?). All I knew was that I would not have to be a mother at age thirteen and I could possibly stuff the awful secret down inside myself even further because there would be no outward signs or consequences, at least for the time being.

I should have known something was up when Frankie said I didn't have to clean my room even though it was Saturday morning. Rosa showed up with Elly and we all piled in the car and they drove us over to the Lehigh Valley Mall where we parked by the Sears entrance. They wouldn't let us look at stuff. They dragged us behind all the merchandise and down a secret hallway and into an office that was all white. The floor and the walls and even the desks were white. It was weird. How did our moms know that Sears had this secret white office? How could they find their white pieces of paper on the white desks? But somehow they did. The reason we were in the white office was to sign up for The Sears School for Young Charmers. Rosa and Frankie didn't ask us if we wanted to be Young Charmers—they just announced that this is what we were going to do, and they made us sign up. We were going to go to Charm School for ten weeks in a row, every Saturday morning from 10 a.m. until noon. No discussion, period.

My stomach twisted into a tight little knot and my fists clenched. CHARM SCHOOL? This level of betrayal by Frankie was just too much. Actually, it was betrayal by all of them. Rosa was thrilled for us, Elly was OK with the whole thing—she was actually smiling—and Frankie had that determined look on her face that she got whenever she made me do something I didn't want to do. Charm school—the ultimate disloyalty. This was so much worse than Dr. Butler that it was off the charts.

The lady behind the desk handed Elly and me pink three-ring binders. They were heavy and scented with perfume. Barf. "Congratulations, girls. You're going to have a wonderful time learning about applying make-up and walking properly and dressing well! And—oh, I'm not really supposed to tell you this, but it's so exciting! You're going to have a special guest for the first class! Miss Pennsylvania is coming!" She actually clapped her hands together with glee.

I never felt so humiliated in my life. I refused to look at my mother or Rosa. I sulked. I stomped around. Frankie KNOWS I hate girl things like dresses and makeup. And now she was forcing me to participate in girl activities by buying my way into the nightmare of charm school. And who thought up the term "charm school" anyway? It sounded like it came from last century or at least from a bad TV show. I liked piano lessons and chorus and PE class. I would die in a class that taught you how to wear a dress or put on eyeliner. I would absolutely die.

I couldn't even get Elly to meet my eye. It probably wouldn't be so bad for her. She liked clothes and boys. I hated everything about all of that. I just wanted to play the piano. Or romp with Wolfie. Or read books.

When we got back into the Sears store part and started walking past the washers and dryers, I grabbed Frankie's arm.

"How COULD you? How could you make me do something so horrible?" I yelled at her, right there in the store, not caring if the washing machine customers heard me. "This is like prison! This is worse than prison! This is enforced slavery, making someone do something against their will!"

"Lennie, don't be so dramatic. It will be fun. Trust me." She didn't seem to understand how upset I was.

"Fun? Fun for who? This is not fun. This is going to be torture."

"Lennie. You're going." Frankie wouldn't even meet my eye. Where is my supportive mother who bought me a kid's marine uniform from the Sears catalog for my fifth birthday just because I wanted one? How could she even think I would want to set foot near anything having the word "charm" involved?

We went to Orange Julius and I couldn't even get anything because I wanted to throw up. We were due back at Sears for the first class, but the mothers wanted to walk over to the Shoe Barn first and look at pumps. Elly seemed completely distracted and absent. She wasn't with them and she wasn't with me and I felt abandoned and miserable.

Back at the white hallway, our mothers really did desert us, leaving us in the clutches of a tall, plump woman dressed all in black whose name was Mrs. Keeler. If I had known what drag queens were back then, I would have realized that she looked exactly like one. She had hair that was also black with a white streak zipping through it. Exactly like the *Bride of Frankenstein*, which I had watched with Aunt Liddy at least five times. Mrs. Keeler's lips were outlined in bright red, and gold clangy earrings dangled almost to her shoulders. Her fingernails fanned all around, ten long red daggers waving in the air. If I had known the Drag Queen name formula then, I could have figured out that her drag queen name would have been Pepper (your first pet) LaBarre (your mother's maiden name). Perfect.

"Welcome, Young Charmers!" Mrs. Keeler said breathily as she led us down the endless, white hallway and into a bright room full of girls our age, all of whom immediately stopped talking and became Looky Loos as we walked in. They were blatantly sizing us up. Elly passed and I didn't. That became obvious when the ringleader of them made room for Elly to sit down and I had to keep walking toward the back of the room. But Elly stayed with me. My true friend forever. Well, maybe.

Mrs. Keeler-Frankenstein-Pepper-LaBarre began her lecture with an admonishment to never be late for appointments because Young Charmers were courteous and aware and would never inconvenience an entire room full of people by holding up their activities.

"But we couldn't help it," I said. "Our moms were looking at shoes at the Shoe Barn and that's at the other end of the mall, so it took us a really long time to get back here!"

About twelve snotty girls turned around and looked at me as if I were another species, which I would soon discover that I was.

"We apologize," Elly said, in attempt to divert attention away from me as well as demonstrating that she was already a Young Charmer because she was being so polite. "It will never happen again."

Mrs. Keeler continued her admonishment against lateness, embellishing it with another one about never-speaking-before-being-spoken-to. One at a time, the snotty girls peered back at me in turn.

Their message was clear: I was not, and would never be, one of them. I would be an outcast. I was worse than dirt. As humiliated as I felt, there was a certain relief in that realization.

Then things got even more horrible. Little pink makeup cases were passed to each one of us. Mrs. Keeler explained very carefully how to open them, identified each item inside, and then instructed us to take turns washing our faces and then applying the products, one at a time and in the correct order, on our clean faces.

"I think I'm going to barf," I told Elly.

"Don't. You'll just get negative attention, and we've already had enough of that." She obediently went through each step that Mrs. Keeler ordered us to do. After I washed my face, I sat there defiantly. Of course, this attracted the attention of the Bride of Frankenstein.

"Goodness, Leonore, you're way behind everyone else."

"I don't really want to wear makeup," I whispered to her. "It's not really my style." Of course the snotty girls, who had the infallible hearing of the Bichon Frises they resembled, heard me say this and started whispering among themselves. Mrs. Keeler's mouth hung open as she looked at me in utter disbelief.

"Then for goodness sakes, why are you here?" Mrs. Keeler said, trying hard to be very nice, but I could see the smoldering coals behind her blue eyeshadow eyes.

"Because our moms made us come." Uh-oh, maybe it wasn't such a great idea to implicate Elly. Now she was going to be guilty by association, and the snotty girls were going to shun her. It was a trait of their genus. I could hear them tittering along with all the whispering. "Uh, I mean, my mom made me come." Too late.

"Alright, Leonore, you won't have to apply any foundation today. Just pay attention, because we don't have much time left in our session, today."

"We don't? I thought Miss Pennsylvania was coming!" I didn't mean this to sound as sarcastic as it did. My comment propelled the snotty girls into complete silence. I was actually feeling relieved and happy that we'd be leaving sooner than I thought.

Those coals behind Mrs. Keeler's eyes burst into flame. "WHO told you that Miss Pennsylvania was going to be here *today*?" She put her hands on her hips and looked more like a linebacker than a refined teacher of Young Charmers.

I didn't want to incriminate the secretary who worked at the white desk. "Uh, no one. I don't really remember, I just heard it somewhere."

Mrs. Bride of Frankenstein took a deep breath and let her arms dangle at her sides in a more ladylike posture. "Well, girls, since our secret is now out, I will tell you that Miss Pennsylvania, Miss Jane Tiffany Weber, WILL be here next week, and she's going to help us with our modeling poses." The flock of snotty girls actually squealed with glee as a group. "Now, please carefully replace your makeup products, close the cases, and we'll see each other next Saturday!"

Elly, who hadn't said more than three syllables, smiled in her direction. We wandered over to the colorless hallway and wondered which way it was back to the washers and dryers, which is where we were supposed to meet Rosa and Frankie.

I was shoved aside roughly as one of the snotty girls decided she wanted to walk faster than us. But then she stopped and whirled around in front of me. "Hey," she said, "are you a lesbo or what?"

I was horrified and inexplicably thrilled that she had called me a lesbo. I froze, not sure what to do.

"Hey, I am talking to YOU. You, the lesbo." She was one of those blond, pretty girls who fits perfectly into her clothes and whose mouth will never need braces.

"I don't have any idea what you're talking about." I lied, figuring that if I had to, I could just push her down and keep on going. Elly was also frozen next to me.

"I know *she's* not a lesbo," she said, pointing to Elly. "But I'm pretty sure you are. So what are you doing here?"

"I told you. My mom made me come."

"Yeah, she's probably trying to cure you of being a lesbo."

The rest of the flock was gathered around now, doing that tittering thing.

Elly, thawing, stepped in between us. "She's not a lesbo. She's just a tomboy."

What was she talking about? And could we please use another word besides lesbo?

"So leave us alone, OK?" Elly grabbed my arm and we crashed through the waves of blond and found ourselves in the fluorescent glare of the Sears main floor. Our moms weren't there yet.

"Thanks," I said to Elly, when we got far enough away from the flock of blond girls.

"I didn't do anything," she replied.

"Yes you did, you knew what to say to them."

"You know, you probably are one."

That stopped me in my tracks. "Why do you think that?" My heart was pounding.

Elly looked at me. "Audrey Fremont. Brigit from camp. You were in love with her."

"I'm not like Audrey." I didn't have an argument for Brigit from camp.

"I know. But Audrey is like you."

Right, I thought. So does that make me one? "But *why* did Blondie say I was a lesbo?" I wondered, knowing the answer.

"Come on, Lennie. Think about it."

So I thought about it, and it made a lot of sense. I don't like dresses or makeup or boys. I could go with that. I hated boys and men because of Uncle Andy and Uncle Bill. I liked when Audrey Fremont touched me at the slumber party and at camp. If she was a lesbo, I supposed that did make me one, too. I was going to have to work this out a little more in my head.

"How come we never talked about this before?" I asked Elly.

She couldn't meet my eye. "Because I didn't want it to be true."

Our moms showed up and my heart started pounding, so I tried to be quiet and calm all the way home. Me, a lesbo. I was amazed that Elly had figured it out before I had.

I was the Charm School loser. After they pegged me, the blond bichons left me alone. I could sit in the back of the room if I didn't want to put the latest goop on my face. I watched Elly with fascination because she liked it all. She looked good and she seemed to have fun. I was happy to fade into the background, and Mrs. Keeler was happy to ignore me. But the week before the class came to an end, my world almost did. Mrs. Keeler announced that there would be a graduation fashion show, and all of us had to model an outfit from the Sears Young Miss department. My stomach fell to the floor at this news.

We were taken on a field trip down the hall, into the store and the actual Young Miss department, where we were given carte blanche to find, try on, and keep an outfit of our choice. This was blackmail of the highest order. The bichons squealed with delight; their biggest challenge was going to be finding only ONE outfit. My biggest challenge was going to be standing upright and displaying myself in some polyester garb while being stared at by parents, friends, family, and worst of all, the little yappy dog girls themselves.

Elly was next to me as we pawed through the teen outfits in silence. I felt disconnected from her, betrayed by her. She was having fun. I was being tortured. I wanted to ask her how she was really doing with the whole fashion show thing, but it was too dangerous with the yappy girls in such close proximity. As I was settling on a lime green polyester pantsuit, Mrs. Keeler came flying over with a red, white and blue two-piece bathing suit.

"Lennie! I've decided that this will be perfect for you for the fashion show!" She shoved the suit at me and then sashayed away toward Donna, the one girl in the class who had a "weight problem." She waved a frilly nightgown at Donna. It was sadistic. Me the lesbo in a two-piece swimsuit, Donna the fat girl in a nightgown, and the rest of the glamour girls would look even more poised and beautiful in contrast.

We had to don our fashion show outfits and line up in the white hallway. We were led to a large conference room where a portable stage had been erected. I was freezing. And humiliated. Strangely enough, there was no mockery coming from the foofy dog girls. They looked at me and made no comments. It was disconcerting. Elly pulled me aside.

"Leslie said you have a good body," she whispered to me. Leslie is the ringleader, the pack leader, the alpha dog of the bichon frise contingent. "She said you were perfectly proportioned."

What body? I couldn't see it or feel it. I wasn't sure I was actually in it. But if Leslie said I was perfectly proportioned, that was enough to keep the pack from mauling me with their meanness.

One by one, we were forced to walk up onstage, pose (special model stance taught to us by Miss Pennsylvania; left foot turned, right heel into left instep, pause), smile, then turn and walk off. It was worse than the curtsey at my first piano recital. I felt like I *was* the clothing I was wearing (miniscule as it was). There was no me in this equation. I could not go through with it. One by one, the yappy girls went up there, posed exactly as instructed, smiled a fake smile, then turned and walked off with heads held high. I watched Elly in amazement when it was her turn. She was beautiful like them. She seemed to enjoy the experience of being stared at. She wore a simple skirt and blouse, not far off from our St. Ursula's uniforms. She looked confident and sure. Then it was my turn.

I was the only bathing suit. I felt Mrs. Keeler's revenge as I escorted myself up to the little stage and stood there, half-naked. I refused to smile. I didn't know how to do the pose. So I stood there in my little two-piece, and fled my body in the same way I did when Andy attacked it. The room went black. My head buzzed. I was doused with shame from some source outside myself. I must have stood up there too long because I suddenly heard applause. The room full of show dog girls was clapping for me.

I took myself back to the dressing room and changed into my regular clothes. I didn't speak to anyone except Mrs. Keeler, to whom I shoved the crumpled Sears Young Miss bathing suit. "I'm never coming back here," I announced to her.

"Oh yes you are, little miss," she said. She really said "little miss."

At that moment I adopted a vow of silence. I would never speak to her again or acknowledge her presence. I would never speak again to any of the bichons. I might speak to Donna and I would most likely speak to Elly. But as far as I was concerned, the charm school experience was now history.

When Frankie and Rosa came to get us, I overheard Mrs. Keeler telling Frankie about my behavior and my appearance at the fashion show, which was our last scheduled charm school event. Frankie nodded her head, seemingly in agreement. Rosa stood a respectful distance away, but I knew she could hear, too. And that steeled my resolve. No matter what, I was finished.

Frankie fought with me in the kitchen. Ted was, as usual, under his headphones. Wolfie was under the coffee table, meaning that she didn't approve of our tone of voice.

"I am NOT going to parade around in a bathing suit in front of a bunch of strangers."

"Yes, you are, Lennie. You have to. It's part of the deal."

"I never made a deal. I was forced into this." And furthermore, I didn't ask to be born. I was going to fire away with that in a moment.

Frankie seemed to consider this. She knew it was torture for me. "It will be good for you," she tried.

"I don't see *how* it could possibly be good for me," I sniffed angrily, like some sophisticated woman in a movie.

"I thought it would be good for you to learn stage presence. Since you're going to be playing the piano in public." This was my mother coming close to an apology for my having to endure lessons in how to apply makeup, and a great distraction for me.

"Really? You think I'm going to be onstage?"

"I have no doubt. And this is why you're going to do it. That's all there is to it."

"I have NEVER seen anyone playing the piano in concert wearing a bathing suit!"

"Lennie! There will be no more discussion about this! You will thank me when you're thirty and famous!" Frankie tossed the dishtowel across the kitchen and it landed in the sink.

Elly came in the back door just then. I didn't want her to gang up on me with Frankie, so I went up to my room. I know they were talking about me in the kitchen. I didn't want to hear it. I had to consider this: Frankie did have my best interest at heart. I loved her for that. But there was no way in hell that I was going to parade around in front of people wearing a polka dot bathing suit. And right in that moment, I had a flash of inspiration. Without even considering the more lethal consequences, I walked to the top of the stairs and I leaped off, into the air, tumbling down the entire staircase until I landed in a heap with my leg twisted under me in a very strange—and painful—way.

Frankie and Elly ran out of the kitchen and clattered over to me. I was scared and in pain but also thrilled with myself. I was going to win this. I could see Ted over in the den, his head bouncing in time to whatever music was blasting through his headphones.

"Lennie! Oh my God, what the hell?! Can you stand up?" Frankie became her professional nurse-self. "What happened?" She hovered over me and checked my forehead and touched my leg gently. The pain started to intensify and my eyes started going black while my ears buzzed. Just like the time I fainted in church because it was so hot and I was starving because we had to fast for twelve hours before communion. I tried to wake myself out of the fainting, and the pain in my leg was so excruciating that I immediately began to sob. When the blackness came back, I let it just take over.

I was dimly aware of them carrying me out to the car. Elly told me later that Frankie screamed at Ted, and when he didn't respond, she went over and yanked off the headphones and screamed at him again. He ran out to the car with Frankie who got in the back seat with me. Elly got in the front, and Ted roared over to the hospital.

I had a hairline fracture of my right tibia and a bad sprain of my right ankle. Lots of doctors and nurses in white bustled around me, pulling Frankie outside the curtain to chat and tell her how much they missed her. A young doctor plastered a cast up to my knee and gave me a pair of crutches and a bottle full of painkillers.

There was not one more word spoken of the Sears School for Young Charmers Fashion Show. I didn't go to watch Elly model her schoolgirl outfit. I never saw Mrs. Keeler again. I watched a lot of television and practiced the piano without pedaling because my right leg had to stick out, and besides, there was no way I could pedal with the huge cast immobilizing my lower leg and ankle. Frankie fed me whatever I wanted, and Elly came to stay with me for the whole rest of the weekend and we played Monopoly and sight-read duets. Frankie never mentioned the fashion show or charm school again. And all Elly said was, "Good thing you didn't break your arm. Or a finger. Or more than one finger. That would have been bad."

9

Offertory

When my cast came off, Charm School became distant history, a fleeting bad dream. Andy couldn't get near me anymore because of high school coming up and my new piano lesson schedule, which was now Saturday mornings at the Miss Ashleys' house. Frankie drove me there, and after my lesson we went shopping somewhere. Or out to lunch. Or to a museum or to downtown Philadelphia to walk around. Once we went to all the historic places like Independence Hall and even Betsy Ross's house. I almost told her a million times, and the thought of Andy doing something terrible to her always stopped me. I decided to just let it fade out of my memory.

One of the last days in algebra class, I let myself think about getting out of Ben Franklin Junior High and moving on in my life. I stretched out my hands in front of me. They were itching to play. Sometimes I would look at them and they didn't seem to belong to me. I don't understand how they remember where to go on the keyboard, but they do. And that's all they ever want to do, play the piano. They look like regular kid hands, but for some reason they seem smarter than everyone else's. My right pinkie finger has a little bend in it. My left index finger has a scar from when I was learning to use my Swiss Army knife at Camp Frontierwood. My hands are mirror images of each other except for those two little details. They are me and I am them, and yet it's like I am me and they are two distinct individuals that I follow around most of the time. They play the music that is inside of me, and I have no idea how they do that.

Miss Draconi handed us a pile of equations to work on that were supposed to help us study for the final. Instead of doing them, I stuck my hands under the desk and worked on Beethoven's *Tempest Sonata*, the allegretto movement. I could hear and see every note even though there was algebra in front of my eyes and not printed music. I had just recently realized that I could do this, look at a piece of music a few times and commit it to memory so that when I play, I see the music in my head and I don't need to carry the paper around with me. The *Tempest* is a bunch of patterns of three that flow like a waterfall in the key of F. I remembered the first time I played it for Miss Ashley #2. She seemed aghast but was really just speechless. I thought maybe I'd done something wrong, but Miss Ashley assured me that all was well. It was confusing, her reaction.

Miss Draconi completely ignored me, though she knew I wasn't paying attention or working on my equations. Of course everyone called her Miss Dragonbreath, but I liked her. I told her one day that I'd rather spend my spare energy on music than on algebra, and she smiled and she said that she would, too. And then she made me promise to get her free tickets to my first concert in Carnegie Hall. So I did, I promised.

Audrey Fremont told me that Liberty Bell High School would freak us both out, but it didn't. For me, it was just a bigger version of Ben Franklin Junior High. I thought about how all the nuns would think the place was Sodom and Gomorrah in disguise as a public high school. Dear Lord, Oh My Dear God, there's necking going on in the small space between two banks of lockers. Dear Lord Oh My Dear God, there are marijuana sales going on at the end of the hallways.

Sister Regina would drop dead of apoplexy, for sure, witnessing all the heathen and evil behavior. I didn't have any particular problem with all the pot. I was pretty used to it from Frankie and Rosa. No big deal. I was curious and a little repelled by all the necking, but I pretty much tried to ignore it.

I definitely didn't fit in with the cool crowd. No one really talked to me much, anyway. I'd go from class to class and pay attention and do my homework. I got permission to go to the chorus room during lunch period to practice. Frankie had to march herself into the principal's office and demand that they let me. The principal, a big man who came from Dallas and wore bolo ties, didn't really understand about kid musicians, and he refused at first. He was going to make me sit in the cafeteria just because that's where you're supposed to be during lunch. So Frankie showed up at his office in her scrubs. She looked very medical and official. She threw around some musical terms and dropped a few names. The bolo tie principal (Mr. Hancock; you can guess what his nickname was) remained unmoved. So Frankie dragged him—and me—to the nearest piano, which happened to be on the stage in the auditorium. It was a very big deal for Mr. Hancock to leave the administrative hall and walk all the way to the auditorium. There, I banged out a Schubert *Impromptu* as fast and showy as I could. The Eb major one, with a million lightning speed runs. When I was finished, Frankie was beaming triumphantly. Mr. Hancock's eyes were huge, and he said, "I had no idea, young lady. No AH-DEE-YUH that you were so talented!"

He came over to me and placed his hand awkwardly on my shoulder. "By all means. You may by all means use your lunch time to practice." He arranged for me to use the chorus room, and then he got me to agree to play at an assembly and at graduation and possibly even a Christmas party at his house.

I practiced and practiced. There was no more mention of how long I sat at the piano. No mention ever again of Dr. Butler. No questions about dating, yuck anyway. And when Elly came over, we'd both practice for an hour before we did anything else. We began to learn the Beethoven sonatas for violin and piano, and I found myself close to tears often. I didn't understand why.

It was during one of my lunch practice periods that Ashton Burstyn walked in. I was working on a different *Impromptu*. Ashton walked right up to the piano and scared the hell out of me. He stared at me and I stifled a shriek. I'd been concentrating really hard, and a face showing up inches from my own really threw me. Especially his. Ashton Burstyn is the coolest guy at Liberty Bell High School. He plays timpani in the orchestra, percussion in the Youth Symphony, drums in the jazz band, and forward on the basketball team. He has a million girlfriends. He is that rarest of combinations—an athlete, musician, and scholar. And, rumor has it, a nice guy.

He came right up to the piano. Shit, I thought, is he going to ask me out or something? I did NOT want him to ask me out. Wait—why would he ask ME out?

"Really great playing," he said. And then he told me his name was Ashton, which I already knew.

"That sounds aristocratic," I said. "Your name."

He laughed. "We live on the South Side." The blue collar, multi-colored section of town.

I didn't know what else to say to him.

"So. Do you want to join our band?" he asked. Just like that.

"What?" came out of my mouth. He was very, very cute. I was noticing this, thinking that I had never thought about the cuteness of boys in general. I was also tucking away the mental clarification that I'd rather look at a cute girl than Ashton. I peered at him and decided that I would spend some time pondering this later.

"What would I have to do?" I asked him.

"You are a really good piano player," he said, not quite responding to my question.

"Thanks. I know." I didn't mean this to sound conceited, I just know.

"I mean really good."

"Well, OK. Thanks."

"We practice at my house. We use an electric piano for gigs."

"You have gigs? What kind of stuff do you play?"

He had not taken his gaze away from me. "Covers, mostly. And some original stuff. Rock. If you can play what you just did, it would be a piece of cake."

The next night, I was sitting at a Roland electric piano in Ashton's garage. There were four guys and me. Ashton stuck something called a fake book in front of me. It had melodies and chords. I was supposed to play the tune and fill in the chords just from the symbols. It was a blast. Playing that stuff *was* piece of cake. When we finished playing *Light My Fire*, the five guys stood there and stared at me.

"Where'd you learn to do that, man?" The bass player asked me. He was what Ted would call a hippie rat. He had long hair that was actually really nice hair, one earring, a ripped t-shirt, and jeans that were torn and looked as though they might fall off. Behind him, Ashton was sitting at the drum set looking like a preppie who was about to go off and play a tennis match.

"I don't know," I answered Hippie honestly. "I guess I can just do it."

"Cool," he said, with real admiration.

Ashton brought over another chart. It was a half notated and half chord chart. "I wrote this," he said, a bit hesitant. "I'm not sure what it will sound like."

We crashed through a sort of rock tune, sort of symphony, sort of jazz chart, and sort of a fantasia all mixed up together. Ashton indicated a strange combination of mixed meters and long, winding melodies. It seemed like it might work with some fine-tuning. I thought of Ted listening to it and trashing it, and I felt rebellious and happy.

"We don't play this for gigs," the guitar player said. His name was Elliot and he was blond and looked like a future lawyer. "We play this for art. Someday we're going to cut a record. It's going to be like Genesis and the Stones and the London Phil mixed together." I could see him with a necktie and a briefcase. Maybe if he let his hair get long and grew a beard he'd look more rock band-ish.

The first gig I played with the band was at the Jewish Community Center for someone's Bat Mitzvah. The only way I could do it was to sneak out of the house. For the second time in known history, Ted did not have a gig. (Ha-ha, I thought to myself, I have a gig and you DON'T!) So he was pacing around the house. Frankie was parked on the couch with a book and probably some drugs in her tea. I went up to my room and told Wolfie what I was about to do, swore her to silence, and went out the window.

Ashton picked me up at the 7-11, our prearranged meeting place. I asked him how the hell he got the name Ashton. He told me it had been his grandfather's name. The grandfather was a painter of large and wildly colored watercolor landscapes. He killed himself in some undisclosed manner. The paintings now sell for thousands of dollars. Ashton felt sad that his grandfather never got to enjoy the fruits of his own artistic labor, so he swore to never abandon his own artistic vision, which centered on making music of a percussive nature. I felt connected to him when he told me that, and I believed him. He looked very un-preppie, wearing jeans and a paisley shirt and a headband. I could see him on the cover of an album. We could be the next Fleetwood Mac, if we could find the next Stevie Nicks.

The Bat Mitzvah party was huge and we got to eat and then play pop tunes for three hours. We each got $40. When I saw Elly later, I showed her my pay and we marveled at the two twenty dollar bills.

"Should I frame them?" I asked. My first money from making music.

"No, you should spend them. You'll be making a lot more than this, believe me."

"You really think so?"

"Yeah, and so will I. It's our destiny."

"How do you know that?"

Elly didn't answer me. She had her jaw set and a fiery look in her eye. Destiny? Well, I guess. I didn't have any better explanation for it.

Elly figured out a Plan. She was going to call up Raphael Bernhard, concertmaster of the Philadelphia Orchestra, to ask for an audition with him to see if she was good enough to be his student. After Sister Regina, Elly studied with Mrs. Nelson, a violinist from the Bedford Camerata. They dropped the "East" from Bedford to make it sound more cosmopolitan. Mrs. Nelson had four little kids all under the age of six, so Elly's lessons were chaotic because the kids always ran screaming through the studio. One day, the biggest one grabbed her bow and ran off with it. Elly and Mrs. Nelson chased him through the house. Elly would then have been murdered by Frank for sure if her zillion dollar bow had been damaged by a wild kid. She came up with the Plan after that lesson and tracked down how to get in touch with Mr. Bernhard.

He agreed to hear her, and I was going to go along for moral support. We'd find my new piano teacher at some later date. Elly figured out how we were going to get to Philadelphia on the train, get off at Market Street Station, walk to the Academy, and wait. Her audition was going to be right after a Philadelphia Orchestra rehearsal.

"What are you going to use for money to pay for these lessons?" Frank snorted from behind a newspaper when Elly told him her Plan.

"Babysitting money," Elly told the front page of the East Bedford Times. She did not tell him that we were selling a little pot that we pinched from our mothers, and that Rosa had promised to contribute from her secret cash stash. Money would not get in the way of her daughter studying with Raphael Bernhard, if he accepted her.

I stood there, watching Elly's sad but determined eyes staring at the unfurled newspaper. I knew exactly how she felt. I wanted to sock Frank and yell, "Pay attention to your brilliant daughter!" But I didn't. I just clenched my fists in my pockets.

Another snort and something unintelligible came from behind the newspaper.

The train wasn't really a train; it was one train car full of people. It was called a bud car, and it somehow propelled itself along the train tracks to Philadelphia, stopping in Allentown and Lansdale and Coopersburg. We got off in the city with a wave of people at Market Street and walked the few blocks to the Academy of Music. Opening the big doors, we heard strains of Dvorak #8. Our favorite symphony, the one I heard for the first time when Elly played it at Youth Symphony and I wept in the audience. My knees went weak with the gorgeousness and power of the music. I also experienced a few waves of relief that it would be Elly auditioning and not me. I looked at her and she seemed scared but determined.

We sat in the middle of the empty house. Dvorak ended and so did the rehearsal. Mr. Ormandy thanked his musicians and disappeared backstage. *THE* Mr. Ormandy, right there in person. I watched him make his way offstage, and I listened to the post-rehearsal conversations, a bit of laughter here and there. The sounds were mostly cases being snapped shut and feet trudging out of the hall. In one instant of pure clarity, I decided that I wanted to be part of that tribe, people who assembled to play music for their livelihood. In that split second, it seemed like the only thing that made any sense in the entire world was to make music. The most important thing that someone could live for, do for the planet, the way to enlightenment, the path to God. And I wanted it more than anything I'd ever wanted in my life. I was just beginning to put words to that want.

The musicians scattered pretty quickly and a tall, handsome man with slightly thinning hair gestured to Elly. He sat back down in the concertmaster chair. I could see from far away that his eyes were an intense blue. His arms were muscular, his biceps visible through the stretched sleeves of his polo shirt, his expression patient and kind.

Elly climbed the stairs to the stage and stood in front of him. I sat down in the end seat of the very first row, sending Elly telepathic encouragement. I couldn't quite hear everything that they were saying. Elly picked up her violin and started to play the *Mendelssohn Concerto*.

She looked—and sounded—like a goddess. Her playing was clean and strong. Inspired. Mr. Bernhard stopped her once, moved the violin a little differently on her shoulder and showed her something to do with her bow, a slightly different way to hold it. When she started to play again, she sounded like a completely different violinist. The corners of her mouth went up in a little smile.

"Bravo," said Mr. Bernhard, loudly enough for me to hear. It echoed through the house, just like Elly's Mendelssohn. "Bravo," he said again. "Very nice." I thought of Frank snorting. The concertmaster of a major symphony orchestra says Bravo and Elly's dad snorts behind a newspaper. The edges of the big picture were starting to come into focus.

I heard Mr. Bernhard say that he would work with her if she agreed to practice a lot. And get a new bow. I could see Elly's body trembling with excitement. She couldn't stop smiling. And then he turned to me. "And you, my dear? What will you be playing?" Oh my God, he is speaking to me. I stared at him. Why would he speak to me?!

"Probably Beethoven or Chopin," Elly answered for me. She was beaming. Relieved, proud of herself, excited about new possibilities with her famous teacher. They were both standing at the edge of the stage, looking down at me.

"Ah, very good. And do you have any Bach" he asked.

"What? I'm not —"

"Yes, let's hear what you can do," Mr. Bernhard commanded. At least that was my interpretation. He was gesturing me toward the giant Steinway that was parked near the back of the stage. I knew from looking at the program that André Watts had just been playing this very piano, rehearsing for his performance of the *Grieg Concerto* with the Philadelphia Orchestra. Was it legal for me to play the same piano that he had? Wouldn't someone come out and yell at me? Didn't they have to tune it before the concert?

Mr. Bernhard opened the keyboard and motioned for me to sit down and play. I got up, pushed all thought from my brain, walked to the piano, and sat on the bench—the very bench the André Watts' butt had occupied—and I started to play the allegretto of the *Tempest*. It flowed out of me, emptied itself onto the keys through my hands. When I finished—I didn't realize I'd had the whole thing memorized—I felt his hand on my shoulder.

"You must study with my wife," Mr. Bernhard said.

"I must?" I felt drops of sweat sliding down between my fairly recent breasts.

"Yes. You must. She does trust my opinion, you know." I knew no such thing, but OK. "I shall see you both in a week, then."

Elly got directions and other details from Mr. Bernhard while I stood there in shock.

"Is there something in the water up there in East Bedford? To have two of you show up on the same day is—rather unprecedented," Mr. Bernard said as he pulled on a trench coat.

We both looked at him.

He smiled enigmatically, transforming himself into a musician James Bond, and left us both on the streetcorner with our jaws hanging open in amazement.

"Can he just pick students for his wife?" It occurred to me after the fact to ask this question when Elly and I were back on the bud car, watching farm fields whiz by.

"Apparently," she said. She was hugging her violin as though it were a little kid sitting on her lap. "Aren't you glad I made up a secret plot?"

"Umm—" I still felt stunned.

"Lennie, do you know who his wife is?"

"Mrs. Bernhard?"

Elly looked at me as though I might be mentally incapacitated. "Isabella Boticelli," she pronounced.

I sucked in my breath. "THE Isabella Boticelli? *The* Isabella Boticelli who is the famous concert pianist? The one who is a Rachmaninoff specialist? The one who you would buy an album from just because she's so beautiful on the cover?"

"You are sometimes a dumb shit," Elly said. "I thought you knew. That's why I wanted you to come, too. I thought maybe you could play for her at one of my lessons. I had no idea he'd make you play today!" This was a huge lie that Elly wouldn't admit to for ten more years. She set the whole thing up. She knew I was going to have to play that day.

I wasn't sure whether to smack Elly or hug her. So I just stood there.

"I knew you were really good, but I had no idea you were THIS good." She said this and looked at me with real admiration.

"Elly, I'm starting to think we don't belong in East Bedford anymore."

"No shit." Elly never says shit.

I wondered how I was going to ask Ted to pay for my soon-to-be-really-expensive-new teacher. And how I would break the news to the Miss Ashleys.

As it turns out, they were expecting it.

"There is NO question that you should be studying with someone of the caliber of Miss Boticelli," Miss Ashley #2 told me. "I do wish, however, that I had been the one to think of such a thing," she added, with just a hint of sniffiness. The three of us were sitting in the living room, each one of the Miss Ashleys at a piano and me on the couch next to the perpetually tempting dish of chocolates.

"Yes, my dear, it will be difficult to lose such a promising student, but I would have urged you on momentarily," said Miss Ashley #1. "We certainly would have done so, wouldn't we, Ethel?" I didn't believe her. And Ethel? In all these years I never knew her name was Ethel. It fit her perfectly.

"We are so very proud of you," they said in unison. They both smiled their pleased teacher smiles at me. We reminisced about me falling off the stage, and I promised to keep them apprised of my piano activities. They hugged me goodbye. Before I walked out the door, Miss Ashley #2 tucked a little bag of chocolates into my music bag. "You can't play the piano without proper fuel," she said. And I saw tears in her eyes before she looked away and closed the door behind me, very gently.

I didn't expect enthusiasm from my father, but I didn't expect derision, either. Or maybe I did and I couldn't admit it to myself.

"You're not going anywhere except the Ashleys for piano," he said.

"Ted, it's an opportunity," Frankie countered. "You, of all people, should understand what this kind of thing could mean for Lennie." I liked it when Frankie said "you of all people." She sounded very authoritative. Then she looked at me and her expression said: Don't worry about it—I'll deal with him.

"I'm not paying for it. Lessons from someone like that will be exorbitant." Ted said "exorbitant" as if he was adjudicating a spelling bee. Ex-or-bi-tant. "We don't have that kind of money. And people like that take anyone for the money."

"Ted, I think the message here is that Lennie has something exceptional."

Big grunt. "Exceptional?" he said, as though this was the last possible adjective that could be applied to me.

"I'll pay for my own lessons," I said. Ted didn't know about my rock band income yet.

Ted grunted again. Frankie shot me another warning look.

"I get paid for band gigs," I said defensively. "Just like you." I had to let him know that he wasn't the only human being who played gigs for money. Frankie rolled her eyes.

This sent Ted over the top. "You will do no such thing. And you call what you do gigging? It's more like whoring. You don't belong in that ridiculous, so-called band." Ted tried to bore holes through me with his gaze. I thought I detected a slight tinge of the very thing that powered Andy. And I didn't like it.

"I'm not quitting the band. And I AM going to study with Isabella Boticelli." I tried absolute defiance. I'd never attempted this before with my father.

He threw his fork down, screeched his chair backward and then stomped away from the table. There was no sound at all for a few long moments.

"I think that went well, don't you?" said Frankie, turning her gaze toward me. She looked a little worried, but also like she was trying not to smile.

Frankie and Rosa drove Elly and me to Philadelphia for our first lessons with the Bernhards. Our fathers were nowhere to be found. Our mothers were more nervous than we were. We didn't talk much on the way there. I was amazed that we found the house so easily from the scribbled directions on a scrap of paper. If Ted had been driving, I know we would have gotten lost and there would have been a battle about stopping to ask for directions and then we would have been late for our first lessons with the famous musicians or possibly even missed them entirely. Ted would have made it our fault. Just thinking about it made my armpits sweat, and I was nervous enough about playing for—what was I supposed to call her? Mrs. Bernhard? Miss Boticelli? Certainly not Isabella.

Our mothers teetered in the doorway, trying to see into the huge house. Mr. Bernhard finally invited them in to wait in the living room while we followed our new teachers to separate studios in opposite corners of the house.

"They aren't going shopping?" Isabella Boticelli asked me as we walked away. "All the mothers go shopping. Are they stage mothers?" She had an accent. Italian. She looked and sounded so exotic that I thought I might swoon.

I assured her that they would be quiet and polite. I glanced back at Frankie and Rosa perched on the edge of the couch, looking much more scared than either one of us. I knew they really wanted to follow us to our respective lessons and sit in, but that invitation was not extended to them. They also probably wanted a joint in the worst way but would never smoke in someone else's house, especially the house of a—no, *two*—famous musicians.

The piano studio was, appropriately, full of pianos. Two six-foot grands were nestled up together, just like at the Miss Ashleys' house. A studio upright sat against one wall and a baby grand stood in the opposite corner as though it had been bad and was being punished. And, taking up one entire side of the studio was a nine-foot concert grand. Five pianos! My hands began itching to play when my eyes landed on the nine-foot. The walls that were not lined with pianos were lined instead with shelves full of music and recordings. There were plaques and awards and signed photographs of Miss Boticelli with famous musicians. Isaac Stern. Bernstein. Du Pré, Von Karajan, Ormandy, Ozawa, Koussavitsky. Wow! I was Dorothy, not in Kansas anymore, only this place was much better than Oz.

I tried to be ready for anything because Isabella Boticelli hadn't actually heard me play yet. She just took me on the word of her husband.

She looked like a deity—long, flowing, dark hair, big brown eyes, very long, manicured fingers, an elegant jacket worn over jeans—a very artistic look. I knew Frankie would record this fashion statement and appear in a similar outfit soon.

"All right, my dear, please play something for me." Miss Boticelli seemed aloof. There was a slight strain in her voice, as though she might be expecting me to be mediocre. Or worse.

I played the *Tempest* again, faster than I'd played it for Mr. Bernhard.

She came over and stood right behind me. "I see," she said. "So, do you know any Bach? I would like to hear a prelude, fugue, or invention."

I played the *C minor Prelude and Fugue* from the *Well-Tempered Clavier* and immediately started a *Two-Part Invention*, the one in D minor.

"Alright, now will you please play for me scales through the circle of fifths," Isabella Boticelli requested.

I played all the scales. Fast. She stopped me at F# major.

"I see," she said again. "Very nice. Now try this." She showed me a way to flip my fingers over my thumb faster, more efficiently. It worked especially with my left hand, which had always been a bit of a problem. I zoomed through the rest of the scales with this new technique. Four octaves, fast, accurate, and clean. Wow.

She put some music up on the rack. Chopin *Nocturne*, opus 9, no. 2. Eb major. I'd studied it with Miss Ashley #1. I played the shit out of it.

"Well," she said. "Well. And what have you memorized?"

I played the opening of the *Grieg Concerto*. It was a brazen thing to do, but I figured I didn't have anything to lose. She listened. She nodded. "And how old are you?"

"Fifteen."

"Ah," she said. "Shall we begin?" I'd been playing for half an hour. She paced around near the piano. "You *can* excel, if you wish. You are somewhat behind if you're thinking this will be a career. But you play more than quite acceptably well, and you can improve. You are well beyond average. Yes, you can excel." Her accent, a little flair of Italian maybe something else, entranced me. "So, Raphael was right," she murmured to herself but I heard it.

"I can?" I asked. *I can excel?* What does she mean by "beyond average?"

"Yes, my dear. You have much work ahead of you, but you have a solid foundation and quite an affinity for the instrument."

"I—well—so, uh—" *Then why did Ted always snort at my playing?*

"My dear, you are much more articulate on the piano than you are with words." She laughed. "No one has ever indicated that you play well?" she asked.

"Well, my junior high chorus teacher— "

She stopped in the middle of flipping through some music and just looked at me. "Anyone else?"

"Um—not—uh, no one has really said that to me." *Well, Ashton did and so did Mr. Hancock. But no one else.*

She didn't say anything. I finally had to look at the floor.

"You really have no idea, do you?" Isabella Boticelli sat down on one of the assorted piano benches around the room. There were many more benches than there were pianos.

"Um, no, I guess not." I peeled my gaze from the damper pedal and looked at the hem of her fashionable jeans.

"Alright, my dear. Let's just work. You'll realize soon enough." *What the hell was she not saying? Realize what?* Miss Boticelli put some music on the rack in front of me. The Bach *Two-Part Inventions* I'd studied a couple years before. My heart sank a little, but she explained that we were going to review a few basics and clean up some technique. This would help, she assured me.

She changed my hand position just slightly. And then she showed me how to color individual notes and then entire chords. She demonstrated how to dance around the keys with more facility instead of just playing them. The hour became ninety minutes. Then two hours. We finally made our way back to the living room where our mothers were pacing.

"There is something extraordinary here," Isabella said to Frankie.

"I agree," Raphael Bernhard said, emerging with Elly in tow. They sent us out to the car so they could talk about us to our mothers without us overhearing.

We climbed into the back seat and sat there just for a moment. And then, in unison, we screamed at the top of our lungs. This—the music, our new teachers, our mothers being completely, one hundred per cent supportive— the possibility of it all. This was big. It was going to be our lives.

That week, Elly and I decided to start acting like Real Musicians. We started marathon practice sessions, four or more hours a day. It wasn't really a big deal; I played at least that much every day. I just worked a little harder, learned how to focus and concentrate. It would be the beginning of a lifetime of marathon practice sessions. On the weekends, we went back to Philadelphia to study with our famous teachers. The Bernhards fed us lunch, asked us about life in East Bedford, which was a galaxy away from Philadelphia as far as they were concerned, and told us about their gigs. We were spellbound listening to stories of meeting Vladimir Horowitz and Itzahk Perlman and Arthur Rubenstein. And they began to turn us into truly formidable musicians. We heard about what Eugene Ormandy had for lunch, and how many cocktails Leonard Bernstein had at parties. And who might be having an affair with whom, though we weren't supposed to know that information and were sworn to secrecy.

Isabella Bernhard insisted that I play through every single scale every day, at least twenty times. Four octaves. Build up speed. Play the circle of fifths plus all three minors. The circle, my lifeline. I loved it. All kinds of rhythm patterns. Complicated finger patterns. Then Hanon and Czerny technical studies. Then technical etudes. Sometimes a few Chopin preludes. Then the big repertoire.

We had a long conversation one day while Elly was with Mr. Bernhard working on the *Sibelius Concerto*, practically unheard of for a high school student to study because it is so technically difficult.

"What do you want from the piano?" she asked me. Point blank.

"I just assumed that maybe I'd go to college and maybe be a piano major," I answered. I hadn't really thought about it much was more like the real truth. And Miss Ferne, the guidance counselor at Liberty Bell High School, took one look at my transcript and said, "Music. Be a music major. You won't make any money but you can get married! Next!" She shooed me out the door, and that was the last I ever talked to her.

"And then what, my dear? Go on to a concert career? You're already a bit late for that. It's not entirely impossible, but—" she didn't finish her sentence and looked thoughtful.

I'd never considered it before, what to do with my life. I just knew I wanted to be a pianist. Whatever that meant. Ever since we moved the pink piano to the basement and got a baby grand for the living room, I just assumed that the piano was my destiny. I never thought about a career because the piano is what saved my life so that I could actually have a life. And since it saved my life, I would always have to play. In that moment, I wanted to tell Isabella Bernhard so bad about Andy. But the words stopped in my throat. My commitment to never tell anyone was still the Prime Directive of my life.

"Think about it, dear. And think about this: go to Indiana next year and study with my old friend, Ludmilla Michalowski."

I practically fell off the piano bench. My heroine, Ludmilla Michalowski!

"Do you KNOW her?" I screeched. Ludmilla Michalowski had been my hero since the first concert I'd ever been to in my life. I had all her recordings. I heard her again in recital in Philadelphia and again with the Philadelphia Orchestra. It had never crossed my mind that it might be possible to study with her, that such a thing was even remotely feasible.

"What's she doing in Indiana?" I asked Isabella.

"Teaching at the University. And carrying on with her numerous extramusical affairs, if I'm not mistaken."

What's an extramusical affair? I couldn't ask her. I'd have to look it up or something. "Why does a famous concert pianist want to teach at a university?"

"She loves it. She's a brilliant teacher. And when she's retired from playing, she'll still have a career. And it's *Indiana*," she said, as though I should understand what *Indiana* meant.

"You must think about these things," Isabella was going on. "The piano is a mechanism. It is an inanimate thing into which you must breathe life. Are you willing to live with that challenge?"

I've never thought of the piano as inanimate. I've seen the piano as a sort of Being, a Being who saved my life back in elementary school.

And then she said, as if she'd read my mind, "But it is more than that, too. Look what the piano is made of. Living tissue of trees, straight from the earth. The stolen tusks of elephants." She stopped and shuddered a little. "I never play ivory-keyed pianos. If I must, I offer a prayer for the beasts that were pillaged. It is offensive to me, yet look at the other instruments of our world. Strings made of gut. Drum heads made of animal skins. Woodwinds made of the flesh of endangered trees. Ahh," she closed her eyes and for a moment I thought she might cry.

"A beautiful touch is one thing you must have," Isabella stated definitively. She officially asked me to call her Isabella, even though my polite self had decided that I should only address her as Miss Boticellier, Mrs. Bernhard. "Look—how you touch the piano determines how it responds to you. You co-create the sound, the music with it. You can't do it without each other."

She played five different A's with five different sounds. She took my hand and showed me the ways to do this. It was amazing to create different colors of the same note by changing a small thing about the way the key is touched. When I got home, I played single notes every possible way I could. As a trumpet. As a hawk. As the sunset. As a flute. I tried notes everywhere, all over the piano, five or ten or twenty-seven in a row.

Frankie didn't say anything as I sat down to dinner. I know that she listens to me practice every day, that she likes it. And she would never presume to ask me anything about the music because she distances herself from anything technically musical. On this day, she looked at me curiously and I knew she was wondering what kind of new, weird thing was going on with my playing. But Ted wouldn't be quiet about it. "You sound like a kindergartener," he announced.

I expected it, so my patience lasted just slightly longer than usual. "It's touch. I'm practicing different types of touch to get different sounds and colors," is all I said. I didn't look at him. I looked at my pasta with plain tomato sauce. Frankie had just gone along with it when I announced that I would no longer be eating meat.

"Touch," Ted spat. "How about playing some music?"

"This is what I have to do before I can play real music." I felt proud of myself for not leaping into a huge argument.

"HA!" Ted slammed his fist onto the table. He would have made a great hell and brimstone preacher. "Look who's telling ME what you have to do to play music!"

I kept eating. Frankie suddenly looked weary of the ongoing battle between her husband and her daughter. She picked up a Redbook magazine. It has been strictly forbidden to ever read at the table while eating, but there she was.

Ted and I ate in silence for a few minutes, but I felt the enormous wedge of tension, thinking it could snap at any second, injuring one of us with its ferocity.

"Those lessons are not cheap," Ted finally said. "I'm not paying for you to play one goddamn note at a time like a five-year-old. Do you hear me?"

I hate when he says, "Do you hear me?" How could I not hear him when he's a foot away? Wolfie the dog got up from her post under the table and went upstairs. I stared into the squiggly lines of pasta on my plate.

Before I could reply to my father, Frankie asked, "Are you enjoying your lessons, Lennie?" The Redbook was open to an article on baked potatoes. It's amazing that someone had to think that up and then write it. There were even lots of pictures of potatoes with different things on them.

"I love my lessons," I said in a scared monotone.

"Frankie," Ted started, beginning to rise from his seat.

"Then don't worry about how they're getting paid for," Frankie said to me, still looking at the potato photos. Openly defying Ted was a brand new sport for her.

I asked to be excused, thinking my parents were about to have an interesting discussion and I did not want to be present for it. I went to the piano. I played scales as fast as I could, not caring about how sloppy it sounded. I played Hanon and Czerny and a few of the simpler Chopin etudes. Then I started again on the touch exercises, single notes and then thirds and then fifths. I wanted to drive Ted crazy. I felt mean and scared and hateful. I played the E's as though I were dropping rocks on the keys. I played the B's as though I were stomping on the keys with my feet, and I played the F#'s with pointy, stinging fingers.

I felt Ted walk behind me on his way to his usual post in front of the stereo, where he put on his new, noise-canceling headphones. I peeked into the kitchen and Frankie was still at the table, paging through the magazine. She looked up and our eyes met.

"Why, Mom?" The full question was really, why is he like this to me? Why does he treat me this way, why isn't he proud of me?

Frankie took a deep breath. There was a reason, and I knew that Frankie knew what it was. "Lennie, think about your grandmother," was all she said. "Just think about how she is. There's your answer."

Oh, no. I couldn't let it go now that I had a flicker of a clue. "I don't get it." Except I could easily imagine her being the same way to Ted when he was little and practicing the sax.

"He didn't get into any music schools. He needed a scholarship—it was the only way he could have gone to music school. He didn't pass any of the auditions he took." Frankie looked scared, like maybe she said too much. Her voice was low and she kept glancing toward the den.

Instead of feeling smug, I felt empty—and so, so sad. And sorry for my dad, who didn't get to do his dream.

I agreed to meet Audrey after school at the 7-11. She wanted to "talk." We got cola slurpees and sat on the curb.

"I got some vodka from my cousin," she told me. Audrey always had a kind of sleazy look in her eye. "Do you want to come over on Friday?"

She meant sleep over. And I didn't even have a good excuse because Elly's grandmother was taking her on a trip to Washington, D.C., to see all the patriotic sites. Elly told me that her grandmother wanted Elly to be American in spite of her Puerto Rican-ness. It was impossible to tell Mrs. Wojciechowski that Puerto Rico was actually a part of the United States. We also didn't have any lessons because the Philadelphia Orchestra was on tour in China for three weeks.

"Well, I guess so," I told Audrey. I couldn't think of any reason not to.

She was weird all week in school. She'd catch my eye and smile a strange smile, and I'd feel a strange flutter in the pit of my stomach—especially when I got to her house and found out that her parents were away for the weekend, and Audrey hadn't even planned a beer party for 50 kids. It was just her and me.

We drank the vodka in some orange juice. She wanted me to play the piano for her, which was a little strange. Audrey didn't have a very long attention span. So I played a couple of Chopin preludes.

"Man, you are good." Audrey would not take her eyes off me. I liked this and didn't like it all at once.

Next we went downstairs to the rec room. We flipped on the TV but didn't watch it. I knew what was coming and felt excited about it. Audrey kissed me. Then we figured out where to touch each other through our clothes. It felt wildly liberating to know that no one would be tromping down the stairs to check on us, that we could drink more vodka and eat whatever we wanted and touch each other wherever we wanted. The most exciting thing was getting our hands into each other's jeans. I had no idea about the slipperiness that awaited me. It was a jolt through my entire body, that wetness. We buried our whole hands in each other's jeans, not really even considering that it might be possible to take them off.

I gradually realized in my bones that this was not Andy, that this was touching without the threat of murder in the background. I had a choice in the matter, and there was no penis weapon involved. It felt good, great. We were both into it, I was feeling good everywhere, I wanted to keep going and going, just to see what could possibly happen next. But Audrey suddenly went blank, like a TV that was turned off right in the middle of a good program.

Audrey shut down completely, and there was no communicating with her. So I got up and wandered around the house. There was a cat sleeping in a chair. There was moonlight streaming in the window by the piano. I sat down at the piano and played through some technical etudes. Somehow it didn't seem like fun to play any Beethoven or Schumann. I was playing a crappy spinet piano, trapped in a house with my semi-friend who had just put an end to an activity that was really intriguing to me. I finally flipped on the TV and there was *The Song of Bernadette*, which I'd seen a million times. I fell asleep in my clothes before she dies, and woke up later under a scratchy blanket.

In the morning, Audrey pretended to not remember what we'd done the night before. It was a terrible acting job. I wanted to talk about it, ask her if she felt as good as I did. But she persisted in telling me how out of it she was, she just couldn't recall a thing. Liar! And I went home dejected, surrounded by a cloud of shame that followed me all the way in the door. Frankie knew something was amiss.

"We drank vodka," I admitted. I thought this might throw her off the trail of her daughter sort of figuring out sex with another girl and liking it.

Frankie stiffened. "Where did you get it?"

"I don't know. Audrey got it." This was the truth.

"So maybe we need to limit your time with Audrey," Frankie suggested.

I did my own little acting job, pouting and pretending to be upset.

"Fifteen isn't old enough to drink," my mom said, stating the obvious. Did she really not know about all the highballs Elly and I stole? And the pot? That we got from her? OK, we *stole* from her or Rosa. What about that?

"I know, but there wasn't anything else to do. And I'm practically sixteen."

"Lennie—"

I interrupted Frankie's impending lecture. At least she hadn't figured out the sex part—if that was, in fact, what we'd done. I went to the piano and played some Mozart sonatas that I knew thoroughly so that I could let my mind wander all around what had happened with Audrey. I was upset and exhilarated, scared and determined to try it again. If it wasn't Audrey, I'd find someone. And I'd file this away in the danger zone of my psyche, near where the Andy file was but not near enough to get it contaminated by him.

I auditioned for the East Bedford Young Artist's Competition along with thirty other pianists, twenty violins, six cellos, two flutes, and one trumpet. The finals were held at the Pennsylvania Center for Musical Arts, the scene of my debut in the Miss Ashleys' Spring Musicale. The Steinway on the stage looked and felt just like the one I'd played when I was seven. It was like seeing an old friend again.

I was escorted into a large classroom to warm up. They put a flute player and a violinist in there with me, which was the meanest possible thing to do to all of us. The flute player looked like she was competing in the Miss America pageant—long blond hair, perky nose, and boobs way too big for a high school student. She warmed up with cascading trills and twitters, a high-pitched nervous sound. I finally figured out that she was playing *Carnival of Venice*, a collection of pyrotechnical variations played at rapid speed. She sounded like a songbird on speed. She was making a lot of noise, but none of it seemed particularly related to music.

The violin boy looked like a future engineer. He had slicked-back hair, glasses left over from fifth grade, and a pocket protector full of mechanical pencils. I know this fact because he told me that he only carried pencils in there so that he wouldn't accidentally mark his music with a pen. He would sooner die than do this. And his name was Percy. I had a rush of admiration for him when he introduced himself. Anyone that can be named Percy, go to high school, and live deserves my respect.

Percy warmed up by playing every scale known to western music. Then he played snippets of a Sarasate piece that is too difficult for someone our age and way too passionate for Percy to handle. His playing was too out of tune and too rhythmic. I wondered what Elly might say, even though I knew.

I won. It was a piece of cake. I saw twitter-flute girl in the hallway after, crying. My prize was $500 and performances with the Bedford Valley Youth Symphony and the Pennsylvania All-State Orchestra. Since Elly is the concertmaster of the Youth Symphony, she was ineligible for the competition. But she won the concertmaster chair for All-State. Our parents apprehensively let us be driven in a van with other Liberty Bell High School musicians all the way across the Pennsylvania Turnpike to McKeesport for three days of rehearsals that would culminate with the All-State Orchestra concert in the McKeesport High School auditorium. Elly, being the only musician from St. Francis Academy for Girls, got special dispensation to ride with the public school kids. There was a cellist named Joli who was beautiful and silent, a trumpet player named Nick who was cool, and a violinist who was completely jealous of Elly because she'd made concertmaster. I was the soloist, so everyone regarded me suspiciously.

The rehearsal started with the *Rosamunde Overture* and Hanson's *2nd Symphony*. The guest conductor, Dr. Williamsburg, was downright mean. He demoted the principal cellist to third desk, and the girl from East Bedford named Joli—who had ridden in the van with us—was promoted to first chair. This was after having each one of the cellos play a lick from the symphony, sort of an impromptu re-audition. And no one could do it except her. I mean, no one could even remotely do it, and she played it fast and note-perfect. This sobered up the entire orchestra. You could hear a pin drop during the rehearsal. It was clear there would be no fooling around with Dr. Williamsburg.

While I was waiting to rehearse my piece, the Beethoven *Emperor Concerto*, the McKeesport High School newspaper interviewed me and so did a reporter from the Pittsburgh Post. I had to have my photo taken with the principal of the school. I got introduced to an entire group of piano students who had come to meet me and hear me play. I was a little unnerved by all the attention. Every now and then, I'd catch Elly's eye. She smiled and I knew she was incredibly proud of me.

After a break, Dr. Willamsburg called me onstage and introduced me. The players shuffled their feet and tapped their stands with their bows. We started the Beethoven and I nailed it. When I finished the first movement, there was not a sound in the room.

"Well, well. Very nice, Lennie," he said. The entire group looked at me.

"And where do you study?" He folded his arms across his chest and his baton stuck out behind him. He looked very Leonard Bernstein. He had to have gotten that pose from him.

"Isabella Boticelli is my teacher." I tried to not be smug, but it was so very satisfying to say this in front of 60 of my peers. Or sort of peers, or whatever we all were.

"Well! So—fine then. That's fine, that's quite fine." He looked flustered. It was as though he expected me to be adequate or terrible, certainly nothing special. I felt Elly looking at my back. We played through the concerto, and Dr. Williamsburg yelled at the orchestra a lot. I could feel him pushing them a little harder than at first. He took my tempos and gazed my way intensely. He dragged the orchestra along, yelling at the basses, the winds, smacking the music stand with his baton.

The first rehearsal day was over at 9 p.m. I hung around the stage, waiting for other kids to finish asking Dr. Williamsburg questions. He stepped off the podium and put his hand on my shoulder. Holy cow. "You show quite a bit of promise, my dear."

"I—uh—well, thank you." I have a problem saying words sometimes.

"Where are you planning on studying after high school?" he asked.

"Indiana, I think. If I get in."

"Oh, you'll get in. No question." Dr. Williamsburg smiled.

"I—well, I—um," I stammered again.

"Get a good night's rest. I'd like to meet with you a few minutes before rehearsal to go over the opening. See if we can get some better coordination from the orchestra. Alright?"

The concert was packed. Frank, Rosa, Ted, and Frankie got seats in the first row. I peeked out from behind the curtains and spied them chatting—except for Ted. Ted was not saying anything. What else is new?

The overture flew by, and it was my time to go onstage. I carefully placed my mittens on an upright piano backstage, along with a glass of water. I wasn't the least bit frightened. I was much more interested in getting my hands on the keyboard. I wasn't happy about the dress I was wearing, which was long and flowy. It was a compromise among Isabella, my mom, and me. I was holding out for pants, but the two of them vetoed that idea.

The orchestra starts with a loud chord, and then I play a couple of bars followed by another big chord. Then more runs. Finally the strings come in and state the theme and we're off. The second after I played the first set of runs, I knew the audience was moving toward the edge of their seats. I don't know how I knew this, just that I could feel them edging toward me. And I liked it—I liked that feeling a lot.

Dr. Williamsburg was wearing way too much cologne. I could smell it wafting all around the podium, toward the piano, and all around the first desks of strings. I thought about this, and how great the horns sounded when it was their turn with the theme. I thought about Ted looking straight through me from the front row. I marveled at myself sitting on the stage, thinking this odd collection of thoughts while I was waiting for the orchestra to get through their opening statement before I played. A short duet with the winds and then it was my turn.

I caught Dr. Williamsburg's eye, and in that moment there was a familiar electrical connection, and then the music took over. And he, and the orchestra, and Beethoven and me—we all conspired to make this music that lived for a few moments and then faded into a memory after the final chord. A split second before the applause began, I felt relief and happiness and the urge to sit down and do it all over again.

After the concerto, Frankie ran up and handed me flowers. The audience kept clapping, and I came out for three bows. I got to shake Elly's hand and Dr. Williamsburg's hand and then someone came onstage and handed me an envelope with the prize money inside. Flashes went off. When the applause died down, it was intermission. I couldn't wait to get my dress off and my jeans on. Frankie would kill me for changing into jeans, but I decided that it was worth it for having to wear that gown-type dress.

Dr. Williamsburg intercepted me in the hallway and practically demanded to be introduced to my parents. Frankie looked so great in spite of a brown plaid polyester suit and very red lipstick. Ted crossed his arms over his chest. It was clear he was bored with the whole scene.

He didn't congratulate me. All he said was, "I like Grieg better than Beethoven." Frankie poked him.

"And what do you think of your talented daughter?" Dr. Williamsburg asked. He was getting lots of answers from Frankie, so he pointed this question at my father.

Ted snorted. He snorted!

"Well, my, my. I suppose I wouldn't have words either." Dr. Williamsburg's neck got all red. I liked how he said "eye-ther instead of "ee-ther." I was concentrating on this so that I would not die of humiliation about my father snorting like that.

We all stood there awkwardly for a moment until one of the stagehands yelled, "Five minutes!" Dr. Williamsburg said something about needing to find his baton and hurried off.

"Might as well hand over the check," said Ted.

"She will do no such thing. It's going right into her college account," Frankie said. "And you were very, very good," my mother told me.

"What would you know about music?" my father said.

Frankie ignored him. "I'm proud of you, Lennie. Really proud." And she walked away from us, leaving me there with my father, who also walked away without saying a thing to me.

Elly and I were playing through some Kodály pieces for violin and piano. She had her music stand set up next to the piano in the living room, and there was music strewn around all over the floor. The music was difficult technically, and we were forging through it, concentrating and communicating with each other with our eyes. The more music I played with Elly, the more I learned and the better I got at understanding nuance and cues. In the Kodály, there were moments of dissonance and passages of beautiful melodies all tangled together. I had moments of feeling like I was flying though the air, it was that exciting and intense. Every now and then we'd hear a pot clatter in the kitchen but it sounded far off, like maybe it was even in another house. But one sound we heard stopped us cold. Elly even dropped her expensive new bow on the floor.

We hadn't heard him come home from work, but Ted must have slipped in the back door without us noticing. He stood in the doorway, leaning against the jamb. And he was laughing. It was not a friendly, inviting laugh. It was a mocking, abrasive guffaw. It was directed at us, at the music we were making.

"What planet did that come from?" Ted snorted. "You call that music?"

Elly picked up her bow. Her eyes looked scared and sad. She wouldn't look at Ted or me.

"Well? What the hell is it supposed to be?" Ted challenged.

"It's Kodály, Dad. He's Hungarian." I said.

"Kodály, eh? Well, it sounds pretty much like shit to me," he said, as though we'd appreciate the compliment or something. He tromped into the kitchen and rattled around in the fridge for a beer.

Elly persisted, unable to leave well enough alone. She followed my father into the kitchen. "Lennie and I are playing this at church next week. Sister Regina invited us."

A loud grunt came from Ted. "Be sure to let me know which mass so I can go to the other one. Or play some Mozart and I might reconsider."

Elly shuffled back to the piano. She was stiff as a board and her jaw was clenched. A lump flew into my throat when I realized she might be doing that so she wouldn't cry.

Ted kept rummaging around in the kitchen. "Kodály. Ha. Shit. Play some real music sometime, like Mozart or Bach or Beethoven. No, on second thought, it's probably too hard." His voice got all whiny when he said "hard," like he was making fun of us, which, of course, is exactly what he was doing. Ted and Frank believed that any music composed after 1900 or by anyone other than someone like Brahms or Beethoven or Mozart was pretty much noise or shit or both. Mr. Kodály never stood a chance.

It was colder in the church than it was outside. At least it felt that way. St. Ursula looked more foreboding than usual from her perch next to the burning candle rack, where I still deposited money regularly even though I didn't really believe anymore that it was doing any good to try and rid the town of Andy. I'd lost my faith in lighting candles long ago.

Elly and I climbed up into the balcony where the choir sat and the organist played and the baby grand piano languished. It was odd for a Catholic church to have a piano at all, but someone had died and left it to St. Ursula's. It was terribly out of tune—more than terribly. Elly rolled her eyes when I played the A. I warmed up with some Hanon exercises and my stomach sank with each new phrase. The piano sounded wounded, worse than a honky-tonk bar piano. No matter how well we played, it was going to sound awful.

The church was dark and empty and freezing. We decided to try to rehearse despite the tuning situation. Elly played the first few solo chords and the notes flew out into the cavernous sanctuary, ringing and beautiful. I joined her with the piano entrance and we jangled through the first movement. The final chord was supposed to be a soft D minor fade out into nothing. The low D was so out of tune that three separate tones sounded. Elly burst out laughing. It could have been worse. One of us could have had the tantrum we wanted to, but it was so much more fun to laugh about it.

Elly had the idea to run over to the convent and get Sister Regina and ask her to listen. Surely she would hear how unacceptably out of tune the piano was and do something about it. She was looked to as the knowledgeable musician around St. Ursula's. That's unfortunate in itself, but we needed an ally, and she was the only candidate.

Sister Regina trooped over from the convent with four other sisters in tow. She stepped into in her Very Important role and let the other sisters know that it was serious business to hear her students in rehearsal and then add significant comments to improve their performance.

We tried it again, the first movement, the honky tonk accompaniment to Elly's melodious playing, and the final, dissonant D minor chord. A discordant stillness wafted through the church and we stared down at the five black figures who hovered near the altar. One of them was kneeling and probably praying for release from the sourness of the music that should have been so beautiful.

"Sister?" Elly leaned over the balcony for her answer.

"Very lovely," Sister Regina pronounced. Elly and I stared at each other in disbelief. "This will be a very nice addition to the offertory on Sunday."

"But Sister," I could tell Elly was being solicitous, deferential, and carefully respectful all at once here. "The piano is so out of tune. Do you think—"

"Yes, the piano is out of tune a bit. But no one will notice that. They'll be thanking God for the gift of communion while you're playing."

"Yes, Sister, but I—"

"Yes, Maria Elena. WHAT?"

"I was thinking, Sister, that perhaps we could have the piano tuned?"

I could feel the air being sucked out of the church, the absolute absence of any breath or movement whatsoever, and the other sisters freezing in place. Sister Regina turned her head very, very slowly, like a raptor, to look at us in the balcony. It was the move and look of a hawk, knowing its prey was captured.

"Are you, Maria Elena, asking that St. Ursula's parish, with all of our limited resources, spend money to tune the piano for your 10-minute sonata?" Sister Regina simply stared at us.

Elly paused. How dare we ask the church to tune the piano when there were starving children in pagan countries? She persisted anyway. "Sister, I think God would like our playing better if it sounded beautiful instead of out of tune."

A huge, painfully slow, and very audible inhalation was occurring below us. After she had filled herself with half the remaining air in the church, Sister Regina spoke. Actually, it was more like a high-pitched yell: "Do you, Maria Elena, actually think you could possibly know what GOD would like? Do you DARE be so presumptuous, Maria Elena?" I knew she was going to throw a "dare" in there somewhere.

"Oh, no, Sister, not at all. I do believe it would be more respectful to play in tune for Him, however," Elly fired right back at her.

Sister Regina stuffed her hands somewhere inside her habit so that she looked like a heap of fabric with a face sticking out. A mean, red, face. "Keep this argument up and we'll have you play on a toy violin, Maria Elena." Uh-oh, Sister was getting mad. Madder. "God will enjoy your performance if it is given in humility. Nothing engenders humility better than persevering with an imperfect instrument, Maria Elena. Do you comprehend, Maria Elena?" Three Maria Elenas in a row. Sister was seething, for sure. "And you, Leonore," she looked right at me. Uh-oh.

"Yes, Sister?"

"You stopped being a St. Ursula's student and went to public school." She said public school as though she were describing shit. "I think it outrageous that you would request such a thing now that you are a part-time Catholic." She turned away from me back to Elly.

"Do you understand how impertinent your request is, Maria Elena?"

"Yes," Elly replied, after a moment. She was lying.

"Yes WHAT, Maria Elena?"

"Yes, Sister Regina, I understand." Elly was gripping a chair and wouldn't look at me. I stayed meek and quiet, trying to figure out if maybe I could read a book and figure out how to tune the piano myself.

"Yes, Sister Vagina," I whispered to the floor.

Sister Regina turned and walked toward the door, her four fellow sisters following like baby geese. Before she exited, she looked back up to the balcony. "I hope you have learned something about being humble, Maria Elena," she said, her words flying upward to find us. "And you, Leonore. You agree, don't you? I assume by your silence that you intend to play on the instrument you were given—loaned, I might add—and be grateful and humble as well?"

My heart started racing. I hadn't tangled with Sister Regina since being in her class years ago. I still felt her power, even though she was down there and I was up in the rafters. "Yes, Sister," I said, just hoping she'd leave and I wouldn't have to agree to any more lies.

"Good," she pronounced. "Be humble and God shall be pleased."

We left after that, climbing down the tiny stairs and into the St. Ursula alcove. As we pushed open the heavy door to the outside, I distinctly heard Elly say, "Fuck it."

We arrived early to warm up before the Mass, not saying much to each other. Ted was coming to church anyway, even though he hated our music. We were playing on the horribly out-of-tune piano. It was still freezing in the balcony. All of the nuns were lined up in the front two rows, bumps of dark fabric kneeling and praying for our imperfect souls. The sky outside was a depressing, Pennsylvania gray. I had the blasphemous thought that hell might be something like this very scene.

Every head in the church swiveled around at the first note we played. All the mass-goers had to see what was going on up there; any music in church besides the dirge-like hymns was unusual. The sounds were so foreign and out of place at the somber mass that our playing was an opportunity for the Catholics of East Bedford to get a little culture. At least that was what I was thinking as I peeked over the railing and saw all the eyes looking at us. Father Chaslowski finally had to ask everyone to return their attention to the front, please, where the somber Sacrament of Communion was taking place.

Our final D minor chord rang out in disharmony through the church. Communion was over, and the priests and altar boys were sitting in their places. And then someone started clapping. It was tentative at first, and then the entire congregation joined in. I could feel the color rise up my face. Someone had liked it, in spite of the shitty piano and the freezing cold church, someone had risked decorum and a possible venial sin to applaud us. Elly threw me a smile and I felt a rush of pride. This is the kind of thing that music can do.

Frank and Ted were waiting for us at the bottom of the stairs. Our moms were further down the steps, being cordial and polite to some unidentified nuns. You can never tell who they are unless you see them face on.

"I still don't think it's music," Ted proclaimed.

"Don't get fat heads just because people clapped," Frank added. "They were just being polite. And you were about as out of tune as that piano," he said, poking Elly in the arm.

I played anywhere and everywhere I could, sometimes with Elly, sometimes with the band, and sometimes by myself. It never failed that, whether I'd heard a piece a hundred times or played it a thousand, at the beginning a thrill runs through me, and then something else happens, like the opening of a fire hose letting all the emotions known to humankind come rushing through. I see things, I feel things, but mostly I know things, like there is such a thing as love. In spite of what happened to me with Andy, I know there is such a thing as love and that if I can feel it, so can everyone else. There's something else, too, something cosmic, like a knowing that we're all in this together and that something like love is the answer—or at least one answer. When I play the piano, I have answers.

Oh my God, I couldn't tell anyone I think like this. Especially Ted. I did try to talk to Elly about it one Friday. We weren't comparing breasts anymore because hers were far superior and we both knew it. Instead, after mac and cheese, we'd take over the living room and play Mozart sonatas or concertos. She understood what I meant and had some of her own ideas to add.

"Nothing else matters except the music, sometimes," I said.

Elly agreed. "You feel everything and nothing, all at the same time."

"Sometimes I feel like the piano is part of me," I confessed. "I don't know where I end and the piano begins."

Elly hugged her violin in reply. "Yeah," she said. "I know."

We played through a Beethoven sonata, all the way. Just reading and playing, no stopping to rehearse or talk or wonder how to shape a certain phrase.

When we finished, Elly said, "I think music can save your life, in a way." And she wouldn't say anymore, but I knew exactly what she meant.

IO

Polka Party

Uncle Henry threw a big bash to celebrate nothing in particular, so we all piled into Frankie's van and went to his house to eat kielbasa and drink beer. It was the first time in several years that Uncle Henry invited any of the band members over, so it was an event. The house was alive with drinking people and polka tapes playing when we got there. Elly and I exchanged a glance that meant, "Let's steal a few highballs." I shot her a look of agreement. We got very good at swiping drinks and sucking them down really fast, then sneaking into the living room and leaving the empty glasses scattered around with all the rest of them. We didn't always know what we were drinking, only that it was strong.

Uncle Henry and Aunt Tammy had an enormous house. Aunt Tammy greeted us at the door. She was wearing hot pants with pantyhose underneath. This was immediately evident because the control tops of the pantyhose extended past the end of her very short hot pants. We nicknamed her Tammy Torpedo Tits. To complete her hot pants ensemble, Aunt T-T was wearing a tube top and a beehive hairdo. The tube top had horizontal stripes so that the blue stripe directly across her nipples made her whole torso look like a flag flying in the breeze. We never wanted a hug from Aunt T-T because of the danger of being fatally punctured.

"Well, hello, girls," Aunt Tammy said as we politely ignored her outfit and torpedoes. "Nice to see you, Elly. And Lennie, are you planning on playing ball with the guys today?" She asked this question looking with outright disdain at my cut-off shorts and Beethoven t-shirt.

"Yeah, Aunt Tammy. I was thinking I might."

She clinked the ice around in her glass. "And I was thinking it might be nice to see you dressed as girl sometime. Wouldn't that be nice? Don't you think, Elly?" Elly dodged this question by slipping into the kitchen. Frankie was behind me and heard the whole thing, though. I'm pretty sure I heard her say "bitch" under her breath.

After I got past the inspection at the front door, it was the usual scene: laughing, drinking people, kielbasa on the grill, the beanbag and croquet games set up in the yard. Polkas blasted from the stereo speakers Uncle Henry moved to the windows of the living room. My parents wandered outside; Elly hung out with Aunt Liddy and her new friend Max. I ran down to the basement to get a couple of root beers from one of the four fridges Uncle Henry has installed down there. It's a big basement with lots of nooks and crannies. I looked in all of the fridges and suddenly someone was behind me. I was shoved roughly up against the fridge. There was a hand clamped on my left breast. Something else pushing up against my butt, hot breath down my back, a hand clamped on my arm.

"Don't say a word. You say anything, I'll beat the shit out of you." I can smell that awful familiar smell: beer, cigarettes, sour sweat, except there was a new twist, some cheap cologne mixed in with all the other gross smells.

I could hardly breathe. It all came rushing back. My body froze, I shut it out of my mind and waited, getting ready to endure until he stopped. My cheek was smashed against the door of the fridge. He was groping my breasts. I couldn't tell if it was is in or out of his pants. I was scared that he would rip my shorts off or worse. He grunted into my ear and I could feel drool down the back of my neck. Warm, slimy. My stomach lurched.

Thank God, there were feet on the stairs. It was Aunt Liddy, calling for me. He slammed my head into the door of the fridge and I saw stars, just like in cartoons. Then he slipped away into the shadows, probably hiding behind the giant furnace that looks like one of those bad special effects robots from one of Aunt Liddy's movies.

"Lennie! Are you down here?" she called again.

"Yes!" I answered, trying really hard to sound normal. My head was throbbing and there were weird lights in my eyes. I rummaged around in the fridge, making lots of clinking noises with the bottles. This particular fridge had root beer and bottles of white wine. That's why Liddy was coming down here, for the wine. I rubbed my head and told her I bumped it. She looked at me suspiciously and then hugged me without saying anything. I saw her sneak a look into the shadows, but Andy was too smart to let any part of himself show. He was like a mean spider, darting in and out of the dimness, waiting to snare his next victim—who has most often been me. A creepy thought began in the back of my mind. I could not believe it never occurred to me before this moment: Has he done this to anyone else? Could he possibly? Why did I not consider this before? I felt a slow angry burn starting at my fingertips and working itself into my chest. Did he do this to anyone else? DID HE?

Liddy and I each grabbed a bottle from the fridge and went back to the yard. I smoothed my clothes, fought the tears that threatened to spring into my eyes. I rubbed the side of my head where he slammed it into the fridge. I kept an eye toward the cellar door to make sure no one else falls into the trap, Elly in particular. But somehow I missed her and I realized that she probably went in search of a drink, too. I imagined Andy the poisonous spider after her so I armed myself with a croquet stick and crept back down into the basement. I tiptoed silently along the wall. No one was near the refrigerators. I saw the furnace with all of its metal arms reaching into the rafters. No sounds except the polkas and laughter from outside. I sensed the power in my arms, knowing that I could kill him with the croquet stick if I had to. I could kill him. I actually could kill him. This thought spread into a feeling throughout my body. It thrilled me.

"Lennie!" Frankie's voice pierced my daydream of smashing Andy's head with the stick I was holding. I thanked her telepathically for saving me from jail.

"Yes!" I yelled back at her.

"Would you grab me a Coke, honey?"

"Sure," I called. I vaguely wondered if she was going to try the Coke-aspirin experiment that I learned about at one of Audrey's slumber parties. Frankie never, ever drank Coke.

I got two bottles and headed toward the door, the one that goes to the house, not the one that goes to the yard. I was still scared but filled with a brand new sense of courage. In one moment, Andy went from being my longtime predator to being my enemy. I was filled with a sense of knowing that I could fight him instead of just giving in. This sent intermittent bursts of adrenaline though me, and I clutched the croquet stick as though it was Excalibur. I didn't want to put it down. I leaned it against my chair, and picked it up when I walked around.

For the rest of the day, he sat in a lawn chair, his eyes hidden behind a pair of stupid-looking aviator sunglasses. I knew he was staring at me with those mean beady eyes. I didn't care. I sent him telepathic waves of hatred and warning. I said things inside my head to him like, "If you ever touch me again, I will shoot your dick off." I silently said the kinds of thing to him that he has said out loud to me. I was thrilled with the realization that I had power, that he was not going to control me anymore. I toyed with the idea of going over there, standing behind him, and saying something outrageously courageous to the back of his head. But I wasn't ready to be in such close proximity to him voluntarily.

My hatred intensified along with my bravado after I downed the remains of half a dozen highballs. By that time, the adults are all drunk, even Rosa. Elly was wobbling all over the place, hugging people. She avoided Andy, though. She sat and talked to Aunt Liddy for a long time. Aunt Liddy seemed so happy with her friend Max. This intrigued me. Max was big. I mean football player big. And she was happy and friendly and smiled all day. Everyone loved her, except for Aunt Tammy, of course. Max drank beer with the men and then hung out with the women in the kitchen, chopping up whatever needed to be chopped up. Her face crinkled when she laughed, so Elly and I told her really terrible jokes that weren't funny, but Max laughed anyway. And she made Aunt Liddy happy.

Aunt Tammy had a real problem with Max. She looked at Max the same way she looked at me, but she wasn't brave enough to insult Max out loud. Tammy wouldn't go near Max. I heard her whispering things to some of the women. She leaned over and said "bulldagger" into Mrs. Kimball's ear. Mrs. Kimball's eyes got really big.

I let my guard down for a fraction of a second when I went into the house to pee. There was no one in there but me because a polka jam was going on in the backyard and the third round of eating had already started. An appropriately drunken "Beer Barrel Polka" wafted in through the open window. I raided the fridge and found one last can of Coke. When I turned around, he was standing there, aviator sunglasses hanging from his shirt like he thought he was some cool Vegas guy or something.

"Come on," he said, as though I would immediately do what he told me. "Go into the guest room." He was commanding me, just like all the other times, hands folded across his chest like an army general expecting me to hop to it.

This time was going to be different, even though it was the only time all day I wasn't carrying my croquet mallet. It was out in the yard leaning against a lawn chair, and I was completely unarmed for this standoff.

"No," I said. I was as close to defiant as I could be. I was freaking out inside, angry and exhilarated, terrified and full of rage. My knees were shaking.

"GO!" he said. He pushed me.

I took a deep breath. My insides were scrambled and whipping all around. "Fuck you, " I said. I did not shout. "You are never touching me again." I started walking toward the door. This was the first time in my entire life that I had ever said FUCK out loud.

His face turned all red and splotchy. He caught me by the arm and spun me around. Then he punched me, with all his might, in the stomach.

Every drop of air left my body and I fell forward, crumpling on the floor. He had knocked the wind out of me. Again. I was eight again, struggling to breathe in the attic. I don't know what was worse, the pain radiating around my gut or the fact that I couldn't breathe or speak or even cry. But I could feel the rage burning through me, and that was enough to stave off the pain and insist to my body that it begin to inhale again.

He slammed out the door. I lay there on the floor, staring intently at the pattern on the linoleum, until the oxygen came back into my body. I gasped a couple of times to get the breathing mechanism to work again. It seemed to take forever for the throbbing in my belly to subside. And as it did, the fury in me mushroomed. The polkas kept playing, no one wandered into the kitchen, and I hugged the floor for a really long time. When I felt OK enough to stand up, I did it slowly and raised my arms to no one in particular, in triumph. This time, I'd won. He was never coming near me again. Ever.

I started to daydream in class. About killing him. I started to think about this all day long in school. We had a substitute for math and another sub for chorus. The boys in the chorus unscrewed the piano stool so that it collapsed and the sub fell off it right onto the floor. I was the one who would have fallen to the floor, but the sub insisted on playing the piano herself because she thought I was bullshitting her about being the accompanist. We were about to sing "Close to You." Instead, we had to read quietly while the principal sat in a chair and glared at us. The boys who sabotaged the piano stool were taken to the office to get suspended. So I had lots of time to think of my new plan for dealing with Andy. I thought about hitting him and punching him, just like he has done to me. I thought about killing him, and I got a little thrill of fear through my body. The thought that I could actually do it was the most amazing thing. I had no idea that I was capable. I was shocked at the depth of my anger, hot and deep enough to provoke murder.

Elly was weirdly silent after our Saturday lessons. My head was still filled with Schubert and how magical the "G flat minor Impromptu" sounded after Isabella worked with me on it. I figured Elly would speak when she wanted to. When she did, I was floored.

"Mr. Bernhard thinks I should change my name," she said.

"Really? Why? Does he think you might be famous?" What an interesting idea, changing a name. I guess I always thought I'd be stuck with Kuklinski.

"Yes. He thinks I should change my name, audition for Juilliard, and enter the Tchaikovsky Competition." Elly didn't meet my eye. She was staring out the window of train.

"Tchaikovsky? The one in Russia that Van Cliburn won?"

"Yes. The next one is in three years. I'll be almost finished at Juilliard then."

"Wow." I had to consider what it might mean to have a famous friend. I felt slight jealousy but more excitement.

"Do you know what my father will do if I tell him?" Elly kept staring out the window.

"Yes, he'll make you quit studying with Mr. Bernhard."

"Right."

"Wait til you get into Juilliard and then do it." I smiled at her.

She smiled back at me. "Right."

I went to New York with Elly for her audition with, of course, both of our moms. We laughed about our first trip to the city and how we thought we'd be dropped off at an orphanage. Rosa still felt terrible about it. She has never forgotten those two mean ladies in the rest room.

"They're probably long dead," said Frankie. "Good riddance!"

When we got to Juilliard, we took ourselves on a little tour around the school. Music poured out of different rooms. Students walked past in ballet garb. Colorful notices about auditions hung on the walls and flyers for concerts and recitals were everywhere. We located the violin audition room and Elly sent us away. She was confident and not scared, just like the day she played for Mr. Bernhard. Our mothers were basket cases, though. Elly made me take them away to wait in the lobby, and it was the hardest thing to see her walk off all by herself, her violin case slung over her shoulder. I had no doubt that she'd be accepted, but I was the one who had to hang out with the moms who shot worried questions back and forth to each other in a fast volley.

Rosa: "Do you think she remembered her music?"

Frankie: "What happens if her hands get cold?"

Rosa: "I think she left some music on the stand at home—yes!—I know she did!"

Frankie: "They say that adrenaline helps stage fright, but it can also make your hands shake. And knees, too. Does she get scared to play? Lennie?"

Rosa: "I hope she practiced enough. Maybe you can't practice enough for something like this. Maybe you're just good or you're not. Dios mio, is she good?"

Frankie: "I hope her skirt isn't too short. What do they think about things like that?"

Rosa: "What about her bow? Could she have forgotten her bow?"

Frankie: "She should tie her hair back so it doesn't get tangled in her violin."

Rosa: "Rosin! Do you think she has rosin with her?"

Frankie: "Rosin! She needs that! What IS rosin, anyway?"

Rosa: "I don't think she's dressed right. She should have worn something else."

Me, finally: "Time out!"

Both moms looked at me as if they'd forgotten I was there. I was getting lots of information about my own upcoming audition and how I would plan on going alone. When the worry volley ended, the three of us sat primly in the Naugahyde chairs and waited. Through the lobby strode Itzahk Perlman, then Isaac Stern, then Dorothy DeLay. And then Elly came sauntering down the corridor like she'd just been shopping or something. She was smiling.

"Well, if I don't get in after that, I'm going to quit playing the violin and enter the convent."

Rosa blanched.

"Just kidding, mom." Elly looked really happy. The general trend is to be freaked out before, during, and after an audition, but Elly was laughing and happy.

We went to lunch at the Russian Tea Room and then wandered over to Patelson's Music House to browse the bins and shelves of music. Since our moms were such good sports, we let them drag us to Sak's and Bloomingdale's and even Macy's. Elly acted like she already lived in New York, fearlessly leading us to and from the subway stops. It suited her, the big city. She seemed to be lighter, happier. I never thought of Elly as exactly carefree, but I saw this in her as she wandered the Juilliard halls, the subway, the New York streets.

Two weeks later, Elly flew with me to Indiana. I don't know how we did it, but we convinced our parents that this trip could happen without their presence. Frankie was the one who finally persuaded the rest of them, I think. She knew what it would be like for me to take auditions with Ted hanging around. So my grandparents Findley gave us the money and even paid for Elly's ticket, and we flew to Chicago, then Indianapolis, and then Bloomington. Before we got on the plane, Frankie presented me with a new pair of plush black mittens.

The Indiana University School of Music was a lot like Juilliard but huge. The sounds – it was not quite a cacophony, more like a garden with every type of music streaming from everywhere. Scales, etudes, every possible instrument playing at once. We wandered the halls and brazenly peeked into the practice rooms. We found a corridor that had only pianos. Hanon, Scriabin, Schubert, Chopin, Bach, Brahms, Czerny, scales, arpeggios—everything was flying out into the hallway from the cracks in the doors. I felt like I'd just arrived home after a long absence. There was nowhere on earth that I would rather have been.

One mistake was eavesdropping on other people's conversations, hearing how hard it is to get into this school, how the auditions are fixed, that the famous teachers already have their studios chosen for fall, how Ludmilla Michalowski was taking only two freshmen and she already knew who they were. I listened to all of these comments replay themselves in my head as I tried to sleep in the twin bed with the scratchy sheets at the Indiana Memorial Union. I knew I was supposed to be scared to death about auditioning, but I couldn't find any fear inside me. There was nothing I loved to do more than play the piano. Fright didn't factor into it, except when we were milling about with all the other auditioners. I saw mittens and tears and trembling hands. I felt sorry for my competitors. As far as I was concerned, the scariest thing that had ever happened to me was Andy. Playing the piano was the exact opposite of that.

A studio door was flung open and my name called. Elly squeezed my arm and said "¡Bueno suerte!" and then I was sucked into a room full of people and one nine-foot Steinway.

"Leonore Kuklinski?" a voice said, confirming my identity. The voice was dressed in a—a caftan, I think, either that or a horse blanket.

"Yes," I replied. "You can call me Lennie."

"You are student of Isabella Boticelli!" A gorgeous woman in an ivory pantsuit asked, her Russian accent heavy. Oh my God, it was Ludmilla! And as soon as I glanced at her, my stomach flipped. My hero, three feet away from me. She looked just like all the album covers and just a little bit older than when I'd seen her in Carnegie Hall.

"Yes. Ms. Boticelli is my teacher." I'm not sure where my sudden politeness came from.

"And how she is?"

"Uh, she's fine. She's great. I mean, I really respect her and have learned a lot from her."

"Yes then, please to tell her hello from Ludmilla."

"Yes, of course." My heart decided to start pounding right then. I was speaking to Ludmilla Michalowski in person. I was trying to understand her accent, her Russian-English syntax. I took a glance at her hands. Beautiful, sculptured, strong. Those hands play Rachmaninoff like no one else on the planet.

"Well then. Begin with scales, please. Four octaves," she said.

I sat down and went through several majors. At the piano, my stomach stopped flipping. One of the auditioners stopped me and asked for minors, then chromatic. Then they started tossing out a variety: F# major. A melodic minor. Eb natural minor. C# harmonic minor. Arpeggios in all the keys. I was so dialed on scales that it was almost fun. They almost played themselves, so I took the opportunity to investigate who was in the room. Caftan Lady. Miss Ludmilla. A man in a dapper suit. Another man who looked like Menachem Pressler and probably was. And two younger-looking people who turned out to be graduate students.

"And what repertoire will you be demonstrating for us today?" The dapper suit man asked me. I found out later he was Jorge Bolet.

"I insist on Bach." Miss Ludmilla Michalowski addressed everyone and no one in particular. "Bach is most important demonstration of how pianist approach the instrument. Please to play Bach."

I played the *Chromatic Fantasy and Fugue in D minor*. There was a low murmur around the table of famous pianists. "Next piece," said Caftan Lady.

I played the Schubert *G flat minor Impromptu* and then part of a Scriabin *Etude-Tableau* and a section of the Chopin *Concerto no. 1*. Someone placed some music in front of me to sightread. It was a Brahms *intermezzo*, and I plowed through. Then something else, the accompaniment to a violin sonata. Prokofiev, I think. It was tricky. Several of them wrote things down as I played. And then my audition was over. When I got back into the hall, Elly was not there. But someone was grabbing my arm. Miss Ludmilla!

"I would like list of repertory which you study with Isabella. I would like you to begin work on all Chopin "Polonaises," have prepared by fall semester. ALL of them. You can do this?" Her eyes were blaring into mine. I think my mouth was hanging open.

Elly came around the bend. The hallways in the music building are circles because the building is round. She stopped in her tracks when she saw Miss Ludmilla speaking to me.

"Well?" said Miss Ludmilla. "You play piano. Do you speak also?"

"Yes! Of course! Chopin *Polonaises*, all of them?" I think I barked this at her.

"Very good. You are practice how much?"

"A lot." Liar. Four hours max. I was taking honors English. "But I can increase that—right away." Her eyes were ripping into me.

Miss Ludmilla grabbed my arm. "Is not enough. More! We have much work to do. All right? The piano is all for you to think about now."

"Yes! So—does this mean . . . ?"

"Of course, dahlingk." I saw the next terrified auditoner coming toward us. So did Miss Ludmilla. "You do not speak this to anyone. I take you as student. I see you in fall. Is not favor to Isabella. Is because you have abilities. I do not accept anyone ever on spot. But you for sure come here—do not go to New York or Philadelphia. You come to study with Miss Ludmilla and something maybe happen for you. We do Artist Diploma, all right?"

"Yes," I said for the twentieth time. My head began to spin. I had no idea what she was talking about. I felt like the small-town naïve kid that I was; things were happening really fast and I was scared. But there was Elly in the background, jumping up and down directly behind Miss Ludmilla.

We spent the evening walking around the music school, spying on people in practice rooms, eavesdropping on more conversations. We perused the music library. We stood in front of the faculty directory at the front of the building and identified all the famous people listed. We bought IU t-shirts from the college bookstore.

"Elly, what do you think is happening to us? You're going to Juilliard and I'm going here. Coming here."

"We're getting the hell out of Bedlam," her new name for East Bedford. "We're actually good at this?!" A question-statement, as though she didn't quite believe it completely. "I think I'm starting to understand what it could mean. Careers. Real careers. As musicians!"

"I'm scared to be here without you." It wasn't the first time I'd thought that.

Elly just looked at me and I knew she was going to say, "Don't be a baby," which she did. "Lennie, you're going to be famous. And I'm going to be semi-famous," she added.

"What? Why only semi-famous?"

"Because I want to be an orchestral player. You can only be semi-famous if you do that. I'll be concertmaster somewhere, though. I know it."

"I know it, too."

"But you—you have to be a soloist."

"I'm not a prodigy. Isabella already told me the scoop on that. I should have started performing ten years ago. I'm already too old."

"Bullshit," Elly said definitively.

"OK," I answered. Who knew?

Wolfie would not come in from the back yard. She was lying under the big blue spruce. It was the day before graduation, a warm evening but not hot. The night was coming, and the temperature was starting to drop a little. I went to get Frankie. She came out in her scrubs, felt Wolfie's pulse, looked in her eyes, checked her gums, felt her belly.

"I don't see anything wrong, honey." She never calls me Honey. "I don't think she's sick," Frankie said. I knew the rest of what she didn't say, that Wolfie was pretty old and that this was her way of telling us it was time.

My mother sat right down on the pine needles. She put her arm around Wolfie, whose eyes were far away. I sat down next to Frankie and put my head in her lap and buried my hand in Wolfie's fur. I did not want to let this happen, experience this. I didn't think I could do it and live, losing Wolfie.

"She was fine this morning. We even played ball." Wolfie was stiff and slow, but she chased the tennis ball in her old-dog way. She couldn't resist a tennis ball, ever.

Frankie petted my hair. I felt like I was five, and I never wanted her to stop. She petted me and I petted Wolfie. And this is exactly why I could never say anything about Andy because I could not lose my mother. But I seemed to be about to lose my dog. My best friend.

"What should we do?" I felt desperate. I started to cry.

"We do what's best for her," Frankie told me.

"You mean kill her." Then I really started to cry.

Frankie was patient with me. I couldn't see her face, but I knew that her expression would be wistful. "I wish all the time that we could do it for people, but it's illegal. No one should be in pain."

"Is Wolfie in pain?"

"I don't think so, but we really have no way of knowing." All we knew for sure is that Wolfie didn't eat dinner and she wouldn't get up. And she seemed to be a million miles away.

She had been her regular self this morning and now we were talking about Wolfie's death, and I had no power to keep her alive. This irrefutable truth made me crazy. A deep place inside of me threatened to erupt, and if that happened I would have to scream and whirl around on the grass like a dervish or a banshee or whoever it is that does the whirling around.

After a long while, Frankie stopped petting my head and said she was going inside. I didn't know it, but she was going to call our vet to see if she would come to the house. I told her I was going to stay with Wolfie and that I would sleep under the pine tree if I had to.

Frankie looked away. Do not fight me on this, I thought. I am not budging. I can't abandon Wolfie. I won't. "OK," Frankie said. "I'll bring your sleeping bag out."

I could not eat dinner. I couldn't go near the piano. Wolfie barely moved. Ted came out once and stood by us. He squatted down and patted Wolfie on the head. He didn't say one single word. Then he stood up and walked over to the fence and looked out at the field behind the house. He might have been crying, but I have no way of knowing. I'd like to think that was true, that he might be able to dredge up some feelings under these circumstances.

I talked to Wolfie. I thanked her for being the best dog ever and my best friend besides Elly. I asked her to please tell me if this was it or if there was something we could do. I knew she could let me know somehow. I believed that dogs should be permanent, that they should be immune to death, that no one should have to go through the parting of human and canine ways. Wolfie picked up her head for just a second. She looked directly into my eyes and we were locked together in a moment of knowing and love. Then she breathed out a long sigh of a breath and the light in her eyes went out.

It took a moment to register. I felt a rise of panic that was just as quickly replaced by an overwhelming sense of peace. She was gone but not gone; I knew this absolutely. It was like her body was finished and the rest of her would continue to run around after cosmic tennis balls.

I lay down in the pine needles with my arm around her. It was weird to feel her body not breathing, to feel the warmth of her fur ebbing into coolness. I felt a huge hole opening up in me, the void where she lived in my earth life that no one else could fill.

Frankie wandered back out. She knew immediately. She kneeled down and patted Wolfie on the head. I knew she'd been crying the whole time. "Bye, sweet girl. I'll miss you so much."

I dissolved into sobs then. Peace or not, I had never felt this kind of loss in my life.

"Your father doesn't know how to do this," Frankie said.

I didn't say anything. I didn't care about him anymore and yet I could feel his pain. He was the one who rescued Wolfie from death by hammer. He used to hang out and talk to Wolfie, throw her tennis balls from the back porch and watch her flip in the air to catch them. I knew he had to be hurting too, and I didn't care one bit.

It was easy to leave home after Wolfie died. Hard to leave Frankie, but easy to leave everything else. It was as if Wolfie's absence opened the door for me to go on into my life. I walked away from that pine tree and never looked back.

II

Miss Ludmilla

Miss Ludmilla was a fucking maniac. At my first lesson, she paced the room. She downed a couple of pills. They could have been aspirin or Quaaludes or LSD, I had no idea. She shrieked. She waved her arms. She came over to the piano bench and hugged me and then shook me and then smacked me on the back of my head. Not hard, just a little whack, but shocking nonetheless. I was overcome by her fabulous perfume and her soft clothing.

"Dahlingk! You play pretty. But where is your soul? Where is your self in your music? I don't hear YOU! I must hear YOU!" She stuck her nose an inch from mine. I was trying my best to understand her. She sounded just like Natasha, of Boris & Natasha on the *Rocky and Bullwinkle Show*.

I pretended that I had no idea what she was talking about. She paced behind me, waiting. I looked down at my feet on the pedals. OK, so maybe I might have had a slight inkling. The thing music is all about. The thing people talk about all the time, but I only vaguely understood. Pouring oneself into playing music seemed dangerous to me. SHE seemed dangerous to me. She saw right through my playing. I just tried to get the notes right and hide behind them.

"You are tie up inside, dahlingk! Here!" She scooted me off the bench and launched into the *Revolutionary Etude*. She was almost blowing the door off the studio. She crashed and banged around the keyboard, and the Chopin flew through the air, almost an assault.

"You can't play this piece timid! [tee-meed] You have to own the piece! You have to have revolution of your own goingk on inside before you can play! Do you comprehend?"

"Yes?" I looked her straight in the eye. She had such a fire in hers.

"This piece is one of hardest in repertory. You are new student to me. But you can play it, I know this without doubt. You have technique beyond normal person. But the notes themselves are boringk. You put self in music, and you will be musician. What are you hidingk?" Her face didn't move away from mine. I was suddenly wondering what it would be like to kiss her.

What was I hiding? Just about everything. And goddammit, she knew it, too.

I was astonished when she handed me a shot of vodka. This was a little too cliché. I sat there like a dork, a dork sitting on a piano bench, holding a shot glass full of vodka, staring at my beautiful, famous teacher. My second beautiful, famous teacher. I felt lucky and bewildered.

She clinked her little glass with mine. She threw back her shot, and I did the same. It burned all the way down, then smoldered inside me. The detached observer part of my brain calmly said: "Well. This is interesting."

"Shut up," I said to this obnoxious part of me. "I am having a Life Experience. Do not interfere with it."

Miss Ludmilla poured two more shots. Oh my God. But she didn't pick them up from the bookshelf. She went back to the piano and gestured for me to sit down beside her.

"Play your sadness," she commanded me.

A zing of terror raced through my entire body. I knew what she was asking of me and I could not do this—let the feelings and the music touch each other.

"You *can* do this," she said, gently. I stopped myself from bursting into tears for no good reason. "Play your sadness," she instructed again. "Play your fear. Play your anger." She looked at me with those fire eyes. "Play some joy. This is there, also."

I almost swooned with the realization that joy was a possibility.

My hands went to the keyboard and suddenly I was playing a Brahms etude. I was summoning some sorrow from the well deep inside and it was flowing out through my hands. I thought of Wolfie and tears flowed down my face. There were so many tears that my throat was not even full of the lumps you get when you cry—or try not to cry. I was sobbing and playing music at the same time and all she said was to do this, and my body obeyed her.

Miss Ludmilla didn't stop me. I didn't even know I knew the piece by memory. I didn't think, I just felt and played. And sobbed. Something came over me, something like possibility and aliveness, and the bigger part of me faded away while the music took the sad and ran with it. When I finished, the last chord echoed. Miss Ludmilla clamped her arm around me.

"Yes," she murmured. "THAT is what we want. THAT was music." Then she got the other two vodka shots and we drank them like tough guys at the bar. She put her arm around me again. Her smell was intoxicating. I couldn't believe I was having those kinds of feelings about my teacher. They were mixed with a million other feelings, too. She *got* me.

"You have a depth," she said to me. She was holding me by the shoulders and looking into my eyes. Hers were blazing. "You have a depth." Then she closed her eyes and her head was nodding, as though she was listening to music inside herself. I sat politely, wanting to play again with this newly released skill of playing the feelings right through me, through my hands to the keyboard.

"Thank you," I said. What else was there to say? My head was starting to fuzz up from the two shots of vodka. I thought to myself that I should buy some vodka and practice drinking it while practicing the piano. If that is how it was going to be, I was going to have to develop a tolerance. And I'd also have to eat lunch before my lesson.

"You see, dahlingk, is more than technique on the keys. I can teach to you how to place fingers, how to lift from chord, how to use pedal perfectly. But if you don't have music to put into technique, there is nothing. There is phrasingk of some machine. There is boredom. You can see this?"

I was on fire with the vodka racing through my veins. "I think so," I told her. She smiled this really benevolent and loving smile at me. I love her desperately in that instant.

Miss Ludmilla assigned some work because our time was almost over. The *Revolutionary Etude*, memorized. All scales, really fast, faster than I've ever played them. Practically the whole Hanon book. And I had to play my feelings in each practice session. This was radical. I was supposed to play them but improvise the music instead of playing repertoire. No Brahms, no Schubert, no Chopin. Improvise my feelings at the piano. My stomach started churning around about this idea, it was completely terrifying and exciting at the same time. I was already planning to hang a piece of paper over the practice room window so no one could look in and identify me, identify the source of this whacky, feelingful music.

I trudged back to Forrest Quad, wondering if my alien roommate would be home. She showed up practically in the middle of the night of moving day, just before the semester started. I was already in my p.j.'s when the door creaked open and a scared face peeked in. I jumped up off the bed, tripped, and said hello.

"OH! HELLO!" She was tall and somewhat dark and very nervous looking. Straight hair, glasses from a *way* outdated fashion, jeans and a t-shirt that had a drawing of the Milky Way and an arrow pointing to the middle of it, saying, "I'm from here."

"I'm Lennie," I said, instroducing myself. "I hope you don't mind that I already unpacked my stuff. I got here early," as in, I've been here for hours wondering when the hell you'd show up, wondering what you'd look like, wondering if we'd get along, wondering if you're a music major, too, wondering if I'd be able to sleep two feet away from someone I never met before in my life.

"NO! NO, it's totally fine. It's OK. Wherever you want to put your stuff is totally fine with me." She headed for the bare mattress and empty dresser. She didn't have much stuff, and no parents were with her to lug her things into the room.

"What's your name?" The whole thing was too awkward to believe. She just kept looking at me and shifting her weight around. I can't remember ever having scared anyone so much just by standing there. And I was incredibly relieved that she wasn't beautiful and snotty. She was plain and frightened. This seemed much more appealing to me.

"OH! It's Jennifer. Jennifer J. Halley. Halley, like the comet. And the J stands for Jupiter." She looked at me and I imagined that she hadn't really wanted that to slip.

So of course I pounced on it. "Your middle name is Jupiter? Like the planet?" I never met anyone named after a planet before.

"Yes." She turned to unpack some bright yellow and green underwear. Wow.

"My middle name is just Marie," I told her. "It had to be something Catholic."

She hesitated. "Catholic? Huh."

"Oh, I don't really—I mean, I don't consider myself religious or anything." I had a flash of Sister Regina's face. She would have passed out cold on the floor to hear me say something like that. After she smacked me.

"Well. I might as well tell you right away. OK? I can't believe I'm doing this." Jennifer paced around for a moment and then faced me. "My family believes that we are actually descended from a master race that originated on Jupiter." She turned away. I heard her whisper to herself, "I can't believe I'm saying this!" She faced me. "I thought you should know. I mean, that would sort of be my family's religion."

Oh my God. "Really," I said. "Wow." Fabulous. First I don't get to go to school with Elly, which had been our Master Plan all along, and now I get stuck in Forrest Quad with an alien. "I'm just from Pennsylvania," I admitted.

"Oh, I'm from Boulder. Colorado." She looked at me and blinked, like she was scared to tell me that. "I know," she said, "here come the *Mork & Mindy* jokes."

I smiled at her. It was exactly what I'd been thinking. "Does Boulder look like what you see on the show?"

Jennifer sighed. "Yes, actually, it does. And my family's house is one block away from Mork and Mindy's house on Pine Street. People come from all over and stand in front of the house and get their picture taken." She looked a little embarrassed about this.

"I can't really imagine," I said.

"No one is really where they think they're from, though," Jennifer went on. "I thought you should know about me being from Jupiter, since we're going to be living together. My family believes that we're all descended from races that populate this galaxy and beyond. I don't really have any information about specific areas like Pennsylvania. Probably most of us in North America come from races that lived on Jupiter and Mars."

Was she serious? She was looking at me with very big, very open eyes. She *was* serious. I decided not to even go there. "What are you majoring in? I'm a piano major," I stated.

"Oh, wow, a piano major. I'm a composer." She smiled this weird, sideways smile at me. "Do you know about the Voyager probes? Two of them are flying through the solar system to Jupiter and Saturn, and both of them have recordings of music by Bach and the Beatles. This is so that any aliens who encounter our sadly lacking technology will know that we have music and the arts in our humble lives? And that we're actually capable of creating music ourselves according to the laws of music theory, which are really just an extension of the laws of the cosmos?"

Scared. I was getting *just* a little bit scared. Why was she talking in question marks?

Jennifer was still talking. "People usually think I'm a little strange? But somehow I just knew that I'd get a really nice roommate who might actually believe me.? She grinned at me. I got a look at the book that fell out of her bag: *Chariots of the Gods.* There was a big flying saucer on the front.

"How did you get here?" I wondered. The middle of the night, just a couple of suitcases, no parents.

Jennifer looked out the window at the dark sky. "Oh, I just got dropped off," she answered vaguely.

Oh, come on. I looked at the sky, too. Really now, come on.

"Um, so, what do you call someone from Jupiter? A Jupitonian?" I wanted to know how exactly to describe her to Elly.

"No, no. We're called Jovians. There's a whole grouping of Jovian planets—that is, ones that have gaseous atmospheres and lots of satellites. Moons, to laypeople." She had the most sincere, open expression on her face. I was touched, in a way.

"Jovians. OK," I said, thinking of the Holst piece, *The Planets,* in which Jupiter is described as "bringer of jollity." Jolly could conceivably be one of the many possible descriptions for the conversation I was having with my alien roommate.

We turned the lights out and talked a little more. Jennifer told me the whole story of the earth being populated by the Jovians eons ago. There were five races of Jovians and that's how we got five different races of humans – black, white, red, yellow and brown. But we earthlings fucked everything up by thinking that one race could be better than another. The real Jovians were appalled by things like slavery, genocide, and ethnic cleansing. So they've abandoned their project (us) and now we're fending for ourselves.

Jennifer *was* there when I got back from my vodka piano lesson. She had an enormous book lying open on her bed. It looked like a collection of star maps. Of course.

"Hi Lennie," she said, sounding a little weary.

"What's the matter?" I was thinking about getting some ice cream from the snack bar in the basement. A cute girl worked there and I went there as much for her as for junk food.

"I have a professor who thinks I'm crazy. I shouldn't have told him about the Jovian colonization of Earth. Now he's ridiculing me in class."

This can't be good. "What's the class?"

"Astronomy."

"Of course," I said, as I was thinking those very words again. Of course Jennifer would find the elective class closest to her heart. Of course she would lie on her bed with a giant star map laid out before her.

"Yes, it's taught by Professor Looney. He's an international expert on everything known about extraterrestrial life. Which isn't much, to tell you the truth."

Was I the only one who thought that Professor Looney teaching about astronomy and extraterrestrials might be a little funny? "So what's the problem?" Actually, one was that I was starting to almost believe Jennifer, and I felt a little protective of her.

"He says the whole concept is a ridiculous metaphysical fabrication.

He says I am no more Jovian than he is. But the problem is that we're all Jovian, originally!"

"I think you're going to have to suspend your true beliefs or flunk this class," I advised.

Jennifer slammed her star map book closed. "Shit," she said. "I thought I could be in on the revolution from the very beginning."

The revolution? "What revolution?"

"Speaking the truth to the people of earth. I thought the best way to do it would be through an academic forum. You know, facts and proof."

"And so far it's not going according to plan."

"Right," said Jennifer. "I'll have to be a little more clever about it. Why do you think Mozart wrote the *Jupiter Symphony*? Why is it that the Jupiter movement of *The Planets* suite is the most powerful and inspired? Because it's where we're FROM!"

I had a vague, weird feeling winding around my chest, making me think that I didn't want to really consider the Jovian origins of mankind. So I told her about the *Revolutionary Etude*—how á propos— and the two shots of vodka I'd consumed at my lesson. And how I thought Miss Ludmilla might drastically change my life.

"Good for you," she said, and meant it. She wanted to hear all about it and so I told her everything, even my flashes of attraction to Miss Ludmilla. From there, the whole rest of the story came out about me liking girls. I figured if Jennifer could come out of the closet about being from another planet, I could probably trust her with the almost-certainty of my gayness.

I couldn't concentrate in music theory class. Thanks to Miss Ashley #2, I pretty much knew everything we were covering in the first semester. Basic harmony, voice leading. Our TA had a tendency to explain everything in triplicate, and I had a hard time keeping my eyes open. So they wandered around the room—and always landed on the girl who sat in the far right row, first seat. We all sat in the same seats every class. It was part of our TA's strategy to dehumanize us. The far right row girl was—well—she was absolutely stunning. Built like an athlete, face like a model, but with intelligent eyes and long, tapered fingers. I tried to figure out what instrument she played. Violin maybe, piano possibly, or something completely unexpected.

I never saw her anywhere except theory class. I couldn't learn her name because the TA also called us by number, as in, "Number 37, could you please harmonize example three on the board?" We turned in our assignments by number. Mine was 14. We wrote our numbers on our quizzes, and I saw that my beautiful classmate's number was 42. So that's how I referred to her in my mind and in my escalating fantasies.

On Fridays after theory, I had piano class, referred to officially as "studio class." The entire population of Miss Ludmilla's studio met weekly to play for each other, hear critiques, and have the opportunity to gather ammo with which to trash each other during the rest of the week. I had had the idea that Miss Ludmilla took only the most promising, amazing, and nice students. I was sorely disappointed by the two Rottweiler senior girls who thought they'd each be the next winners of the Tchaikovsky Competition. Surprisingly, instead of being at each other's throats, they teamed up together against the rest of us. There was one other freshman besides me, a timid guy named Keith who wore bow ties every day. Keith was scared of his own shadow, and he was interested in mastering the pianoforte literature, which meant he pretty much only played repertoire from before 1800. I secretly thought it was because he didn't have the chops to play anything technically challenging, but that could have been just my growing snottiness.

The sophomores and juniors were quiet and studious. No one stood out to me. Everyone played frighteningly well, and no one was terrible. But of course, no one could be. Then there were four graduate students who were studying for a variety of degrees, and me—the only artist diploma. I was intrigued by Tatiana, a woman from Kiev who looked perpetually worried and spoke Russian with Miss Ludmilla as often as possible. None of the rest of us had any idea what she was saying, gesturing, or crying about. Tatiana played like a firestorm, crashing around the keys, never missing a note, making the most dramatic music I'd ever heard coming from a keyboard. If she did make a mistake, she'd smack herself in the forehead, burst into tears, and then run from the room. Even Miss Ludmilla could not put a stop to this leaving behavior.

My first performance in studio class was the Schumann *Papillons*. I played the hell out of it, if I do say so myself. At the end, the last chord rang out and I could feel—something—from my peers. It felt like hostility mixed with envy mixed with a little bit of admiration. It was all there. Miss Ludmilla thought otherwise. "Please to play first bar again. Again!" She strode around the recital hall stage with her hands in her jacket pockets, brow furrowed, head bobbing slightly in time to the music.

"Again! Again!" after I'd played it about ten times in a row. I didn't get what she was looking for. I noticed the grad students perking up with interest. I was getting grilled and they were enjoying it.

"These are not butterflies! They are roaches! More delicate!" Ludmilla yelled. And the more she yelled, the less delicate I was. When she finally let me get up from the piano bench, I noticed that I was sweating—and shaking a little. I don't think it was from fear. It was more from being unnerved. I knew the piece, I could play the notes, and she kept finding fault with it, kept demanding a touch I didn't feel.

It was the first time I'd experienced Miss Ludmilla doing what all my classmates did: ripping the music to shreds until it didn't resemble anything that my heart felt. It was de rigeur to laugh at the attempts to make music, critique the shit out of someone's technique, tear little things like hand position or facial expression apart. Above all, belittle all attempts at creating music out of the notes on the page.

This is what made me sweat and tremble. Not playing for people, not fear of a memory slip or that I couldn't do it or that I wasn't good enough. It was the deeply cutting commentary of my supposed peers. And when Miss Ludmilla went in that direction, I was surprised and scared, not knowing how to react.

The applause from my classmates was tepid. I could tell that they enjoyed my trouncing a lot more than my playing. I trudged to the very last row of the recital hall. I had to get away from them. I had to stare at Miss Ludmilla and ask myself why the hell she had just torn me to pieces in front of the vulture people, my classmates. I threw myself into a seat, almost sitting directly on top of Joop. (I'd started calling her Joop at dinner one evening when she was explaining the origin of fruits and vegetables. It had been an argument between two Jovian botanists, and the resulting variety had been an unexpected bonus.)

"Joop! What the hell are you doing here?" My heart started pounding in addition to all the other weird physical symptoms. I'm glad I remembered to whisper, though it didn't seem like anyone noticed us in the back of the dark hall. The person playing after me was one of the nondescript juniors, who was plowing through a pretty boring rendition of Beethoven's *Tempest*. It was more of a breeze than a tempest. Miss Ludmilla was sitting on the edge of the stage with her head in her hands.

Oh my God. Now I'm doing it, too. I sound just like them.

"Did you hear me play?" I asked Joop. Of course she did.

"Of course I did, that's why I'm here," she said. "You were stellar."

"Is that some kind of cosmic double entendre?"

"I guess. But I mean it. You play rings around these people."

I wasn't going to go for the rings comment. I didn't have it in me to crack a Saturn joke in that moment.

After the placid *Tempest*, there was Keith the freshman who played a Scarlatti sonata. It was eerily beautiful, soft and ethereal as though he really was playing a pianoforte and couldn't get much volume. When he finished, Miss Ludmilla addressed us: "Dahlinkgs. I don't know what you are doingk, but nobody is practice. All of you—get off your asses and work. Do not come in here unprepare again! All of you!" She strode off the little stage and went slamming out the back of the recital hall, making it clear she was not interested in chatting with any of us.

I felt like she'd slapped me personally. Unprepared? I knew *Papillons* backward and forward. Could she be talking to everyone but me? But she said "all of you." My stomach twisted in a knot.

"Let's get smashed," Joop suggested. We left the music building and ran across the street to Bear's. One of Joop's grad student friends was waiting tables, and he served us shots of tequila and two tall drinks called Blow Jobs. They were delicious.

"Is this how it is? We get torn to shreds when we're least expecting it?" I could not believe Miss Ludmilla yelled at me like that.

"I don't know," Joop said. "But I think so."

"It's so mean."

"Right."

"You seem to be taking it in stride. Maybe composers are nicer."

Joop laughed. "I wasn't the one who just got fried up there. Last week in composition seminar, my toccata got dissected right before my eyes."

"You had to write a toccata?"

"Yes. And it wasn't fun." Joop raised her glass and clinked it to mine. "Welcome to the real world, Lennie."

"Thanks a lot," I said, and drank my illegal drink.

We were sipping the Blow Jobs in silence, pondering this, when most of the oboe studio walked past us and settled into the giant booth right behind us. 42 was with them, and I swear she looked right at me as they walked by. So, she's an oboist! I never would have guessed. They were talking about making reeds and how you couldn't do anything if you had a sharp reed because it was too short, but you could always clip the tip of a flat reed although you'd run the risk of making it too bright. 42 actually had a reed sticking out of her mouth, like it was a friendly lollipop or something.

"They're all such nerds," said Joop, sort of gesturing at the oboe players. "They all have pinchy little mouths and strange eyeglasses. It's got to have something to do with oxygen deprivation, don't you think?" Joop's gaze followed one of the male oboists, whose oboe case hung from a long strap on his shoulder like a purse.

I wasn't about to reveal my growing interest in 42, so I didn't say much. She is definitely not a nerd, though. "There's something about the sound," I said to Joop. "It's so haunting, don't you think?"

"That is true," agreed Joop. "I don't think many composers write that well for oboe." She said this pretty loudly, and the comment drew silence from the oboe booth. They all looked at us.

"You are so right," Purse Boy said, joining the two conversations together. My heart started pounding because I might have to interact with 42. Get to, I mean.

"The tessitura is so narrow," said Joop. "Most composers don't really understand that."

"You are exactly right!" Purse Boy was getting pretty excited. "Two and half usable octaves! You should never write anything pianissimo below first-space F. And high D. That's my limit. It's impossible!"

"But there's that high G in *Tombeau*," said Joop. This drew silence and awe from the oboe table.

"It's amazing that you know that," 42 said. Joop smiled. It WAS amazing, the things she knew.

"Dvorak either hated his second oboe player or else had a really good one," a very plump girl with blond Brillo-pad hair contributed with a slight lisp from the opposite side of the booth. "He wrote lots of low C#s. Like in the cello concerto. Very exposed and scary. What kind of drinks are those?"

"Blow Jobs," I said, and then got really embarrassed because 42 looked at me with the absolute cutest little half smile I've ever seen.

"REALLY?" Miss Dvorak squealed. "What on earth is in them?"

Joop got up and offered her a sip. Uh-oh. We were combining booths.

"I don't know a thing about oboes," I said to no one in particular. There were at least eight of them. It seemed weird, eight oboe players in one spot. You don't see that much, like eight elephants or eight whooping cranes.

"What do you play? You don't look like a singer," Purse Boy said.

"She's an incredible pianist," Joop answered for me. The oboes all looked at me.

"Well, I am *a* pianist," I qualified.

"She studies with Michalowski," Joop would not shut up.

There was a collective intake of breath. "Wow." This came from across the table. I'm pretty sure it was 42. My heart started to beat fast. Apparently studying with Miss Ludmilla is a big deal.

"We all have the same teacher, of course," Miss Dvorak said. And then she went around the table introducing everyone. Her name was Nancy. Purse Boy was Tom. There was a Larry, a Lisa, a Laura, a Jim, a Kathy, and a Beth. That was 42's real name: Beth.

Baskets of French fries started arriving, along with pitchers of beer and a few more Blow Jobs. The conversation went back to the oboe's small range of usable notes. Then to the *Flower Clock*, which apparently requires an excellent pianist to handle the difficult piano reduction. Then Joop got into an argument about writing harmonics into a composition. The oboists said it should be up to the player to choose whether or not to use a harmonic; Joop insisted that a composer could ask for that effect. I could feel my eyes glazing over and wondered how to politely leave so I could play my *Papillons* over and over. Before I could figure it out, 42 leaned over to me.

"If you ever want to play through some rep, let me know," she whispered. I'm pretty sure that's what she said. I couldn't hear clearly.

"Really?" Oh no, too enthusiastic.

"I think it would be fun. I know you could play *Flower Clock*." She smiled and that was that. And then she was gone.

"So have you done it yet? With anyone? I mean, with a guy? Well, or even a girl?" Joop asked me this one night when it was very dark. We were lying in our beds, chatting in the pitch black. It must have been 3:00 a.m., and we awoke simultaneously and started talking. It was so much like something that would happen with Elly. The dark was total. No moonlight shining in our window, not even any lights from the rooms across the quad.

Since Joop knew I was gravitating toward women, she told me that the original master race had no problem with homosexuality, and in fact, the Native American concept of Two-Spirit is the belief that homosexual or transgender people have both male and female living in them and so are spiritually elevated. I needed to really think about that one.

I answered her truthfully. My only real "doing it" experiences had been with Audrey and that didn't get very far. I didn't really think I could consider the things I'd done with her as officially "doing it."

"Pardon me, but how do you know you don't like men?" A flash of Andy came into my head. But that wasn't real sex, another part of my head said, trying to make a little sense of it—as if that could ever happen.

"I guess I don't," I answered, wondering what a mutual, loving experience with a man might look and feel like, realizing that I had never once considered the possibility.

"How about you?" I asked, not quite wanting an answer. Maybe there was some odd Jovian sexual ritual or apparatus that I might not want to know about.

"I've been having sex with a guy named Zag from my theory class since the fist week of school. It's been very cosmic." Joop's voice got a little husky. She was in some graduate level theory seminar since she knew everything already.

"Zag? As in Zig?"

"No," was all Joop said.

"How come you never told me?" I was a little hurt. She could tell me about being from Jupiter but not about having something so earthly as sex with a mysterious guy named Zag.

"I don't know, Lennie. I haven't told anyone. Zag is so—I don't know. Different."

"OK," I said. Different? Different than Jupiter herself? "Did you tell him about—you know—the colonization of Earth and all that?"

Joop took a deep breath. "No. I didn't."

"Huh. I guess that might be wise."

"Yeah," she said.

I tried to stare at the ceiling, but it was too dark to tell if I was looking at it. I felt a little tug of jealously in my chest.

"Hey," Joop said, "Zag has a friend you might like."

"A guy?"

"Yeah. A really sweet guy. Not scary. And he's a virgin, too."

"Do you think it would be definitive? Do you think I'd know for sure if I did it with him? Or do you think I'd stay ambivalent and confused?" I wasn't really ambivalent. I was just trying hard to let it be possible that I could like men.

"I think you could gather a lot of evidence," said Joop.

I lay there in the dark considering this. I wouldn't have to go looking on my own and trying to flirt or anything. Not that it would be difficult on a college campus to find some guy who wanted to have sex with no strings attached. All I'd really need to do is walk into any frat house and it would be immediately available. But this friend of Zag sounded—I don't know—safer, I guess.

"What's his name?"

"Timothy."

"What's his major?"

"Harpsichord. He reads figured bass better than anyone I've ever met. And he paints, too. Watercolors."

I agreed to meet Timothy in the lobby of the music building on Friday after the orchestra concert. When he walked up to me and tapped my shoulder, I practically jumped into the air. He was very cute. A little trembly. Tall, thin, lanky. Artist clothes. Paint on his pants, his fingers. We went to Bear's and ordered drinks and we didn't talk very much, just a little about pianos, harpsichords, and painting. He did abstracts that looked a lot like wild flowers. Not wildflowers. Wild, crazy, colorful, strange flowers.

We both knew what we were up to, so we didn't stay long at Bear's and went to his place, an old house on Third Avenue that he shared with about ten other people. He lived in a room with a jazz trumpeter who was never there. Timothy told me about him, and he seemed sad and wistful about it.

We drank almost a whole fifth of vodka mixed with a variety of juices. Orange, cranberry, apple (not very good), grapefruit (strange but surprisingly tasty), and tomato. When we were both almost falling down drunk, Timothy said, "Well, would you like to try having intercourse?" Just like that, as though we were doing a science experiment.

Which, actually, wasn't that far from the truth.

I burst out laughing, trying to pretend that my stomach had not just done a giant flip. Timothy looked a little taken aback. So I quickly said, "Sure. Of course. I'd love to." Like he'd just asked if I wanted him to pass the mashed potatoes. Then I realized that he looked more frightened than me.

"What do you think we're scared of?" I started to unbutton my shirt. I didn't have one ounce of desire or interest in this activity. But I had to go through with it—for the experience of it—so I wouldn't be technically a virgin anymore. So I could fit in. So I could figure out if my crushes on women were a phase or a mental illness or an abomination or a fate worse than death.

Timothy turned around and took off the rest of his clothes. He snapped the light off and I was disoriented for a moment until the streetlights filtered in and my eyes adjusted. He was holding the covers up for me, so I slid in next to him. He jumped when our bodies bumped into each other. We both got very still. Maybe he could hear my heart pounding. The room began to spin. Slowly at first, and then it picked up speed. If I stared at the overhead light fixture, I could almost control the speed of the whirling.

Timothy sighed a big, long sigh.

"That bad, huh?" I don't know why I chose this to say.

"Look," he said. "I'm really just doing this because—well, I—I mean you're really nice and cute and everything but—"

But what? I was thinking—hoping, really—that there might be a chance of canceling this whole experience, leaving, never seeing him again because the music school was so enormous that I'd never have to run into him. I have no idea where they keep the harpsichords, anyway. I could possibly never see him until graduation.

"Your roommate suggested that we meet because—well, because—"

I got brave and reached out and put my arm across him. He flinched. "Because WHAT?"

Another huge sigh. "Because I don't know if I really like women. Because I think I might be gay. Oh, God. I know this is really using you, I feel terrible—"

It was my turn to hold my breath. It was as though he slapped me, but I liked it.

"You think you might be GAY?!"

"I'm so sorry, this is terrible, I know. It's a terrible thing to do to someone. But your roommate told me the same thing about you. She thought maybe we could work it out."

"WHAT?!" I felt immediate relief and betrayal in the same moment.

There was a silence that happened between us. Then we started laughing. We both realized how weird it was to be lying in bed with a naked person of the opposite sex.

"I think I'm in love with my roommate. The trumpet player," Timothy confessed.

"Have you ever been attracted to any women?" I wondered.

"No, I don't really think so. I try to be, but I don't think I can do it." He started caressing my belly. It was a little strange but it felt good. "Have you?" he asked. "Been attracted to any men, I mean."

"Not that I can think of," I confessed.

"You like women for sure then," he concluded.

"Yeah," I said, not including the actual, extensive number of women I'd been attracted to. "Right now, there's this girl from in my theory class. Her name is 42. She's dark, brilliant, and beautiful. I've only spoken to her once." I told him about Bear's and how she wants to play music with me.

"Oh, you have that theory TA who numbers people." We both laughed about that.

"Do you think she digs girls?" Timothy asked.

"I don't have any idea. I just look at her."

Timothy laughed. "I know how that goes."

Timothy had the brilliant idea to get up and play music together. I followed him down the hall into a room that contained a grand piano, two harpsichords, a giant stereo stystem, and a couple of chairs. Timothy sat down at the bigger of the harpsichords and started playing. Couperin. *Les Baricades Mysteriuses.* It was so beautiful. Light from the streetlight filtered in through the window along with the slightest breeze. I was completely comfortable being naked, listening to his sad, brilliant music. I still felt drunk, but the room stopped flying through the air.

As he played, Timothy's penis sort of hung out on his leg. It attracted my attention because it was so—there. I haven't seen any others in person besides Andy's, and his was more of a weapon than a body part. Timothy's was friendly-looking. It was a lot bigger than Andy's, surrounded by some downy fur. It lay there companionably on his thigh while he played. More Couperin, then some Bach. Toward the end of a three-part invention, the penis began to come to life. At the last cadence, it was completely standing at attention.

"Wow," I said, both about his playing and his penis.

He looked down. He didn't try to hide it or cover it up. "Yeah. Thanks."

I became what I consider to be outrageously brave and asked him if he wanted to try doing it since the opportunity had sort of obviously presented itself. If we managed to succeed, then we could both honestly say that we'd done it.

I got up and stumbled toward Timothy. No more spinning, but the floor felt like the deck of a ship. I straddled him and we fit ourselves together surprisingly easily. It was painfully intimate, looking right at each other. So we both closed our eyes. I had flashes of feelings I couldn't understand, fear and joy and then images of Andy that I brushed away. Then some anger, realizing what I'd been robbed of.

"I don't really know what to do with these," he said, lightly touching my breasts.

"Don't worry about it." I let more feelings come and then started to really get into the sensation of him inside me and it feeling OK. Pretty good, actually. Really, really good after a few minutes.

With our eyes closed, we grasped each other and rode it out. Timothy came in a surprised gasp. I didn't, but I was fine with that. I got what I wanted: what it really might be like with a man. The knowledge that it was OK, and that was the thing—it was just OK.

We had fallen off the harpsichord bench onto the shag rug and we lay there in a heap. "I don't know what to say," Timothy said.

"Me either," I agreed.

In spite of what had just happened, we were still awkward about touching each other.

"So," he began, "I really dig you and everything, but—"

"It's OK—don't say it."

"The thing about us just being friends?"

"Yeah."

"I was really going to just thank you for making me realize—"

"That you like me but you like guys better."

"Yes."

"Me, too. But girls. I like girls better." I got a shot of something thrilling race through my body. Just to say it out loud to someone I barely knew—but had just fucked. There was an irony in there somewhere.

Timothy got up and went to the piano. He started to play Schubert, *Leibesbotschaft* this time. It was so lovely that my heart threatened to break. I felt a flood of what seemed to be love for him. When he stopped, I sat next to him on the piano bench and played *Mozart 21*, the adagio. He didn't move away. He reached over my hands and added a few of the orchestra chords. When we reached the end, we both had tears in our eyes.

We put our clothes back on, but I couldn't go.

"Would it be OK if I just stayed?" I asked him.

"Of course." Timothy put his arm around me like a father might do with his daughter, protectively, and that was how it stayed for the next four years.

When I got back to my room as the sun was coming up, Joop was looking through a book about the solar system. Jesus. She glanced at me, expectantly. I suddenly felt furious with her and grateful to her all at once, but the fury won out.

"What makes you think you can just announce to people that I might be gay?"

She looked up from her planet book. Her big Jovian eyes were full of sincerity—and a little touch of fear.

"Oh, Lennie, it doesn't seem like that big a deal."

"It IS a big deal. Who would want to be gay with the way people treat you? And how do we know it isn't completely wrong and I'm a freak of nature and I could go to hell?" I felt ridiculous saying this, but I was scared about it, deep down. I don't want to be gay. I want to be who I am but I don't want to be an abomination.

"I told you. You're not a freak—you're a Two-Spirit."

"I don't know what I am."

"You're a chickenshit."

"You're an alien."

She tackled me and started wrestling. I went limp. She pinned me down and got her face really close to mine. I was aware that I still had vodka breath and she was going to kiss me anyway. It was one of those movie pre-kiss pauses where we looked deeply into each other's eyes, searching for whatever it is they search for in the movies. The thought I had was that I was mere millimeters away from kissing an alien.

I started laughing. Then she did, and we rolled around in a heap on her bed. I realized in that moment that I'd gathered two allies for my journey through music on earth, the latest detour of which was veering full out into Gayland.

"I don't give a shit if you're gay," Joop said, hugging me.

"Well, then I don't give a shit if you're from Jupiter."

"Elly?" I said into the phone. The voice that had answered definitely wasn't hers.

"Just a minute," it said.

I waited a moment, listening to rustling sounds.

"Hello?" said Elly's voice

"Who—?"

"Lennie, that was Herman. We're—uh, well, he's my—um. Well, we're dating!"

"*Herman*? You're dating someone named Herman? When the hell did this happen?" I'd talked to her exactly one week earlier.

There was a pause, some shuffling noise, and then a kiss. Definitely a kiss. "See you later." Another pause. "Me, too!"

And then, "Lennie? Are you still there?"

"Yes, Elly." I'm still here, picturing this guy named Herman kissing you goodbye as he leaves your room and goes off to practice. All I can really see is Herman Munster playing Bach's *Toccata & Fugue in D Minor* on an organ covered with cobwebs. "Herman?" I said again.

"Yes! He's amazing! He's a senior. He's a violinist, too. We've been going out for a—well, about a week now. We play duets every day."

I just didn't have a good feeling about this, and not just because his name is Herman.

"Is this the guy you beat out for concertmaster?"

"Well—yes. But he doesn't have any hard feelings about it."

"Are you sure?" I realized that I was twisting the phone cord.

"Yes, Lennie. And listen to this. We went over to Lincoln Center last night and sat at the fountain. It was so warm, and the night was so beautiful And he confided the most amazing thing to me."

Elly was starting to sound like a character from a Brontë novel. "What?"

"Well—" Elly paused. "I guess I can tell you."

What? Was there any doubt? Was she actually considering not telling me something? Was there *anything* we couldn't tell each other? With the exception of Andy, of course, Elly knew everything there was to know about me. I felt awful to think there was something she might want to keep from me. Really sick to realize it had something to do with this Herman guy.

I could hear Elly take a breath on the other end of the phone. "He told me that he's convinced that he's the reincarnation of Hector Berlioz. Isn't that incredible?"

OK, so my roommate is from Jupiter, I just fucked a guy who is every bit as gay as me while sitting on a harpsichord bench, and my best friend is now dating Berlioz. I held the receiver out and stared at it as though it was the source of everything bizarre in my life.

"Lennie?"

"Berlioz? You mean he thinks he's Berlioz in a brand new body?"

"Exactly."

"And you believe him?"

"Of course I believe him. He knows every note of *Symphonie Fantastique*."

"Jesus, Elly, *anyone* can study the score and learn every note of it. Plus, you're Catholic and we don't believe in reincarnation."

There was a weird silence. "I think he might be telling the truth, and the Catholic Church might not have all the answers to everything."

Holy shit. Actually, I was much less concerned about Elly's eternal soul than I was about her physical self having anything to do with the Return of Berlioz.

"Elly—"

"Do NOT lecture me, Lennie. You've never met him. He's so sure of this that there are passages in *Fantastique* that he's corrected. And get this: He thinks that I've come back as Harriet Smithson because that's how much he's obsessed with me."

Harriet Smithson was an actress that Berlioz fell madly in love with and pursued mercilessly. Every freshman music major knows that he then smoked opium and wrote *Symphonie Fantastique* about her. For her. That he was "emotionally deranged" about her. Then he eventually married her and they were both miserable because she could never live up to his idealization of her and then he dumped her and she soon died in despair. (That chapter in my music history text read like the *National Inquirer*.) And this is the person my best friend thinks she's dating? Why would Berlioz return to the planet as some no-name violinist?

I asked Elly that very question. She almost hung up on me.

I felt scared and desperate and too far away. "Elly. Listen to me. Have you ever previously had one inkling that you've come back to earth as Harriet? Have you ever given this possibility one second of consideration before this?" I was getting agitated, pacing around and twirling the phone cord into an unrecognizable blob.

"Well, I did name my turtle Harriet."

When we were seven, Elly had one of those tiny pet-shop turtles that eventually grew into a giant version of itself. We took the foot-long turtle to Monacacy Creek and released it into the wild. I can still see Elly crying, "Harriet, Harriet! I'll miss you!" The turtle never looked back, leaping happily into the creek and swimming away—pretty fast for a turtle.

"I don't think that's sufficient evidence that you yourself were Harriet Smithson, famous actress of the 19th century." I was the one who was considering going to talk to someone at Psych Services, but it seemed that Elly was the better candidate.

"I don't think you understand at all, Lennie."

"I guess I don't." I decided not to tell her about Timothy. Losing my official virginity to a fellow searching-potentially-gay person didn't seem important or relevant to anything anyway. Not when Elly was dealing with a crazy delusional person.

We hung up and I sat there worrying. Joop coaxed me to go over to Nick's where we ordered big baskets of fish and chips and beer. She always knew where to not get carded.

Joop waved a fry at me. "Now, this Herman guy. Is he a brilliant composer?"

"I don't really think so," I answered. Elly had dodged that question. "She said he was a really good violinist."

"Does she know that Berlioz started out as a flute player?"

I never knew that. "So, the guy has to be crazy. Or at least delusional."

Joop had malt vinegar dripping down her chin. "I hate to ask this, but—is Elly—is she OK looking? Is she insecure?"

"She's gorgeous. And when we were six, she had the vocabulary of a 30-year-old."

"Then why would she want to hang out with some loser guy?"

"I've been wondering that myself." I've been fretting about that, actually.

We got back to the dorm and I went down to the snack bar. No one was there and the cute girl behind the counter gave me a banana split for free because she said I looked like nothing on earth could cheer me up. I ate the whole thing, watching *Night of the Living Dead* on the TV in the lounge. I missed Aunt Liddy, missed the real Elly, and wondered if I'd ever find anyone—a woman anyone—who might have the slightest interest in me. Who might want to put their arm around me or cuddle up with me and watch a bad horror movie or play music with me late into the night as we gazed into each other's eyes. Would 42 even be a possibility? I wondered about it so hard that I finally trudged over to the music building and found my favorite practice room, the one with the perfect-action seven-foot Steinway, empty. I slid onto the still-warm piano bench and started pounding out a Brahms intermezzo, playing my feelings out in A flat major just like Miss Ludmilla wanted me to. I played some full-out fear and sadness until the morning light filtered into the room. I played so much fear and sadness that I lost time doing it and didn't realize that tears flowed down my face until I felt the wetness of my shirt against my chest.

I decided I had to settle this thing once and for all with a professional opinion, so I marched myself over to Psych Services after a particularly boring music history class. We'd been discussing castrati—it seemed appropriate somehow. I needed to know what exactly to do and thought that a professional shrink type might have an idea for me.

The Psych Services offices were in an old house on Jordan Avenue. It seemed like they'd tried to cheer up the dark and slightly creepy interior with lots of plants and a few bright prints. I might have run away but the receptionist practically jumped on me, inviting me to fill out a form and have a seat. Maybe they didn't get much business on a walk-in basis. Or possibly I just looked crazy. Anyway, I was the only customer there.

As it so happened, they *did* have someone who could see me right away. The woman in lime-green polyester stood up from the reception desk and led me down a dark hallway. The building was eerie to begin with, and for some reason they didn't light the narrow hallways, so the basic creepiness was multiplied tenfold. Ms. Lime Green Polyester took me to a doorway and knocked. Then she left me standing there, alone in the hallway.

The wooden door opened and a man with red hair, a red beard, and a red and green plaid shirt ushered me into a small room that had a table, two chairs, and a bare light bulb hanging from the ceiling. On the table were some pens and a yellow legal pad. That was IT. Not even a coffee mug. Not a painting on the wall. Not even a plant. I felt like I'd wandered into a basement interrogation room and that some CIA agent was about to pepper me with questions.

This is a very bad idea, I am thinking as The Man in Red gestures to one of the chairs at the table. I sit down, and a cassette tape recorder materializes from a briefcase I hadn't seen because it was so goddamn dim in there.

"My name is Stuart," Mr. Red Guy said from a mouth that was completely hidden by hair. I suppose it could be spelled "Stewart," but I didn't ask.

"My name is Lennie," I contributed. I looked at him pointedly, questioningly, if you get what I mean. I wanted him to know I was suspicious of a guy who would spend his time in a dim interrogation room on a college campus when he looked more like he should be a lumberjack in the Canadian Rockies. I knew I'd be seeing a shrink-in-training, but I couldn't figure out how he got through the casting call.

"What brings you here, Lennie?" Stuart asked. He turned on the tape recorder. I stared at it. I did not want it to tape me. He caught my glance. "Do you mind?" he asked.

"I sort of do," I told him. I thought maybe it best that no one at the university be able to have any knowledge of my possible lesbianness because I think it's still pretty much illegal everywhere. "Hmm, well, okay," he said. "My advisor likes us to record the sessions in case there is ever any question."

"Question about what?" I asked, knowing this would fluster him even more.

Which it did. He made a few sounds, sort of hem-hawing. He never answered me with words or even a look. The tape recorder went back in his bag.

He looked very unsure and I felt sorry for him. I briefly thought about making up a different reason for coming in, something not quite as complicated as being homosexual and not knowing exactly how to proceed with it. I didn't want to upset him. Maybe he would have been more comfortable with someone a little easier, like Jennifer from Jupiter.

Stuart/Stewart tapped a pencil on the table. Then he asked me again what brings me here. So I took a deep breath and told him that I was worried that I might be gay. This was not exactly the truth because I'm sure of it, but I wanted to go easy on the guy.

"Hmmm, what do you mean by worried?" He actually stroked his red beard.

What is there to further explain about the term "worried?" "Well, it's not exactly something I'd choose to be. I mean, look at the way things are for gay people in the world. Who the hell would want that? Wouldn't it just be easier for me to be with a man? My roommate has a serious boyfriend now and I'm eighteen and I think I should know by now which airline I'm flying for sure, if you know what I mean."

Stuart/Stewart did not know what to say. I could tell because his hands were shaking a little and he stopped making eye contact with me for a moment. He tried to regain his composure and said, after a few throat-clearings, "Well, has anything ever happened to you to make you think you weren't normal? Uh, er, in that way, I mean."

Oh, great. Professional confirmation that I am, most certainly, abnormal. OK, semi-professional confirmation. "What kinds of things?" I asked, innocently.

"A poor relationship with a male relative. A poor relationship with your father. Some sort of abuse at the hands of an older male."

Whoa. Uncle Andy on top of me, a gun, hitting, not being able to breathe, "Don't you EVER tell anyone or I'll do the same thing to your mother..." I was not about to tell Stuart/Stewart any of this. But I understood what he was getting at. I didn't say anything, not a word. Ice picks of fear started poking around in my gut.

"Because, uh, er, well, it can happen that an inappropriate sexual experience at an early age can skew one's healthy sexual orientation, you see." He still would not look at me.

"And what if everything was just fine, thank you, and I had a perfect childhood?" I decided to be defensive because I was NOT going to tell him about Andy. It had been buried long enough. I knew it was pretty pathological on some level, but could it have made me queer? I didn't see the connection. I did not *want* to see the connection.

Stuart/Stewart stifled a little laugh. "No one can possibly have a perfect childhood," he announced definitively.

"Mine was fine," I declared. I decided to get the hell out of there because this was not helping me and, in fact, it was scaring the shit out of me.

"Childhood aside," Stewart/Stuart was gaining some steam, "what evidence do you have that you have feelings for women?"

I wasn't going to give in to his questioning. I had a flash of Dr. Butler and her many teeth. Shit. I'd been exactly in this position before, hiding the same subject matter. "Uh, let's see—maybe the feelings themselves?" I said, feeling a little proud of my sarcasm.

"I see," he said, and touched his beard. More flashes of Andy, who did not have a beard but shared the same kind of icky energy.

"I think I'll just go, OK?" I stood up and started retreating toward the door. I didn't want to turn my back on him. I was freaking out completely with the epiphany that I was abnormal because of what had happened to me as a child.

"You still have twenty minutes left." He seemed way too relieved. I felt mad about that. He can drop this news on me and then be relieved that I want to bolt out the door? Isn't he supposed to help me out? Be professional? Be concerned about my emotional welfare?

"That's really OK. Maybe it's just a phase. We were just talking in the dorm one day," I lied. "I just haven't gone out with many men yet." I got out of there as fast as I could, ran past the lime green pantsuit woman and out the door and straight to the library. On the way there, I looked brazenly at every single woman I walked past. "I could love you," I said in my mind to each one of them as they walked by.

I went up into the stacks and climbed up some rickety stairs to a section of really old books. I slid down to the floor and started to tremble, letting the tears stream down my face. I don't want that to be the reason. I don't want what he did to me to have anything to do with who I fall in love with. I don't want Andy to be the reason my stomach does little flips when I see someone like 42 or the flute player from Argentina or even Audrey Fremont. When I melt because her lips are so soft that I want to cry. When I feel so full of passion and desire that I think I'll go crazy if I don't touch her. I don't want it to be wrong, pathological, evil, and all those other things that society thinks of gay people.

I was scared to look, but I went down to the card catalog and started searching. Homosexuality, causes. Nothing. A few religious diatribe books. Causes of lesbianism. Same thing. Lots of references for the Kinsey Institute. Which is on this very campus! An entire department for the research of human sexuality. Well. That sounded somewhat promising. I checked out *Sexual Behavior in the Human Female* and *Homosexualities: A Study of Diversity Among Men and Women*. I didn't even care that the checkout girl eyed me with glances I couldn't interpret. Maybe she thought I was a pervert. I tried to look very scholarly, but my knees were shaking. Maybe my hands were, too. I looked at them and wondered for a moment. They've never trembled when I play the piano. Not once in my memory. Do these hands belong to me? They felt foreign. They began to itch to get to the keyboard. And with that thought, the rest of me relaxed. No matter what, the piano was always there, waiting for me.

I was trying to get the full story of Herman out of Elly, but she was evading my direct questions. She was madly in love with him, that much was clear. She was telling me about *Harold in Italy* and *Les Troyens*, two huge Berlioz works that Herman thought needed revision.

Oh for Christ's sake, I was saying inside my own head. If this guy really was Berlioz, why wasn't he writing new music instead of revising old pieces that, incidentally, are excellent?

That's all Elly would say about him. She changed the subject and told me how worried she was about her comparative religion test. She took the class because she thought she knew everything about Catholicism and she wouldn't have to compare at least that religion. But she had a mean professor who seemed to like to torture the musicians in his class.

"Really fun," said Elly through the phone in the dark.

"Don't worry, you've never flunked anything in your life. So what else about this Herman guy?" I was baiting her. "Any undiscovered Berlioz manuscripts lying around?"

Elly was reticent. She didn't want to talk about him except in the most vague terms. "Lennie, don't make fun of him. He really believes it."

"But do you? I mean, really. How could he possibly prove something like that? Does he dress like Berlioz?" I added that, trying to be funny but actually being obnoxious.

A long silence. "I don't know if I really believe him. I think so."

"So are you having sex with him?"

"Lennie!"

"Well, are you?"

"Yes, of course."

"What do you mean, of course?"

"It's what you DO in relationships." As if I wouldn't know this or have any experience with it. I felt pissed at her for saying that. And then of course she had to turn it around to me so I finally told her about Timothy. I casually added in that this is how we both determined our gayness, by sleeping with each other. She didn't say anything, even about the harpsichord bench, which I actually think was really erotic.

"Do you have a problem with me being gay?" I finally asked the dark room. I was scared to hear the answer.

"I've known about it forever."

"That's not what I asked."

More silence. My stomach twisted. "I don't have a problem with it, Lennie," she finally said. "I just worry about you in the world. It's—well, it's not very friendly for you, you know."

"Yeah." It was not what I'd expected to hear. Tears welled up in my eyes.

"And you can't get married and I can't play at your wedding. That's the worst thing." I could hear Elly trying not to cry now. "I can't play some sappy thing or even some beautiful thing at your wedding because you aren't going to have one."

I'd never even thought about anything like a wedding. Me being married to anyone, man or woman. Flash of walking down the aisle with 42—this was not a bad image, really.

"Are you thinking of marrying Herman?" Well, I had to ask.

"No," Elly said immediately. "I'm a better violinist and I don't think that would work."

I was relieved. I let out a loud sigh.

"I miss you all the time," she said.

"I miss you, too. All the music around here and Gingold and Buswell and fifty thousand violinists all over the place and none of them are you." My throat got tight. I was going to cry.

"Yeah, the famous people. We have them, too. Did I tell you I met Isaac Stern? I was scared of him even though he was a lot shorter than I thought."

"Did you play for him?"

"No, just audited a master class. He was brutal."

"Yeah, they can be brutal, can't they?"

"Lennie, I think you could be famous. You have no idea how amazing a musician you are. I'm pretty good, but you—you have the thing it takes."

"You sound like Miss Ludmilla."

"Believe her."

Elly yawned and we hung up. I lay there and replayed a Beethoven Sonata in my head, the one I was working on for studio class. There were passages I didn't like, things I wished I could play better. It was OK for the most part, but the thing that was the most OK was that I was so sure of myself and my playing that I felt connected to—well, I don't know what. The cosmos, Joop might say. God, the nuns would tell me. Source, Timothy would add. Whatever it was, it was me and it was not me and the only way I could feel it was at the piano.

12

France

I don't know why we always kept the phone ringer on loud. So when it rang at 3:00 a.m., we both shot out of bed and fumbled around trying to grab it. Joop got there first, and when she picked up the receiver, I could hear whoever it was screaming in a tiny but powerful voice from all the way across the room.

"What? Who? STOP SCREAMING! I can't tell who you are!" Joop got very firm with the caller. Then she handed the phone to me. "I'm pretty sure it's Elly."

"Hello?" I said, my heart pounding. Was someone dead? Did she get a gig?

"LENNIE!!" She wailed. "MY LIFE IS OVER! MY CAREER IS RUINED! I'M JUST CALLING TO SAY GOODBYE BEFORE I KILL MYSELF!" Elly was crying and screaming, wailing, blubbering, and swearing along with a few other assorted noises.

"Tell her we're going to call the police and tell them she's threatening suicide and they will knock her door down and save her," Joop announced from her bed. She did not climb back under the covers. She was wide awake and obviously planning to coach me through this call.

I looked at her.

"That's what they do. You call the police and tell them someone is suicidal and then they go and save them. It doesn't matter that we're in Indiana and she's in New York. All it takes is a phone call." Joop recited this patiently, like she was telling me how to go about baking brownies.

I told Elly what Joop said, but it had no effect except to propel her into another round of unintelligible crying and babbling. I just let her go on and on, praying that she wouldn't hang up on me.

"It's going to be a hell of a bill," said Joop. The phone receiver was lying next to me, and we could both hear Elly clear as day. When I could recognize a few words, I picked up the phone and tried to get whatever the story was out of her.

"Herman," she started, but she was hyperventilating. Joop took the phone and instructed her to get a paper bag and breathe into it. Amazingly, she calmed down pretty quickly.

"Strictly an earth thing," Joop said. "Hyperventilating never happens on Jupiter because of the much more refined respiratory system which is not hooked into any emotional centers."

"Elly, you should move to Jupiter," I said to the phone.

"Maybe I should. Maybe I WILL." She started crying again.

"Can you tell me what happened?" I asked, gently as possible.

She blew her nose. "Did you just tell me to move to Jupiter?" she asked.

Joop laughed a silent laugh across the bed.

Deep breath in New York City. "Well, Herman promised me dinner at Windows on the World. We were going to celebrate the final concert. Lennie, *Capriccio Español*, I worked for months on the solos. It's *full* of violin solos."

"I know, Elly. I know." What did that son of a bitch do to her? Drug her ridiculously expensive meal? Lace it with Ex-Lax, like someone in the trumpet studio did before the orchestra auditions? I might have to kill Herman so he could come back as some other dead composer in his next Earth life. Or maybe he could come back as a maggot.

Another deep breath. "So, we had reservations early, as soon as they opened. Herman hired a limo, we got dressed up in our concert clothes, and we were going to have this fabulous dinner before the concert." Her voice caught here. "I'm never going out to dinner before a concert again in my entire life," she pronounced.

"That sounds like a good idea," I agreed.

"So, we each had a gin and tonic. It was early, so I thought one was OK."

"Elly, we're underage. How did you get served?"

The silence on the phone translated her reply, which was: "Are you kidding me? Have you ever heard of fake IDs and too much eyeliner?"

"Then we had some appetizers and he was telling me how much he was into me and how proud of me he was and what a great career I'm going to have. Then how scared he is to start going out on auditions, so scared that he might stay in school and do a masters program. He HAS to compose, he's so convinced about the Berlioz thing that it's interfering with his ability to live in the 20th century. He's convinced that he's a misunderstood genius, and he has to do something about it. He even started wearing those floppy bow ties like in the 19th Century. Then he finally started telling me that he should have been concertmaster of the orchestra, not me. That he resented me for winning the seat."

I looked over at Joop. She was listening intently to Elly, too.

"Even though he's so proud of you?" I asked.

"Yes, even though he's so proud of me. Proud to be with me." Elly was crying again. She went on in between sobs. "Then before I knew it, we were having wine with dinner, and then he ordered a bottle of champagne. I think I had kahlua and coffee for dessert. I don't remember dessert anymore. I don't remember the spectacular view. I don't remember worrying about how much I was drinking."

Uh-oh, I was thinking.

"But I do remember him telling me that since he's Berlioz and I'm Harriet Smithson, that he realized that he's still mad at me for something I said in 1835 and that I was going to have to pay for it."

That fucker. That fucker!

"So when we started to leave the restaurant, I could hardly stand up. I don't remember the limo ride back to Juilliard for the concert. I don't remember getting my violin out."

Fucker fucker fucker fucker. . .

"Lorin Maazel was the guest conductor. I do remember seeing him backstage and he looked really mad to me. I couldn't figure out why—he's such a nice man. I walked onstage to tune the orchestra. When I got to the podium my foot slipped and I ended up doing a complete split—right there in front of the orchestra and the audience and everything—and I almost dropped my violin but Herman helped me up. Then I asked for three—or maybe four—A's. The oboist was really pissed. At one point he refused to play another one. There was complete silence onstage and everyone stopped tuning. The principal cellist yelled at me to sit down. I couldn't figure out what the problem was. I think I was talking really loudly. And then I tried to conduct the orchestra with my bow!" Elly groaned after she said that. "Can you imagine what that must have looked like?"

I could always handle those leftover highballs better than Elly. She could sometimes be drunk on part of a beer. My heart ached to imagine her onstage at Lincoln Center, falling down drunk, waving her bow at the incredulous musicians.

"Then everything got really quiet and I started laughing and couldn't stop. But Mr. Maazel came out and we started the overture. Lennie, it was *Leonore #3*. I was playing it for you! The bad thing is that I said it out loud to the violin section just before the downbeat. 'This is for my friend Leonore.' Only I think I probably slurred my words. And I might have said it really loudly. More like I shouted it to all the violins. I'm playing Leonore Number Three for my friend Lennie! She's named for this overture, you know!"

"Thanks, " I said, imagining her doing a split right onstage. She must be very limber. And then speaking before the downbeat. It's unheard of. Not done, ever. "He didn't stop conducting?"

"No, he just glared at me and kept going. Except I couldn't even play!" What a surprise, I was thinking. "I was out of synch with everyone else's bowings and it was a terrible mess." Crying again. "Lennie, the stage manager came on right after the overture and pulled me offstage They weren't going to let me play the Rimsky-Korsakov. He said Mr. Maazel was furious. He and some other stagehand dragged me to a dressing room and made me sit there and drink a ton of coffee."

And this meant that all the violins would adjust forward, putting Herman in the concertmaster chair so that he would play the solo violin parts for *Cappricio Español.* Elly didn't have to explain that part to me. The asshole! I was right! He had to have been planning to sabotage her all along. He plotted and seduced her and made his move when the time was right.

"What else was on the concert?" I wondered.

"*Symphonie Fantastique* after intermission."

"THAT FUCKER!" Mr. Fake Berlioz wanted to seat himself in the concertmaster chair to play 'his' symphony. AND, he'd been practicing all the *Español* solos so that he could just slip right in there and play them perfectly. He would be the hero, filling in for the incapacitated, drunken concertmaster.

"Yeah," agreed Elly. "That fucker. Except I was the one that poured the alcohol down my own throat. He didn't do that, I did it myself."

"He knew exactly what he was doing. And he got what he wanted all along, right?""He got what he wanted. And I should have believed you. And now I'm going to probably be kicked out of school."

"You could come here," I said, a little too fast.

"I don't know what I'm going to do. I don't know how I could possibly walk down the hallway again. Everyone thinks I'm a complete fuck-up."

"Elly. You were set up. Sabotaged. Go talk to Mr. Maazel. Or whoever the orchestral studies director is. They'll understand. And maybe Herman will get disciplined."

Silence from the other end of the phone. "I've already decided. I'm going to take a bunch of auditions. There are auditions for orchestras all over the world every weekend here in the city. I'm getting out of here. I don't know where I'm going, but I can't stay here. Not after what happened and how stupid I was."

It was as if she hadn't really heard me. "Elly, you weren't—"

"It's OK, Lennie. I know what I have to do now. Thanks for talking to me." She started crying again and hung up, leaving me alone in the middle of the dark night. Joop had fallen asleep sitting up on her bed. I know she was trying to be helpful and vigilant, but she was snoring with her mouth hanging open. I didn't have the heart to wake her, so I tipped her over and she fell peacefully onto her pillow.

Elly called again while I was in the middle of studying for my music history exam. I was feeling particularly hostile towards Berlioz, even though I know Herman had made the whole thing up. I was certain that he was a lying sack of shit, as Aunt Liddy would say. I couldn't make myself get the least bit interested in the idée fixe in *Symphonie Fantastique*.

"Lennie! I got a gig! I'm going to be assistant concertmaster of the Sinfonia de Rennes! In France! I don't know exactly where Rennes is in France yet, but - France! Lennie!"

This was quite a contrast from our previous conversation. "How did—"

"I told you, I went to a bunch of auditions. Everyone auditions in New York. I tried out for Singapore, the Filarmonica de Caracas, some orchestra in Spain, and one in New Zealand. They just called me from France to offer me this job! And I'm going!"

"When?"

"Now! I can't believe I'm going to be living in Europe."

There was no mention of Herman. Of finishing school. Of other Juilliard friends. Something about the tension in Elly's voice made me not ask. She filled me in on some of the details, that the orchestra needed an emergency replacement and it was for assistant concertmaster. She had to leave immediately. She wasn't going to finish the semester. She apologized to Mr. Maazel, who was actually gracious and understanding. And she said Fuck You to Herman, who coolly ignored her in the lobby, surrounded by several other potential Harriet Smithsons.

"Elly, are you sure—"

She interrupted me. "Don't try to talk me out of this. You weren't there. You don't know how ashamed of myself I am. This is the only possible thing to do. I have to leave. Are you going to be happy for me or not?"

"What about Frank and Rosa?"

"What ABOUT them? This is not up to them."

I didn't want to ask really, but I wanted to know if they'd been in the audience to witness the drunken spectacle. I didn't think so because Frankie hadn't said anything about it to me.

"What does Mr. Bernhard think?"

"It's not up to him, either. I'm going and that's that. And I'm changing my name, too."

"To what?"

"I don't know yet."

I felt helpless. I couldn't fly out to New York. I had finals and juries and a competition in Chicago. "Elly, I'm scared for you."

"Don't be, Lennie. It's just France."

The summer loomed for me. Elly was gone, playing some summer festival in Belgium with her new orchestra. Joop was going to be interning at Arecibo in Puerto Rico, listening for signals of alien intelligence while working on her first symphony. Timothy was going to some early music festival in Oregon, and 42 won the audition for Spoleto. Not that we had official plans to spend any time together or anything, but I felt sort of wistful about her being in Europe along with Elly and I was staying behind.

Miss Ludmilla piled on the repertoire. She wanted me to learn *Rach #3*, the impossible concerto. So I got dutiful, working on it for hours every day, listening to recordings, studying and memorizing the part. I listened to everyone's recordings, André Watts, Isabella Boticelli, Miss Ludmilla, Byron Janis, even Vladimir Horowitz. They were all so different and so amazing. I was excited to create my own interpretation, which, at the moment, sounded like a combination of Ludmilla Michalowski and remnants of others. Learning the notes was the easy part. I got to the point where I could hear the orchestra accompanying me, every wind run, every lush string background. All the tutti passages. My phantom orchestra accompanied me all the time, into every practice room. I could hear every timbre, every nuance they played. Finding my own voice was the challenge.

Elly came up with the brilliant idea that I should visit her in Rennes after the tour. Since it was summer, the orchestra schedule was more erratic than during the regular season. We could see the sights of Paris, play chamber music with her friends, and sip French wine. I jumped at the chance, and Frankie bought me a plane ticket without batting an eye.

Elly was waiting at Charles DeGaulle airport, where she started screaming as soon as I stepped out of the jetway.

"I have missed you SO much! I have so much to tell you and show you. I can sort of speak French already. You look really GOOD!" We hugged and hugged and I cried because it was so wonderful to see her. And also because I felt scared of her in her new French attire, which consisted of the shortest skirt known to womankind and a tight, bosomy top.

She whisked me into the city and dragged me immediately to Notre Dame where we looked at all the statues and sculptures and saint relics until I almost passed out because I hadn't slept since leaving Bloomington twenty-seven hours earlier. I was refreshed by a baguette sandwich and some delicious French coffee, and then we talked about how Sister Regina would have a stroke if she saw us in Notre Dame without hats on. And with Elly practically naked, I thought to myself. Dear Lord Oh My Dear God.

We took the Metro to Gare du Nord and caught the train to Rennes.

"I have to tell you something before we get there," Elly said. I was trying hard to keep my eyes open with the rhythmic click-clacking of the train.

"You have not met the real Berlioz." That was a mean thing to say.

"No, Lennie. But I am fucking the conductor."

You know how people on TV or in the movies spit whatever they're drinking all over the place when they hear something shocking? Well, that's what I did right there on the train. Good thing it was only bottled water. Good thing only Elly and I occupied the four seats that were facing each other.

"You're WHAT?! Nevermind, I heard you. Don't say it again."

"OK." She crossed her arms and looked at me sort of defiantly. There were water spots all over her clothes, skimpy as they were.

"So. What should I say? That's great?"

"Say whatever you want. But don't judge me."

What has gotten into her? When have I ever judged her? I never even called Herman an asshole out loud to her. Ok, once. I told her this.

"He's fifty-seven."

"JESUS, Elly. What else?"

"He's famous. Do you want to know who he is?"

"I'm sure I'll find out soon enough." I got a clenched feeling in my belly, and wondered if this trip was a bad idea. I watched the French countryside whiz by, a chalet here and there, vineyards, quaint little towns. And then, quickly, Rennes, a bustling city that was full of centuries-old buildings. Elly shepherded me to her tiny apartment on Rue Victor Hugo, complete with pigeons roosting on the windowsills and a bidet in the bathroom.

Elly went to call the mysterious famous conductor, and I let myself feel awash in confusion and fear. Where did my friend go? She'd been in France less than six months. Where was our ease and sisterhood? Were we going to be casualties of growing up and growing apart? I felt like I didn't know her all of a sudden, didn't know what to say. We didn't even talk about music on the train ride, something that always connected us. I don't care that she's fucking some old conductor—it's weird, but she can do whatever she wants. Is that what's come between us? Who we sleep with?

I let myself fall asleep on a futon near the pigeon window. I didn't hear Elly leave, and when I woke up twelve hours later, there was a note on the table next to a bag of croissants and a little pile of francs so that I could buy coffee and take a taxi to the rehearsal hall. She spent the night with him, of course.

When I got there, the orchestra was on break. Elly ran over to me and hugged me, and I began to think that maybe my fears of the previous day were completely unfounded. I met the conductor, and he *was* famous. Jason Samuels, the dashing, not-quite-Leonard-Bernstein. He'd recorded with Miss Ludmilla, and was known best for his Strauss and Mahler. He globe-trotted, guest conducting all over the place, and had made quite a name for himself recording all sorts of repertoire with different orchestras and soloists. He was the second American to ever conduct the Vienna Philharmonic.

Elly introduced me to everyone in the orchestra. One of the horn players offered me the use of her piano for the time I was there. Her name was Patrice, and as soon as she made the offer, Elly pawned me off on her for the evening because she wanted to be with Maestro Jason.

Patrice didn't waste one second. We had dinner at a charming crépe restaurant where she had to order for me because the only word on the menu that I understood was "vin." And then she seduced me over dessert, a smooth molten chocolate dripping sensuous concoction. She reached across the table to dab at a drop of chocolate on my lip, and that, as they say, was *that*. We went back to her place in her toy car, some sort of Renault that only semi-comfortably seated two. As we drove, she pointed out landmarks in the city that was very beautiful and charming by twilight.

Patrice. Dark. Brown, sparkling eyes. A sumptuous mouth. Do all wind players have mouths like this? I thought of 42, who could be part Patrice. And her hands. Strong and intelligent looking, as though they gave many clues to the rest of her. She was, of course, French, from some little town on Ile de Ré. And she'd studied at the Paris Conservatory. She's been in the Sinfonia since graduating from the Conservatory. Did Elly know that Patrice was gay? Or was it some sort of fortuitous coincidence? Fate that we were thrown together? Maybe this fucking-the-conductor thing was just what we both needed.

None of the experimenting that happened with Audrey came close to my escapades with Patrice. She was smooth, seductive, sexy. That accent, my God, she spoke French to me and she could have been saying the grocery list and I would have melted at her feet. We spent the entire night naked, rolling and roiling in this lust I didn't know I possessed. Patrice laughed at me, saying something half French and half English about having just uncorked me like a fine bottle of champagne, which, of course she would know all about.

"How old are you?" I asked her. She seemed young but like she knew a lot. The French call it La G-Tache, for example, and I had no idea I had one until Patrice pointed it out to me, staring directly into my eyes while I experienced the most mind-blowing orgasm of my life, the first orgasm in the company of another human.

"Vingt-huit." Twenty-eight. Wow, an older woman. She knew everything about where to touch me, where to guide me to touch her. What to say, how to move. I wanted the night to last forever and felt angry when the dawn broke, spectacular as it was, soft light growing.

Patrice did have to practice her horn some because the orchestra was doing a Strauss festival with Maestro Jason, playing *Ein Heldenleben* and *Til Eulenspigel*. So I spent part of a day practicing *Rach #3*, and when I stopped to take a break there were three orchestra wind players sitting in the kitchen drinking wine with Patrice. They had been listening to me, and they all wanted to play chamber music. Within moments, we were reading through the Mozart *Quintet for Piano and Winds*.

Playing chamber music with Patrice was like having sex a different way, and by the time we were finished reading the Beethoven quintet for the same combination of instruments, I was ready to throw out the other three players and rip her clothes off.

"Je t'adore," she said to me, coming and coming. I felt like I'd stepped off a plane onto a new planet where my body didn't know any bounds of physical pleasure. It was so new and so exhilarating that I didn't see Elly for most of the first week I was there. She finally stormed into Patrice's apartment, where I'd stayed to practice during one of their orchestra rehearsals.

"You come to visit ME and you spend all of your time fucking someone!" She didn't even say hello to me. "What kind of friend does THAT?!" Elly was furious, her hair flying and her face crimson and angry.

"Excuse me, but practically the first thing you said to me when I got off the plane was that you were fucking the famous conductor. You made arrangements to get rid of me the second day I was here! So I guess that makes YOU a friend who would do that." I was so pissed that I was shaking while I yelled this at her.

"He's going to be leaving in a few days! This is the only time I have with him!" Elly spat back at me. "I thought maybe you'd UNDERSTAND."

"Well, I found someone who seems to be interested in spending time with me, which is more than I can say for you!" I was getting madder and madder. The argument was completely stupid and groundless and I wasn't going to let her win it.

"You're just being selfish like you always were." Elly crossed her arms and planted herself and I could see the defiant little kid in her. But the selfish comment was too much.

"WHAT?! Selfish? When the hell have I ever been selfish in our lives?"

"I got you your teacher. Where would you be if I hadn't gotten you in with Isabella? Studying nothing music with those two old biddies in Bedlam?"

"Elly, I have thanked you a thousand times for that. What the hell else could you possibly want from me?"

"We were supposed to go to school together. You could have just as great a teacher at Juilliard but no, you had to go to some farmland in the middle of nowhere."

"Elly! Ludmilla Michalowski! *Indiana*! I HAD to go there!"

"I needed you and you weren't there for me."

"I tried to warn you about that Herman asshole. You wouldn't listen."

"You didn't know a thing about him. He was sweet at first."

"He was a lying sack of shit." It felt good to say that out loud, thanks Aunt Liddy. "Berlioz?! How could you be so goddamn stupid and gullible?"

"Stupid and gullible? Look what you're doing! Fucking the female Cassanova of the orchestra! You're in line to have your heart broken, Lennie. You're the stupid and gullible one."

My jaw must have dropped open. Yes, I'm sure it did.

Elly was on a roll. "Yeah, you're supposed to be here visiting ME, but you're too interested in your lesbian sex fix that you're abandoning me. Again!"

That was mean. My lesbian sex fix? I could see Patrice looking in from the other room. I felt nauseated that she had to witness this.

"Why don't you just leave me alone? We can talk about this in the morning when we're calmer." My hands were shaking, along with my knees.

"FINE. I'll be at the patisserie on the corner at 8:00. If you're not there right at 8:00, I'll assume you don't give a shit about me and you can find your own way back to the States. I swear, if you don't show up I'll never speak to you again."

Fucking in the heat of anger and other assorted feelings can be a huge rush. Patrice and I went at it for the entire night. She was tireless, I was discovering that I was tireless, and I couldn't get enough of her. Or maybe I couldn't get enough of what we were doing.

"Are you going to break my heart?" I asked her.

"No, chérie, you are going to break mine," she said, and she looked sad.

"But you're the Cassanova of the orchestra."

Patrice laughed. "I think Elly talks about herself." God, that accent! "She has had every man of the brass section, every conductor, every friend of someone who visits. I am very far behind her in the conquests."

"Really?" So Elly is fucking everyone, not just the famous conductor? What the hell is she doing?

Of course I slept through my meeting with her at the patisserie. Of course she refused to speak to me in person or on the phone. At the orchestra concert that night, Elly showed up in Place de la Gare with my suitcase and made a huge display of dropping it at my feet before the concert began and then turning on her heel and stomping away from me. She did not say one word to me. Not one single syllable. She didn't meet my eye. It was familiar, that flounce that she did, but she'd never done it to me before. Only to her parents or an obnoxious guy. But now I had officially gotten it directed at me—the flounce—and I was too paralyzed to even call out after her.

I wanted to beg her to speak to me, beg her to please not let it end like this. I wanted to apologize to her, grovel to her, prostrate myself on the ground in front of her. But I couldn't move, and I was invisible to her. Non-existent. It was like she wiped me off the slate of her life, like I no longer took up any space anywhere near her.

That night they played *Liebestod* and the *Elgar Cello Concerto* (with Jaqueline Du Pré!) and *Sibelius 2*. The music sounded wrenching and full of grief. I felt like I was in the middle of the cliché: You look like you just lost your best friend. And I had. I watched her play. She was full of fire and determination. She looked like Elly but she didn't act or feel like Elly. And I was dead to her.

Patrice took me all the way to Paris in her miniscule Renault. It was a huge act of generosity because gas was so expensive and it was so far. And we had no idea if we'd ever see each other again. She had her job in the orchestra, even though she was afraid Elly would try to get her fired for being gay, and I worried about that, too. "It *is* France," Patrice rationalized. "The sex is not such a big deal." Coming to the States with me wasn't really an option. Me staying there was not even mentioned. And so we left things way up in the air when we parted at the terminal. She got out of the car and we embraced and kissed for a long time. No one gave us a second glance. I love France.

The plane took off and I could see all the famous icon spots as we flew over. "Au revoir, Eiffel Tower, Champs Elysses, Tulairries, Louvre, Rive Seine, Notre Dame. Au revoir, Elly. I hope I speak to you again someday, but I doubt that I ever will," I whispered to the window. We flew into the clouds after a few scenic moments. My heart felt hard, exhausted, sad.

I couldn't really picture it, life without Elly. It was like losing an appendage, a relative, my sister. I didn't know who I was without her. I wondered how I would explain this to Frankie so that she would understand. It was like breaking up our family. Like a divorce.

I stayed awake all the way across the ocean, through a screening of *A Star is Born* and then the strange loud quiet of the airplane, a peacefulness in spite of the constant hum of the engines. I had to wait two hours at JFK before I could hop a plane to Indianapolis and then a little prop jet to Bloomington. It was tornado season, and as the small plane was coming in for a landing, we zoomed back up into the air. The woman next to me threw up, the guy in front of me started to cry, and the pilot told us, in a shaky voice, that we were having trouble because we'd almost been taken down by a tornado tailwind. "Taken down?" Even after hearing this, I felt no fear, just a numbness around my heart, a strange hardness and a compete lack of fear. I wanted to be at the piano more than anything. Maybe there I would feel something.

I dumped my things in my room and went straight to the music building. I played every piece of music I had in me, starting with the Chopin ballades and the *Arabeske in C Minor*. Yes, it was there, a flood of fear and rage, starting near my heart and flying down my arms through my fingers. I just played and cried and wondered what the hell I would do without Elly. When I couldn't play anymore, I walked the circle of the music building, round and round.

Miss Ludmilla was in her studio. She often practiced late at night, and there were times I'd just sit on the floor outside her door and lose myself in whatever she was playing. It always had such powerful magic. Tonight she was playing Scriabin. I waited for the slightest pause and then knocked loudly on the door, which flew open immediately. She grabbed my arm and yanked me inside. I could hardly speak, my eyes were filling with tears.

Miss Ludmilla locked the door again and got out the vodka.

"We need to talk, yes?"

Miss Ludmilla took my hands in hers. She has never done such a thing before. Hands are off limits for shaking and even touching. But she grabbed mine and looked into my eyes, which were beginning to overflow.

"What is wrong, Lenyah?" Her face was full of concern.

"I don't know." And then I started to cry for real.

"Yes, you do know. There is something deep in you troubling you. A suffering," she said. "Always I have known this. And I would not ask but for you, I think it stops your music. For some people it makes their music. For you, is like damper pedal. Now, you either tell this to me in words, or you scream or you write on paper or you have tantrum. But you let it out or it will stop your music and your love life and you will burn out and dry up, become prune of young woman and then you might as well be dead." Might as *vell* be dead. Miss Ludmilla let go of my hands and reached over to pick up her shot glass. She sipped her vodka demurely. I'd never seen her sip it before, she usually threw back shots like Ivan the Terrible or Dr. Zhivago or someone like that. She sat on the couch and looked at me. This was the longest uninterrupted soliloquy that I had heard her deliver in the whole time I'd been studying with her.

"Do not keep things locked up in body. Is not good for you or your music," was her coda.

So I told her. Everything. It came out in a jumble. I told her about leaving Patrice in France. About me being a—what do I call me now? A lesbian? About Elly dumping my things at the concert in front of the whole orchestra. Then about my father mocking and disdaining me. And then, after a huge breath—all about Andy. When I was done, I noticed that more than half the bottle of Stoly was gone, my face was on fire, my mouth was numb, and tears were streaming down my face.

Miss Ludmilla put her arms around me and we both stumbled over to the piano bench.

"Now," she whispered to my drunken head. "Now, you must play.

Play what you just tell to me. All of it."

My hands hit the keyboard, violently at first, as if I could discharge a lifetime of pent-up anger and grief in a few chords. I played Scriabin, and then Prokofiev, the third sonata. And then I fell into a Mozart sonata, number 12, the one with the backwards circle of fifths progression in the middle, a minor circle from C to F to Bb to Eb to Ab and then I strangely modulated from there to the Chopin Eb Nocturne. Gentle, pastoral, the calm after the storm. Landing the plane safely after the tailwind. I played *me*, and she listened and didn't say a word.

I woke up the next morning on Miss Ludmilla's couch. She had covered me with a soft cashmere blanket that smelled delicious, like her. There was a note on the piano in her beautiful script: "Lennie— you are free now. Is time to soar. L."

Oh God, she didn't hate me. She didn't think I was crazy. She covered me with a blanket. Before I even peed, I went to the piano and played a Chopin nocturne. Something felt different, the weight of my hands. The weight of my soul.

13

Kinsey

Joop found us an apartment down on Henderson. It was good to get out of the dorm, and I didn't even care that there was a giant hanging mobile of the solar system in the living room. We scrounged an old baby grand that had been passed down through generations of grad students. It had lived in our complex for at least a decade, being moved from apartment to apartment by the management who rents exclusively to music students.

We brought our first load of groceries home from the Safeway and bumped into each other in the tiny kitchen, trying to figure out where to put everything. I put a recording of Ashkenazy on our little stereo, mostly to drown out the flute player next door who was practicing trills. It sounded like a flock of birds on speed.

"Lennie, you're going to have to get over this. You have a lot to do this year," Joop said.

I was pouting because yet another letter to Elly had been returned. I hadn't heard a word from Patrice and figured that I had just been a notch on her bedpost. And 42 wasn't anywhere and I couldn't find out where she went. Was she still in school? Did she get a gig? Did she ever come back from Italy?

"Yeah. Right." I said. I was feeling listless. My practicing was flat. I couldn't figure out what else was wrong besides the Elly Issue. OK, and the Patrice Issue. "Get over what? The fact that I don't know who I am and no one seems to love me?"

"You know who you are. You just can't accept it."

"So? Do you have a brilliant suggestion?"

"As a matter of fact, I do," Joop said. She was sitting at our thrift shop dining room table with manuscript paper strewn all about.

"You do?"

"Yes. Come on." She carefully capped her special pen and dragged me out the door. We headed down Third Street to campus and strolled into Morrison Hall.

"What are we doing here?" I had been in very few of the campus buildings except the music ones. Morrison seemed to be one where academic classes occurred. It felt weird to me. Chalkboards and books and scholarly looking people. No music in the air.

Joop tugged me along and we entered a nondescript office. There was a plump, secretaryish looking woman behind the desk. She could have been my mom's age, probably older. She was wearing pink polyester.

"May I help you?" she asked. It sounded like "M'elp you?"

"Yes," Joop replied. "To your knowledge, is there anything wrong with being gay?"

"JOOP!" What the hell? I looked to the plump woman and she was smiling. I was wondering what she might know about being gay anyway. "Joop!" I tried again, whispering really loudly. "What are you doing?"

The plump woman smiled at us. "Why, absolutely not, of course. There are certainly plenty of religious protestations to homosexuality, but there is no conclusive evidence that it is deviant. In fact, the American Psychiatric Association has recently dropped homosexuality from its list of disorders." She smiled a yellow-toothed smile, and I got the impression that she could have been talking about vacuum cleaners or potting soil, she was that nonchalant.

"See? Now can you get over it?" Joop said to me.

I stammered, too surprised to know what to say. Or ask. I looked around the office for a quick escape and then spied the sign over the door that said "Institute for Sex Research." We were standing in the foyer of the Kinsey Institute. I felt relieved because for a moment it seemed as if Joop had shoved me into the first occupied office she saw and asked the receptionist this outrageous question about being gay.

"Ah, I see," the woman said. Excuse me, but she looked like she should be a waitress or a mother or something, not a sex researcher. "I see what might be happening here."

"You do?" Joop said.

"You—" she pointed at me, "are wondering if you're gay?"

"Not exactly," Joop answered for me. Fine. I just stood there. I couldn't believe this was happening. "She IS gay, but thinks something is wrong with that, so she's moping around and wallowing in self-deprecation. She's a brilliant pianist, and this is getting in the way of her music. Is that about right, Lennie?"

More stammering.

"Come on back," said the Pink Polyester. C'mon bay-ak.

I wanted to flee, but Joop grabbed my shirt. We were escorted into an inner office. There was a very attractive, intellectual-looking, athletic woman sitting at a desk in front of a stack of files. Across from her was a guy who appeared to be wearing a touch of makeup. He also wore a tie and a small stud in his left ear.

"This is Amy and this is Dustin," the waitress said, gesturing to them. "I'm sure they can answer any questions you might have." She smiled again and went back to her reception post.

Joop asked them the same question she asked Pink Polyester—if there was anything wrong with being gay. Dustin laughed and Amy furrowed her brow as though she'd never heard such a thing. She cocked her head and looked like a dog trying to understand human English.

"See?!" said Joop. "When will you get it?" I met her eye, and she looked so frustrated and so full of concern for me that the giant brick wall inside me started to crumble a little.

Dustin and Amy rattled off a few facts and information that I'd never heard before, like the Kinsey scale of sexuality. Joop was a one and I was a five. No big deal, according to our tour guides. I felt lighter, like I might be able to possibly begin to maybe believe this stuff. But I had to ask one last thing. The main thing. The deciding factor.

I sucked in a big breath. "OK. So if I had—um, an unfortunate sexual experience as a child, is that what made me gay?"

Amy got that puzzled puppy look again. "Do you mean that you were sexually abused as a child?" Nothing like getting right to the point.

Joop looked at me with such love I thought she might cry.

"Yes, I guess that's what you would call it." Images of Andy that I'd worked so hard to push away flew into my field of vision. For the second time in as many months, I was saying it out loud to someone.

Dustin jumped in. "No. Unequivocally no. That doesn't make you gay. That just means you had a sicko adult in your life."

"Wherever did you get an idea like that?" Amy asked. So I told her about Stuart/Stewart at Psych Services. She wrote something down on a notepad. She looked pissed.

"Well, I'm going to apologize on behalf of the profession. That's just wrong. Incorrect. Unfortunate misinformation. Basically, a nasty lie."

They talked to us for an hour. I wondered about reimbursing them for all the free advice. "You walking out of here and feeling like a normal person is all we need," Dustin said.

"And comp tickets for your entire career," added Amy.

"Are you guys going to be shrinks?" asked Joop.

"Actually, yes," answered Amy.

"Do you talk to anyone who wanders in here?"

"Not that many do. But yes."

"Cool."

Joop and I went over to the music school and found a room with two pianos. We romped through some Mozart and then improvised something that Ferrante & Teischer might play, echoes of "Born Free" and "Love is Blue." I was starting to feel giddy, like I didn't know what to do with this new and unexpected freedom in my psyche. A second, deeper level of freedom, on the heels of my cathartic night in Miss Ludmilla's studio.

"I can't even *pretend* to play with you, you're so beyond my league," said Joop. She looked wistful. "I'm giving up. It's like trying to play tennis with Martina."

"Well, I've never composed anything." I tried.

"Shut up and play *Rach 3* for me," she commanded.

I happily blasted through the beginning of the first movement.

"Holy shit," said Joop. "You're on fire. You're a queer on fire."

She pulled out a joint and lit it, the flame of the lighter illustrating her point in miniature.

Miss Ludmilla ordered me to enter the concerto competition. This was highly unheard of because the unspoken rule of the contest is that it's for grad students only. It was more than highly unusual that an undergrad even enter—you have to be nominated by your teacher. Winning would be impossible. But that is exactly what I did. I won. I blew away all of the violinists and cellists and pianists and one lone flutist. I played the *Rach 3*, after working on it incessantly after France. I had a connection with the piece itself and I practiced it relentlessly. I had to play parts of it for every studio class, and my classmates started realizing that something was up with it. No one could learn it that fast, they said.

After I won, there was whispering in the halls when I walked by. The piano grad students, who normally wouldn't condescend to speak to a sophomore, became ingratiating. There was always someone lurking outside my practice room. And when I opened the door to leave, at least six people scattered like roaches do when you turn the light on.

"Lennie! I knew you could do it! I never had any doubts!" Frankie screamed into the phone. My parents were driving all the way from East Bedford to Bloomington. The prize for winning the concerto competition was $1000, a performance with the IU Philharmonic, another with the Indianapolis Symphony, and professional representation for a year. I was going to get gigs with orchestras, play recitals, and try to build a career for myself.

Before the first rehearsal with the orchestra, the piano studio threw a dinner for me at Miss Ludmilla's house. Someone made pasta with marinara sauce, known to be a staple of mine. What I didn't know was just how easy and clever it would be for someone to lace my portion of the sauce with a smattering of angel dust until - I sat down at the piano and watched the keys swim up to meet my eyes. The orchestra started playing and the music made absolutely no sense to my brain. It was as if they were playing in an entirely different tonal system, one full of quarter and micro tones. And then the piano took off and started to fly through the musicians; I had to grab onto the keyboard to keep from falling off the bench. We were parting a sea of bows and bells and music stands. I was flying above them and between them, and I could read everyone's part at once.

I think I was playing, but maybe I was singing. Or both?

An ocean of color danced in my eyelids. I watched the notes on the page in Technicolor, even though there was no printed music in front of me. I became the music, it became me.I looked up at the ceiling. There were notes up there, too.

I could see Ludmilla gesturing in the back of the hall. When she waved her arms, trails of light decorated the air. She ran to the stage when the orchestra took a break.

"What! What the hell? Len-yah! What the hell you are doing?! You don't sound exactly like shit, more like lunatic! WHAT THE HELL?!" Ludmilla had on some sort of billowy jacket that floated through the air and surrounded her like a violet aura. Her hair was wild. Her eyes were huge. She looked absolutely gorgeous to me. I was so in love with her and I told her this as I clapped my arms around her and held her tight. She had to push me away. She dragged me off the stage and stared into my highly dilated pupils "What!? You are high? You are drunk? What kind drugs you are take?"

Drugs? I didn't take any! And how I was feeling was—well, really, exceptionally, strangely—high. And drunk. And something else I couldn't identify. But I couldn't be, I wasn't. I had an important rehearsal. I'd never do something so irresponsible, especially when the piano was involved. But I was hallucinating, for God's sake.

I smiled at Miss Ludmilla and told her she looked beautiful. She was surrounded by unearthly, swirling colors. I was feeling really, really, euphoric. I wanted to kiss her. I wanted to kiss everybody.

"Len-yah – I am going to slap you! Len-yah! Wake up!" She was holding on to my shoulders, yelling into my face. Through my stupor, I realized that she looked scared to death. That made me want to cry.

"I demand to know! What happen? What kind drugs you take before rehearsal?"

"No drugs!" I insisted. My face felt droopy and I couldn't feel my mouth or focus my eyes. "I wouldn't even take beta blockers," I told her. "I would not take an aspirin! A Tylenol!"

Joop materialized and grabbed my arm. The next thing I knew, I was in Miss Ludmilla's studio, and the two of them pushed me down on the couch. They fed me coffee and made me drink a lot of water. For the second time, I spent the night on her couch, but this time she stayed with me all night. So did Joop. By the morning, they had it figured out.

While I hallucinated a bit more and then slept it off, Ludmilla dragged in every one of her students and interrogated them, KGB style. There was a shakeup in the piano studio and the two Rottweiler seniors were sent packing. She got the Rottweilers to produce the drugs and gave them the choice of leaving school or getting arrested. They left. She called the cops anyway.

I was devastated that someone would do such a thing to me.

"Lenyah, do not take this so personal. They are so jealous they can't play like you, so they do this. Small people. Give to them no mind." She was livid, and she was mortified by something like this happening in her family of students. Ludmilla alternately lectured me and comforted me. She was furious but also sad that two of them could have stooped so low.

"Good riddance," Ludmilla said. "They kiss careers goodbye."

The second—and final—rehearsal went much better. The conductor was a guest, not a regular faculty member. He was French, Jean-Pierre Something-or-other, and I noticed that the two violists right in front of him were focused on his—well—his package and not the music at all. Monsieur Jean-Pierre sat on a stool to rehearse, therefore displaying his ample crotch to the fascinated violists, who whispered to each other. Whisper, stare, whisper stare. Smile.

No one said anything about my drugged version of *Rach 3*. But it made the student newspaper because of the expulsions. The news had flown around the music school at lightning speed, and the scandal centered on my assailants and not me. I got a lot of sympathy for playing through a drug haze and got something of a reputation as a warrior, someone who could play under any conditions and not fall apart. The stories that went around had me taking an LSD trip, being poisoned with arsenic, or eating a whole pound of marijuana.

"That would have been fatal," Joop told me, folding up the IU student paper. "Besides, eating pot doesn't give you the same result as inhaling it. Your saboteurs chose exactly the right substance to effectively compromise your playing."

Maestro Jean-Pierre was kind to me. I felt a little bad for having the mean thought that of course Elly had fucked him somewhere along the way in France or else she would for sure if she ever crossed his path. He took my tempos, dragged the orchestra along, rubato-ed beautifully, giving me lots of space for entrances. There's a moment a few minutes into the first movement when I dialogue with the oboes, and I took my eyes away from the keyboard long enough to glance at the principal player. My God, 42! I hadn't spotted her the night of my drug trip.

Our eyes met for a nanosecond above the running thirds, and either she sent me a spark or vice-versa. But there it was, our timbres intermingling, and in the middle of this wild concerto I wondered what it might be like to lock lips with an oboist, her in particular. It was a fleeting thought—I had to keep my concentration. But later that night, trying to come down from the rush of playing that piece with a real, live orchestra, I thought about it again. And again. And the next day, I lurked around the oboe studio, hoping to catch a glimpse of her. Or something.

I got to the hall early. The tuner was just leaving. It was the old guy, the head piano tech. Mr. LeFavre. He stopped me as I walked up to the Steinway.

I had never heard him utter a word to a student before. He usually only spoke to the famous piano faculty, and it was unheard of for him to tune for a student performance.

"I've been here a long time, Miss Kuklinski."

"Yes, sir," I replied. I almost said "Yes, Father," out of habit but caught myself.

"I have heard many a piano player in my time. I have worked on many an instrument, and believe me, I can tell who plays which piano, and who knows how to play."

I looked at him. I'd never thought about that before, that inside the piano there is evidence of who's been there.

"You, miss, are the real thing. You might as well plan on doing nothing else in your life."

"I—uh—I'm—"

"I was in the audience for the competition. I'm honored to have met you." He patted me on the arm, the exact thing that Miss Ludmilla does because of the no-hands thing. And then he walked offstage.

I sat down at the Steinway and warmed up with scales and Czerny, thinking about what he said. I had no plans for what to do with my life and would have been embarrassed to tell him that. I had dreams of being onstage, yes. But they were distant, hazy. And I realized that I'd been afraid to imagine a life of performing because—well—who really gets to do that?

Someone came and told me I'd need to go to a dressing room because the house was about to open. Instead, I stood in the wings and watched the seats fill up. The piano grad students all sat together in the front right next to the keyboard, so I could see them all lined up, ready to tear apart my performance.

Backstage, Frankie tiptoed over and adjusted my girl tux. That's what she called it, a beautiful black suit she purchased at Macy's in New York City especially for this concert. I was about to be something of a scandal because women just don't wear pants to perform. Frankie thought it was just fine to buck the system, and she made a special trip to Manhattan just for me. She didn't say a thing to me about Elly, which I appreciated. I know she saw her in New York. I could have asked. I didn't. She kissed me on the cheek and went to find her seat.

"I'm so proud of you," she tossed over her shoulder as she left. I know she didn't face me to say it because she was already crying.

"I love you, too," I said to her back.

Maestro Jean-Pierre escorted me out after the overture to some tepid applause. I sat down at the piano and everything else fell away— the grad students, the drugged pasta sauce, the fact that my father hadn't spoken one word to me since arriving in town. I was dimly aware of Joop sitting next to my mom. And then Maestro Jean-Pierre looking to me for the signal to begin and me giving it and hearing the strings and clarinet for the two bars before my entrance, that beautiful melody that happens before the acrobatics begin. I was transfixed and completely absorbed in the music. Gone, and I didn't know where I was until the second movement started and I heard 42's stunning oboe solo. Monsieur Jean-Pierre waved his body around on the podium with the lush strains, and I had to focus myself on where we were in the music so I wouldn't forget my entrance.

The third movement was fast, but it felt good as all the notes fell into place, exactly where they belonged. I felt the little glissando startle the front row grad students. When the brass came in, the energy built and built, and we played off each other, the orchestra and I, and it was like a great train chugging along, daring anyone to get in the way. Even in the unlikely middle section, where the meter gets strange and the running thirds don't seem to match what's underneath at times; even there it was perfectly synched. We pressed on, the momentum of the piece pushing us all toward the climactic ending, not really faster but with more intensity than at the rehearsal. A huge swell, another, the final bars, the final chords, and the Maestro grabbed me off the bench and swooped my arm into the air like a prizefighter and the audience was on their feet. Even the grad students! Bravos, whistling, clapping. Someone ran out with flowers, Miss Ludmilla appeared from the back of the hall, walking down the aisle toward me, people looking at her, applauding me. I came out for four, maybe five bows. The last time, the Maestro made me sit down and play an encore.

"This is what you DO!" he instructed me, so I played the first thing that came to mind which was a *Papillons,* and there was a hush and then more applause when I finished. By the time I got backstage, I was floating somewhere north of my head, watching all sorts of people congratulate my body. Hugs, pats on the back, smiling.

My parents were suddenly there, my father tight-lipped, exactly like he was after my very first recital and the Young Artists concert, except this time I was a big competition winner, and I'd just played one of the most difficult concertos in the repertory and played it well, if I do say so myself. He couldn't even bring himself to say one word. So we stood around tensely while I got congratulated by various faculty and interviewed by reporters from the student paper and the Bloomington paper and even a guy from Indianapolis. He said, "Your parents must be very proud," and Frankie exclaimed that she was, and I saw her kick my father in the shin and take his arm. "We are extremely proud," she said, and my father managed a tight smile and still didn't say a word.

Miss Ludmilla had a little reception after the concert, and after my parents left I spotted 42 hanging around in a corner. After being congratulated for two solid hours, I'd had enough and I asked her if she wanted to play that Françaix piece.

"Right now?" She was incredulous. So was I. But I wanted to play more music.

"Right now." I was adrenalized and feeling brazen. In my mind, asking her to play music was the same thing as asking her if she wanted to have sex.

She said yes. So we trooped up to my favorite Steinway room in our concert clothes. She handed me the piano part.

"I've been carrying this around with me for about a year, just in case you ever wanted to play it," she confessed. This elevated my pulse a bit.

I knew I would get my fantasy wish to kiss an oboist. I knew it would happen after we played music together. I knew Joop would give me plenty of space back at the apartment, I knew Frankie and Ted were leaving at the crack of dawn and I'd already said my goodbyes. Well, one goodbye. So while 42 messed around with her reeds or whatever it is that they do to them, I sat on the piano bench and planned our romance. It was going to be a hot one.

Her first note sent a shiver through me. She had a gorgeous, dark, and penetrating sound that vibrated all the way to my heart. The first movement of the piece was slow and beautiful, and 42 gazed at me as she played. I couldn't meet her eyes because I had to read the billions of notes splayed out on the page, but I could feel her watching me. I knew she was a great player because of the Rachmaninoff, but I didn't know if we'd fit together musically. My fears were unfounded because I could feel everything about her—music pouring out of her and traveling the airwaves to me.

When we finished the last movement, I said the most cliché thing without even realizing it. "You must have really great chops." Oh God, really. I really said it.

42 laughed. And replied in the only possible way: "Want to find out?"

14

Bedlam

I was having one of those lessons where Miss Ludmilla wanted to talk and plan more than play the piano. All of a sudden I had a recital opportunity in Cincinnati and a performance of the Beethoven *Choral Fantasy* with the Evansville Phil. She wanted me to take every gig that came my way. "Until you get establish, and the Cliburn will help."

The Van Cliburn Competition. I have a year to get ready.

My gaze was drawn to the window and I spied none other than Leonard Bernstein strolling across the parking lot toward the music building. It was like a press photo come to life, Lenny with a big smile and a crowd of fans around him. It was pretty common to see celebrities all over the place around the music school, but seeing him in particular unleashed something stuffed deep inside me. Sudden memories of being little and seeing him on TV. Sadness, grief over my lost friendship with Elly. Thrill to see him. Sadness about my absent, sullen father who took me to the Carnegie Hall concert all those years ago and couldn't even say one syllable to me after the Rachmaninoff. The wonder of now studying with Ludmilla Michalowski and living the dream that started all those years ago. Watching the real, live Lenny come toward the building felt like coming full circle.

Miss Ludmilla followed my eyes out the window. She ran to her studio door and poked her head out. "Maestro!" she called.

Holy shit. She was beckoning to him. And he sauntered over, flanked by half a dozen adoring young men. Wow, he was amazingly handsome up close.

She kissed him once on each cheek. He smiled broadly. "I want you to meet my student. Lenny – Lennie!" Len-yah, Len-yah! She grabbed his hand, grabbed my hand, and clasped them together in a handshake. The hand embargo was off! The real Lenny had a funny, warm smile.

Ted would have shit his pants to see this.

Ugh, punched-in-the-stomach sadness . . .

"Glad to meet you, Lennie," he said, laughing.

I mumbled a few things about being honored to meet him, and then Miss Ludmilla launched into the story of how I'd been in the audience when I was seven to see her first performance with the New York Phil. Lenny laughed more, recalling something funny about that concert set. He actually remembered what was on the program: Shostakovich, Rachmaninoff, and Mussorgsky-Ravel. And the dress Miss Ludmilla wore. (Who could forget that, even more than a decade later?) And then he made himself comfortable on the couch and instructed me to sit down at the piano and play him something.

I hesitated for the slightest moment until I felt Miss Ludmilla, standing right behind me, poke me gently in the back.

It felt like an audience with the Pope or something. Dreamlike. I sat down on the familiar bench, looked at the familiar keys. Touched them. And then my fingers started to play the Scarlatti *E Major K531 Sonata*. It's such a simple piece, no pyrotechnics, but one of the most beautiful, effortless, evocative pieces I knew. I just played it without thinking. Cascading harmonies, like a harp. Triplets everywhere. The piece doesn't really belong on the modern piano, but we all play it anyway because—well, we can and because we can't resist. And

Horowitz plays it all the time. That's saying something.

The real Lenny looked pensive, like he wanted to jump on the piano and play, too.

"OK, I'm interested. Play something else!"

This time my hands chose the Chopin *G Minor Ballade*.

He listened and traded a look with Miss Ludmilla, and all the handsome young students held their collective breath—I could feel it—and then out of the blue he invited me to come to Tanglewood sometime. "Maybe play a little something with the student orchestra. How about the *Schumann Concerto*?" Just like that. "You can take a few lessons with Murray." Perhia! "Or—well, I think Leon might be around this summer, or Alicia." Fleisher! de la Rocha! "You wouldn't mind, would you, Ludmilla?"

"But of course not, dahlings. Lenyah can use new perspective for summer learning." Miss Ludamilla, always gracious. She would tell me later if this was not the truth. She would forbid me from working with someone she disapproved of. Her ego never entered the picture—she wanted the best for her students and I knew this without a doubt.

What do you say to Leonard Bernstein besides "Yes!" Thank you is what I added. Things like this don't happen to people. Students. Me. Or maybe they do?

I couldn't wait to race to the phone to call Elly, we'd talked about moments like this for years. And then my heart crumpled. There would be no calling Elly.

Then Mr. Maestro Bernstein sat down at the other piano and played with me through part of the four-hand version of *Candide* –I swear, he made music just by being in the same room with a piano. When he played, it was magic. I tried to absorb every note of it, everything pouring out of him. He seemed extra-human to me, someone so very evolved and I made a mental note ask Joop about it. She might have a theory as to Leonard Bernstein's cosmic origin.

He left amid handshakes and many smiles. He promised me that someone would contact me about Tanglewood. I had just fucking played the piano for Leonard God Bernstein and gotten myself invited to Tanglewood. Holy shit!

"Did he really mean that?" I asked Miss Ludmilla, who nodded yes.

"Good for you, Lenyah, good for you!"

"Did he really just ask me—"

"Lenyah! Start to think more of yourself!" Miss Ludmilla yelled this at me. "Accept what is happen to you in your life! Alright?!" She flipped her billowy jacket around, irritated. "I am losing patience if you are not thinking highly of yourself! Enough already!"

I had no idea what to say.

"Listen to me! Your father, he is not God! Stop listenting to him in your head!"

Then she made me sit down on the spot and read through the *Schumann Concerto*. She took it apart measure by measure and when we were finished with that, she went to the other piano and pounded out the orchestra reduction while I played the solo part again. She was ruthless—and fantastic.

All the while I was thinking about what she'd said about my father. I felt small jolts of electricity through my hands, like something was getting disconnected.

42 was lurking outside the studio door when I finally emerged. I was so glad to see her.

"You're going to be famous," she said.

I told her about Tangelwood and what had just happened with Maestro Bernstein.

"See? I told you." She was smiling so sweetly at me. "Lennie! I'm going to Tanglewood, too! I'm going to study with Gomberg, and I'll be playing in the student orchestra!"

We both jumped up and down like little kids. A couple of opera singers were walking by at that moment and whispered something to each other. But we just kept jumping and jumping, like nothing else in the world mattered except being very, very happy.

Frankie urged me to stop for a few days in Bedlam—oh, I mean East Bedford—before heading up to Tanglewood. I hadn't been home in ages, so I went—just for her. Ted and I were pretty much just not speaking anymore, which was fine with me. I couldn't identify one specific reason for the ice, but I figured it was because I wasn't absorbing any of his criticism anymore. I knew it was all bullshit, but why he'd continue it when I'd had so many successes, I couldn't figure out. So I just ignored him and he ignored me. And with Miss Ludmilla's coaching, I could withstand his glares.

"He always wanted you to be successful, and now that it's really happening, he can't stand it," Frankie told me. She was standing in the kitchen in a suit and pantyhose, the whole deal. No more scrubs. My mother was now on the faculty at the nursing school. She was in line to be the dean, too.

"He does the same thing to you, doesn't he?" I asked. There had been noticeable frostiness between my parents since the concerto competition.

"Yes, he does, especially now that I make more money than he does."

I wanted to ask Frankie why she stayed with him, but it didn't feel like the right time. Although, when would the right time be?

Rosa was going to be hanging out with Frankie for the evening, their Friday night ritual still intact, and I wanted to give them a little space. I didn't want to have to talk about Elly and what happened in France, so I left and wandered down to the annual East Bedford Arts Fest. I guess I really wanted to give me space. I walked the few blocks downtown and felt as though I were visiting another country. Or planet. It looked familiar, but in a *Twilight Zone* sort of way.

Main Street was lined with booths and vendors, artwork hanging and displayed everywhere. And on every street corner, there was some sort of music going on: duos, trios, rock bands, polka bands, and sometimes just a lone guitarist singing with a warbly voice. And there they were: The Continentals. They were playing on the main stage to a crowd of mostly older people. I stood rooted to a spot on the pavement, remembering how I thought their music was such magic when I was little. I wandered away while they were in the midst of "The Chicken Dance," played exactly the same way that they had always played it, except now there was a woman dressed up in a chicken outfit leading about four hundred people in the chicken motions. Sigh.

Up near the Bank of Bedford, there was an interesting duo of oboe and guitar. The timbre made me think of 42, so I sat down under a tree, closed my eyes, and listened for a while. They played some sweet tunes with a modal tinge. I started thinking of Tanglewood and my heart beat a little faster with that excitement. I'm going to be playing with Leonard Bernstein, holy SHIT! I closed my eyes and saw the Shed, heard the orchestra, played the *Schumann Concerto* in my mind, which clashed a bit with the live music that was happening just a few feet away.

"Lennie," a voice somewhere above my head said. I opened my eyes and looked directly into Elly's. I scrambled to my feet.

"My God. Elly?" As if I didn't know exactly who she was.

"Lennie," she said again. "What the hell are you doing here?"

"Well—what the hell are *you* doing here?" We stood there looking at each other. I wanted to grab her and hug her, but I was afraid she would stop speaking to me again and we'd only just started five seconds before.

"The orchestra is off for six weeks. I was going to surprise you at Tanglewood."

"WHAT?! You were? I thought you weren't speaking to me. Ever again in our lives"

"I wasn't. I was so furious with you that I wasn't ever going to even *look* at you again. Ever. Only I realized that it wasn't you I was furious at. And then I realized what a selfish bitch I was when you were there. I realized about a million other things, too."

She grabbed me and we hugged and cried for a really long time. We sank down to the ground and proceeded to catch up on a year's worth of each other's lives. There she was, in the flesh, right in front of me. She looked great. She looked like herself. No more slut clothes. Her eyes met mine, no looking off into the distance for something, someone.

The oboe and guitar duo packed up and were replaced by a trombone quartet. The trombones began with an arrangement of "Mrs. Robinson." Yikes. It was not difficult to drift away from that. Elly and I strolled around the booths on Main Street, arm in arm. We eventually found ourselves near the polka tent where The Continentals were still onstage.

"Did you know they were playing tonight?" she asked me.

"Yes. I was here earlier and experienced 'The Chicken Dance.'"

"Ah. 'The Chicken Dance.' They play it every hour on the hour, did you know that?"

I didn't know. How weird and sad, I was thinking.

We stood and watched our fathers play for a while. Their trance was familiar to me, the way they furrowed their brows and seemed to look far off into the distance, the way I've seen classmates play Mozart in recitals, as though it was the most profound expression of the most profound music ever composed. Only it was not Mozart; it was the top of the hour and they were again playing "The Chicken Dance" to 400 people who were bobbing around, flapping their arms.

I heard Elly sigh over the din, just as I had two hours before. Elly standing next to me was the most natural and the most shocking thing all at once. We meandered away from the polka tent and toward a lemonade stand. We both got strawberry lemonades with sugar around the rim of the cup and found a spot along the creek, away from the crowds and the polkas.

"Lennie. I have a lot to tell you." Elly was looking at the dark water in the creek, not at me. "But first, the main thing. I'm so sorry we parted like that. In France. I cried so much about that. I felt mad and terrible. And crazy."

I was remembering her dumping my suitcase on the ground in front of the entire orchestra. The quiet ride with Patrice, four hours to Paris to the airport. The numb plane flight, taking forever to get back to Bloomington. "It's OK," I told her. It still felt slightly not OK, but I didn't care. I wanted her back in my life.

"I figured out a lot of stuff this past year," she told me.

"I figured out a few things myself," I replied, thinking of the definitive visit to the Kinsey Institute. Looking at Elly, I was overwhelmed with how deeply in my core I loved her—and needed her. And I was amazed by her transformation back into herself. I could see into her eyes again.

"Lennie, I have to tell you something else. The reason I was a crazy, promiscuous bitch. The reason I was so shut down. I was flipping out from the moment I landed at Juilliard. The minute I got away from here. Bedlam, I mean. I had to hold it all together here, and then when I got to New York and met Herman and got seduced by him, it all started to unravel."

I wasn't exactly following. "What started to unravel?"

She took a big breath and her eyes filled with tears. Again. "I came back here to get help. To confront him. I couldn't keep going, fucking everyone who crossed my path and being scared of everything and running away. I was crazy and getting worse."

I still didn't get it, but my heart was starting to pound. Something was registering in my subterranean self. "What?" was all I could manage.

"Lennie, the whole time we were growing up—" She wouldn't look at me. "Frank—my father—he would—"

I am not hearing this. NO. NOT HER. TOO.

"It didn't happen that many times. Oh, what am I saying? It happened, that's bad enough. He would get so mad and he would rage and throw things around and one time he pinned me down and grabbed at me and then all of a sudden it became—it turned into this sexual thing. He would—he forced himself on me. And the next day he would ignore me like he usually does." Elly was crying now and hugging her knees.

I was so paralyzed with disbelief and anger, I could not even reach out to her. Anger magma ran through my insides, hot, getting hotter. Swirling around. It was going to have to come out somewhere.

"Frank? Frank?!" I said the one syllable with as much warm slime as I could. I grabbed Elly's arm and I think I might have yelled something or maybe that was just in my head, and then I stifled the urge to run through the flapping chickens up to the stage and—what? Tackle Frank? Pound his face in? Kick a hole in his bass drum, at the very least.

My hands were fists. I really wanted to hit something. Him. "Always be careful of your hends," Miss Ludmilla instructed me. "No sports. No skiing. No hitting. No chopping vegetables." I didn't care. The urge to punch was all I could feel. "Your hands are your livelihood. Your expression. Be always careful of them." But all I wanted to do was pound Frank with them. And Andy. It was the next logical thing, as if anything about any of this could be termed logical.

"Your FATHER." Like I was speaking it to try it out.

"My father."

I was shaking. "Jesus Fucking Christ," I swore.

"He hurt Rosa, too, just to scare the hell out of me. I've been not knowing how to live with that since we were ten."

"What do you mean, he hurt Rosa?"

"The time she had to go to the hospital? It wasn't my uncle."

"WHAT?!"

"I think Frankie knew it wasn't my uncle. It was Frank. He did it because I threatened to tell someone."

"Jesus Fucking FUCKING Christ!" Could there be a worse expletive?

"I wanted to tell you so bad, the whole time we were growing up. And I couldn't because I was too scared. I believed him. I saw what he did to my mother." Elly was trembling. "I knew he could do worse to me, that he could possibly even kill Rosa. Or both of us. Now that I've been away, I can't believe I lived like that for my whole life. Hating my father and being scared to death of him. And living down the hall from him, never knowing when he was going to turn into that monster person."

By this time I had begun to weep. For me, for her, for the two little girls that couldn't tell each other. For the two little girls trapped in a sick secret, scared to death for all those years.

"Me, too," I managed to say between sobs. I'd been waiting for my whole life to tell her.

"What?" It didn't take long for Elly to realize what I meant. "Frank? He molested you, too?" Elly was incredulous. "How? How the hell could he—?"

"No, no, not Frank. Andy." Sobbing now, shaking. We sat there by the creek, arms around each other. She sobbed, I sobbed. We wept together. Elly's lemonade tipped over and made a little river trail to the water.

"You mean there was more than the barn and the parking lot?" Elly asked.

I told her. Every single week, after every single piano lesson. I told her everything. And then she told me even more about what Frank did to her. People steered clear of us. I don't know if we were loud or hysterical or just gave off the energy of Do Not Disturb. I was vaguely aware of the same old goddamn polkas playing in the background— the beat kept by a rapist. A goddamn fucking child molester rapist. I kept feeling huge urges to go up there, kick his drum set, stab him with a drum stick.

"I'm so sorry," I said. For no particular reason except that I knew exactly what it had been like for her and for me. Understanding suddenly that our bond had always been much deeper than childhood friendship or even pseudo-sisterhood.

"I'm sorry, too." More crying. I just let the snot happen and the pain-magma in my belly expand, the anger in my fists smolder. Her pain was mine—no line of demarcation between us.

"He said if I told, he would have Rosa sent back to Puerto Rico. This was after he beat her up." I remembered that night, cowering in my room under the covers with Elly and Wolfie and the pile of peanut butter sandwiches.

"Sometimes I wondered about you. Because of the barn," Elly said. "And the parking lot. And that party at Uncle Henry's—I know something was weird there for sure. I thought it might be happening to you, too. But I couldn't bring myself to say anything! I wish I could have been braver. I'm so sorry, Lennie." No platitude, I knew she really was sorry. And so was I

We didn't even really notice when The Continentals packed up and cleared the stage, dusk fell, and a cover band came on and played everything from Elvis Presley tunes to songs from *Saturday Night Fever.* We talked and talked, telling each other everything, every last detail. The time Frank kicked Elly down the stairs and the time Andy kicked me down the stairs. Hiding in bathrooms to wash the semen off our legs, hands, shirts. Learning how to cry so that no one heard. Being hyper vigilant about who walked in the back door. Worst of all, dying to tell each other and protect each other and not being able to.

"Do you know what saved me, Elly?"

"Music," she replied, not even needing to think.

"And Wolfie the dog."

"Yes, and Wolfie the dog."

I told her about chanting the circle of fifths, over and over, interspersed with hail marys or acts of contrition or multiplication tables or the key signatures of minor scales.

"I wish I'd thought of that," she said. "I really wish I'd thought of that."

We sat in the dark and watched the moonlight on the creek. Crickets sang. The world around us seemed the same and wildly different at the same time.

Elly told me the story of the past year. After I left, she went even crazier in France. She began to be late for rehearsals or miss them entirely. She used tons of cocaine, started drinking nonstop, and stopped counting how many guys she slept with in one night. She was extreme even by French standards. It turned out that Patrice was the one who finally rescued her after a guest conductor left her stranded in a hotel in London where the orchestra was on tour. Patrice kept track of Elly's violin, nursed her through coming down from whatever drug and alcohol combination she'd ingested, and took her to some sort of detox crisis center. Patrice stayed behind with Elly for the two weeks after the tour, keeping watch on the unraveling of Elly.

"And then she put me on a plane and told me I had to come home and tell you, that I had to mend things with you. So here I am. I knew you'd be here because Rosa has kept me up to date on your life. She and Frankie knew we'd eventually start talking again."

I thought I might never stop crying in my life. And by the way, merci, Patrice.

"Rosa. Frankie. We have to tell them," Elly said.

This is when we realized it was something like the wee hours of the night. There was no more music, the crowds had gone home, it was quiet and still humid in the Pennsylvania dark. We hooked arms again and started walking in the direction of Ted and Frankie's house. We weren't sure if Rosa would still be there. As we strolled down Broad Street, a cop car came driving by. They shined the spotlight on us. Two cop faces peered at us. We must have looked crazy. Disheveled, still crying.

"You two ladies all right?" the passenger seat cop asked. "It's 2:00 a.m."

The Elly I knew and loved made a stunning and magnificent return: "We actually are not at all alright. Would you happen to know the statute of limitations on prosecuting a child molester?" Was she serious?

The cop got out of the car. "Where is this child molester? More importantly, where is the child?" he said, looking around. He had his flashlight out and his hand on that stick thing they use to bonk uncooperative suspects.

"Oh, they're not here. See, we were just talking about what happened to us as children, and there's nothing that I'd like more than for you to arrest my goddamn fucking pig father. And her goddamn fucking pig uncle," she said, gesturing to me.

Watch the fucking pig thing around cops, I was thinking.

"Well, the cop said. He seemed flustered. He went around to the driver's side and conferred with his partner.

I felt something rise up in my chest. I had my friend back. I had an explanation. I had a lifetime of fear and anger to express. I was going to Tanglewood in two days, officially invited by Maestro Lenny Bernstein.

The cop came back over to us. "Ma'am—"

"I'm not a ma'am. I'm twenty-one."

"Yes ma'am. I mean, miss." I had never seen a disconcerted cop before. "When did the alleged—uh—crimes take place?"

"When we were children. About twelve years ago."

The cop went back to his partner, who was standing outside the car at this point. They conferred again. Then the partner came over to us and said, "We are unable to arrest the persons in question, but you are advised to go down to headquarters and consult with them about submitting a report and possibly pressing charges. They will be able to advise you as to the viability and statute of limitations regarding your complaint."

I was wondering if they have a course in police school that teaches them to talk like that.

Elly stared at him. "Well. Thank you. That helps a lot."

"Yes, miss. Now, it is late. Do you two have transportation at this time?"

"My house is two blocks away," I said

"You should head out now, and we'll follow you to your home." It was pretty much a directive. The cruiser idled in wait for us. As we started to move away from them, the driver cop stuck his head out the window. "I don't know what will come of this," he said, "but tell your—uh, your father—that what happens to child molesters in jail is not very pretty." The cop set his square jaw, like he wanted to say a lot more.

"Thank you," said Elly. "I will be sure to do that."

We held hands, the cop car a short distance behind us, and crossed the intersection at 8th and Broad, the same place we'd almost been run over in hopes of going to heaven in a state of grace. Our moms weren't surprised when we walked in the back door of my old house and found them at the kitchen table playing gin rummy. Our dads weren't back yet. They were probably still out drinking.

We told them everything. Bam, just like that. This time, for me, there weren't many more tears. A renewed lava flow of anger, for sure, especially after seeing both of our mothers dissolve, weeping, as they understood what we were telling them.

Rosa couldn't even speak. Every time she did, she began to choke and gag. Frankie's eyes were a mix of blaze and grief. "I knew something wasn't right, Lennie. I knew it, I could *feel* it. I couldn't figure out what it was. And I didn't do a goddamn thing about it." She apologized over and over. And over. I didn't want her to apologize. I just wanted to be done with it. I wanted Frank and Andy to go to their unpretty fate in a jail somewhere, preferably Alcatraz. Frankie let a river of tears cascade down her face. She got up and pulled a bottle of Jack Daniels out of the cupboard. She paused there for a few moments at the open door, coming back to the table with Frank's favorite beer mug, the one he always used when he was at our house. Frankie suddenly whipped it into the sink where it crashed into a million pieces. She put her arm around Elly. "It's a start," she said. And then she burst out crying, big, mournful, heaving sobs.

I wondered if it was worse, Frank being Elly's dad and Rosa's husband. There was nothing of Andy's in Frankie's house. If there was, I'm sure my mother would have incinerated it on the spot. My heart ached even more than I thought it could. For me, for Elly, for our mothers who were thinking they had been terrible mothers, knowing that they hadn't been able to protect their daughters. I wondered what that must feel like. I sat there in the numbness of not quite believing that the truth was finally out.

We sat around the table and drank the whiskey and cried more and then started planning. We went to the guest room and made up the bed for Rosa. Elly would stay with me in my old room until I went to Tanglewood, and she would follow me in a few days.

Frankie stopped in the mid-air fluffing of a pillow. "Just exactly where the hell were your grandparents, Lennie? Just exactly WHERE THE HELL WERE THEY when this was all going on? Huh? Where WERE they?"

"I don't know, mom."

"Jesus Fucking Christ," my mother said. So, that's where I got it.

I'd never thought about it. My stomach flipped, remembering the times I tried to hide in the kitchen with Gramma. Or make myself small in the living room, blending in with the furniture so Andy wouldn't realize I was there. Why didn't they wonder what I was doing or where I was all that time? Did they know something and turn the other way? My stomach threatened and then began to rebel. It was full of whiskey and fire, and I had to race to the bathroom to throw it all up. Frankie was immediately there, holding on to me from behind. Rosa and Elly stood in the doorway. I puked my guts out. It felt like years of toxins pouring out of me. It probably was.

15

Tanglewood

When I woke, Elly was sleeping an inch away from me. The fuzz of the morning cleared away gradually, and the events of the night before came back into focus. Frankie must have gotten me into bed, tucked me in. I still felt the queasiness in my stomach, the fear around my heart. I was so glad to see that Elly was right there next to me.

From the voices in the living room, it was clear that something was stirring down there. The little bedside clock said 9:00 a.m, a bit early for our dads to be awake and functioning the day after a gig, but I heard both of their voices interspersed with Frankie and Rosa's. Feeling like I was eight again, I snuck down to the landing and listened. I closed the door on Elly. She looked so serene in her sleep.

Frankie was doing most of the talking. I could hear that catch in Rosa's voice, like she was going to choke again. When she did speak it was completely in Spanish. And it was loud.

"What the hell?" Frank's voice.

"She's leaving you, Frank. What is it about that that you don't get?" Frankie was using her charge nurse voice. It was the same voice that answered the phone when I called her at the hospital. You cannot get away with anything around that voice.

"Come on, I didn't DO anything. Cut me a little slack here. I don't even know what the hell she's talking about."

"Well, for starters, it could possibly have something to do with the fact that you molested your daughter repeatedly throughout her childhood. IS THAT ENOUGH, FRANK?"

"Don't speak to him that way, Frankie," Ted instructed.

"I will speak to him—and you—any goddamn way I please."

"Not in my house, you won't!"

"Let's just see how much longer it's going to be your house, shall we, Ted?"

There were some scuffling sounds and some unintelligible words. I could hear Frankie seething under her controlled professional voice and her sarcasm. It probably wouldn't be long before the shouting started.

Rosa started up the steps. She was wrapped in a blanket. She looked like a tired, sad Indian princess. I stayed on the landing. I wanted her to know that I'd heard. We locked eyes. In her sadness and bewilderment, she said to me, "It will all be OK, niña. We'll get through this." And I began to cry because in her pain, *she* was comforting *me*. Here she was, trying to come to grips with the fact that her husband is a child molester and that she didn't protect her only daughter from him.

We both went in to sit on the bed and look at Elly until she woke up, which was immediately, because Frank suddenly barged in, yelling. "Tell them! Tell them I didn't do this!"

There had been no time between sleep and waking for Elly, and she looked stunned. There was her father, acting like a madman, still in his polka band outfit, standing at the side of the bed and demanding that she admit she lied.

"Tell them, Elly. Tell them I didn't DO this." Frank was all red and sputtery.

"Didn't do what, dad?" Even though she knew exactly what he was talking about.

"What they're saying I did!"

"Oh, you mean what I told them you did? You mean about molesting me? Why would I tell them you didn't when you did? All the time!" Elly turned to me. "This is not the way I imagined confronting him." She grabbed a sweatshirt off the chair and pulled it on, covering herself up.

"What do you mean, confronting me? About what?"

"About what you did to me, Dad."

"I didn't DO ANYTHING TO YOU. I'm starting to get mad about this now." Frank stamped his feet. His face was scarlet. His eyes could not stay still.

I could feel Elly tremble next to me—with anger, not fear.

Ted pushed his way into the bedroom, followed by Frankie, who was holding a baseball bat. A baseball bat? "Why don't you just leave him alone?" said my brave, brave father.

"Leave HIM alone? You're in *my* room," I reminded him. I was starting to feel heat rise through my body. My ears caught fire.

"It's MY house," proclaimed Ted.

"As I said, we'll see about how long that remains to be true," Frankie countered. She hardly ever repeats herself.

"I'm warning you, Frankie," said Ted.

"You're warning ME?" Frankie shouted.

While my parents assumed a standoff posture and yelled at each other, Rosa seemed to be trying to get as far away from Frank as she could. But there was a wall in the way. Frank spluttered and Rosa hesitated, not wanting to look at him or speak to him. She couldn't contain it. She completely ignored my bickering parents. "How COULD you? How could you do this to our daughter? Our child? What is *wrong* with you? You're a monster, you're worse than a monster, you're sick, you're disgusting. And you come in here and say these things to her? Like you are the innocent one and we're making up lies? You come in here, uninvited, and want her to lie about YOUR innocence?" Rosa shed her blanket and found her strength.

"I'm telling you, I didn't do what she said." Frank had a scared look in his shifty eyes. "Yes, you did." Elly somehow stayed composed.

"I DID NOT! I don't know what the hell you're even talking about!"

"OK, here it is: You hit me. You touched me. You relieved yourself sexually with me. You molested me. You forced yourself on me. You violated me. You RAPED me. That's what you did. I was ten years old and that is what you did to me!" Elly's composure evaporated, thank God.

Her father stared at her, eyes wide, fists clenched. Ha, I was thinking. What are you going to say to that? What are you going to say to that, Mr. Big Man Child Rapist?

"You're all crazy," is what came out of his mouth. And he turned and left. He stomped down the stairs and slammed the front door so hard that a vase fell off the mantle and shattered on the brick hearth.

"Are you satisfied now? Are you proud of yourselves? You ARE crazy. All of you. You don't accuse people of this kind of thing. You're insane." Ted followed Frank's exact steps, crashing out of the house after his friend.

"You don't accuse people of this sort of thing unless they do it," Elly said in a monotone.

The four of us took a collective breath. We all sat on the bed for a while, not talking.

When Elly and I left for the six hour drive to Massachusettes, our moms were starting to put things in cardboard boxes.

I followed the music to a small building. The Chamber Music Hall, it said on a small sign out front. There was a wind octet onstage and they were in the middle of rehearsing the Dvorak *Serenade for Winds*. And there was 42, playing principal. The music, so rich and full of Slavic harmonies, gave me the kind of chills that don't come from the cold. The sonority was so different from what I was used to, which is, of course, mostly piano. But here, the oboes, bassoons, horns, and clarinets, with a couple of strings thrown in, produced an organ of sound and depth of harmony that went right into my bones. I could have listened for the rest of the day. The anxiety and drama of the weekend were replaced by a calmness that was spreading through me, making itself at home, and I was amazed at the space within me that I was now free to explore.

I slipped into a seat in the back of the hall. The front door was open to the summer, which is how I found the music in the first place. The sun streamed in, Dvorak washed over me, and I became enraptured watching 42 play. She made it look easy. Sometimes oboe players look like they're going to explode when they play, but not 42. The beautiful, dark sound flew out of her instrument in an effortless way, and I let myself get lost in a momentary reverie of fantasy with her—and me— as the naked stars.

I took three long, deep breaths before I went onstage for the first Schumann rehearsal, Miss Ludmilla's recipe for instant calm. I hadn't seen or talked to Mr. Bernstein beforehand, but he greeted me like an old friend when I approached the piano. He introduced me to the orchestra as Lennie, and there were a few snickers from the players. I recognized the familiar wariness they had. I'd have to prove myself at the keyboard before anyone would be the slightest bit convinced that I was a worthy soloist. The first few measures seemed to do the trick. There's a big chord in the orchestra followed by some dotted chords in the piano, then another forte chord and the theme in the principal oboe. It felt like 42 was singing it right to me, and I was so mesmerized by her sound that I delayed my next entrance for a fraction of a second. Mr. Bernstein noticed, but I'm not sure anyone else did. After that, the piece flew together like we'd already rehearsed it.

It was astounding to see Mr. Bernstein leaping around the podium like it was a trampoline. He coaxed music out of the orchestra that I didn't know was possible. And I wanted to follow him even though it was their job to follow me. He knew this and he played with me about it, and I managed to smile my delight to him.

I don't think much when I play, but space was starting to open up for that, too. I imagined Miss Ludmilla out in the seats, encouraging me. We'd had a discussion about what I was going to wear before I left Bloomington and I told her—again—that a gown or a dress was out of the question. She fought me on this for only a day or two, knowing how important it was to be comfortable when you play. She gave in to the girl tux Frankie got me when I won the Concerto Competition. She gave in with a certain amount of feigned disapproval, insisting that I had to show my shoulders and cleavage now that I was in the big time. I thought of this around bar 89, where there are a series of flowing arpeggios in the piano and soft melodies in the winds. I had to stifle a laugh, and I'm sure the tense little flute player was forming an opinion that I was crazy, something she would certainly share with the rest of the woodwinds at the break. I knew 42 would come to my rescue, however.

But I didn't get to talk to 42 at the rehearsal break because Mr. Bernstein took me aside and said something about maybe scheduling me for a few concerts during the year. I thought sure, great. And then: DURING THE YEAR? During the year, he conducts the Boston Symphony or the Israel Philharmonic or the New York Phil. Oh Dear Lord, Oh My God.

I told Elly about this after the rehearsal, and she screamed, one of those high-pitched alarm screams. I didn't care, despite the strange looks from the two violinists strolling by.

"Lennie. You ARE going to be famous," Elly proclaimed.

"Yeah. Maybe I am!" I conceded.

The concert was the most fun I ever had in my entire life. It started out that way, anyway. The middle of the first row was taken over by Frankie, Rosa, Elly, Aunt Liddy, and Max. I peeked at them right before the concerto, and they were all smiling the biggest smiles I'd ever seen on any of them. Liddy had her flask out in plain sight on her lap, which was completely illegal in the Shed—and in every other concert venue I know of. I knew she was nervous for me. In the seconds that the orchestra was re-tuning, I had a quick stab of wistfulness that Ted wasn't there, that Ted had never been there, really, and now he was going to be off in his own land. That place he'd rather go than be with Frankie or me. Or Frankie. But I brushed the thought aside quickly. I had a job to do, Schumann to play, an audience to win over, and a conductor to impress.

An unheard-of thing happened at the end of the first movement—a smattering of applause from the educated audience who knows to never applaud between movements. I was thrilled and unnerved, so I jumped into the second movement a little prematurely, but the orchestra was right there. Mr. Bernstein was toweling off his forehead, but he tossed the towel and brought the strings in perfectly. He winked at me and went along with my jump-the-gun tempo.

And then something happened, some darkness suddenly fell over me in the Intermezzo. It started during the section where the cellos sing the second phrase for a moment, and then we trade it back and forth. The brand new space in me collapsed and I was little again, grabbing on to the invisible notes on the page to pull me up from some depths that I thought might drown me.

"Just play," I urged my hands, knowing that they could play the concerto without the rest of me. They automatically went where they needed to but I was losing the music. The firestorm of feelings from the weekend before were unseating the ones I needed to get through the performance. I felt something brand new: panic. Three more deep breaths. A look that was a question from the podium. Then a little whisper of a voice far in the back of my head starting chanting: C, G, D, A, E, B, F#. My hands are playing, I see the notes of the concerto in my head, I hear the circle of fifths in some other remote survival place in my brain. I keep on playing, I shut everything else out, and then I hear Miss Ludmilla coaxing, urging the human part of me to touch the music part of me and *sing*. Four little chords, the strings answer. Four more, they answer again. Then the clarinets and bassoons playing the second theme again, major, then minor, then major again, just a few bars before the attacca that signals the third movement.

I took off, playing the third movement much faster than we'd rehearsed it, and every cell of my body came alive again. Mr. Bernstein pulled the reins in at the little marcato section, and I realized that I could slow down a bit, there was nothing to run away from anymore. I relaxed again and and let the build-up to the forte section get huge, waiting for my dialogue with 42, and as soon as I heard her a swell began inside of me and the lights in my head came on again as I reached the surface. Horns answered by woodwinds, the tutti stating the theme before I come in and take over for the last time. Forte octaves in the left hand, marcato strings again, another big buildup, this time to the end. Accelerando, the circle of fifths passage, major, minor, major. Running sixteenths and dancing through the keys to the final cadences. Final chords, timpani, and a long, sustained last chord that rang out through the hall and touched the night through the open air of the Shed. There were a few seconds of silence and then the first thing I saw was Frankie leaping to her feet, her arms raised in triumph. She wasn't even clapping—she was parading around like she'd just won a race or scored a touchdown. Elly and Rosa were getting up, too, and the whole place was applauding and people were standing up. I must have, too, to bow.

Applause, shouts of "Bravo!" and someone bringing me flowers. When I came out for a second bow, the whole row—Frankie, Rosa, Elly, Liddy, Max—were all on their feet with their arms raised, the pose of a team of winners. So I looked at them and I did the same thing, raised my arms in the air, one hand clutching a dozen roses that had materialized from somewhere. And Mr. Bernstein grabbing my other hand and yelling "Bravo, Lennie!" over the roar, ushering me back for another bow and another. I started hearing it from all over the place, Len-nie, Len-nie, Len-nie! They were chanting! Even the orchestra! And Mr. Bernstein runs out, throws my arm in the air like I've just scored a knockout, and they're chanting and maybe they're chanting Len-ny or maybe Len-nie but it didn't matter.

Mr. Bernstein told me to play an encore and the string players were tapping their stands with their bows and the wind players were shuffling their feet and so I sat down at the piano and the Shed quieted down, which shocked me, they WANTED to hear me play more. So I thought for just a moment and I picked the Chopin *Etude in C# Minor*. I played it fast, two minutes of fireworks, and suddenly there was more applause, and when I stood to bow and look into the audience, I saw a familiar figure walking down the aisle toward the stage. I could hear whispers of recognition ripple through the crowd as they realized it was Ludmilla Michalowski. She was coming toward the stage to congratulate me! She told me she'd be in Russia, I didn't expect her here. Not in a million years! And there she was, flowing clothes and her trademark smile. The audience was beside themselves, they began applauding for her.

I stole a glance back through the orchestra and 42 had her oboe stuffed under her arm and she was clapping wildly. I shook hands with Mr. Bernstein again and the concertmaster again and the other string players and everyone seemed to be smiling. When I went offstage, I didn't go back on, I was barraged with congratulations. Suddenly there was Miss Ludmilla again, her arms around me. There was a small crowd following her.

"Lenyah," she said.

"Thank you for coming," I said.

"Something happen, yes?" she asked me.

"Yes, something happened," I confirmed. A lot of things happened.

"Good," she says. "Excellent." She was beaming. I suddenly thought of the Schumann *Papillons* that I played so terribly at our first studio class.

Miss Ludmilla got the telepathic image and she said, "You remember when I tear apart first Schumann you play for me?"

"Of course," I said. "I'm glad you did."

"Yes. Now you play pretty good Schumann."

We both laughed.

I saw Frankie and company making their way toward us. Their arms were still in the air.

On the road trip caravan back to Bedford, we stopped twice to pee and grab a cone at Dairy Queen. There was an urgency to keep going. My car, Frankie's, and Liddy's, all in a row down the interstate. When we pulled into the driveway of the house I grew up in, something was immediately, noticeably, different.

"Did he leave?" I asked my mother.

"I threw him out," said Frankie. She hadn't said one single word about this at Tanglewood. "I wish I'd done it when you were little. I wish I'd had the courage. I'm sorry, Lennie."

"Mom—"

"Things would have been a lot different. Don't ever compromise yourself, Lennie. Ever. Not for any reason in the world." She was looking out the car window, not at me. At some place far away from both of us.

Walking into the house, the first thing I noticed was the absence of the stereo equipment.

"Where did he go?" I asked. Not that I was going to do anything about it.

"I'm not sure. Somewhere with Frank, we think." Frankie got out the pot stash. We were going to get high together. While she rolled a couple of joints, I played her my favorite Chopin impromptu, *Gb Major, Op. 30 no. 9*. Then Elly and Rosa pulled up with a carload full of stuff. My mom and Rosa were going to be roommates. Max appeared and started carrying things into the house.

Liddy pulled my mother aside and whispered to her. They pulled Rosa and Max into their murmuring. I distinctly heard one of them say, "The Grove."

Elly figured it out. "The Band Picnic! It's today!" she said, as though she'd been planning to go and simply forgotten "What are the four of you plotting?"

They all stood motionless, looking like robbers caught in the act.

"We thought we'd stir the pot, so to speak," said Max

This cracked Aunt Liddy up. "You can't cook," she laughed.

Frankie looked seriously at Elly and me. "Do you *want* to face your father again, Elly?" Then she looked over at me, and I realized that, of course, Andy would be there.

"I'm OK, considering," said Elly. "The therapist recommended a lot of planning if I was going to confront my abuser. My father. It didn't exactly go as planned."

"You have a therapist?" I asked. "They have therapists in France?"

We all got a smile out of that. Then I told everyone about my failed attempt at therapy with Stuart/Stewart, and in the process, came officially crashing right out of the closet.

"Oh, Lennie," said Frankie. "That was never any big secret. I always knew," she said.

Up at Tanglewood, Frankie and Rosa told Liddy and Max the story of what happened to Elly and me as kids. Max sat there and shredded a Sunday New York Times in silence while Liddy, on the other hand, went wild. She raged on and on, similar to the drama that unfolded when Elly and I told our mothers everything in the middle of the night. Liddy threw stuff around the hotel room and Frankie just let her.

"I KNEW it, I KNEW it. I KNEW something was not right. That son of a bitch. That pig." Liddy went on and on, hurling every insult she could think of. I had never seen the fierce side of my sweet and gentle aunt, and Frankie said it was awe-inspiring. She alternately stormed and then she cried. "I'm sorry, I'm sorry I didn't protect Lennie." And, "You know, I'm going to have to kill him now."

Max reached out and took Liddy's arm. "No, you're not going to kill him. I am. I could kill them both." Max said this with such calm. Of course she could do it, no question. So they cooked up the plan to go to the Grove, to confront the rats in their natural habitat.

The six of us collected ourselves and got ready to leave the house. I thought it might be the way that a posse would form in the old cowboy days. When some justice needed to happen, the town rallied together and went to mete it out, gathering a group of determined vigilantes. That's how we got in the car and headed to The Grove. We were on a mission. We were a mob out for justice. We silently gathered forces and imaginary weapons and met at the car at the same exact time.

When we got to The Grove, the parking lot was full and The Continentals were already drunk, playing polkas in the pavilion. It all looked the same. The pool. The barn. The pavilion. The tag football field. Elly and I reminisced for a few minutes about all the years we looked forward to this event, the highlight of the summer for us. Playing Beautiful Ladies, roasting marshmallows, yearning to play in the band with our dads.

"It all looks so much smaller now," Elly remarked. We were wandering near the barn. She was right. In my memory, it was an enormous, dark cavern. In reality, it was just a sweet little barn converted into a play space. It looked friendly. The smashed beer bottle was long gone, all traces of that experience erased by time.

The posse stayed in close eye contact. Frankie and Rosa helped themselves to drinks. Liddy was well underway already with her own personal stash of white wine. Max looked like she might explode at any moment. Like she could just stick her arm out and annihilate someone with the sheer power she had packed in it.

"Well, well, look who's in town! The famous concert pianist," Aunt Tammy sidled over, beehive hairdo over a foot tall. I had the weird thought that her hair must crash into the bedboard when she sleeps and so how does she actually get any sleep, anyway? Everything else at The Grove had shrunk except Tammy's hair, which was getting higher.

"Hi," I said. I didn't want to talk her her. I was wearing shorts and a t-shirt, and her next comment would be about that.

"Gosh, Lennie, is this how concert pianists dress? Did you wear this kind of thing onstage at—what is that place, Tangled Roots or something?"

I knew it. "You know, Aunt Tammy, that's a pretty good idea. I think I might set a new fashion trend. And it's Tanglewood. It's famous but people who only listen to polkas don't know that." I was irritated by the way she said "pianist," like pee-ANN-ist.

Tammy spotted Frankie strolling toward us and she cleverly navigated a quick escape as far away from me as possible. She didn't even take the time to retort to my sarcastic comments. I liked that she didn't want to tangle with Frankie.

My mother seemed really tight, like a stretched rubber band. I knew what she was waiting for, the exact right moment to snap and get the desired effect. Rosa stood by, not like a rubber band waiting to snap but more like a warrior ready to defend. I knew in my heart that she would never utter another word to her husband again as long as she lived, her husband who was already an ex-husband; all they needed was the paperwork. I knew it was hard for her to be anywhere near him, but she was a loyal and important member of the vigilante mob.

I was the first one to spot Andy, sitting near the grill, his chair surrounded by empty beer bottles. I looked directly at him, and for the first time, I didn't have a wave of fear or adrenaline coursing through me. Instead, it was a wave of nausea mixed with revulsion. And something that might be pity, I couldn't exactly identify it.

Liddy saw Andy at about the same time. She didn't waste a second. She marched over, hauled her arm back, and slapped him hard across the face, so hard that he fell backward in his lawn chair onto the ground. The band, just breaking for a new round of drinks, ran over to the where the commotion was happening.

"That's just the beginning, you son of a bitch," yelled Liddy. One of the band members, Mr. Kimball, I think, grabbed Liddy and tried to pull her away from Andy. She would have none of it. And Max was giving him the evil eye, so he let Liddy go.

My feet were glued to the grass. I wanted to get closer and could not. I didn't want Liddy to do this for me. I needed and wanted to do it for myself, but I was suddenly incapable of moving my body. What would I do if I could? Hit him? What would I say? All those years, all those fantasies of stealing his gun and shooting him, or at least telling him off, or telling my parents, or calling the police. I couldn't move because I knew the truth was about to be spoken and I still, I STILL thought he would do it, that he could and would kill us all. For a few scary moments I was unable to tell yesterday apart from today, there was no difference. No time had passed. I was too scared to jump down into the rose bushes beneath the window. I was eight or maybe I was twenty-one. I was ten, I was twelve. I was terrified. I made him into my enemy and fended him off once. But I was still afraid. Still absolutely paralyzed.

"What the hell is going on here?" Frank was the first one to address Liddy. It was perfect because she now had two targets and plenty of energy for both.

"YOU! You're just like him! You should be ASHAMED! You should be SHOT."

A circle was forming, just like for a playground fight. It was Andy, Frank, and Liddy in the ring, but only for a moment. Frankie, Rosa, and Elly stepped in. And I stayed rooted. My heart was pounding out of my Chopin t-shirt.

Andy finally scrambled up from the ground. He was pissed. I knew that look. He reached his arm out to grab Liddy.

"Don't you DARE touch her," Frankie commanded. Amazingly, Andy put his arm down.

"What the hell?" he spat.

And then I saw it. Just a tiny spark of fear in his eye. The game was over. That little flicker of apprehension in his expression reminded me that I had a whole reservoir of courage way down inside me. I took the ten or so steps to come face to face with him.

I saw it get bigger. His fear, his knowledge that he was finally, FINALLY going to have to answer for what he did. "What the hell, Uncle Andy, is this . . . " My voice spoke all by itself. "I told them what you did to me when I was little. And now I want to know why. I want to know how you could hurt a little kid like that, week after week. I didn't cry, I didn't collapse in tears. I didn't feel like running away or throwing up. I stood my ground, right in front of him and his beer breath.

The circle seemed to be getting tighter. There was tension in the air, the kind you can feel, the kind that sticks to your skin.

"Oh, you too?" Frank stepped up. He was drunk and ready for a fight. Andy was happy to let him hog the spotlight. I might have been the only one to see the beads of sweat on Andy's upper lip and the way his jaw trembled and his hands started to shake. I knew him, the way he operated. The heinous, forced intimacy we shared gave me a perspective on him that I didn't want but didn't know how to shut away yet.

Elly. "Yes, her, too. Andy did the same thing to her that you did to me. The SAME THING. And we're not going to stay quiet about it anymore."

"Oh, for Christ's sake," said Ted. And then, the most astounding thing happened: Frankie hurled her drink right in his face. Ted stood there like a statue, letting the whiskey drip down his cheeks onto his shirt.

"Now JUST A MINUTE," Aunt Tammy threw herself in the middle of the boxing ring. "What on earth is going on here? Lennie, are you making up some story about your poor uncle?"

That lit a fire under me. I'd been calm, feeling my way to my strength. But I wasn't going to listen to that beehive pile of shit anymore.

"Making up stories? Making up STORIES, Aunt Tammy? How could I possibly make up a story like this: Andy drags me to his attic and tries to rape me when I was eight. Only not once, not twice. Repeatedly, week after week after week. And then he told me that if I ever said a word, he would kill me. Do you think that's a made up story? DO YOU?"

She burst out laughing. She burst out LAUGHING! "Well, Lennie, if anything like that really happened—and I'm sure it didn't—it must have been because you came on to him. You must have been asking for it!" Tammy stepped toward me. I backed away automatically, her points a little too sharp and close.

"I was EIGHT YEARS OLD! How the hell could I be asking for it?"

Tammy retorted without skipping a beat: "I'm sure you learned your tricks from your slutty little Porto Rickan friend here."

There was a pause while the impact of that settled in. And then I realized that the real fight was not between me and my pointy aunt—it was with Andy, and he was trying to slip away from the crowd. He was slinking away, trying to escape! Elly and Rosa had their jaws hanging open with the ferocity of Tammy's insult, unable to even respond.

"Hey!" Liddy yelled at him. "Get your ass back here!" Remarkably, Andy stopped. Maybe he realized that there was ultimately nowhere he could hide.

"I think you should all calm down," Ted, still dribbling booze, tried to instruct us. But in fact, the melee seemed to be just beginning.

"Calm *down*, Ted? CALM DOWN? Do you care what happened to our daugher? DO YOU?" Frankie was just revving up, I could tell. First a drink in the face—what could be next?

"Oh Frankie, listen to yourself. You're just one of those women's libbers who can't keep their mouths shut." Tammy again. She was so determined to never be thought of as a women's libber that she displayed portions of her bra on purpose, just to be sure people knew she wore one. As if anyone's tits could have anything near that kind of shape on their own.

"Frankie, he's my brother. Don't talk about him that way." Ted said. "And Frank is my best friend. You girls should think about the lies you're spreading about them." He crossed his arms over his chest. My officially separated parents commenced an evil staredown.

Watching Frankie was like watching a volcano that was calculating its eruption for maximum effect. Steam and rumbling, it was inevitable but you just didn't know quite when the top might fly off. My mom has this great way of letting the tension build and build and acting almost calm while everyone around her is ready to bolt. But this time she couldn't contain it. She took a deep breath and blew sky high. She roared at my father and started pushing him. The whole circle moved with them. Ted was thrown off balance and fell. Frank lost his footing and fell on Andy. The rest of the band hovered around Frank and Ted, unsure of what to do or how to act. Then some man I didn't recognize caught Frankie and held her arms behind her. This lasted for exactly five seconds before Max intervened and picked the guy up by his shirt. His feet actually dangled off the ground for a moment.

"Now everyone, just STOP THIS!" Aunt Tammy was taking control. She shrieked at the top of her lungs. "STOP THIS FOOLISHNESS RIGHT THIS INSTANT!"

As she was screaming, something interesting was happening to the circle. It was becoming lopsided, with most of the people crowding around Elly, Rosa, Frankie, Liddy, Max, and me. The remaining people stood by Ted, Frank, Andy, and Aunt Tammy. Even Uncle Henry was closer to the more populated side of things.

"Now Lennie, I think you've caused just about enough trouble for one day. You should just leave. You've become much too big for your britches and we don't want you here anymore telling these lies." Tammy pointed to the parking lot with one of her dagger fingers. I noticed that her pointy tits were askew, one higher than the other.

"Fine, just one thing before I go." Frankie started to protest, but I started walking toward Aunt Tammy. Elly was immediately next to me. We herded her closer and closer to the edge of the pool, and with a little telepathic surge between us, reached out and shoved her in. The resulting splash was so very, very satisfying. She blubbered about in the deep end, where she surfaced immediately and spluttered and splashed and yelled at me even more. No one made any move to help her get out of the water, where she floated about like a Shitzu that couldn't swim.

The crowd got really quiet and then began to scatter, dispersing the playground fight circle. There were a few tentative toots from a sax, a few notes from a string bass. But the band didn't play again, and all conversation seemed to stop. Tammy flailed on in the pool, her mascara streaking to her chin.

"Well, I think we're finished here," said Frankie. She poured herself another drink for the road. Aunt Liddy took one, too. She hardly ever drank the hard stuff.

"Thank you, Max," I said to the big woman who dangled men by the scruff of their necks. I would always remember that.

"My pleasure," she said, hugging me. "Wish there was more I could do." I know that she meant that with all her big heart.

As we headed toward the official posse steed, Frankie's old Chrysler, I caught a glimpse of Andy huddled back in his lawn chair. He was crying. He gestured to me to come over to him. Another familiar wave of revulsion washed through me, now mixed in with something new, something that felt like pity. As I turned toward him, I was instantly surrounded by five warrior women.

"You don't have to do this," Frankie whispered into my ear.

"I know, Mom."

He stood up and he looked and me, and then he looked away and then he sort of looked at Liddy, Frankie, and everyone else. Finally, he looked at the ground and spoke. "I'm sick," he said in a whisper. "I'm sick and I'm sorry about what happened."

"You mean 'what you DID,'" Frankie corrected.

"Yeah. What I did. I'm sorry."

"You could go to jail. You SHOULD go to jail. I'm looking into it." Frankie stared him down just like she had my father.

Andy didn't say anything. He cried and could not look at any of us. "I'm sorry."

This was supposed to make me feel better, feel vindicated and heard and like I'd won. But the words themselves meant nothing to me. I felt empty. And calm. Like now maybe it could be over for me.

Andy shuffled, sniffling and mumbling. All of a sudden, he looked to me like exactly what he was: a sick, pathetic loser. All those years of being terrified of him, wounded by him, wishing I could tell on him or kill him or, best of all, erase him from my world. And now, here he was, crumpled and wretched. I couldn't find one drop of compassion for him even though he was growing more pitiable by the second. I wanted to be done with him, but a brand new thought crept in, one that I'd never considered before. What if someone had done the same thing to him? Maybe that's why he was so weak and scarred that doing it to someone else was the only way he could exist.

Well, it's a thought.

"I'm sorry for you, too." That shot out of me from the depths of I know not where.

I took a breath and marched myself to the car. Liddy and Frankie lingered for a minute, and I don't know what else they said to him. I saw Uncle Henry reach down and fish Tammy out of the pool. I was amazed to see her with wet, flat, stringy hair. She looked like she might potentially be human, except that her pointy bra was completely turned around and she now sprouted two new points from her back. She was rather scrawny, I was surprised to learn.

Elly took this scene in, also. "Some transformation," she said, and took my hand.

We left The Grove with Frankie, Rosa, Liddy, and Max, and we didn't look back.

16

Finale

Roasting on a Puerto Rican beach. The beach chairs are arranged in a semi-circle near the water's edge. I looked around at my companions feeling disoriented: how did I get here? Frankie sat looking out at the ocean, too, and I could only guess at what she was thinking. Elly, Rosa, and Rosa's sister Teresa chattered away in Spanish, catching up on Elly's entire life. Max and Liddy dozed on the sand, looking calm and restful. And Joop was deep in conversation with 42, probably about the technical limitations of the high range of the oboe or something esoteric like that. Joop was taking the weekend off from Arecibo, where she went every summer to listen for signs of extraterrestrial life. This year she was writing a piano concerto in her spare time. The concerto is for me, and I will premiere it at the IU New Music Festival in the spring and play it on my concert tour that starts in two months. Joop promises to make it unbearably challenging and full of cosmic harmonies and Puerto Rican rhythms.

The weather is perfect, the ocean dancing. All the bad stuff is behind me, like finding out about Frank and confronting Andy and losing my father ultimately, finally. The amazing things are behind me, too, like *winning* the Cliburn. I feel like I'm standing in the calm after the hurricane and I'm not sure what to do next. We came here to rest and I don't remember the meaning of the word. My body is still at the competition. My hands don't know what to do without a piano. My head doesn't know what to do out of the piano trance.

I had a freakout two days before leaving for Forth Worth. What's the point of a piano competition, anyway? As far as I was concerned, I'd already won the biggest battle of my life. I announced to Miss Ludmilla that I was going to withdraw from the Cliburn.

Ludmilla would have absolutely none of it.

"Nonsense, Lenyah. Is how you get career. You go!" She swished around and ordered more vodka, as was her custom during these talks. If we had been in her studio, she'd be pouring. Instead, we were at Bear's. Everyone who passed us paused to take in the amazing sight of Ludmilla Michalowski in a college bar drinking shots of vodka.

"But – "

"Nyet! No buts! You have come this far. You are going to be stop by little bit of—what? You are lazy now? You are scare? Of course you are scare! Is big deal!" And then she lectured me about potential and my responsibility to use the gifts I was given; otherwise, it would be a slap in the face of the divine. Oh, and something about her refusing to take no for an answer.

"Think of this, Lenyah. One hundred pianists from around world. Is very selective process and you are already chosen. What you are do instead? Watch television? You will go, and now you will drink your vodka." She raised her glass and held it in the air until I raised mine, clinked it with hers, and threw the fire down my throat. "Good," she said.

So I went. Me and 99 other pianists from around the world.

42 was standing over me, holding my snorkel gear. Joop already had her mask on. I told her she looked like a weird astronaut, and she

smiled a squashed-face smile beneath the rubber snorkel. I followed the two of them into the water, paddling over a field of brain coral, sea urchins, and thousands upon thousands of wildly colored fish. Joop was a strong swimmer and I kicked hard to keep up with her. She dove down once to get a better look at a sea turtle. 42 followed her. I was left alone on the surface, watching them.

42 rose to the surface and swam toward me, her snorkel poking out of the water. Joop splashed over next to us.

"I was wondering what it would be like if you could swim as well as you play the piano," Joop said, treading water.

"What do you mean? I swim just fine!" I protested.

Joop and 42 laughed.

The three of us floated around in the ocean, heads bobbing, fin feet swishing.

"Have you taken it in yet?" Joop asked.

Two mask faces stared at me.

42 began to sing the first movement of Rach 3, the piece that won me the competition. Joop joined in, harmonizing. We bobbed around the water like that.

"No," I finally said. What would it feel like when it sunk in? A $25,000 prize. Management for three years. A concert tour already scheduled, to begin with a recital in Bedlam. Uh, er, I mean East Bedford. Oh, and one more thing: my father showing up at the finals.

42 lifted up her mask. Her eyes sparked and reflected the blue of the water.

I hadn't thought about any of this during the 17-day competition. 42, Joop, my dad, Andy. I wasn't thinking, period. It was me and the keyboard, me and my hands, me and the music. Nothing else existed, and when thoughts of Andy or my father or even 42 came into my mind, they were immediately replaced by sixteenth notes or chords or running passages of thirds. My psyche put the rest of me in a sort of involuntary meditation for two weeks, where I paid attention to my breath, my hands, and the music. That's it. I don't know who I spoke to or what I ate or how I got from my host home to the recital hall. I barely remember getting dressed in my girl tux. I barely remember Miss Ludmilla's sudden appearance backstage before the finals. A remote part of me that had been in storage for 17 days wanted to rush up and hug her, but I held back; I held my concentration because it was almost over.

I saw him when I sat down to play *Rach 3*. The finals, the concerto with orchestra. The competition was down to six of us and I felt unreasonably calm. But seeing him jarred me. I never look at the audience, but something made me glance to the right and I saw him in the third row, he only break in my trance, which quickly took over like a backup generator kicking on when the power goes out. I saw him and then I didn't see him anymore; I just played. Blocked everything out and it was me, my hands, the notes in my head, the black and white keys and the orchestra behind me. Frankie, Elly, and Rosa in the first row.

It was like a courtroom drama when they take forever to read the verdict. The little slips of paper get handed around. The jury looks blank, or tries to. The temperature in the hall rises because everyone is sweating with anticipation and unfelt fear. Finally, they adjust the mike and they read from the scraps of paper: the crystal award goes to the woman from Romania who carried around beets and bananas in her bag. I think that's all she ate the whole time. The silver medal: the guy from Russia, incredibly handsome. Applause, more tension. The head judge, a woman wearing a suit with a frilly collar stands up and says, "The gold medal winner..." and the entire auditorium takes a simultaneous breath, "is Lennie Michaels."

I hear something like a gasp from someone and the announcement doesn't immediately register because I've forgotten for a moment that I changed my name, but only until the audience bursts into applause and I hear that high-pitched scream that can only be Elly's and then the full realization of what has happened topples me almost to the floor.

And I see him again out of the corner of my eye, standing up by himself in the third row. He is clapping along with everyone else and he throws his arms in the air in triumph and claps more and for the first time in recorded history, he is looking at me and he is smiling. I think there might be tears in his eyes, but I can't see that far.

The rest is confusion, cameras, applause, people I've never met congratulating me. People milling about, all talking at once. I get swept down a hallway, more photos, arms around me, smiling, and champagne comes from somewhere. I'm ushered to some sort of reception where everyone applauds as I walk in the door. I see Frankie, and make my way toward her and then there's my father and he grabs me and we hug for a long time. He says something into my ear and I can't understand him but the fact that he said *something* is amazing. The fact that he showed up, he sat in the third row, he clapped and raised his hands in triumph. He hugged me, he congratulated me, he smiled at me. He was there.

I get swept over to some reporter and then there's Van Cliburn himself—and the rest, as they say, is a complete blur. Somehow we land in Puerto Rico and then I'm wearing a swimsuit and then I feel the sun on my body, reinforcing the fact that I do have a body after all.

And I might have a father again.

Joop is screaming into her snorkel and pointing furiously. A pod of dolphins is swimming by, a few of them leaping joyfully into the air. My eyes inexplicably fill with tears.